PEDLAR'S ACRE;

OR

THE WIFE OF SEVEN HUSBANDS.

A ROMANCE OF OLD LONDON.

LONDON:

PUBLISHED BY E. LLOYD, SALISBURY-SQUARE, FLEET-STREET.

PEDLAR'S ACRE;

OR,

THE WIFE OF SEVEN HUSBANDS.

CHAPTER I.

THE COUCH OF DEATH. — THE SLEEPING POTION. — REMORSE. — THE CHARCOAL
FIRE, AND THE BOILING LEAD. — THE VICTIM'S LAST CRY.

HE winter's wind whistled around the ancient chimneys of Pleasaunce House, which stood upon the brow of Richmond Hill. The drifting snow-storm fell thickly upon every possible projection, even of a brick on the outward walls of the mansion, that could give it a resting place — the ancient trees dashed their denuded branches together as the wind caught them in its wild career — scudding clouds covered the blue vault of Heaven; and the melancholy roar and dash of the river

Thames upon its banks, as it heaved up with its highest tide huge flakes of ice upon its surface, came floating upon the night air.

The month was November, and all nature wore its most sterile aspect without; but what were the shuddering and the wild noises of the snow-storm compared with the jangling roar of human passions within Pleasaunce House?

The old and time-worn, yet magnificent, mansion that went by that name was the abode of Sir Thomas and Lady Margaret Shard, a wealthy couple; but their union was unblessed by the smiling faces of offspring, and Sir Thomas loved the wine-cup better than he loved his lady.

*　　*　　*　　*　　*

The clock in the tall turret to the eastward of the house strikes the solemn hour of twelve, and all is still within the ancient abode, which had more than once been the honoured lodging place of England's royalty.

Situated in one of the wings of the house—the wing that for splendour was most to be admired, and which contained the loftiest and the most magnificent apartments of Pleasaunce, as the place was familiarly called—there was a bed-chamber of such gorgeous proportions and fittings, that it would have been difficult throughout the length and breadth of England to have found its parallel.

A dome-shaped roof carved and gilt into a thousand rich devices — Corinthian columns, raising their tall slender beauty far up beyond the dazzled sight—costly panelling, upon which the choicest artists of Italy had exerted all the resources of their rich imaginations—a floor covered with tapestry that might have wrapped the limbs of royalty, and then seemed a fitting garment —numerous chairs, tables, cabinets, and ottomans, resplendent with gilding, all combined to make the room look more like some large casket of rich and rare beauty from the Orient, than an ordinary bed-chamber.

And yet this was the state bed-chamber of Pleasaunce.

In the very centre of the room a magnificent couch rested upon the floor, with massive carved lion's feet for support. Its coverlet was cloth of gold; and from the centre of the domed ceiling above there hung by a gilded chain a gorgeous canopy of velvet and gold, and deep silken fringe, and tassels of bullion, which formed the upper portion of the bedstead, if such it might be called, for the term bedstead conveys no sort of idea of the charming taste that prevailed in the decoration and the arrangement of that sleeping couch.

Tall statues of Grecian nymphs held candelabra, in which blazed wax lights, lending a softened charm to everything in the room. Upon an ample hearth blazed and crackled a pair of pine logs, among which had been cast some cedar and cinnamon slips, which sent forth a grateful perfume as they were consumed.

Such was the state bed-chamber of Pleasaunce, in the reign of Charles the First of England, and before the dragoons of the Commonwealth made an assault upon the house and dismantled it, and actually littered their horses in that very chamber which we have been at the pains to place before the mental eye of the reader in all its rich and rare antiquity.

But there was soon to be a blot upon the beauty of that apartment. Man was to mar what man had made.

Up a flight of steps which led from the delightful garden of Pleasaunce, there came a reeling and boisterous step—a window was thrown open, and a rush of cold air, accompanied with snow, and rain, and sleet, rushed into the room; and after that chilling shower came a man, neatly attired, but with his apparel torn in various places, and his face flushed with wine.

The snow lay in the folds of his cloak, and the broken feather had a mass of it within its curling folds.

"Ha, ha!" he cried, as he dashed the window shut again—"ha, ha! a capital night for a Polar bear, or a—a—what's the name of the beast, or bird, or fish, that bears cold the most? It's not me, though. It's not Sir Thomas Shard of the old Pleasaunce. No, no!

"'Let's be merry—let's be merry,
　　Kissing ripe and joyous lips;
Let's be merry—let's be merry,
　　While great Jove his nectar sips.'

To be sure—to be sure; Jove always used to get drunk, and that was what made it so comfortable a thing in this world. So I mean to get drunk, for a man when he is drunk is twice a man, according to all accounts, for he is a man beside himself. Ha, ha! a deuced good joke that— ha! Upon my life, that mercer in old Cheapside has a daughter that is enough to turn the head of an anchorite! such eyes — such lips — such dimples—such flowing ringlets! Oh, ye gods! she is a darling, 'pon my soul she is! Oh, dear!"

Sir Thomas Shard flung himself upon a chair by the side of the fire, and stretched out his feet to the blaze. Then he drew half his sword from its sheath, for the other half was broken off in a brawl that he had been in before he reached his home, and looking at it carefully, he shook his head, saying—

"Now there is a good blade gone. I only hope it is in the internal anatomy of the rascal who had the confounded impudence, just before I reached my coach, to ask me what I wanted with the mercer's pretty daughter. 'What do I want?' says I; 'what do you suppose now, stupid, that I want, eh?' 'Oh,' says he, 'the girl's mine,' said he. 'Ah, take that,' says I; and so there was a row—I think there was a row—by Jove! there is a row in my head!"

The tipsy master of Pleasaunce rested his throbbing head upon his hands; and then, after a pause, he said—

"I wonder where my lady is? She used to be on the look-out for me, and ever be ready to load me with reproaches; but I don't see her now. Perhaps she is getting used to my funny little ways now of coming home in the middle of the night, and don't mean to take any notice of 'em; and yet, how she looked at me this morning! What a freezing look! I don't wonder at it snowing afterwards. Ha, ha! that's a good joke! I'm unusually witty to-night. But—but, how my head swims round and round. I am afraid it will ache in the morning."

"No, Thomas," said a soft voice, "it will not ache to-morrow, I assure you it will not."

Sir Thomas Shard started to his feet, and standing close to his chair, he saw Lady Shard in an elegant night-dress, over which she had thrown a gorgeous mantle of ermine, fastened with a diamond hasp.

"What—my lady—Margaret—you—"

"Yes, Sir Thomas, I am here," said Lady Shard, in a soft, sweet voice. "I heard you come in."

"Oh—ah!"

"And so I came to you, for I have been sleeping in the cedar chamber."

"Yes—oh, yes; in the cedar chamber."

"I hope you have enjoyed yourself very much in the city?"

"Oh, uncommon! I saw such a—no, d—n it!—it's an extraordinary thing, my lady, ain't it, how ugly all the city girls are?"

"Are they, now?"

"Oh, uncommon—uncommon! particularly the mercer's daughter—particularly the mercer's daughter. Ah, I rather think, though I have had a little drop, I am a little too cunning for my wife—ha!"

"Well, that's a pity," said Lady Shard; "for in such a case, the poor wenches may have some difficulty in getting husbands."

"Well, I should think they would. Perhaps you think I'm drunk?"

"Oh, no—no; when first I heard your voice, I ceased to think about it."

"Oh, you did? Very good, very good. Moreover, then, Lady S., you will be so good as to get me a bottle of Burgundy; and I tell you, that the sweetest—no, I mean the ugliest—oh, what a lie!—girl in the city, is a mercer's daughter in Cheapside."

"Indeed?"

"You don't believe it. I can see by your manner you don't believe it, that's flat!"

"Oh, but I do, Sir Thomas."

"Don't Sir Thomas me, ma'am! I am sorry to say that, in my opinion, you have taken a drop too much to-night. I don't mean to say that you are so drunk that you don't know pretty well what you are about; but you have taken a drop too much; so go to bed—go to bed, and—and sleep it off—off—ah!"

Sir Thomas staggered to the magnificent couch, and tripping over one of the bullion tassels that lay on the side of it, he rolled on the coverlet of cloth of gold, and fell into a deep drunken sleep.

Lady Shard stood gazing at him, and trembling as though she were in an ague. She then struck her breast with her clenched hand, and uttered a strange faint kind of scream; and then she approached the fire, and tried to warm herself by its cheerful blaze.

"He sleeps—he sleeps," she said; "his head will not ache to-morrow."

With a slow and gliding step, she approached the side of the bed, and leant over it to listen to the breathing of Sir Thomas Shard. There could be no sort of mistake about it—for he slept soundly.

Again Lady Margaret struck her breast, and uttered the strange cry, and then she crept to the fire, saying in a moaning tone—

"Cold—cold—oh, so cold!"

She rubbed her chilled hands one over the other; and she listened to the storm without as it roared and rattled past the window. Her face was ghastly pale; and when the wind moaned fiercely for a few minutes, she too moaned, as if in imitation of the sound.

The clock struck one.

Lady Margaret Shard started at the

sound, and again crept up close to the couch, and inclined her ear to catch the sound of the regular breathing of her husband : it was quite evident that he slept heavily and profoundly.

"He sleeps—he sleeps !—No—no—no ! His head must not ache to-morrow ! How the wind howls ! Are the spirits of the dead riding upon the blast ? Is it possible that the dim, shadowy phantoms of those who have lived this mortal life, and then gone from it, can show themselves to human eyes ? Oh, no—no—no ! It is but a dream of the imagination; or else, surely, I should have seen them !"

She turned slowly round and looked into every corner of the chamber.

"If there were such things, I should see them now," she said.

Nothing but the sighing of the wind, and the roar and splash of the disturbed rain, and now and then a groan from her husband as he slightly shifted his position upon the couch, came upon her ears.

"It is time," she said.

With a stealthy step she approached the candelabrum and blew out every one of the lights, and the flashing flames from the pine-wood fire sent a sufficient light into the chamber to make every object in it plainly visible.

This light from the fire, though, was deceiving and uncertain, and it cast strange shadows, that seemed to be full of strange life, upon the walls and the dome-shaped roof of the gorgeous room. The rich gildings, though, and the many colours in the splendid apartment, had conveyed to them a still richer colour by this fire light than the wax candles had been able to bestow upon them.

Lady Margaret looked at the slumbering face of her husband, and then she said, in a low tone—

"No, it is decided. His head will not ache to-morrow."

CHAPTER II.

THE APPARITION OF THE STATE-CHAMBER.—THE DREADFUL DEATH.

AS Lady Margaret said these words she slowly left the room.

A kind of semi-darkness now reigned in the state-chamber, for a tall, flickering light that had come from a piece of pine-wood had died out, and there was little to illume the room except the glow from the mass of red-hot cinders of the wood that had been burning all the evening.

Still that was sufficient to send a reddish halo over the whole place, although far off from the fire, where the shadows of the canopy and of the magnificent couch fell, was nearly total darkness.

This effect arose from the source of what light there was from the fire being so low down that it sent the shadows rather upwards than otherwise.

About a quarter of an hour elapsed in silence and peace within that room, and then a strange creaking noise might have been heard, and from behind one of the tall Corinthian pillars a long, narrow door in the wainscot opened, and a figure attired in a gray cloak with a hood to it, that nearly covered the whole face, crept into the room.

In addition to the hood, the figure had upon its face a half-mask of crape, so that nothing but a small portion of the mouth and the chin were visible.

With a slow and stealthy movement the figure crept on until it reached the side of the couch on which lay Sir Thomas Shard.

It so happened that at that moment he turned uneasily over to his side, having his back to the fire-place, and as he did so he muttered—

"Another cup! Only another cup to the health and joy of the mercer's fair daughter ! God, she is beautiful !"

Some other inarticulate expressions escaped the lips of the sleeper, and then the deep and regular breathing ensued again, and all was as before.

The tall figure in the grey cloak spread its arms for a moment or two over the sleeping man; but whether it invoked a curse or a blessing it is impossible to say.

The wood-fire was now rapidly sinking down into such a state, that the red light given from it was each moment growing more and more sombre. The figure in the gray cloak approached the hearth, and with the iron tongs that were commonly used for the purpose of aiding in the arrangement of the logs of the old wood fire, it displaced one of the half-charred pieces of pine wood; burning beneath it was a hollow and glowing red cavern of combustion.

From the folds of the cloak, then, in which there must have been a capacious pocket, the figure took a small iron ladle, such as is commonly used for holding molten lead.

"Oh, God!" said Sir Thomas, in his sleep; "she is divine!"

The figure slowly turned its head and gazed at him as he lay upon the couch, and then a strange half-groan, half-sigh, came from its lips. The iron ladle was placed upon the glowing cavity on the fire that the removal of the half-burnt log had left.

With a hissing noise, now, a small flame curled round the bowl of the little ladle, which soon began to get of a dark-red hue. Then the figure in the cloak took something from another pocket of the garment, and cast it into the ladle.

It was a lump of lead.

In the course of a few seconds the soft and ductile metal yielded to the influence of the heat to which it was exposed, and settled down into a little pool of molten lead, upon the surface of which was a glossy-looking film of prismatic colours.

Again Sir Thomas Shard moved uneasily, and in a strange tone spoke, saying—

"No, no! Do not tell me of death! The mercer's daughter is an angel; but I may not see her!"

The figure in the cloak listened to catch each word that he uttered, and then when all was still again, save the howling of the wind, and the soft and solemn patter of the sleet and snow upon the window panes, it lifted the ladle from the fire, and with a slow and solemn step approached the couch upon which the sleeper lay.

It was then that in a low voice, that sounded like the solemn dirge of some organ in a vast cathedral, the figure in the cloak spoke:—

"Six in the grave, so cold and hollow—
Will a seventh in due time follow?"

It was difficult to say if this dismal sort of chant was the result of insanity, or if it came from the lips of a supernatural being.

Nearer—nearer, still stepped the figure, until it got right to the side of the couch. The little flame in the fire still spurted up, and cast a deceiving light upon all things in the room. Sir Thomas Shard lay upon his left side with his back to the hearth.

His right arm was placed partly over his face and forehead.

And now the cloaked figure just gently shook the little iron ladle, as if to be sure that the small portion of lead it contained was in a liquid state. It moved to and fro like water.

"Sweet eyes!—oh, sweet eyes!" moaned Sir Thomas Shard; "but eyes so beautiful——"

The figure advanced the ladle to the back of his head. The little iron vessel had a long lip-like spout to it. By one tilt the molten lead was sent on an errand of death, right into the right ear of the slumbering man.

For a moment there was a hissing sound, and a gush of vapour from the ear, as the frightfully burning fluid made its way through the ventricles into the very brain of the sleeper. Then he sprang up from the couch and uttered two such shrieks as must have been heard far and wide, even through the storm.

Clasping his head with both his hands, he sprang into the air, and then fell to the floor and rolled over, biting at the rich carpet in his wild agony. He rolled on to his back, and the body with a fearful convulsion was arched till the back bone crackled again; and then with one convulsive sob it fell to the floor quite flat like a log of wood.

The spirit of Sir Thomas Shard had fled to its maker.

With the ladle still in its grasp the cloaked figure stood tall and erect at the head portion of the couch, half hidden by the descending drapery of the canopy.

The fearful death-struggle of Sir Thomas Shard, with all its fearful concomitants, had not lasted more than half a minute, and then he lay dead and still upon the floor.

The cloaked figure crept to the panel in the wall behind the Corinthian column, and got rid of the ladle in some sort of way, and then came back into the room.

It was with a strange staggering sort of gait that the figure now moved; but if it was mortal, it had evidently made up its mind to every horror, for it stooped over the body of its victim, and by a great effort succeeded in lifting it on to the couch.

For a few seconds, then, the cloaked figure regarded the face of the dead. Then, still staggering like one in a giddy paroxysm of the most awful terror, the figure went to one of the candelabra, and got a wax candle, and lit it by the glowing embers of the fire. Approaching the body, then, it held the light so that a good view of the ear that had received the molten lead could be obtained.

A bright speck of a metallic character was plainly to be seen, deep seated in the ear.

The figure held the wax candle on one side, so that drop by drop the melted wax fell into the ear, and in a moment or two the metallic appearance was covered up.

To replace the candle in the candelabrum, and to glide, then, towards the fire, was the work of a moment. Suppressed cries burst from the labouring bosom of the cloaked figure, and it wrung its hands in a very paroxysm of grief.

It was then that a sharp knocking was heard at the door of the chamber, and the figure started for a moment and listened.

The knocking was continued.

With a rush and a bound the cloaked figure reached the door, and shot a small night-bolt into its socket. Just as it did so, an attempt was made on the outside to open the door.

"Hilloa!" cried a voice. "Did you call, Sir Thomas? Sir—sir! is anything amiss? Gregory woke William, and William roused me up, and said there was a cry for help!"

The cloaked figure did not reply, but creeping along the floor till it reached the secret panel, it passed out of the chamber. The panel closed with a sharp noise, as the spring that held it shot into its place again.

The knocking at the chamber-door continued now, and by the sound of voices without, it was evident that several of the domestics were there assembled.

"Sir Thomas," cried one, "are you there, sir?"

"It will be only proper," said another, "to rouse our good lady; she is sleeping in the cedar chamber."

"Where is her own page, Cyprian?" said a third.

"Here," said a voice; "what is the matter?"

"Oh, Master Cyprian, did you not hear a scream?"

"A scream did you say? I have heard two such screams as I hope never in this world to hear again. They sounded as though they were in my very ears, though I do sleep in the other wing of the mansion. Is Sir Thomas at home, think you?"

"We don't know, Master Cyprian; but as the screams seemed to come from this part of the mansion, we think we ought to see if Sir Thomas be at home or not. Do you knock, Master Cyprian."

"I will."

The page knocked and kicked at the door.

"What ho! Sir Thomas! Sir Thomas!" All was still.

"This won't do," said the page. "I will run to my lady's chamber in the cedar room, and awaken her up. I feel certain something is amiss."

"Do so, good Cyprian."

The page ran though the long corridor to Lady Shard's chamber; and while he was gone, the servants, who had collected in some fear around the door of the state chamber, indulged in various surmises as to what the screams could portend.

In the course of a few minutes the page returned, closely followed by Lady Shard, in the ermine robe that she had worn when last introduced to the reader.

"Oh, heavens!" she cried, "what is the meaning of all this? What has happened?"

"We don't know, my lady; but there were screams from, as we think, this chamber; but the door is fast, and no one answers."

"Break it open instantly."

This was an order that the servants, whose curiosity was fully awakened, were not slow in obeying; but the door was of solid oak, and would not yield easily.

CHAPTER III.

LADY SHARD IS INCONSOLABLE FOR THE DEATH OF HER SIXTH HUSBAND.

AFTER in vain trying, by their united force, to break the door down, one of the servants, at the suggestion of the page, Master Cyprian, went for a crowbar, with which he soon returned.

"That will do it, my lady," he said.

"Oh, yes—yes; but where is Sir Thomas? Have any of you seen him come home?"

"No, my lady."

"Yes, my lady, I heard him come in at the window of this very room, and he was quite merry."

"Merry was he ?"

"Yes, my lady ; and singing a kind of song."

"Oh, that I had known he had come home ! But my mind much misgives me that something has happened to him, or that he is taken very ill. Be quick and open the door at any risk."

The crowbar did its duty well, and the door of the state chamber was forced open at some damage to its beauty, and to the utter destruction of the bolt which was on the inside.

When it was fairly opened, the servants drew back as by general consent, and the man who had the crowbar with him held it in an attitude of defence.

"What is it that you fear?" said Lady Shard. "Sir Thomas, if in health and living, will harm none of you, and if sick or dead, he cannot."

"Why, my lady, we—we——"

"Yes, my lady, we——"

"That's just it," said another.

"You are a pack of cowards, all of you," said Cyprian, the page, as he took a light from the hands of one of them. "I suppose you want our good lady to go in first, and so encounter what of surprise or danger there may be? You call yourselves men, and flout at me because I am but a boy; but I will show you that I have more courage than any of you."

"You had better be careful, Mr. Whippersnapper," said one.

"Yes," said another, "the devil will have you."

"Silence, all of you," said Lady Shard. "Is this language to use before me? For shame of you—when death or sickness may be in the house. Come, Cyprian, we will go together ; of a surety, you have more courage than all the lazy knaves."

At this rebuke the servants looked rather foolishly at each other, and the page gave a nod of satisfaction as he rushed into the room, followed by Lady Shard.

The other servants, now that the page went first, were ashamed to stay outside entirely, so they followed their mistress into the apartment; and as three or four of them had lights besides the one that Cyprian, the page, carried, a tolerable radiance was cast over the apartment.

"Call to your master," said Lady Shard to the page. "If he be home he may possibly reply to you."

"Sir Thomas!" cried the page, as he held up the light he carried as high as he could above his head, and that was not very high—"Sir Thomas Shard! If

you are here, sir, be so good as to say so."

No reply was vouchsafed to this appeal.

"He is not here, my lady," said the page ; "and, after all, the cries that have alarmed us, and so completely roused the household, may not have been in this house."

"We will hope they were not," said Lady Shard; "at the same time, that we will likewise hope that no poor creature is in suffering near to it. Some of you will feel it to be your duty, I hope, to look about the neighbourhood of the mansion."

"Oh, my lady—my lady !" cried the man who had the crowbar, and who had broken into the room with it, and, upon the strength of being so armed, had approached the couch upon which lay the dead body of Sir Thomas Shard.

"What is it ?" said Lady Shard.

As she spoke, she kept her breath so closely shut, and looked so very pale, that it was awful to see her.

"Here is Sir Thomas, my lady, asleep or dead !"

"Dead !" cried everybody.

"No—no!" said Lady Shard. "He is surely asleep."

"Not after all this knocking, and row, and talking," said one. "No mortal man could sleep in such a racket.'

"Yes," said the page, "if you took as much spiced canary as our good master, Sir Thomas, takes at times, before he gets home, you would sleep so sound that the last trumpet would fail to awaken you."

"It will fail to awaken him," said one of the servants who had looked intently in the face of his master, "if he sleeps as soundly upon hearing it blow as he is likely to do while any mortal voice lasts."

"What mean you ?"

"He is dead."

Upon this announcement, Lady Shard stepped forward and knelt by the side of the couch, and looked in the face of her husband. That face was quite calm and serene-looking ; but there could be no mistake about it being the face of the dead.

"Heaven help us all!" she said.

"Amen !" said the servants, as they gathered round her and the couch.

The page then raised his shrll voice, saying—

"But strong men, in their prime of life and strength, do not die in this way without a cause."

"No, they do not."

"Rouse yourself, my lady! who knows but that our master, Sir Thomas, may have been murdered?"

"Murdered !" shrieked Lady Shard; "Who murdered him ?"

"That I don't know, but——"

"But what, Cyprian ? Speak out."

"As sure as there is a heaven above us, we shall all know some day or another who did it."

"Oh, yes," shudderingly muttered Lady Shard, "some day we shall."

"And the sooner the better," said the page. "You, Gregory, run into the village for Master Londonmere, the cunning leech; you, Thomas, go to Sir Ralph Shard, at Westminster, and tell him his son is dead ; you, Luke, run to Sir Ingestrie Lees, the magistrate and ask him to come at once, and tell him there has been foul play, we think."

The servants looked at each other rather hesitatingly ; but Lady Shard, as she rose from her knees, and clasped her hands, cried out—

"I confirm all these orders—go—go!"

Upon this they started upon their several errands, and then the page stepping up to his lady, said—

"Oh, madam, if you would only weep !"

"Weep ?"

"Yes—oh, yes, try to shed tears; they would so relieve you; anything is better than this awful despair !"

"Awful despair !" echoed the lady.

"Yes, dear lady, it is awful; of course, this is a shock to you of the most strange and serious character ; but, oh, recollect that we are all mortal, and must all die some day !"

"Oh, Cyprian—Cyprian, tell me——"

"What, my lady—oh, what?"

"I have been kind to you."

"You have, indeed."

"Then—then——"

"Speak out, my good, kind mistress, and tell your faithful Cyprian what you would have of him."

"I merely wanted to ask you, boy, what you thought was the probable cause of the death of your master ?"

"Well," said Cyprian, "to the best of my belief, I—I——"

"You what ?"

"I don't know."

"You play with my feelings!"

"By heavens I do not; but, in truth, I cannot think what can have hurried him to the grave in this way, unless in some affray, which possibly, having too much wine, he might have been engaged in

before he got home, he received some hurt, which has afterwards caused his death."

"It may be so."

"It is the only thing I can think of, my lady."

"Alas—alas ! I am very sad ! I will to my chamber now, Cyprian; and when the good leech from the village comes, I will see him. Oh, what will the world say of me ?"

"Of you, madam ?"

"Yes, good Cyprian; you know that I have had other husbands."

"Why, a—yes."

"You have heard that ?"

"They do say, lady, that this is the sixth."

"They say truly, Cyprian; and yet I am not thirty years of age; but now, when the obsequies of my poor lost husband are performed, I will retire to a nunnery, and pass the remainder of my life, which I pray will be in prayer and repentance. I will, good Cyprian, I will to my chamber again. Oh, what a night of horror is this !"

"Farewell, good madam."

Cyprian and his lady parted upon the landing-place outside the door of the state-chamber.

"Well," said the page, "may I be flayed alive if I know what to make of all this. Here am I, page to a seemingly noble and virtuous lady, who has had six husbands, and is not thirty yet! Lord bless me, what an extraordinary lady ! Well, she talks of going into a nunnery ; but I don't think she will. Heavens ! if she gets a seventh husband after all this, I should say he will be an uncommonly bold man, that's all."

In the course of the night, now, the doctor of the village of Richmond, for such it then was, and a poor one too, came to the mansion ; and, after an interview with Lady Shard, he examined the body of Sir Thomas, and decided that he must have died of a heart pang, which had stopped the circulation for so long that it could not recover again, for there were no marks of violence upon the body at all to account for death in any other way, and the appearances were not those of apoplexy.

Lady Shard gave the doctor a munificent fee, and he left the mansion quite well satisfied with his visit; leaving a written paper, with his opinion as to the cause of the death, behind him.

Early in the morning the aged father of the late Sir Thomas arrived at Pleasaunce, and betimes a magistrate and several other gentlemen ; but nothing could be made of the affair, except that Sir Thomas was dead, and that his widow was in great grief.

Lady Shard's maid deposed to sleeping in an ante-chamber of the room called the cedar-chamber, and that her lady went to rest at ten o'clock, and never left her room at all till she, the maid, roused her, in consequence of Cyprian, the page, coming into her room, the door of which she had unthinkingly left unlocked, and pulling her by the nose as she lay in bed, and telling her that something was amiss in the house.

This evidence of the maid's must have been wrong, either from circumstances over which she had no control, or wilfully. We shall find out as we proceed which is the case.

Suffice it to say, that an inquest was held upon the body of Sir Thomas Shard, and a verdict of "Died by the visitation of God" returned; and he was committed to the tomb of his ancestors in Westminster Abbey; and Lady Shard looked more lovely and stately than ever in her widow's-weeds, although there was an expression of grief upon her face that did not seem as if it would go quickly.

CHAPTER IV.

THE GRAND WEDDING AT THE CHURCH OF OUR LADYE AT SOUTHWARK.

THE long and dreary months of the winter have passed away, and it is just six months since the time at which Sir Thomas Shard died so mysteriously in his great house at Pleasaunce.

The sun of a bright and beautiful June morning is shining upon all things, and, by the magic of its beauty, lending a charm to the meanest objects. The river Thames is sparkling like a lake of gold. The gardens that sloped down to the banks of the stream are all in the full luxuriance of their richest vegetation; and old London looks in the sunlight like a city of some much fairer clime than ours.

But it is in and about the church of Our Ladye at Southwark that the greatest amount of bustle and excitement and hilarity seems to be going on, for there a marriage is about to be celebrated, which, if we may judge from the preparations attendant upon it, must be of no ordinary state and importance.

Crowds of people of all grades and conditions thronged the church doors—bands of music pealed forth joyous tunes—flags were flying from all the houses of entertainment in the vicinity—and such a scene of excitement and bustle was rarely ever seen upon any such an occasion.

Within the church the preparations were great and gorgeous in the extreme. The communion table was decked with flowers, and some of the pews which were to be occupied by the bridal party were elaborately fitted up with silk and velvet.

It was rumoured that the bride had given away a thousand pounds to the poor of the neighbourhood to make merry with on that day, and that by her liberal largess she had won all hearts.

It was quite clear that such a wedding had not taken place for many a long day in the old church, and it was equally clear that the bride or the bridegroom must be very rich to be able to stand the vast expenses of such a bridal.

The crowd increased each moment, until it got to be so great, that the difficulty of moving about in it came to be impossible.

But still it kept on increasing, and as in this country the people are quite proverbial for stopping to gape at anything whatever, there is no wonder in the fact that a wedding, which is ever an attractive thing to both old and young, should have its charms for the giddy multitude to a greater extent than anything else.

Various rumours were afloat among the crowd with regard to whose wedding it was, for, strange to say, no one seemed to be very well informed upon that subject.

"You may depend," said one, "it is some old maid who has got more money than wit, and who has made up her mind to marry a young man."

"It may be so," said another, "but to my mind it seems more likely that it is some old dotard, who in his second childhood has taken a young girl for his wife."

"Ah, my good friends," said a little weak looking man, "if that is the case there is very little difficulty in coming to a correct conclusion as to how she will serve him."

"That's true enough," laughed the crowd.

"But what do you say," suggested another person, " to its being neither an old maid nor an old bachelor who is about to be married, but a widow?"

"A widow?"

"Yes, a widow."

"But how do you know that?"

"Well, my good friends, I don't mind telling you all about it; but first of all I must state to you that it is one of the greatest secrets that ever was, and so you must not mention it again to any one."

"Oh, no—no."

"Well then, my aunt, you see, has a sister who married the sexton of old St. Paul's Church."

"Yes—yes?"

"And he has a cousin who is sexton here at Southwark, you comprehend."

"Yes—yes?"

"Well, my aunt's cousin—no—that is, my cousin—Dear me, where was I?"

"Go to the deuce with you for a fool," cried another man in the crowd; " my idea is that you don't know a word about it. If you do, why don't you say it at once, without plaguing us about your relations?"

"Yes—yes, say it at once!"

"Well, I will. You must know that a gold pin has been given to each of the people belonging to the church for them not to say a word about who was going to be married till the ceremony took place actually, and that's how I came to know it."

"Well, who is it then?"

"Why it's a widow."

"But who?"

"Oh, that I don't know."

The people were so enraged at the want of knowledge now on the part of the individual who had presumed upon engaging their attention for so long, but one knocked his cap over his eyes, another tore a good rent in his doublet, a third saluted him with a hearty kick, and it is hard to say where the popular fury might have ended, if just at that moment the clash of music had not come upon their ears, and suggested to them all the notion that the bridal party was about to make its appearance at the church.

This silenced the outcries of the mob, and had the effect of rescuing the unfortunate man who had attempted to give information that he did not fully possess.

The music was of the most soul-entrancing character. It at times swelled up into a wild and martial kind of melody, and then sunk to the soft cadences of a love ditty.

The good folks who had come to attend the wedding were quite entranced with the character of the music.

The fact is, that as nothing had been spared in any particular to make this a grand and splendid wedding, so in the matter of the music the most lavish expense had been gone to, and the best musicians had been paid their own terms for attending upon the auspicious occasion.

The sounds that so delighted the people were brought about by the agency of no less than thirty trumpeters, each on horseback, and who tuned their instruments so well together, that the effect was truly superb.

It is said that—

" Music hath charms
To soothe the savage breast;"

and certainly it must have, for it soothed on this occasion the wild and reckless spirit of a London mob, and after that exhibition of its power, we may consider it capable of anything.

Previous to the arrival of these thirty trumpeters there is no question at all but that the vast mob were in what may be called rather a sportive humour.

That is to say, it was disposed to commit any enormity or any violence for the sake of a little wild and reckless amusement, accoding to the nature of mobs in general.

But the musicians halted just outside the church porch, and then they played so sweet and gentle an air, that you might have heard a pin drop as the gentle swelling notes came upon the breeze.

The mob was silent, and then there was a cry of—

"Way for the bride! Way for the bride!"

Following in the train of the bride there came armed men—lackeys all blazoned with gold—pages—and, in fact, every species of attendant which the state and the luxury of those times enabled the rich to attract around them by the magnificence of the scene.

But hardly had the eight milk-white steeds of the bride stopped at the church door, when there arose another cry, and this time it was—

"Way for the bridegroom! Way for the noble bridegroom! Hurrah! here he comes!—here he comes!—Make way there! Here is the bridegroom!"

A train of splendidly attired horsemen appeared now, and at their head a cavalier, in a dress of white satin all covered with silver lace and rich embroidery. He wore a Spanish hat with a magnificent plume of feathers in it, and looped with a diamond of very great beauty and lustre. The hilt of the sword that hung by his side was studded with jewels; and take him for all in all, so richly attired, and so gallant-looking a young bridegroom, had scarcely ever crossed the portal of the old church.

And now, as the mob made way for him, and, without in the smallest degree knowing who and what he was, cheered him just for his good looks and his rich apparel, he turned and acknowledged the salutation, by lifting his plumed cap from his head, and gracefully bowing to the multitude.

This won their hearts directly, and the women, in particular, were loud in their expressions of admiration of him.

They all got a good look at him when he raised his cap, but not before that, for the plume of feathers in it had the effect of casting quite a shadow over his face.

The bridegroom, then, appeared to be about thirty years of age, of a tall and swarthy person, and a frank, open kind of aspect.

The small, coal-black moustache upon his lip added very much to his appearance; and take him altogether, he seemed, indeed and in truth, a very proper gentleman

There was a bright kind of smile, too, upon his lips, as though he felt that that day he had achieved a something that was worth the winning.

In this manner, then, the bridegroom went to the church-door, and then springing from his horse, he advanced to the door of the chariot in which the bride was, and pushing the lackeys on one side, he himself opened it, and bowed low to the lady within.

CHAPTER V.

DISCOVERS WHO THE BRIDE AND THE BRIDEGROOM REALLY ARE.

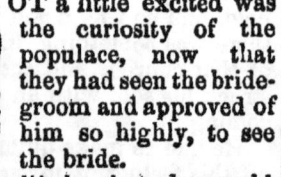

NOT a little excited was the curiosity of the populace, now that they had seen the bridegroom and approved of him so highly, to see the bride.

It was not at all likely that she would meet with the same amount of approbation that the handsome bridegroom had, especially from the ladies.

But the carriage-door is opened, and the bridegroom bows so low that the plume in his cap seems as if it would sweep the ground, and then a mass of white satin and lace steps out of the carriage.

That is the bride.

A veil covers her face—indeed the veil was fastened first of all to the top of her head-dress, and then it was large enough to descend quite to her feet, so that she was, so to speak, quite wrapped up in it, which, of course, was rather a disappointment to those who were desirous of getting a good look at her.

One or two voices only cried out—

"Long life to the bride! Hurrah!"

But if this was done for the purpose of coaxing her to look round, and in acknowledgment of the courtesy to show her face, it utterly failed.

She leant upon the arm of the gallant-looking bridegroom, and at once entered the church.

"Ugly! you may depend," said a woman in the crowd to a neighbour.

"To be sure," said another. "If she was not she would never be so mighty particular about showing her face. When I was married I let everybody look at me."

The crowd laughed at this speech, for it implied, on the part of the utterer of it, that she had certainly no bad opinion of herself.

But we will now attend to what is passing within the old church itself.

There are numbers of well-dressed people in the church, and the priest at the altar ready to perform the ceremony which should make the bride and the bridegroom one in life. There was a hushed and holy kind of stillness within the sacred edifice as the procession of the bridal party moved up the long aisle of the stately building.

The bridegroom held the veiled bride by the hand; but it was strange to see that the only persons they were followed by were lackeys and servants.

No friends—no relations were there to bless that union with their presence. The bride and the bridegroom appeared to be alone in the world.

This had a very odd look, indeed.

But now the altar was reached, and then the bride said in a low tone to her intended husband—

"Have you no friends here, Martin Lassamour?"

"None."

"Not one?"

"Not one."

"But why is this? If I came alone, from the peculiarity of my position, surely you need not have done so."

"I will tell you the honest truth. I did ask some friends to come, but they one and all refused."

"Refused?"

"Yes; they made one excuse or another, so that I was compelled to see that they did not want to come, and I forbore to press the matter."

"It is very strange."

"It is. But heed it not. It is you alone I came to meet in the church—it is you alone that I care for. Let them all go, the false and fickle friends, who are fit for nothing but the wine-cup and the wassail. You and I will live for each other."

"Oh, Martin! if, indeed, you will preserve such sentiments as these, all may—all will be well—but——"

"But what?"

"Nothing!—oh, nothing! The ceremony must now be proceeded with at once, I suppose."

"All is ready," whispered one of the official persons connected with the church.

"Then we are not disposed to delay," said the bridegroom, and as he spoke, he lifted the veil from before the face of the bride.

There were several in the church who did not know who the bride was till then, and with a shudder they muttered to themselves, when they saw her face, the name of—

"Lady Margaret Shard!"

Yes, the bride of Martin Lassamour, the gallant and handsome-looking young cavalier, was no other than the wife of six husbands—the enormously wealthy Lady Shard, who had been but so short a time a widow, and who now was seeking for consolation in the arms of a seventh husband.

A bold man must Martin Lassamour have been truly.

There was a suppressed kind of murmur in the church, and a flutter of garments as people changed their places with an uneasy kind of feeling.

The Lady Shard, with her cold, impassioned glance, looked around her at the faces she saw, and she did not seem to be in the smallest degree aware that her position was rather a peculiar one, nor did it seem to strike her that most of the looks she met with were indicative of dread and suspicion.

Perhaps she felt deeply, though, for all that.

Troubled waters are deep sometimes, and present a clear and glassy surface to the eye when in their inmost depths all may be wild strife and tumult.

If the Lady Shard really did feel deeply the condition she was in—if she really did feel that the public suspicion was strong against her, on account of the deaths of her six husbands, she must have possessed the most admirable fortitude and self-command to appear upon this really trying occasion so very calm and cool as she looked.

But her ladyship was, it must be borne in mind, a woman both of education and ability.

The stillness that had reigned in the church previously to the arriving of the train of the bride was none in comparison to the death-like repose that was now within it.

The faintest whisper would have been heard if any one had spoken, but no one did so.

Martin Lassamour had been a soldier. He had gained a name upon the battle-field, and he was a bold cavalier; but yet there was something in the awful stillness of that church, and the people in it, that struck his soul with an undefined sense of coming ill.

He had to make quite an effort to shake off this feeling of mysterious dismay.

The lady looked him calmly in the face.

"Martin?"

"Yes, Margaret; you—you spoke?"

"I did. I want, now, to ask you one question."

"A thousand if you will."

"Do you repent?"

"Repent?"

"Yes, do you now, at the eleventh hour, repent your engagement to me?"

"Oh, no—no!"

"Question your own heart, Martin, closely. You know that my misfortunes have given a bad odour to my name; you can see even here in the church that I am avoided altogether, or looked upon with distrust. It is not too late, if you wish it, to draw back."

"Margaret, for what do you take me?"

"An honourable gentleman."

"Then ask no more. I came here to wed you of my own free will, and of my own free choice, and not all the cold looks or doubtful aspects of the whole world should prevent me."

"I am yours—yours, Martin, for ever."

A sickly smile passed over the features of the lady, and then, with her hand still in that of Martin Lassamour's, she stepped up to the altar.

At that moment there was a trampling of feet at the church door, and a shout from the people without. A figure advanced swiftly up the long aisle, and stood close to the bride and the bridegroom.

This new comer was a tall, stout man, of some sixty years of age, and his rubicund visage sufficiently testified to the fact that he had lived well, if he had lived long.

The dress of this new comer was certainly not at all adapted to grace a bridal, for he was splashed from head to foot, and appeared to have ridden hard. He wore the general attire of a country gentleman, and by the costly character of some of the appointments of his dress it was evident that he was well to do in the world.

Lady Shard changed colour slightly at the sight of this stranger.

As for Martin Lassamour, he merely looked at him with the curiosity of a man who wonders why some one of whom he knows nothing at all should mix himself up, or attempt to mix himself with his affairs.

"Lady Shard," said the new comer, "you know me?"

"I do. You are——"

"The uncle of the late Sir Thomas Shard, your husband."

"Yes."

"Who has been dead six months or thereabouts, and now you are about to marry again. Now, hark you, madam. My poor nephew was your sixth husband, and this poor devil whom you are going now to marry will be your seventh, unless he slips his neck out of the halter at the last moment, which he had better do if he has any sense left him."

CHAPTER VI.

LADY SHARD BECOMES MISTRESS MARGARET LASSAMOUR.

ITH such distinctness was this rather uncorteous speech, to utter at a wedding, pronounced by the elderly gentleman, who had evidently ridden hard to get there in time to say it, that Martin Lassamour looked at him in amazement.

"Sir," he said, "who are you?"

"I am Sir Ralph Shard, sir, of Cotton Court, in the good county of Berks."

"Then, sir, you will hear from me."

"Very good, sir. That is just as you like. I never dislike the fact of hearing from a gentleman, and I must pay you the compliment of saying that you look like one. But, sir, I am old enough to be your father, and I was old enough to be the father of the lady's late husband, and I said to him the day of his wedding—'Thomas, my boy, you will soon be in the family vault along with the other husbands of the lady you are about to marry,'—and lo, he is there; and now, sir, I have had a hard ride to get here in time to give you a piece of advice, and that is, to take warning, and don't make the seventh husband of the widow of six."

"Is that all you have to say, sir?"

"All? Zounds, is it not enough? What more would you have?'

"Nothing, but your absence."

"Oh, I am going."

"And, sir, I beg to tell you that your intrusion here is by me considered an insult."

"Why, man, you are out of your senses."

"Perhaps so, sir. That is a point upon which it is exceedingly difficult for any one to determine. But I hope you will be so good as to stay in town until to-morrow."

"What for? To amuse you by letting you try to thrust a rapier through me? Oh, dear, no! I have done my duty. I warn you, young sir, that's all. Perhaps I have been a fool for troubling myself about you, but ought to have just let you go to the devil in your own way; but a man must act up to his nature, and it was mine to try to do you a good turn, so it don't much matter how you take it. As for you, madam, you are——"

"What, sir?" said Lady Shard.

"A very lucky woman."

The old baronet, for such indeed he was,

now at once turned on his heel, and left the church.

Martin Lassamour bit his lips with vexation, and then the lady said to him in a calm and gentle voice—

"There is still time to take the advice of this old man, who is so angry with me because his nephew, my late husband, left me his heiress instead of him."

"'Ah, that is it?"

"Yes, Martin."

"Sir," said Martin Lassamour, addressing the priest. "Reverend sir, will you proceed with the ceremony?"

The priest inclined his head, and in the course of another ten minutes, at the furthest, Lady Shard had abandoned her name of that quality, and become plain Mrs. Margaret Lassamour.

Yes, the words were spoken—the irrevocable words which made Martin Lassamour the seventh husband of the lady whose wealth scarcely any one ever knew the extent of.

Indeed, it is quite doubtful whether she herself knew exactly the amount of her possessions.

The fact was, that all her previous husbands had been men of considerable property. The whole of them had left wills in her sole favour, so that she was enormously wealthy; and the only one whom she had married who was penniless, was Martin Lassamour.

Martin by no means imposed himself upon the rich widow as a person of any situation. On the contrary, it is possible that in speaking to her upon that subject he rather under than overrated his means, for he was of a frank and free temper, and never in his life had stooped to a meanness or to a deception.

In fact, he was one of that class of men then so common in Europe, who, while they might with justice be called adventurers, had nothing in common with the bad qualities and the lapse morals which we are now in the habit of associating with such a name.

At that time the younger sons of many good and noble families became what were called adventurers. That is to say, with little but their good name and their sword to exist upon, they went through Europe, accepting military and other appointments at the various courts as they could get them.

Such a man, then, was this Martin Lassamour, who had wooed and won the rich widow of the late Sir Thomas Shard so soon after the death of her late husband.

To be sure, Martin Lassamour had had plenty of warnings on the subject.

He could not say that his friends had not told him who and what the Lady Shard was. It was impossible that he could ever allege that he had made the match with his eyes shut.

Some had not scrupled to say at once, that there could be no doubt of the fact that she had murdered all her six previous husbands, while others contented themselves with only wondering at the extremely odd circumstance of a woman of thirty years of age only being so very lucky.

But in defiance of everything, as we have seen, young Martin Lassamour, who was one year younger than the lady, actually did marry her.

We shall soon see how he sped, after such rather extraordinary nuptials as those which had been celebrated at the old church at Southwark.

There was a look of satisfaction upon the face of the lady after the ceremony was over, which showed that, notwithstanding the way in which, up to the last moment, she had seemed to be willing to let Martin Lassamour draw back, how very much pleased she was at the fact that he had not, in reality, done so.

She appeared as if in a moment she had shaken off all that look of gloom which was upon her face, and awakened to a new life.

Did she really love that young and gallant soldier? It would seem as if she, in truth, did so.

And now the bridegroom, according to custom, saluted the bride; but no one else in the church showed any inclination to take advantage of the occasion, and to do so.

"Now, my love," he said, "we will leave at once for your home at Hammersmith."

"Your home now," said the bride.

"No, yours still. You, and you only, are mine. It would be very wrong and very base of me to assume any kind of authority over your rich possessions."

"When I give my heart, Martin," said the lady, "I give all. You, and you only, are my lord and master now, and I am your slave—your property—your wife, to obey you in all things, and in all things to defer to you."

This was really so sweetly spoken, that Martin Lassamour was more than ever inclined to be pleased with his bargain, and to think that the world must have been very censorious, indeed, to judge of the lady as it had done.

"What if she has had six husbands?" he said; "she could not help that. If they would die it was surely no fault of hers, poor lady ; and is she to be held up as such a monster of iniquity just because her husbands have all died ? Pho ! Stuff !"

With such spurious reasoning, Martin Lassamour tried to still the voice of alarm that, in spite of him, would make itself heard in his bosom.

The fact was, that he could not possibly conceal from himself that in marrying the wife of six husbands he had done an act of bravado, such as most men might well have shrunk from, and such as in any one else he would have condemned, no doubt, in the most unmeasured terms.

In this he was urged by two considerations.

The first was the more generous.

The lady was of a fine and commanding style of beauty, such as excites the great admiration of every man. Indeed, strange to say, there are tastes in the world which seem to prefer a woman in the exact ratio that she is unfeminine.

Thus, then, the beauty of the Lady Shard, although quite an undoubtful fact, was rather of the masculine order ; and it so happened that this Martin Lassamour was an admirer of such women.

It is well for them that there are men in the world who value them for just that masculine air and appearance for which others detest them.

Consideration the second was the boundless wealth of the widow.

Of course there were not wanting many kind friends of the young cavalier who put this down as consideration the first ; but we think we know Martin Lassamour a little better than they do. At least, we are disposed to take a more just and charitable view of his conduct in this transaction, which, of course, laid him open to much censure.

It was, then, with such hopes and such doubts, fears and expostulations, that young Martin Lassamour entered upon the rather fickle and stormy ocean of matrimony.

And yet he was a brave, bold man, and he did not allow himself to be cast down by any vague suspicions concerning his wife, or by any surmises concerning the mode by which she had become for six times a widow.

"If she should," he said to himself, "become for the seventh time a widow, it will be, I suppose, in the natural order of things, and cannot be helped ; but I will not believe for a moment that there has been anything in the shape of foul play in the business."

It will be lucky for Martin Lassamour if he can bring himself to continue in the blessed belief of his wife's innocence.

CHAPTER VII.

CHANGES TH   ENE TO A MORE HUMBLE STATION OF LIFE.

NE month has now elapsed, our readers will be pleased to consider, since the nuptial day of the fair lady of Pleasaunce House, Richmond, with the young and handsome and adventurous Martin Lassamour, her seventh husband.

The month had flown by quickly. Each passing moment had appeared to have its own peculiar pleasure, and not one had lagged or seemed to pass heavily.

It was quite a new life to Martin Lassamour. The tall trees—the sweet garden—the mass of flowers—the songs of the birds, and the murmuring of the fountains in the grounds of Pleasaunce House, were all to him sources of the very best enjoyment.

But this was just because all these sights and sounds were so fresh and new to him.

They formed to him altogether the most striking contrast to the adventurous and changing kind of life he had formerly led that they possibly could, and it was not in nature that the young man should not, to some extent, enjoy the scene.

But at length the very monotony of enjoyment began to pall upon him.

The old familiar friends and the boon companions—the struggle with poverty—the expedients from day to day to live, and the hair-breadth escapes from what, at times, looked like certain death, must all have had their charms.

The young adventurer was too easy and pleasantly situated now, and it seemed to him as if he had really got to the end of the better, because the more active part of his life.

Such a state of things would never do.

And yet Martin Lassamour's own judgment condemned him, and he often said to himself—

"Why, what a brain-sick fool I am! Have I not been striving all my life to attain to some such position as I am now in—a position of gentlemanly ease and competence? and now that I have it, with a handsome wife into the bargain, I am getting dissatisfied!"

Martin Lassamour had not reached that height of philosophy which teaches those who wish to read the lesson aright in their daily lives, that it is not the possession but the pursuit of earthly pleasures which is pleasant.

But he was quietly finding that truth out, and in a little time it was sure to be to him quite apparent.

But we will not anticipate. Sufficient for the time is the evil thereof.

It so happened that on the evening of the day which was the first month of Martin Lassamour's wedded life, a storm broke over the roof of the quiet mansion of Pleasaunce, and then it was that, starting to his feet, he cried out—

"Ah! this is something. This puts a little new life into me. I like a storm."

"Martin?" said his wife.

The tone in which she spoke stopped him in a moment in what he was about to say. He hurried to her, and saw, or fancied he saw, that she looked a little paler than usual.

"You are ill," he said.

"No—no! It is you that are ill."

"I?—oh, no! I am quite well."

"You are sick at heart, Martin. Do not heed the rage of the elements without; but sit you down by me; I wish to say something to you."

"Yes. Your wishes are my commands. I hope that I have said or done nothing to offend you?"

"Nothing whatever."

"In truth I am right glad to hear it, for from your tone and manner, my dear Margaret, I was afraid I had."

"Oh, no—no—no."

"But yet you have something to say to me?"

"I have."

"Then I am all attention. Let the storm rage without: I am better pleased to be here listening to your voice."

"Are you so?"

"Yes, I am, dear."

"Oh, Martin! is it me, or is it yourself that you are now trying to deceive?"

"Margaret?"

"Nay, do not feel offended. I am a woman, and it is said that nature, in lieu of the bodily strength and activity of men, has gifted us with a keener sense of observation, and a much more lively feeling for changes in the aspect of those whom we love, and whom we watch——"

"Watch?"

"Nay, do no interrupt me. Hear me out."

"I will."

"Then, Martin, you are tired."

"Oh, no—no; not of you."

"I do not say you are so—I do not, indeed, think you are so; but you feel that this mode of life, so different from what you have been accustomed to, is irksome to you. Now that's the simple truth, is it not?"

Martin Lassamour was silent for a few minutes, and more than once a faint denial rose to his lips, but his better nature got the better of such base promptings, and he replied—

"It is the truth."

Lady Margaret lad her hand upon his.

"Martin, I like you all the better for your candid admission of what I knew to be a fact. I think that it is quite natural that you should have such a feeling. This is a new sort of life to you, and I told you before our marriage, that you would soon feel devoured with ennui."

"You did."

"Well, you thought otherwise, Martin, but I knew you were wrong, so you see that my words have become true. I am not at all surprised or mortified, or in any way disappointed."

"You are too good to me."

"Not at all—not at all. What I looked forward to, and what I expected from the event, has happened, that is all. But I do not think that you love me the less, Martin, for all that."

"Oh, no—no. Indeed, I do not."

"I know it."

"On the contrary, your every action only convinces me more and more of what a treasure you are. Your sense, your devotion, and your mildness, all add to my affection of you."

"And your love?"

"Yes, I was going to—to say that; and my love."

"I believe it. And now, Martin, I have to make a few observations to you, and to end with a proposition."

"What is it?"

"Stop a bit. The observations must come first."

"As you please, dear Margaret."

"You are my seventh husband."

"Hem ! I—a—know that."

"I will not say, Martin, that I had no affection for any of your predecessors, for if I were to say so, it would not be true. I had some for them all."

"Yes—yes ; but—a—don't you think—"

"What?"

"That it will be just as well to let the other six sleep quietly in their graves, and not revert to them all in this sort of way, eh?"

"It is necessary at this present juncture, or else I would not, I assure you."

"Well, well, if it be necessary ; but do you know, when you speak of them it feels to me as if a lump of lead——"

Lady Margaret uttered a scream.

"Good Heavens ! what is amiss?"

"Nothing !—oh, God, nothing ! It was—it was a flash of lightning, that was all ; and—and you know, dear Martin, I don't like lightning. I am a sad coward in a storm, I fear. There, don't you hear the thunder ?"

"No—it must be very slight—nor did I see the flash of lightning you speak of."

"But I did, Martin. What were you going to say ? Pray finish."

"Well, I hardly know now."

"It was about the—a—the—a——"

"Oh, the six predecessors, that was all. I didn't know that I was going to say anything further about them, than that I would of course like to hear what you had to mention on the subject if you thought it necessary, but that for choice I would rather avoid the subject."

"Yes, but——"

"But what ?"

"You said something about—a—a lump of lead, I think, did you not ?" said Lady Margaret.

"Oh, yes. I was explaining that the mere mention of them gave me a cold feel like a lump of lead, that was all."

"Oh, that was all?"

"Yes, and foolish enough, Mistress Margaret."

"Very, because bad may be best."

"To be sure it may. But go on, dear one, and if I must be pithy about the gentlemen of whom the only pleasant thing to think is, that they are out of this world, and so being permitted to have the good fortune of calling you mine, I am quite willing to do so, only make an end of them as soon as you can, and change the subject to the far more agreeable topic of yourself, my own charming wife, Margaret, and I shall be all the more pleased."

CHAPTER VIII.

LADY MARGARET GIVES MARTIN LEAVE TO ENJOY HIMSELF A LITTLE.

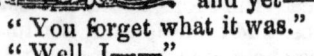LREADY is said what I have to say of them, Martin," said the Lady Margaret, after a brief pause.

"So much the better, and yet——"

"You forget what it was."

"Well, I——"

"No excuses. I will respect your memory. I said that I could not say I no affection for them, or any of them ; but that no feeling that I ever had for them was ever near to the love I have for you."

There was truth in every tone and accent of this speech, and Martin Lassamour crossed the old fire-place, and placed his arms round the neck of his wife, saying—

"And I have murmured to think the days long when with you, Margaret—you who have been so good, so kind, and so generous to me !"

"Oh, Martin, do not speak thus ! Do not."

"Nay, but I ought ; for do I not owe to you a large debt of gratitude ? Did you not give your hand to me, poor and over-head in debt as I was ? Did you not place me here master of all you possess ? Oh, yes, Margaret, I ought to be grateful to you, and I am."

"And do I owe you nothing, Martin ?"

"Nothing at all."

"Oh, yes, much. Did you not, in defiance of your friends' obloquy and public opinion, wed me ? Did you not, in spite of all that could be rumoured against me—for nothing could be said : it was all merely rumour—did you not wed me and present me with your honourable name ? Oh, yes, Martin, you did all this when you led to the altar the wife of six husbands."

Martin made a gesture of impatience.

"For the love of me," he said, "do not mention the six husbands again, I beg of you."

"I will not."

"That is right. Oh, if one could but forget them, what a capital thing it would be."

"It would. Oh, God, yes, that would be a blessing ! But now, Martin, knowing that you love me, knowing that you feel that I love you, and knowing that I may put confidence in your faith and in your honour, I have a proposition to make to you."

"Name it."

"It is this; that you go out into the world and enjoy the society of your equals —it is, that with abundance of means at your disposal, and as a gentleman, you go and seek those sports and those pastimes in London, which you have been accustomed to. All I ask of you is one thing."

"Oh, Margaret——"

"Nay, hear me out."

"I will—I will !"

"All I ask of you is, that you never are absent from this house after the present hour of the evening ; and—and that you will never let me know that you are unfaithful to me."

"Margaret, can you think me so base ?"

"No, I do not—I do not !"

"I do not know how to thank you for this kind proposition, Margaret ; but I think it will have a good effect upon me, and that will be to wean me gradually from all the foolish pursuits which I was in the habit of calling pleasures. I think that it will have the effect only of binding me more closely to you, for in the content of your quiet and endearing wifely affection, with the risks of my intended visit abroad, I shall become to understand your true nature."

"Then you will go ?"

"Yes, I—I think I will now and then."

Margaret Lassamour sighed deeply.

"You do not, after all, wish me to go ?"

"Martin, I cannot tell you an untruth. If I were to say that I wished you to go, for the sake of your going, it would not be true, for the fact is, I am partially fond, and would fain ever have you by my side ; but my reason yet tells me that you ought to go. But I ought to ask you to beware of another thing."

"What can that be ?"

"The wine-cup."

"Oh, make yourself quite easy on that score. I beg to assure you, Margaret, that I never was a drunkard. I would not have the health and the calm nerves I now have, if I had paid over-attention to the wine-cup."

"It is well. The storm is over, I think, Martin ; I will now retire to my chamber, and I hope dear—dear, Martin, that we thoroughly understand each other now ?"

"Oh, yes—yes !"

"Enough, then. If you go to-night, take this key. It will let you in by the little gate, and it opens every door until you reach the state bed-chamber, where you will find me, no doubt, or I shall be in my own room that you know of."

"Yes—yes ! but I do not think——"

"What ?"

"That I will go to town to-night."

"Nay, but I think you will ; and so, farewell, dear Martin, till you turn your steps hitherwards again."

With a slow and stately step, the Lady Margaret left the room, and Martin Lassamour was alone. For the space of about five minutes, he paced the chamber to and fro, and then he said—

"I don't half like this. It all sounds quite right, and kind, and considerate, and all that sort of thing, and yet I feel very uneasy. Is it at my own conduct or at hers ? I am afraid I am behaving unkindly to her in accepting her proposition. She sighed deeply when I did so accept it. I ought not to have done so ; and yet to shut myself up for ever, so to speak, in this old house—oh, no, I could not do that."

A roll of thunder at this moment shook the heavens, and Martin, glancing from the window, saw that the storm was anything but over.

"A rough night," he said, " and yet the ride to London will be to me all the pleasanter. I like the rough voice of the full-mouthed thunder, and the vivid flash of the forked lightning. Yes, I will go— that is, I think I will go. I wonder what she will think of my going ?"

Martin paced the room again for some time in silence, and then he said, abruptly,

" Of course she wants me to go, and if I don't go now, I shall have to live all the same scene over again, and all the talk about those infernal six predecessors of mine ! Bah ! how I seem to hate the whole lot of those six ! Six husbands before me ? It will be my sting.—I wonder what on earth they all died of ?"

Martin Lassamour threw himself into an arm-chair, and seemed in deep thought for some time, and then rising, he rang a silver hand-bell.

A servant appeared.

"Oh, Arthur?"

"Yes, sir."

"Saddle me the best riding horse in the stables at once, do you hear, and bring it to the garden gate."

"Yes, sir."

The servant retired.

"Yes," said Martin, "I will go to town— I will go to the theatres—to the good tavern, too, in Pall Mall. By Jove, they sell good wine there, and there are some clever sports, too, always to be met with; and what if I lose a few gold pieces at play, too? It will be nothing to me now. Yes, I will, at least for this one evening, have a few hours of joviality with my old companions. To be sure, they would not come to my wedding any of them, and they said rather injurious things of my wife; but what of that? They don't know her as I know her, and I can afford to laugh at all that."

There came a tap at the door of the room.

"Come in," said Martin.

Cyprian, the page of the Lady Margaret, made his appearance, and with a low bow approached Martin Lassamour, as he said,

"My mistress sends me with this to you, noble sir, and sends her love to you."

As he spoke, Cyprian placed upon the table before Martin Lassamour a small packet, which seemed to be rather heavy.

The packet was carefully tied up with silk and sealed, according to the fashion of the time.

"I will attend to it," said Martin, rather from not knowing very well what to say, than that he thought there was really anything to attend to.

The page withdrew.

"What can this mean?" he said, as he hastily opened the packet, the first object in which was a well-filled purse of money, and on the top of it lay a small piece of folded paper.

Martin eagerly opened the paper, and read the following words from it:—

"My Martin,—I send you withal to appear as you ought to appear among your friends. Remember one o'clock.

"Your own

"Margaret."

The purse sent him contained in gold and notes more than a thousand pounds in value in all. Martin sat with it in his hand for some time, and then he started to his feet and hurried from the room.

In five minutes he was going at a round gallop to London.

CHAPTER IX.

MARTIN LASSAMOUR MEETS WITH AN ADVENTURE ON HIS ROAD TO LONDON.

IT would appear as if the storm which had taken place while Martin and his wife were conversing together was but the forerunner of one of greater magnitude.

When Lassamour left Pleasaunce House he felt that there was a strange sultriness in the air, and along the horizon there was a streak of reddish light, that looked very strange and threatening in contrast with the deeply-black clouds immediately above it.

Some frightened birds flew swiftly past his face, and afar off he heard the muttering of thunder.

The horse was evidently in a state of agitation, and kept starting at every shadow that crossed his path.

"By Jove," said Martin, "the storm, I think, has yet to come, and I shall catch it before I get to London. Well, that don't matter — I can call somewhere and change my apparel, so that will be the worst of that; and as for the storm itself, why, in good truth, after this month's ease and quiet and calmness, and repose and luxury, anything is desirable to me for a change."

The reader, from all this, is able to come to a very good conclusion with regard to the character of Martin Lassamour.

In order to put a stop to the rather fidgety conduct of his horse, Martin clapped spurs to him, and made him set off at a good round gallop, which soon sent him some good four miles on his journey to London.

Now, it must be borne in mind, that although ten miles' riding took any one from Richmond to London, or from London to Richmond, then as it does now, yet that it was a very different looking ten miles then to what it is now.

The ride or the drive to Richmond is now nothing in the world but a journey past villas, and well-built houses, and trimly laid-out gardens.

At the period of which we write, though, it was quite a different thing, for some parts of the road were as lonely as though they had been a hundred miles off from any human habitation, and there were several patches of woody country to go through where even in daylight the sun was all but completely shut out from the earth.

In fact, the road was one which probably then lay under the reputation of being beset by lawless characters; and any peaceable and well-disposed persons, if they had to travel to Richmond, went in companies, in order to protect each other against the attacks of depredators.

This state of things—which there are folks who persist in calling the good old times—has happily passed away, and people may now, with only an occasional exception, pass through the breadth and length of England upon their own proper business or lawful pleasures, without the shadow of any sort of hindrance.

Surely modern civilization has then to be thanked for something in this one particular.

But Martin Lassamour had no fear.

The young husband of the great lady of Pleasaunce House was one of those persons who rather, if anything, required a certain amount of work contingent upon anything that he set about.

The probability is, that in wedding the Lady Margaret Shard there was a sort of additional charm to him in the widow, from the fact that so much strange mystery surrounded her.

What would, no doubt, have made other men shrink aghast, no doubt to his adventurous spirit was rather an additional recommendation.

We do not take upon ourselves to say that solely on such a ground as this Martin Lassamour wedded the widow; but we are quite certain her peculiar position was to him no kind of drawback, if it were not a superadded charm in the affair.

It was this seclusion that the young cavalier had had in his elegant abode at Pleasaunce, though, that had become irksome to a degree.

Now that he was alone, and in the fresh and free open air again, notwithstanding the roughness of the night, he felt like a schoolboy let out to play.

Indeed, such was the state of hilarity of the young adventurer, with a thousand pounds in his pocket, a good horse under him, and good health and spirits, that in the midst of the storm he set about singing, in a loud voice, a half-bacchanalian, half-amatory song of the period, better known among the rather licentious young gallants of the taverns and of the theatres, than to sober-minded, decent folks.

It was while, with no mild voice, he was chanting this ballad, that Martin Lassamour reached that part of the road which was more densely wooded than any other.

To be sure, by making a little detour, he might have easily enough have avoided the wood; but it was not in the nature of Martin to go out of his way for any little abstraction, so he at once spurred his horse into the little wood.

There was such a death-like stillness now in this place, that even Martin felt the influence of it, and although he did not stop singing, yet his tone was much lower than it had been.

His imagination was certainly, to some degree, affected by the silence of the spot.

Presently his horse either trod in a hole in the ground, or it saw some shadow which had the effect of, for the moment, terrifying it; for it shied, and nearly fell, and, in fact, the probability is that it would have fallen, but that it had a rider on its back of the most perfect skill in the management of a steed.

"Hilloa!" cried Martin Lassamour, as he patted the neck of his steed. "What is the meaning of that, old friend? You ought not to stumble."

The horse seemed to be nervous and fidgety.

"Let me see," said Martin, suddenly looking about him. "I hope I am on the right road."

This was one of those doubtful speeches that a man makes to himself when he begins to feel pretty sure that he has made some sort of mistake as to his route; and, in fact, to look about him, or to attempt to look about, at that time of darkness in such a place, with a hope of finding out a lost path, was one of the difficulties of travelling which it would not take any one many minutes fully and entirely to appreciate.

"By Jove!" said Martin, "I can't say that I know whether I am going east, west, north or south."

He half shut his eyes in order to concentrate their power of vision.

But that was of little avail; for let him look on which side of him he would, there was the same prospect of tall, black-looking stems of trees, while overhead their foliage appeared to unite to form a canopy of the blackest and of the most impervious character.

"Hem!" he said. "Pleasant this."

He had brought his horse to a standstill, and it was well that he had done so, for at the moment there came so terrific a clap of thunder, that had the creature been in motion there is very little doubt but that it would have fallen.

The young cavalier seemed to shake with the force of the concussion in the air.

As it was, the horse made a sudden plunge, which would have overturned many a rider; but Martin Lassamour preserved his seat.

"Woa!" he cried. "Woa! Why what in the name of the fiends have you to be frightened at in a clap of harmless thunder, I should like to know?"

By patting and coaxing the horse, he got it to stand quite still, with the exception of trembling, which the cavalier could not control.

"I wonder how long the storm is going to last now?" said Martin, as he tried to catch a glimpse of the night sky through the trees.

It was in vain, though, to attempt to do so.

Martin then smiled to himself, as he said—

"I trow that my Lady Margaret will think that such a night as this ought to bring me back to Pleasaunce House, instead of going to London; but if she has such a thought, she does not know me yet."

Putting his steed in motion now again, Martin Lassamour thought that his best plan would be to get out of the wood, and so, by reaching the open road, see if he was going right for London, or had left his proper route.

Hardly had he got half a dozen paces, though, among the trees, when a strange screaming, yelling voice, broke the stillness of the night air, and he thought he heard the words—

"Hold—hold! Mind my little ones!"

"Little ones?" he cried. "What on earth is the meaning of that, I wonder?"

"Ha—ha—ha!" roared something with an unearthly sort of laugh, and then all was still again. It was not a human laugh that—of that there could be no sort of doubt.

CHAPTER X.

MARTIN LASSAMOUR HAS A STRANGE ADVENTURE ON HIS ROAD.

ARTIN LASSA-MOUR was anything in the world but a superstitious man.

But, then, he lived in an age when the wild and the wonderful had a much greater amount of credulous believers than in our own times.

No wonder, then, that when he heard this strange and truly demoniac kind of laugh, he rather hastily drew rein, and felt anything but quite comfortable.

It was not for many moments, though, that Martin allowed any species of fear to prey upon him, and then he cried out in a loud voice—

"Who and what are you? Speak in intelligible language, if you have aught to say to me."

"Martin Lassamour," said a voice.

Martin started, for it was a strange, hissing kind of voice, and so close to his ear as it seemed to be, so that he involuntarily put up his arm to keep the speaker off from nearer contact with him.

"Martin Lassamour," said the voice again.

"Yes. I am he," he said.

"'Tis well."

Martin waited now for a few moments in silence, with the expectation that something would follow this; but as nothing came of it, he said, in the course of about half a minute—

"Well, I am he."

"Wait," said the voice.

"Wait?"

"Yes, wait!"

"And for what, pray?"

There was no reply in words, but a very faint and very beautifully coloured crimson light, not far from him among the branches of the trees, and seemingly in the very midst of the long finger-like leaves of an old fern, appeared to be a pictorial kind of reply to him.

"What is that?" he said.

"Hush!" said the voice.

The light did not increase in size, but its lustre every moment increased in brilliancy, until it was so brightly beautiful that it was painful to look upon.

And yet Martin Lassamour felt a sort of fear as regarded it, and he could not take his eyes away from it if he would.

"Martin Lassamour," said the voice again.

"Yes," he said, "I am he. I am not in the habit of denying my name. Tell me what is the meaning of all this?"

"You shall know."

"Many thanks."

"Deride not, nor think nor speak lightly of that which you know not. Beware! beware! beware!"

"Of what?"

"Lead!"

"Oh, indeed. Well, many a better man than I have fallen by a bullet, and if that is to be the mode by which my spirit is to be released from its mortal pains, why so be it."

"No, not by the bullet—not by the deadly bullet shall your days end, Martin Lassamour, husband of the wife of six husbands."

"Hold!" said Martin, suddenly. "You would much oblige me, be you whom you may, if you would so far study my feelings and my wishes as to say nothing of my six predecessors."

"And why not?" said a voice so close to him, that he felt certain he had but to stretch out his hand to touch the speaker.

He did so stretch out his hand, but there was nothing to grasp but the thin and unsubstantial air.

"Where are you?" he said.

"Here!"

The voice was now on the other side of him.

"Ah, yes, I have you."

Again he was foiled.

"Here," said the voice again, and again it was on his right side, where it had originally sounded.

Martin made an effort to grasp the person who spoke, if indeed it were a person,

but he said in a grave tone of voice, not without some emotion—

"Who or what you are I know not. You may be mortal or you may not; but if you be not, it is not well to jest with one who is still in the flesh, and who has mortal fears and feelings still about him."

"Well spoken," said the voice.

The tone of the voice was no longer mocking, as it had been before, but there was an air of gentle sadness about it that was very sweet.

"What want you with me, then?" added Lassamour.

"Much."

"But first tell me who you are?"

"I may not."

"Well. Do you live?"

"Oh, yes—yes."

"But not as men live? You are not human?"

"Question me not, Martin Lassamour, but listen to me with all your soul."

"I will."

"'Tis well. You are the seventh husband.

Martin Lassamour uttered a groan.

"Still those six predecessors of mine," he thought, "are to be thrown in my face."

It seemed as if the unknown being who spoke to him heard the purport of his thoughts, for it replied to them at once, saying,—

"Better hear often of the six that went before you, than be spoken of by the eighth who might follow you."

"Why, yes, I grant that."

"Then listen."

"I do—I will!"

"Beware of her whom you have wedded. If you would know more, take this fern leaf. It was plucked on the eve of St. John, and is from the miraculous root which gives eyes to the soul in sleep. Take it and keep it in your bosom when next you sleep in the state-chamber—alone! alone!"

"What fern leaf? I see nothing."

"You have it."

"Indeed, I have not."

"It is done! Farewell! oh, farewell! And beware—beware of her whom you have given your name to."

"Yes; but——"

A yell, so strange and startling and unearthly that it seemed, for the moment, as if it pierced his brain like a sword, sounded in his ears. It was either that the horse heard the yell as well as his rider, and set off at mad speed in consequence, or, by the sudden impulse which was given to Martin Lassamour by it, he struck the spurs he wore deep into the flanks of the startled animal; but, in either case, the effect was the same, for the creature set off at a mad gallop.

Two minutes sufficed to carry Martin Lassamour quite clear of the wood.

The clouds opened and revealed a patch of blue sky, into which sailed a gracious and beautiful full moon; and in an instant, as if by magic, trees, hill, road, mansion and river, were all revealed to the gaze of Martin Lassamour.

He was on his high road to London; and as his steed did not seem inclined to relax its speed, for a mile or two he let it have its own way, and galloped on, full of strange thoughts about what had happened to him in the little wood.

The storm-clouds that had made the early night look so dreary, had completely blown over; and by the time Martin Lassamour reached the great city, a lovelier evening could hardly have been conceived. The horse, as well as his rider, appeared to feel all the luxury of the delightful change in the state of the air.

The mad speed at which the cavalier had gone was relaxed into an easy and pleasant canter; and Martin Lassamour could hardly persuade himself that the scene through which he had passed was real.

"Was I dreaming," he said, "or did I hear and see all that I thought I heard and saw in the wood? Upon my faith, I think I must have nodded on my horse's back, and so fancied it, for it partakes too much of the character of the wild and the wonderful to be relied upon as true.

There was one strange circumstance, too, that had all its effect in inducing Martin Lassamour to be very doubtful about the reality of his adventure in the little wood, and that was that, although so much stress had been laid upon his possessing himself of a certain leaf of fern, no effort had been made to be sure that he took it.

"I have no leaf of fern," he said, "and as the whole affair seemed to be for the purpose of inducing me to take such a leaf, why my not taking it convinces me pretty well that I must have got into a kind of reverie in the wood and dreamt it."

Martin was just of that careless sort of temper that he was ever willing to accept the curt explanation of anything that troubled him.

CHAPTER XI.

LASSAMOUR IS RATHER LATE HOME FROM HIS REVEL IN THE CITY.

HERE was an old tavern in London at which Martin Lassamour had been accustomed to spend much of his very precariously-earned money, and where he was in the habit of associating with many of those boon companions whom he had shaken off, or who had shaken off him, at the period of his marriage.

The fact is, this community of *bon vivants* looked upon it as a sort of high treason against good-fellowship to get married. They soon found that when one of their members entered into the matrimonial condition he was no longer fit company for them, or, as the phrase might have been reversed, they were no longer fit company for him.

It had been a sad blow to them to find that Martin Lassamour, who had been the life and soul of their frolicking meetings, had taken to himself a wife.

In Martin they had ever found the ready wit to plan enterprises of fun, frolic, and daring, and the ready courage to carry them out, so that with his absence one half of the spirit of their meetings had flown.

The fact was, that although not distinctly formed into a club for any express purpose, the young men who met at this tavern were of the class called Mohocks, that set London in such a ferment in an after reign.

These Mohocks were bands of young men, with plenty of money, plenty of time, and no characters, who banded themselves together for the purpose of doing anything that was contrary to law, order, and social decency, for their own amusement, after dark.

The ill-organised police of London, at that period, were anything but in a condition to contend with such bands of men.

At a time, too, when all who claimed, whether upon good or bad grounds, the title of gentleman wore swords, it was no easy matter to contend against some twenty or more half-drunken men with such weapons.

It was, then, not exactly to so very wild and lawless a crew that Martin Lassamour had belonged; but they in many respects resembled the Mohocks of a future era; and it is well to feel that they differed from them in the one important particular, that Martin's friends indulged in practical jokes, which were intended to be jokes, while the Mohocks indulged in all sorts of vices.

There was quite a blaze of light from the principal room of the tavern as Martin Lassamour pulled up his horse at its entrance.

"Hilloa!" he cried, "hilloa! Mark Apsley, where are you, man? Is this the way you attend to old friends and customers?"

"Oh, Lord!" cried the landlord, coming out into the street. "Bless us and save us, if here is not the right worshipful and gracious Martin Lassamour. The sight of your worship is good for sore eyes. Well, I never! and how is your worship?"

"Quite well, old fellow," said Martin, as he flung himself from his horse. "Let my steed be well seen to, for I don't know exactly where you could light upon his fellow."

"Goodness gracious, no! Oh, what a beauty! Here, Tim! Tim!—Tim, I say!"

"Yes, master," said the ost'er's boy, making his appearance, with strong indications of having been at his usual employment, namely, draining the wine measures.

"Take the worshipful Martin Lassamour's horse, you rascal, and see to him well."

"Yes, master."

"Do, Tim," said Lassamour, "and on your head be it."

"On my head, sir?"

"Yes, you d—d rascal."

"Yes, sir."

Tim led the horse into the stable, and Martin Lassamour, with a feeling of pride about him, entered the tavern.

Truly that was the first time that Lassamour had ever been able to enter it in such bran trim as he was then in.

The appearance of the young man was striking in the extreme, and he well set off the handsome clothing which he now wore.

His dress was far from being gaudy, but it was rich in the extreme. Every article he wore was the very best, and the most expensive of its kind. The buttons and loops of his apparel were of solid gold.

He wore diamonds upon different parts of his dress, to a large amount of money.

A ring upon his finger he knew that his lady wife had given three hundred pounds for—the jewel that looped up his cap was probably worth as much—his sword had a hilt of silver richly gilt—and, in fact, with the thousand pounds in his purse, and all his jewels about him, Martin Lassamour was quite a walking fortune in a small way, and he felt that he was so.

Truly, Martin ought at that moment, when he felt so much pride in his gay appearance, and the wealth that had been spent upon him, to have thought upon the fine lady at Pleasaunce House, who was no doubt counting the weary hours till his return.

But the young man's thoughts did not go home just then. He was, on the contrary, full of glee at his escape from his splendid prison, as in good truth the magnificent house at Richmond had come to seem to him.

He forgot even the strange adventure in the little wood on the road to London, so intent was he upon surprising his old associates with his presence.

The landlord, anticipating great credit for so doing, made an effort to pass him to announce him, but Martin Lassamour caught him by the nape of the neck, crying out as he did so—

"Hilloa! whither so fast?"

"Oh, only—to—to—that is——"

"What?"

"To let them know that your worshipful worship has arrived. That is all."

"Indeed?"

"Yes, noble sir, and so——"

"Silence. I will let them know myself."

"Oh, then, in that case, I—a——"

"May go down stairs again."

"Truly so, noble sir."

"And, do you hear? when you come up again, which let be soon, if you please, you will bring with you as much as you can carry of that rare old claret that you only keep for great occasions, and that you charge such a price for, that it will be enough to weigh your soul to perdition at the day of judgment."

"Lord, have mercy upon us!"

"It is true."

"Nay, but, worthy sir——"

"Stuff! Give me none of your lying excuses."

"Lying? Oh, Lord! oh, Lord! The idea now——"

"Of what?"

"Of any one for even half a moment accusing me of lying! I who am truth itself! Oh—oh! And as for the price of the claret, I can only say that——"

"You will take care that I pay for it."

"Well, a——"

"That will do. Charge your price: I can and will pay it, for I am rich now, as you perhaps know. I have married a rich lady, who does not stint me in the use of her wealth, I can tell you."

"Yes, sir, so I hear, worshipful sir. Why, they do say that out of the last six husbands she had, she must have made a million of money, noble sir."

"Silence!"

"Sir?"

"Hark you: if ever again you name the six husbands in my hearing, I will straight walk out of your house, and you will never see me cross its threshold again."

"Oh!—oh!"

"Understand me now. This is no idle threat, and no jest. I am quite sincere, and I will keep my word, with the little addition, perhaps, of breaking your head as I go. So you had better be careful."

"I will, noble sir. Lor bless me, I shall, now that your worship has spoken of it, as soon think of mentioning the si——Oh, dear, no, I didn't say it."

"Beware!"

"I will—I will. As much claret as I can bring up stairs, your worship ordered?"

"I did; and mind you that it is of the best."

"It shall be—it shall be. Dear heart, but I feel quite happy, and twenty years younger, to see your worship. Why, the place has not seemed like itself for the past month or so, since your worship has left us. Well, well, this is quite a happy night, I declare, and I feel half out of my wits with joy."

CHAPTER XII.

MARTIN LASSAMOUR FINDS THAT HE HAS THE LEAF OF FERN.

AND now, indeeed, Martin Lassamour did forget his fine lady-wife at her grand estate of Pleasaunce, as he opened the door of the apartment in which the boon companions he had scarcely ever expected to see again sat.

At sight of him there was at first some such a stare of astonishment as one might have supposed his apparition would have been greeted with, had he been supposed to be dead.

During that stare, though, at him, the various persons in the room had ample time to see the very flourishing condition of their old associate, and that was a species of information by no means lost upon them. There were the diamonds—the rich clothes—the prosperous look, which never can by any possibility be assumed if it has no reality, and never can by any possibility be mistaken.

No sooner, then, were these evidences of the changed fortunes of Martin Lassamour apparent, without the shadow of a doubt, than the whole party, with one accord, gave a loud and ringing cheer of welcome.

Martin was vain enough to be intensely gratified at this, and he lifted his plumed hat as in recognition of the shout.

"Bravo!" cried one, "bravo! Another cheer more for our well-beloved friend and comrade, Martin Lassamour. Bravo! one cheer more!"

The one cheer more was given with such a hearty good-will, that the old house shook again, and the lights danced in the chandelier that hung from the ceiling.

"Thanks to you all," said Martin, as he advanced into the centre of the room. "Thanks to all."

Twenty hands were outstretched to him to shake, and he hardly knew which to take first.

"Why, Martin," said one, "where have you been for this age? Surely not with your wife?"

"Ha! ha!" cried the others.

"The wife of six husband!" cried one.

"Ha! ha!" laughed the whole party again.

Martin Lassamour held up his right hand for silence, and that action, together with the slightly heightened colour of his cheek, at once induced them all to be still and listen to him.

"Old friends and comrades," he said, "I have something now and at once to say to you, before we exchange another word together. Will you listen to me?"

"Yes—yes."

"To be sure we will."

"More wine, friend?"

"Silence—silence."

"Hear the noble Martin Lassamour!—Hear him!—hear him!"

"Gentlemen," said Lassamour, "when you are quite at leisure, and quite disposed to hear me, I will go on."

"Yes, yes. Now—now!"

"Very well, then. I shall assuredly come among you as of old, if you wish me so to do."

"Yes, yes; oh, yes!" cried the whole party.

"Very good," added Martin. "I do believe that you sincerely wish to see me among you as I used to be: I do believe that from my soul."

"You may, Martin."

"Then we may look upon that part of the affair as settled, gentlemen; and I now come to the condition upon which I intend to come."

"The condition?"

"Yes, the condition. Now, gentlemen, I am very far from being so arrogant as to wish to impose any condition upon you for my own pleasure or gratification. All I wish is, that you should know upon what understanding I will come here, and if that does not suit you, I can stay away."

"Name it—name it!"

"I will. It is that you never mention my wife, or her previous husbands, either in jest or in earnest, or on any pretext whatever, in my hearing or presence."

The guests looked at each other in silence.

"Come," added Martin, "does the condition please you or displease you?"

With one accord, then, they broke silence in a unanimous assent to the condition imposed upon them by Martin Lassamour, and he drew a long breath of relief at the thought that he had overruled all murmurs and all objections with regard to his rather extraordinary marriage.

"Then, gentlemen," he said, "you know me as you used to know me—as Martin Lassamour, one of yourselves. It is true that I shall not be often with you; but I wish that when I do come, I may find from you all the same good fellowship and the hearty welcome that I used to find."

"You shall—you shall!"

"Upon my faith, I believe it."

The opening of the door, now, and the appearance of the landlord, accompanied by a couple of his drawers or waiters bearing a number of bottles of the well-known and as well admired claret for which it was very seldom that any of the present party happened to be in sufficient funds to pay for, raised the popularity of Martin Lassamour to the very highest possible pitch, for they saw, in a moment, by the looks of the landlord and the smile upon the face of Martin that it was his order, and that he meant, or had paid for it all.

We need not follow the career of Martin upon that evening. Suffice it to say, that he drank sufficiently of the rich wine, and that he was seduced into play, at which he lost every farthing of the one thousand pounds that his munificent lady had placed at his disposal.

Heated with the wine, and a little vexed at his losses, Martin Lassamour sprang to his feet, as a clock in the house struck the hour of twelve.

"What is that?" he cried. "What hour?"

"Twelve!"

"Fore God, so it is! My horse—my horse! I have far to ride! My horse!"

"But, Lassamour, you won't go yet?"

"Yes—yes!"

"Oh, no—no! We don't mean to stand that sort of thing. It won't do, old fellow. Bar the door, gentlemen. He don't go yet."

Martin hurried to the door just as several of his boon companions ran to it and fastened it. A flush of colour came to his cheeks, and then he turned a little paler than was usual with him, as he said in quite a calm and cool voice—

"Gentlemen, when I tell you that it is my wish to go, and go I must, I trust that there is no man here who will go through the farce of attempting to stop me."

"Ha—ha!" laughed some of the more riotous of the set. "That won't do. No! no! He don't go yet for a good two hours."

Martin Lassamour placed his hand upon the hilt of his sword, but in an instant he took it away again, as he said—

"I appeal to those who are sober enough to understand that when a gentleman says he intends to go, he is not to be prevented by the idle badinage of some who have drunk too deeply of the good wine."

This appeal was not without its effect. Some half dozen of those who had been more anxious to win the money of Martin Lassamour than to drink the wine, and who were, therefore, sober enough to see the gross impropriety of trying to detain him, and who had a suspicion that any further attempt of the kind might be so offensive as to keep him away again, now interferred, and a kind of squabble ensued, in the midst of which the door was pushed open from without, and a tall, swarthy, dark-looking man, rather fashionably attired, stood on the threshold.

"Hilloa!" he said, "what is all this about?"

"Hurrah! for Sir Warrenne de Vo-lence," cried one, calling thus out at the top of his voice the name of the new comer.

This Sir Warrenne de Volence was a man who, it is true, did at times form one of the party at the old tavern, but his bad and quarrelsome disposition never made him very welcome.

Against our friend, Martin Lassamour, he had a special dislike, for having gambled away his means, this De Volence had sought to repair his ruined fortune with the wealth of the Lady Margaret Shard, and had been refused proudly by that lady only one week before her marriage with the young and gallant Martin Lassamour.

No wonder that the sight of Martin was wormwood to him.

CHAPTER XIII.

MARTIN LASSAMOUR REACHES PLEASAUNCE HOUSE BEYOND THE APPOINTED TIME.

E VOLENCE wore a blackened scowl upon his face, which was by no manner of means dissipated by the encounter with Martin Lassamour.

As for the rest of the mad-brained party, they appeared to think that a collision between the former rivals was now all but certain, for De Volence had used very disparaging conversation concerning Martin, and they seemed to all jump to the conclusion that he must by some means know of it, although he certainly did not.

Possibly De Volence himself, upon the supposition, true enough in many cases, that defamation, let it be uttered where it will, commonly finds its way to the object of it, seemed to think that Martin Lassamour must know that he had spoken very slightingly of him behind his back, and he evidently stood upon his guard.

"What!" he said. "Lassamour here?"

"Yes—yes," cried several, "and a good fellow he is too. Long life to him!"

"Oh, indeed."

"Sir Warrenne de Volence," said Martin Lassamour, "will you have the goodness to get out of my way?"

"Sir?"

"I say, will you get out of my way, as I am about to leave the room, and you occupy the threshold of the door?"

"Oh, Heaven forbid that I should detain you, sir, when you wish to run away."

"Sir?"

"I say what I say."

"But did you mean, sir, to insult me by what you say? for if you do I must request, as my time is limited, that you will have the candour to say so at once."

"Oh, dear, no, my good sir. I can well imagine that the married man is in a hurry to get home. Perhaps the lady has a will of her own. Ha!"

"Sir Warrenne de Volence," said Martin, slowly and calmly, "will you have the goodness to attend to what I say for a few minutes without interrupting me?"

"Oh, certainly! Say on."

"Then, sir, I do not allow any one to jest with me, or to mention in any tone of levity or disrespect, either myself or the lady who is my wife."

"Oh!"

"You comprehend me, sir?"

"And if I presume to mention her, even notwithstanding this little dissension? What then?"

"Why then, sir, I shall kick you."

"What?"

"Kick you!"

"Zounds! Blood and fury! the very hint of such an insult requires blood to wipe it out! Caitiff! adventurer! fortune-hunter! seventh husband of a strumpet! have at you! I will rid the fair lady of another spouse to-night!"

It was quite clear that Sir de Volence thought to take Martin Lassamour at unawares, and inflict either death or so much injury upon him before he could draw in his own defence, as to render the contest between them not at all doubtful. With such a base intent he let his hand creep to the handle of his sword, and even as he spoke, he drew it from its scabbard with such quickness, that it was quite clear he had had an intention to use it so soon as he dared to do so with any hope of asserting afterwards that he had sufficient provocation so to do.

Before any one could intefere in the slightest degree for the protection of Martin, Sir Warrenne made a lunge at him, and but for the quickness with which Lassamour stepped aside, that moment would have been his last.

"Villain!" cried Martin, as he seized the hilt of his sword to draw it.

Alas! the sword was a new one, and it stuck rather closely to the scabbard, so that De Volence had yet another opportunity of making a lunge at him, which, no doubt, would have been fatal, but that one of the company, a mere youth of the name of Lamont, rushed forward, and snatching from the table a rather massive candlestick, flung it, candle and all, full in the face of De Volence.

"Take that, assassin!" he said.

De Volence received the candlestick right in the centre of his face, and the blow was so well aimed and so great, that over he went as if he had been shot.

"Bravo!—bravo!" responded from all parts of the room now, and a general clapping of hands ensued.

Martin Lassamour had got his sword drawn by this time, but there was no occasion to use it, for his antagonist was either insensible or pretended to be so.

Turning to young Lamont, Martin said—

"My good sir, I owe my life to you."

"Oh, don't mention that," cried the young man, as he drew his sword and placed himself by the side of Lassamour. "I won't be still and see a man play such an assassin's game as this rascal would have played."

"Come with me," said Martin Lassamour, placing his hand upon the arm of the young man, "come with me. Gentle-men, good-night; my time is, inceed, not my own just now, or I would awaken Sir Warrenne de Volence. I leave him, though, with the less reluctance, that I know he knows well where to find me; for it will be at the house of her to whom he went a wooing and got rejected. Will any of you, too, tell him, when he rises, one thing?"

"Yes—yes—oh, yes!"

"Tell him, then, that if my young friend, Lamont, here, should meet with any accident during the next twelve months or so, that I shall lay it at the door of De Volence, and call him to such an account as shall necessitate his settling his affairs in this world. Come, Lamont. Follow me!"

So saying, Martin Lassamour left the room, taking his young preserver with him.

It was half-past twelve.

Martin Lassamour uttered a groan.

"My dear, sir," said Lamont, "what is the matter with you? Did the villain hurt you?"

"No—no! but time is flying."

"Yes; but the night is young."

"It is to others, but not to me. I brought you away because I wanted you to be out of the way of that savage, De Volence. Promise me, will you, that should he challenge you, you will send for me?"

"I will."

"Thanks—thanks! Call upon me when you will at Pleasaunce House, Richmond, and the sooner the better. Adieu! I have no time to say another word to you."

He shook hands heartily with the young man, and then striding to the door of the inn, he called out—

"My horse—my horse, I say! Oh, quick—quick!"

Martin Lassamour promised to be too good a customer to the tavern to be neglected, and his good steed was soon brought out to him.

Without, then, waiting a moment to say a word to any one, he mounted, and set off at a mad gallop towards the Richmond road.

Martin Lassamour knew that he could not do the distance in the time before him; but yet he wanted to be as little behind the time as possible.

"By Heaven!" he said, "had it not been, now, for that rascal, De Volence, all would have been well. I could have ridden it in the whole hour easily; but now it is out of the question. It is just possible, though, that Margaret may not notice my being a little over the hour of one."

It was with a feeling of deep chagrin that Martin Lassamour heard one o'clock peal from the clock of a church tower while he was yet a good four miles from his home.

"Oh, but this is provoking," he said—"on the first cccasion, too, on which she has behaved so handsomely, and I may say, so nobly to me—placing a thousand pounds in my pocket, and only asking me to be at home by the hour of one, and yet I lose the money and break my promise! It is too bad. I don't know what I shall say to her when I see her beautiful face in the morning."

Although, by the striking of one o'clock, Lassamour felt that it was no use struggling to save his credit at home, yet he went on at such a pace that the four miles were soon over.

He drew up his foaming and panting steed at the little gate in the garden wall, of which his lady had given him the key.

"By Jove, though," he said to himself, as he opened the gate, "I must call up some of the fellows to mind my horse for me, and take him to his stall."

As he spoke, he opened the gate, but the moment that he did so, a voice said to him—

"Welcome home, sir !"

"Ah, who is that?"

"Cyprian, my good master."

"Oh, my lady's page?"

"The same, sir."

"Is—is your lady up, good Cyprian, or —or—has she retired for the night, can you tell me?"

"She was up till one, sir, and then she left the hall, and retired, as I heard, to her own small chamber. She desired that you should be shown to the state bed-room, where some refreshment is laid for you."

CHAPTER XIV.

MARTIN LASSAMOUR HAS RATHER A STRANGE VISION IN THE NIGHT.

NOW Martin would fain have asked the page how his lady seemed to bear his absence; but, although the question came to the tip of his tongue, so to speak, he somehow forbore to put it.

A pride, that was very proper in its way, restrained him ; and, besides, he knew that Cyprian had been in his lady's service before her marriage with him, Lassamour, and he did not feel quite sure that anything he might say would not be reported to Margaret.

"Very well, Cyprian," he said. "I can find my way to the room by myself. You look to the horse."

"As you please, sir. Sober !"

"Eh?"

"Sir?"

"I thought you said something, Cyprian."

"Not I, my good master."

Lassamour, by the light of the moon, which was still in the heavens, tried to look in the face of the page, to see if by such an examination he could detect if he had spoken or not; but a cloud at the moment swept over the face of the luminary and baffled him.

"Cyprian?" he said.

"My good sir."

"I thought you muttered the word sober."

"Oh, dear, no, sir."

"Very well. Good night."

Martin Lassamour walked away through the garden in the direction of the house; but he felt quite certain that Cyprian had uttered the word sober, notwithstanding the sturdy and apparently calm denial of it by the page.

It was an irksome thing for him to think so, but now Martin Lassamour could not but come to the mortifying conclusion that Cyprian had been placed where he found him in order to impart to his mistress the state in which he, Martin Lassamour, should reach home.

"Confound it," cried Martin. "I don't very well see how I can object to it, or what I can say about it; but this system of espionage is not to my taste by any means."

The probability is that if Lassamour had not been sober, so that the conduct of the page had been the other way, he would have been much more angry upon the occasion; but as it was he only felt a degree of chagrin at the fact that he was watched in order to be reported upon.

Martin soon found his way to the state bed-chamber.

He stood in that same room in which Sir Thomas Shard, the sixth husband, had breathed his last.

The darkness of the room, and the general features of it, remained the same as when we first introduced it to the reader.

Upon the hearth burnt a brisk and pleasant fire of cedar logs, which threw out a grateful perfume, and upon a little table near to the fireside was a slight repast, with a bottle of choice Spanish wine.

The lady was not there, though.

Martin Lassamour felt uneasy.

"I suppose," he said, "Cyprian will find some mode of letting her know that I am at home, and she will come to me."

Minute after minute passed though, and come she did not, and then he said,—

"Well, I don't see any very great indecorum in a man seeking his own wife, so I will just take a glass of this Spanish wine, which I happen to know is of the right sort, and then I will seek her chamber, since she does not seem disposed to seek mine."

As Lassamour lifted the bottle with the Spanish wine, he saw a small folded paper lying beneath it on the table.

A glance let him see that the address upon it was to himself.

"What is this?" he said. "What can this mean?"

Eagerly he opened the paper and read as follows:—

"One o'clock.

"Martin, I am not angry—I am, perhaps, a little vexed. Let us not meet till the morning.—Yours, &c.,
                          "MARGARET."

He dropped the little note to the floor, and sank into a seat in an attitude of musing.

It was a tall, old-fashioned chair with a wilderness of easy cushions in it, and Martin Lassamour leant back in it, and fixing his eyes on the crackling logs in the grate, he said to himself—

"Humph! She is not angry, but she is vexed. I guess the one feeling is not very far off the other. What ought I to do? What—ought—I—to—do?"

He was silent for a time.

"Perhaps," he said. "I ought to seek her at once, and try to laugh the affair off; or tell her sincerely how that brute in human shape, De Volence, detained me; and yet, no—no. If I do, she will be in dread of a duel between us, and will be trying to exact from me some promise or another, that it will be difficult to resist."

He was silent for a still longer period of time, and then he said in a low tone—

"I think, after all, I had better fairly do as she wishes, and wait till the morning, and then in broad daylight I can tell her just that I could not get here, and there will be an end of it. Yes—yes, that will be the best, after all."

The flames in the wood fire gradually subsided, and left nothing but the red embers on the old fire-dogs of the ample hearth.

Martin reached out his hand and took another goblet of the old Spanish wine.

"This wine," he said, "agrees pleasantly enough with the claret that I did not, thank the fates, take too much of, and so, as Master Cyprian has had the kindness to testify, I am 'sober.' "

It was quite clear that Martin Lassamour was not at all too well pleased at the hearing of this accidental expression concerning his condition from the page.

"Curse his impertinence," he said, after a pause, and then he took another drop of the rare Spanish wine.

How still the old house was.

To be sure, now and then from without there came a sighing sort of sound which was nothing but the night wind among the tall trees that were not far from the windows of the room in which Martin sat; but that, certainly, was the only sound that at any time disturbed the solemn repose of the hour.

The feeling that had prompted Martin to delay seeking his lady, even in defiance of the sort of prohibition against doing so contained in the note he had found upon his table, soon proved a practical refutation in the progress of the time.

"I cannot go now," he said. "If I had gone at once, and on the impulse of the moment, it would have been all very well; but after reflection it will not do; so I must even obey her, and trust to the morning."

He took off his sword and laid it on the table before him, as he said—

"Well, I suppose I shall require some rest, at all events, and I may as well go to bed."

Martin Lassamour was certainly getting rather sleepy, and no wonder, too, considering how far he had ridden, and what company he had been in.

He yawned several times as he sat looking at the fire, and then he suddenly started, for he thought he heard a strange noise in the room.

"Who's that?" he cried.

All was still.

"Is any one here?"

No answer.

It then struck him that some one had tapped at the door of the room, so in order to make quite sure upon that point, he called out—

"Come in !"

Nobody obeyed this permission, and then Martin, after taking a steady look all round the chamber, made up his mind that it was nothing.

"Pho!" he said, "I am half asleep, I suppose, and some gust of wind has shaken a door or a casement, and made me fancy some one was at hand. The best thing I can do is to go to bed."

The state bed in that room was, in good truth, a very magnificent affair indeed, and looked as it it invited kind repose.

Martin Lassamour looked about upon the ample hearth to see if there were any billets of wood with which he could replenish the fire, but there were none, so he was compelled, after a kick at the dying embers, which put them closer to each other, to let it go as it might.

With the slowness of a man scarcely half awake, Martin Lassamour took off his doublet.

"Ah," he said, in a low tone of voice, "they do sell a good sort of claret where I have been to-night; but if that rascal, De Volence, makes the place his resort, it will never do for me to go, or it will be the death of one or either of us, or, perhaps, of both. Yes, perhaps, of—What is this?"

Something fell at his feet as he unbuckled the garment beneath his doublet.

Martin Lassamour stooped hastily, and picked the something up. It was a heavy fern leaf, looking quite fresh and soft as if just plucked from a tree.

CHAPTER XV.

MARTIN LASSAMOUR KNOWS NOT IF HE DREAMT OR SAW A VISION.

Y what unaccountable and mysterious agency this fern leaf had found its way to his breast in such a fashion, Lassamour was quite at a loss to conceive.

But there it was in his hand, and all the circumstances connected with his singular adventure in the wood on his route to London came strongly and fully upon his memory.

He sunk back into the large arm-chair in silence with the fern leaf in his hand.

A crowd of strange thoughts came through his mind in mad confusion.

After a time he spoke.

"This is very strange—it is more than strange. What on earth am I to think of it ? Am I awake, or am I merely dreaming of this matter? Martin—Martin Lassamour, rouse yourself, and do not be made the fool of superstition in such a fashion."

The embers in the fire-place appeared now to be upon the point of expiring, and the lamp upon the table had a very sickly aspect to his eyes.

But there was the piece of fern in his hand. There could be no possible mistake about that. It, at the least, was such a tangibility that he could not fancy its existence by any stretch of imagination if it had none in reality.

Martin sat in this position, then, for about ten minutes or so in deep thought, with the fern leaf in his hand and his eyes fixed upon it.

How long he would have sat there in such a reverie it is hard to say; but his reflections were disturbed, suddenly, by his hearing something in the room like a deep-drawn sigh.

Martin started.

The sigh came again.

"What is that ?" he gasped. "Am I alone?"

As he asked the question his eyes slowly wandered around the room, as if in search of some one who was to give him an answer to it, and then they rested upon another antique arm-chair, similar to the one he occupied, and which stood on the other side of the fire-place.

He recollected having, only some few evenings before, laughingly requested that there might be two such chairs in the state bed-chamber now that the lady of the house was no longer alone.

Yes, the eyes of Martin Lassamour became fixed on this old chair with a strange sort of fascination, and as he looked at it, he felt as if, for a moment or two, his very breath was suspended.

The chair was occupied!

How, or by whom it was occupied, Lassamour would probably have found it hard to say; but that some strange, shadowy, misty form sat in it, there could be no doubt.

As Lassamour looked at this form, it grew more and more distinct each moment. From being a misty, indistinct-looking object, it grew into something like shape and substance to his eyes.

At last, he saw that there sat opposite to him a cavalier, well dressed, and with all the appointments of a gentleman about him.

The face was awfully and deadly pale, though, and there were blue lines about it which were shudderingly suggestive of the grave.

It was an awful thing to sit there and look at that dead-looking face.

Martin Lassamour felt the blood creep around his heart, and he was paralysed for the moment. It seemed to him as if he was held down by the weight of some spell that it would be as vain to attempt to break, as to remove the earth by his individual strength.

And there, then, sat the unfortunate Martin Lassamour with his eyes rivetted upon the chair opposite to him, and every sense absorbed in the contemplation of the strange and unearthly-looking figure that sat in it.

Still more and more distinct the figure grew, and as it did so there shot up from the embers of the wood-fire in the grate a strange flickering kind of flame, that played upon the countenance of the ghastly looking visitor.

The figure sat like a statue.

And now a strange idea took possession of Martin, that if he could by any means summon strength enough to speak to this figure, that it would reply to him again.

He thought too that it had something to say to him that it might be well worth his while to hear, and therefore was it that he made a prodigious effort to speak.

It seemed to Lassamour as if that effort of his to speak were the most fearful one he had ever made; but the strong will at length predominated, and he managed in half choking accents to say,—

"Who and what are you?"

Simple words one would think and say they were to utter, but, oh! what an effort they cost Martin Lassamour!

The spell of silence, though—of that strange and awful silence which had sat upon the figure in the chair, was broken.

Slowly the apparition, for such surely it may and must be called, moved its hand, and pointing to Lassamour, it said in a deep-toned awful voice—

"I am the first!"

All was still again.

The figure appeared as cold, as stony, and as lifeless as before, and as incapable as before of uttering a word.

Then it struck Martin Lassamour that it was just possible, by some strange condition of its existence, the figure might be able to make replies to questions asked of it, but not to say more than would constitute such a reply.

He did not know exactly how or in what kind of way such an idea took or got possession of him; but it did somehow.

Martin then proceeded to act upon this rather odd supposition. So he, with somewhat less an effort than he had before made to speak, succeeded in saying—

"What mean you by 'you are the first?'"

"The first husband!"

"Oh!"

The truth, or something that seemed to be like the truth, flashed upon the mind of Martin Lassamour, as he told himself, though he did not utter the words out aloud :—

"This is Margaret's first husband; the first of the six predecessors, that everybody will keep teasing me continually about."

The figure slowly inclined its head twice, as if it could perfectly well define the thoughts of Lassamour, and meant to imply an affirmation to them.

"You are the first husband of—of Margaret?"

"I am," said the figure.

"Then your name is—is——"

"Archibald Renton!"

"Yes, I—a—heard that she had a Mr. Renton for a husband once; and—and—"

SIR THOMAS SHARD APPEARS TO MARTIN LASSAMOUR.

"Yes, yes. Oh, yes!"

"You died?"

"I died!"

"If, then, it is not impertinent," said Martin, feeling a kind of desperation which, if it were not courage, at all events stood pretty well in the place of that feeling—"if it is not an impertinent question, may I ask of what you died?"

The figure now began slowly to fade away.

"Stop!" said Lassamour; "that is the question of all others that I most wish you should answer me. I pray you to do so."

The figure grew still more distinct.

"I implore you to answer me!"

It was all but gone.

"Hold!" cried Martin Lassamour. "Hold! Tell me if the strange reports about my wife are true. Did she, or did she not do murder to rid herself of her six husbands?"

"Murder!" said the voice of the apparition, and then it was gone.

The chair was vacant.

Martin Lassamour felt a cold sweat bedew his limbs, and his heart beat with vehemence. He still kept his eyes fixed upon the old chair.

"God! it comes again!" he cried.

He saw a strange vapoury-kind of form in the chair. Each moment, as before, it grew more and more clear and distinct, until at last he could trace the outlines of a human figure.

"No—no!" he gasped, "no more: I have no more to ask of you, now."

Still the figure grew more and more distinct, and as it did so, a new terrror beset Lassamour.

It was not the same figure that he had already spoken to.

This new apparition was that of an aged man, or, at all events, of a man much older than the first one. His head was bald, and he seemed to wear some sort of official costume, with a gold chain round his neck.

In the course of about a minute the figure had got quite clear and distinct, so that Martin Lassamour had no sort of difficulty in seeing it in every respect clearly.

There it sat, glaring at poor Martin Lassamour.

CHAPTER XVI.

MARTIN HAS VISITS FROM MARGARET'S SIX HUSBANDS.

IN good truth, this was rather a terrible position for Martin Lassamour to be in.

Gladly, now, would he have relinquished all idea of getting any information from the apparition before him, provided that by so doing he could have at once, and for all, have got rid of him.

But as it came of its own accord, it was likely to stay until it had carried out the objects of its coming, whether they happened to be agreeable to him, Lassamour, or quite the reverse.

The figure, like the former, said not a word.

"It, too," thought Lassamour, "must be spoken to ere it can speak, and it is my doom to speak to it."

He thought if he did not speak to it that there was just a probability of their sitting and staring at each other till the crack of doom.

With a feeling, then, of desperation, Martin Lassamour soon gathered courage to say something to the figure.

"Speak—oh, speak," he said, "if you have aught to say to me."

"Ask!" said the figure.

From this reply Lassamour gathered that he must put some interrogation to his strange visitor, so he said at once to it—

"Who are you?"

"I am the second."

"By Heaven, I guessed it!" gasped Lassamour.

The figure was silent.

"What on earth, then," cried Martin, "do you want with me?"

"Ask! It is for you to question."

"Oh, that is it? Then, let come what may, I will question you, spirit as you are. What is your name?"

"Sheriff Green."

"Yes. I heard that she did marry a sheriff of London, and got with him an immense fortune, which he left her in the course of six months."

"He did."

"Well, then, since you will be questioned, pray, what did you die of, Mr. Sheriff?"

The figure began to melt away.

This was the usual finishing peculiarity of all the ghosts, that the moment Lassamour put to them the only question that really was of any importance to him to get an answer to, of a clear and intelligible character, they began to go.

"Stop!" cried Martin. "You professed to answer me what I should ask, and I therefore demand of you that you should answer me this! Did you die by fair means or foul?"

"Foul!"

The figure was gone.

The chair was empty once again.

"Foul!" gasped Martin Lassamour. "It said, foul! Oh, is this a madness? Oh, this is too, too terrible! I shall go mad with such communion with the dead! And yet was my question answered in such a way as I can depend upon? Is the mere repetition of a word used by myself sufficient to found a—Ah! no, no! —no more!"

Another shadowy form was in the chair.

As before, Martin Lassamour could not keep his eyes off the object, which, as the others that had gone away, gradually from appearing to be more like a kind of mist than anything else became something like a human form.

In the course of about another minute, a pale, dark man, in a very plain suit of black, with a sword by his side, sat in the chair glaring, as the others had done, at Lassamour.

Poor Martin thought he might as well now begin with him at once, assuming that he, like the others, required to be asked specific questions before he would reply.

Rousing himself, then, for the fearful interrogation, he managed, without any circumlocution at all, to say to him—

"Who are you?"

"The third!"

"Yes, I know it—that is to say, I guessed as much. What is your name? or, I may more correctly say, what was your name in life?"

"Doctor Adolphus Bacon."

"Oh!"

The figure looked cold and still in the face of Martin Lassamour, who now, after drawing a long breath, said—

"Doctor Adolphus Bacon, will you tell me if it was by fair or unfair means that you came by your death?"

Even as Lassamour spoke, the apparition of the once-lived and well-known Doctor Bacon was fading away from his gaze, and he felt desperate at this evasion of the last question, and the only important one, on the part of the apparition.

"Stay!—oh, stay!" he cried.

"Unfair!" said the ghost, as it still slowly faded from his sight.

"You shall stay," said Lassamour; "I will be fooled no longer in such a fashion—you shall stay and answer me, or, ghost as you are, I will try the effect of cold steel upon you."

As he spoke, Martin tried to grasp his sword, but he found that his arm had no power in it, and that he was in the large old chair in which he sat more helpless than a child, for he could not move hand nor foot.

"God, what is this?" he said.

The figure faded right away, leaving Martin, as the others had done, with the repetition of the word unfair, which was one of the words he had himself used in framing the question to him.

An undefined kind of apprehension now took possession of the mind of Martin Lassamour that he himself was dead, and that this was, so to speak, his first kind of communication with the land of spirits.

The impossibility of moving any of his limbs had, no doubt, engendered this very terrible notion in his distracted mind.

It was a very terrible notion, though, let it spring from what it might. No wonder that it very nearly went to the length of being its own fulfillment.

"No—no!" cried Martin. "I want no more. I have nothing to ask of you all."

The chair began to fill with another shadow, and Martin groaned deeply.

Gradually, as before, this shadow filled up its first outlines into the form of a human being, and this time it was rather a young and handsome-looking man, dressed in the extreme of the fashion.

"I will not speak to this one," said Martin to himself; "I will let it go or stay as it thinks proper; but I will not speak to it."

This was a determination much easier to make than to adhere to, as Martin soon found.

The stony, terrible gaze of the figure seemed to look into his very soul and to chill his blood. After persevering for about three minutes he could withstand it no longer, and so, more with a view of getting rid of the apparition than that he cared for its replies, he groaned out—

"Who are you?"

"The fourth!" said the figure.

"Yes, I know that. Your name?"

"Sir Charles Leeson!"

"Ah, yes! and, my good, sir, were you killed, or did you die, at your age, of a natural death?"

"Killed!" said the figure, and it melted away.

"No more, I say!" screamed out Martin Lassamour. "I will see no more! Heaven protect me! Why should I be made the sport of fiends in this way? Is it wanted to drive me mad?—for, if so, some speedier method might be found! I will see no more!"

The chair filled again.

Now with a shudder Martin Lassamour closed his eyes for moment.

"I will not look," he said, "I will not even look, and then I cannot be expected to speak."

But this was by far too great an effort of will or of philosophy.

The mere thought that, sitting opposite to him, and glaring at him, was a being of another world, waiting for him to address, was too much to be borne, and after the space of time we have mentioned, which, in truth, appeared an hour to Lassamour, he opened his eyes, and there sat another figure.

He knew this one by sight.

The only one of the former husbands of Lady Margaret that he did know now sat before him.

"I know you," said Lassamour, "and would ask you something. Your name is Oliphant, and you are the fifth husband of Lady Margaret?"

The apparition said nothing.

"I comprehend why you do not speak," said Lassamour. "What I have just said to you is not in the form of a question; so, to get rid of you, I beg to ask if you were murdered by my wife?"

"Murdered!" cried the figure, and it vanished in a minute.

The sudden cry of "Murdered!" that had come rather startlingly from the lips of this apparition, jarred upon the nervous system of Martin Lassamour.

But he knew that there was yet another to come, and it did not surprise him when he saw a misty form in the old chair, and that that misty form in a few moments assumed the likeness of a man in the prime of life, but of rather a sallowish and dissipated look. The dress of this last apparition was draggled in mire.

CHAPTER XVII.

THE PEACE OF MIND OF MARTIN LASSAMOUR HAS FLED FOR EVER.

ARTIN LASSAMOUR knew well enough who this was that sat in the chair before him.

It was Sir Thomas Shard.

But yet with a dogged kind of resolution, as if he felt that it was his fate to do so, Lassamour resolved upon asking of him the same questions that he had put to the others, so he said—

"Who are you?"

"Sir Thomas Shard!" said the figure.

"Ah, yes—of course; and you are—"

"The sixth husband of the Lady Margaret."

"Yes, I know it. Well, Sir Thomas, I am going to ask you the decisive question, which, from experience of a pretty extensive character, I know will cause you to vanish, no doubt, as quickly as you came."

The ghost looked quite cold and silent.

"And yet," said Martin, "I don't know but that now you are here, Sir Thomas Shard, it may be desirable for me to ask you something else before I part with you for ever, probably."

The ghost took no sort of notice of this half and half sort of appeal to it.

"Then, Sir Thomas, speak," added Lassamour, with a sort of calmness that was very awful to contemplate, for it was very unnatural indeed. "Am I alive, or dead?"

"Alive."

"Ah! Is this a dream or a reality?"

"A reality."

"Will Margaret have an eighth husband?"

"No."

"Then I shall outlive her?"

"Yes. If——"

"If what?"

"You are warned in time."

"Warned in time? Well, it won't be the fault of you or your five predecessors if I am not, I take it. And now, Sir Thomas, will you permit me to ask how you came by your death? I know the question will frighten you away, but yet, as I have nothing more to ask of you, I put it to you."

The figure did not fade away.

On the contrary, it looked as distinct as before, and to the horror and consternation of Martin Lassamour, it slowly rose from the old arm-chair.

As it rose, the figure kept its eyes firmly fixed upon him with an awful stare.

"What would you?" said Lassamour. "What mean you?"

The figure advanced a step towards him.

"Off! off! I say!"

"Martin Lassamour?"

"Yes—yes. I am he!"

"You asked me what was the cause of my death, and I will tell you, but it must be in your ear."

"No—no!"

"Your right ear."

"No—no! approach me not. Your presence at arm's length is sufficiently terrible. Approach me not! The air is icy cold about you: it chills the blood in my heart. You will kill me! I forego the question: I do not ask anything of you!"

The figure stepped closer to him.

"In your ear," it said—"right in your ear, that conducts to the brain, the answer must come. In your ear—deep in your ear. Ha! ha! I will, I must tell you all. It is my mission, and I will!"

The figure made a dart towards Martin Lassamour, who, in the terror of the moment shook off the paralysis that had appeared to sit upon his limbs, and sprang to his feet.

"Help! help!" he cried. "Help—lights! oh, lights!—I can bear this no longer!—help!—help!"

He seized his sword, which lay upon the table before him, and drawing it from its scabbarb, he made a lunge at the apparition with all his force.

* * * * * *

A sudden trampling of feet—a blaze of light—the sound of voices—all came upon the senses of Martin Lassamour, and he found himself standing with a drawn sword in his hand, in the midst of half-a-dozen of the domestics of the household.

The morning sunbeams were darting into the room through the casement. The fire had long since been out, to all appearance, and so had the lamp.

Fruit, cold meats and wine were on the table, and the huge old arm-chair opposite to Martin Lassamour was empty, only he had thrust his rapier right through the back of it.

"Where am I, and what is all this?" he said.

"At home, sir," said Cyprian, the page.

"At home?"

"Yes, sir."

"And—and it is morning?"

"Early morning, sir."

"Yes—I think—that is, no——Oh, God, was it a dream or not?"

The servants looked at each other with puzzled expressions, as they saw the wild bewildered look of their master, and Cyprian only looked as if he were more sorrowful than surprised.

Martin Lassamour placed his hand over his eyes for a few moments, and then suddenly looking about him, he said—

"Cyprian?"

"Yes, sir?"

"The time—what is the time?"

"Some minutes after six, sir."

"Heard you nothing?"

"We heard your cry for help, sir, and at once made our way into this room, fancying that the cries proceeded from it."

"Yes—yes; and what did you see?"

"We saw you, sir, with a drawn rapier in your hand, and with looks of alarm upon your countenance, sir."

"Nothing else?"

"Nothing."

"It is more than strange."

"What is, sir?"

"Why, a—a—nothing—nothing."

The servants looked at each other aghast, and one of them, then, by a significant touch to his head, signified that in his opinion the brain of Martin Lassamour was affected.

"Go—go, all of you," said Martin.

The servants left the room; but as Cyprian was going, Lassamour called him back.

"Cyprian?"

"Yes, good sir."

"You have been long in your lady's service?"

"I have, sir."

"How long?"

"Ten years, sir, and I am yet but a boy, so to speak; but I was only eight years of age when I first became page to her."

"Oh, yes. Ah, and that was in the—a—time of——"

"Her second husband, sir."

"Oh, indeed. His name was—was——"

"Sheriff Green, sir."

"Yes, by Jove, I know it. I saw him to-night!"

"Sir?"

"I say I saw him to-night."

"Good gracious, sir, he has been dead and buried these eight years or so, I should say."

"Very likely."

"But, sir, you don't mean to say that—that——"

"I saw him."

"You alarm me, sir. You give me quite a turn, sir, I assure you. It is all a joke or a dream, surely, sir."

"I think it neither; and as for alarming you, good Cyprian, if you had seen what I have seen this night, you might, indeed, say something on that head; but why do you look at me so oddly for?"

"Sir, I—I——"

"Well, go on."

"I don't know what to say to you, sir, but——"

"Come, come, Cyprian, why this hesitation? If you have anything to say to me, out with it, boy, at once, will you."

"Sir, I fancy you a gentleman of the strictest honour, and as such, if you will give me your word not to repeat it to my lady, I will tell you something."

"I promise, on my honour."

" Then sir——"

The door at this moment opened, and the Lady Margaret appeared on the threshold of the room.

Cyprian stood aghast.

Martin Lassamour himself, for the moment, did not know what to do or to say.

It was was not at all likely that the confused looks of both the page and her husband should escape the penetrating glance of such a woman as the Lady Margaret, nor did they.

She glanced from one to the other of them for a moment or two in silence, and there was a slightly heightened colour on her cheek.

Cyprian tried to cover his confusion by a very low bow, as he moved to the door to leave the room ; but Lady Margaret, drawing herself up to her full height, said in a commanding tone of voice—

" You will stay."

CHAPTER XVIII.

SHIFTS THE SCENE TO A DWELLING OF A MORE HUMBLE CHARACTER.

INGERING by the door stood the page; he had no resource but to obey this order.

"I am afraid, Martin," added Lady Margaret, addressing her husband, "that I have an apology to make to you."

" An apology to me ?"

" Yes, Martin; I think I interrupted you in something you were saying to our young friend, Cyprian, here."

" Oh, no—no !"

" No !" said Cyprian ; "it is not so, lady."

" Indeed !"

" On the contrary, it was something I was about to say to him."

" May I ask what ?"

" Yes, lady."

There was such a cool, commanding look about the Lady Margaret as she spoke, that up to this present moment Martin had let her have it all her own way; but yet he felt anything but pleased at the sort of authority she assumed.

Now, however, his feeling of ire got the better of his prudence, and he said—

" I have yet to learn that I may not address a few words to one of the servants of this house, or that one of them may not speak to me, without giving to your ladyship an account of what it is about."

Lady Margaret bowed.

"You may go, Cyprian," she said—"you may go."

Cyprian left the room, seeming, in good truth, not at all sorry to get out of it.

When he was gone, Lady Margaret turned her flashing eyes upon Lassamour, and said in a low tone—

" Well, Martin ?"

" Well, my lady?"

" Have you nothing to say ?"

" Yes. I broke a promise that I made to you, and whether it was a foolish or a wise one, it was a promise, and so I have to apologise to you."

She bowed again.

" I did not reach home till half-past one o'clock last night."

" I know it."

" I hope, then, that it is not an irreparable fault."

" No."

" It is with great pleasure I hear you say so, Margaret."

There was a tone of returning tenderness about Martin Lassamour, for he felt that he was rather in the wrong, after all, and that his lady, who had done so much for him, and who had behaved so liberally to him, deserved at his hands all the consideration he could possibly give to her.

No doubt she noticed this change in his feelings, for she spoke very gently, as she said—

" Martin, what I say I mean. When I asked of you to return home before one of the clock, I had a reason for so doing ; but I hope that this will not be repeated. I hope that on another occasion a gentleman will take some little pains to keep his word."

" Madam ?"

" Nay, do not be irritated now. It is past and over for this once; but do not let it occur again, I beg of you; and there is yet another thing."

"What may that be?"

"Oh, Martin!"

"Oh, Margaret!"

"Nay, sir, do not mock me; but I beg—I implore of you to avoid the wine-cup."

"Avoid it?"

"Yes."

"Good madam, would you have me, then, refuse like a churl to drink a cup of wine with a friend?"

"No, Martin; it is the abuse of good wine that I now speak against, not the use of it. But let this discussion cease now; it is surely sufficient for the time, and it is painful to me."

"And to me."

"Then it is over."

She smiled, and held out her hand to him, which he took, silently congratulating himself upon the fact that at any rate she had not asked a single question about the money that she had given to him on the evening before.

To be sure, he would feel anything but pleased if she had asked any such question, but the fact that she did not made him more fully appreciate the generosity of her disposition.

"Margaret," he said, "I know that I am headstrong and wilful. The fact is that I have led so wild and so desultory a life before I knew you that it will take a little time to curb me down to the ordinary and proper placidity of married life. All I ask of you, dear Margaret, is to have a little patience with me."

"Oh, Martin," she replied, in a tone of deep emotion, "if that is all that is wanted, I will have abundance of patience with you."

"It is all."

"Then you may be sure that my love for you will easily enable me to practise such a virtue. We will yet live for each other."

"Indeed I hope so."

"It is settled that we shall," she added with a smile; "and now tell me what Cyprian was saying to you?"

"Indeed I cannot, for he did not say it."

"But you and he had been talking?"

"Yes, I told him what I now tell you quite freely, that I fell asleep here in this chair, and had a very troublesome dream—a kind of nightmare, I fancy."

"Indeed?"

"Yes; the remembrance of it haunts me now."

"Then you do remember it?"

"Why, a—that is, a——"

"Martin, do not tamper with truth in this fashion. You do remember it, or you do not."

"I do, then."

"And you will tell it to me?"

"No, Margaret."

"No?"

"Decidedly no. You must be quite satisfied with my assurance that it is not a proper dream to tell you."

Martin Lassamour, by thus implying some kind of impropriety in the subject matter of the dream, thought to effectually silence all inquiries of Margaret upon the subject, but he did not succeed in that. The probability is that she saw that it was a subterfuge, and it had the effect of widening her curiosity.

"Martin," she said, "proper or improper, I want to know what you dreamt of."

"Nay, I cannot tell you."

"You can if you will."

"But I—a—ought not."

Martin was resolved that, come what would of it, he would not disclose to her what the apparitions of her six former husbands had seemed to say to him.

She flung her arms round his neck, and looked smilingly up into his face, as she said—

"My own Martin! I know that you cannot—that you will not refuse to tell your Margaret what it was you dreamt of."

"I must."

"Now, my dear Martin, I will coax it out of you. Come, naughty, bad boy, Martin, what was it?"

"Excuse me."

"No, no, I won't, indeed. You know that curiosity is considered to be one of the great characteristics of my sex, and, if so, why should I not possess the feeling? So, my own good, dear, kind Martin, you will tell me?"

"No."

"No?"

"I cannot."

"You will not?"

"I do not like to use so harsh a phrase, my dear Margaret, but the fact is I have made up my mind not, and I will keep my determination."

She flung herself from him in a moment.

"Adventurer! dastard! profligate!" she cried. "Is it for this that I have taken you from the very kennel, and tried to make of you a gentleman? But, beware, sir! you know not the spirit you have raised, and which you may in vain try to quell again!"

CHAPTER XIX.

MARTIN LASSAMOUR FINDS THAT HIS SITUATION IS NONE OF THE PLEASANTEST.

S O completely taken by surprise was Martin Lassamour by this ebullition of rage on the part of the Lady Margaret, that he staggered back a few paces, and did not arouse himself till she had left the room.

"Humph!" he said. "So it has come to this, has it, and only a month married, too!"

He sunk into the chair that was next to him, and groaned aloud.

"Alas! alas!" he said; "I fear that I have married a she-dragon instead of a woman. Can I ever forget the fury that shone from her eyes? This is pleasant indeed!"

Martin laid his hand upon his head. It ached a little, just to let him know that either the claret or the Spanish wine had been imbibed a little too freely, and he gave himself up to thought for a time.

"What on earth is to be done now?" he said. "Would to Heaven that I had never married her. But it was my own head-strong folly that induced me to do so, and of course, like every other fool when he makes up his mind to such a course, I would listen to no reason, and quarrelled with all who persuaded me, and what is the result?"

He rose and paced the room with hasty and distracted steps, and then, as he looked from the window, he said—

"Let me consider what it was that she had the excessive kindness to call me. An adventurer — a dastard, and profligate. Very good, my lady, and I think you had the kindness, too, to say that you had picked me out of the kennel. Very good again—very good and kind, indeed."

With rather a furious gesture Martin Lassamour left the room, and strode to the breakfast parlour, and the moment he got there he seized a silken bell-rope, and gave it such a furious pull that it came away from its fastening into his hand.

A couple of servants answered the summons with looks of wonder.

"Breakfast!" roared Lassamour, in a voice of thunder.

"Honoured sir, it is on the table before you," answered one of the servants.

"Very well—be off!"

"Yes, honoured sir."

The servants left the room, and Martin sat down to the well-laid breakfast table, and ate voraciously, just for the sake of having something to do.

"Ah," he said, "I don't know but what I ought to send a message, I mean an order to my wife to come to breakfast; but I don't want her, and so I won't."

Perhaps Martin Lassamour had a slight kind of suspicion that the order, if he had sent it, would not be obeyed.

If so, it was highly prudent on his part not to send it at all.

But be this as it may, there can be no doubt in the world but that Martin Lassamour passed a very uncomfortable half hour at the breakfast-table; and then, starting to his feet, he went to ring the bell again, but the destruction of the long silken cord on the former occasion rendered it impossible for him to do so, and he roared out—

"Who waits?—who waits?"

The same two servants that had before answered his summons entered the room

"Order my horse!" cried Martin.

"Yes, sir."

"The same I rode last night."

"Yes, sir."

"Be quick."

"Your orders shall be obeyed, sir."

"They had better."

The servants were evidently disposed to treat him with the most faultless respect. It is possible that they had received orders of a special character so to do; but it is certain that he found it impossible to find fault with, or to pick a quarrel with any of them.

His horse was duly brought to the great gate of the house, and after making rather a hasty toilette, he mounted, and turned the creature's face towards London.

"When I shall return home," he said, "is not in my own mind very distinc:.

"No, sir," said the servant.

Off he rode.

"Confound everything and everybody," said Martin Lassamour, as he set the horse to a gallop, and found from that rather violent kind of exercise a degree of relief from the oppression of spirits under which he was suffering.

What he meant to do he had not settled upon : but as he rode along, he said to himself—

"I wish, now, that I had told her at

GAMIEL GANDER GOES A WOOING TO THE FERRYMAN'S DAUGHTERS.

once what I really did dream of, I should then have seen how she took it. But was it a dream?"

That was the puzzler, after all.

"Was it a dream?"

This was just the sort of question that Martin Lassamour might put to himself to the end of all time, and yet not be able to answer satisfactorily.

There were many circumstances against the supposition that it was a dream, and many in favour of it. How was he to unite the conflicting evidence, and to come to anything like a conclusion on the matter?

"If it was a dream," he said, "it is certainly the very strangest that mortal man ever had. If it was a reality, it is a warning of such a character, that I shoud be mad not to take notice of it."

But still the doubt remained, and but that now Martin Lassamour heard the sound of a horse's feet rapidly approaching him on the road, he would have gone on puzzling himself on the subject.

And now he looked anxiously forward

to see who, at that early hour, was coming from London.

Round a turn of the road there appeared a horseman, mounted upon a light and lady-looking gray nag, and as he neared Lassamour, the latter saw that the rider was no other than the young man named Lamont, who had, no doubt, on the preceding night, saved him from the assassin-like fury of Sir Warrenne de Volence at the tavern.

"Hilloa!" cried Martin Lassamour, in a loud voice, for the sight of any one to whom he could talk freely was just then the most welcome thing that could by any possibility meet his eye.

The young man paused.

"Hilloa!" shouted Lassamour again. "Master Lamont, do you not know me?"

"Oh, yes!"

The young man put spurs to his steed, and was by the side of Lassamour in a moment.

"Martin Lassamour," he said, "a good morning to you. May I have the pleasure of hearing that I see you quite well?"

"You may, my good friend; and you?"

"Oh, yes, quite so. I fear, though, that I am interrupting you, and that you are out thus early on some special affair of your own."

"Not at all."

"I rejoice to hear it, for I was coming to you."

"To Pleasaunce House?"

"Even so."

"Then come back with me, or—or I will go on with you, if it will suit you as well to ride to London again, my good friend."

"As you please, sir; I am quite at your service and directions, so far; but, indeed, I should not have troubled you at all, but that I made you a promise."

"You did, and it was one that I am glad to see you recollect. You promised to call upon me."

"I did more."

"Indeed?"

"Yes, good sir. You made me promise you that if I heard anything of Sir Warrenne De Volence, you should be the first to know of it."

"Oh, yes, I did."

"I have heard from him."

"You do not mean to say that he has challenged you?"

"He has."

"And you will meet him?"

"Meet him? Of course I will. Can you imagine for one moment that I would do otherwise?"

"No. And yet——"

"And yet what?"

"This is my quarrel, good Master Lamont, and not yours, and when I made you promise that you would on the instant let me know if De Volence troubled you upon the subject, it was with the feeling that he had no sort of right to do so, but that it was to me he ought to send his message."

CHAPTER XX.

[INTRODUCES TO THE READER TWO NEW CHARACTERS.

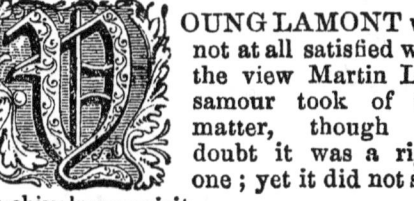 OUNG LAMONT was not at all satisfied with the view Martin Lassamour took of the matter, though no doubt it was a right one; yet it did not suit his chivalrous spirit.

"You will pardon me, I am quite sure, Martin Lassamour," he said, "for what I am going to say."

"Oh, yes—yes; say on."

"Then, my good friend, since De Volence has thought proper to send me a message of a hostile character, I can do nothing but meet him, let the real cause of quarrel be what it may."

"You are right," said Lassamour, after a brief pause. "At all events, you are so far right, that you are going to do just what I should do myself in such a case, and all I can say is, that I will go with you."

"For that kindness, a thousand thanks."

"No. No thanks at all. Did he send a written message to you?"

"He did."

"Have you it with you?"

"Oh, yes! It is no honour to carry about with me such a rascal's signature; but it is here. I pray you read it, Martin Lassamour, and you will see what he says."

The young man handed to Martin a note, which contained the following words:

"Sir Warrenne De Volence to Master Adolphe Lamont, greeting and defiance.

"If Adolphe Lamont will meet his mortal foe at any time and place he may please to appoint, to measure swords with him, he may prove that he is no coward. De Volence awaits a written answer by the old Ferry House at Lambeth, at the tavern of the King's Arms."

"That is all," said Lamont.

"And enough, too," replied Lassamour; "now, my good fellow, I think you know enough of me to be satisfied to place this matter in my hands."

"Oh, yes—yes!"

"You perceive that this is the most irregular kind of challenge that it is possible one gentleman can send to another —no swords are named in it; and, in fact, it is not a proper challenge at all."

"I thought it odd."

"Then what, for the sake of argument, would you have done with such a letter if you had not known me?"

"I would have written a reply, appointing some hour and place, and there have met him."

"Indeed!"

"Yes; but why do you say, 'indeed?'" said Lamont.

"Because I strongly suspect that you would, by such a course of proceeding, have missed the opportunity of ever measuring swords with De Volence."

"How so?"

"He has the repute of being a hirer of assassins; and as this letter is so strange a one, it lends a colour to such an accusation. It is more than likely that when you got to the place of rendezvous, you would have found yourself set upon by assassins, and there would have been an end of your career."

"Can this be possible?"

"I think it is so; but I will trust him in every way. Heaven forbid that I should judge even such a man as De Volence hastily, or upon mere hearsay and report! So I will adopt such a course as shall enable him to show that he has some notion of honour in him if he likes."

"I am very much beholden to you; but who comes here in such hot haste?"

A horseman came dashing along from Richmond, and as he neared them, Martin Lassamour saw, rather to his surprise, that it was no other than Cyprian, the page to his lady.

Cyprian drew rein when close to his master, and touched his cap.

"Well, Cyprian, what is it?" said Martin.

"This from my lady, sir."

Cyprian handed Lassamour a note, tied up with green silk, and neatly folded.

"Excuse me, good Lamont," said Martin, as he perused the note. "Were this from any one but a lady, I would keep it till we had parted."

"Nay, heed me not."

To tell the truth, Lassamour was rather curious to know the contents of the note that had been sent after him with such hot haste, and he read the following lines with mingled feelings—

"My own MARTIN,—Have you a heart to forgive me? If you have, come back to me; but if not—if for the hasty words I have spoken you please to cast me off for ever, I will leave Pleasaunce House, and go and live in obscurity wherever you may please to direct, and be still your repentant and your loving wife,

"MARGARET."

It was quite out of the question, with such a man as Martin Lassamour, who had many generous impulses in his mind, that there should be anything but one answer to such an epistle as this.

Turning to Cyprian, he said—

"Will you speed back to your good lady, and tell her that with my best love, and my greatest haste, I will soon be with her?"

"Yes, sir."

Cyprian was off like an arrow from a bow.

"Lamont," said Martin, "ride home with me now, and pass a day at Pleasaunce House. You will be right welcome for my sake; and after we have dined, we will go down the river in my lady's barge, and have some pleasant talk together, and as we go I will tell you how I will manage matters with this rogue, De Volence."

"I accept your invitation as freely as I know it is given," said Lamont.

They both turned their horses' heads in the direction of Richmond again, and were soon at the great gate of Pleasaunce House.

It is needless now to say how the Lady Margaret won over Martin to forgive her for the harsh things she had said, by the gentle courtesy with which she received his young friend, Lamont. Let it suffice that there appeared to be a perfect oblivion between them of the scene of the early morning.

The costly dinner passed off right pleasantly, and then Martin said, gaily—

"I have promised our young friend here a seat in your stately barge on the Thames, Margaret. Have I said too much?"

"Oh, no—no, Martin. I have no barge now.

"No barge? Why, there it lies, gently undulating on the surface of the river. I can see even from here the bright sunshine gleaming on the gilding of its prow."

"Yes. And so can I."

"Then how is it, my Margaret, that you say you have no barge, now?"

"I have parted with it."

"That is provoking."

"So it is."

"It is, indeed, Margaret—very."

"Well, I can't help it. It belongs to another."

"And pray who is that other?"

"One Martin Lassamour, who is my lord and master, and to whom I have parted with all I possess, as well as with my heart, which beats for him alone!"

"Ah, Margaret, how you have deceived me!"

Martin smiled as he spoke, and looked with renewed affection in the face of his wife. All the dark visions of suspicion against her were forgotten: he only saw before him the beautiful and loving woman who had thrown a brilliant fortune at his feet, and who hesitated not to tell him that all was his that she posssessed.

"Then," said Martin, "we will have my barge out, shall we, Margaret?"

"Yes, Martin."

Lassamour smiled as he gave the necessary orders; and then Margaret retired to prepare for the little voyage down the Thames.

"You have a treasure in your gentle lady," said young Lamont, when they were alone.

"Oh, yes—yes! I have, indeed," said Martin.

"By my faith, between you and me, Martin Lassamour, I do not wonder at the facility with which she has been able to make seven men, now, adore her."

"Seven?"

"Yes, you know you are the seventh."

"My good friend, take some wine, and if you love me, mention not that."

CHAPTER XXI.

TAKES THE READER TO OLD LAMBETH FERRY HOUSE.

WE will now leave Martin Lassamour and his friend, and the fair and accomplished Margaret, the wife of seven husbands, to proceed on their pleasure excursion in the gilded barge on the Thames, while we introduce the reader to some other personages of our story.

Close to old Lambeth Palace there existed, then, a ferry across the Thames.

A house, with no end of old gables and enormous sloping roof-tops, and with a pretty enough garden surrounding it, stood not far from the water side.

In that house dwelt Langdon, the well-known ferryman of Millbank and Lambeth. With him resided his two blooming daughters, Patience and Amy, who were the acknowledged belles of the neighbourhood.

Patience was just twenty years of age, and Amy was eighteen. They kept house for their father, and that circumstance, together with the early loss of their mother, had imparted an air of seriousness to the young girls, which, otherwise, they might, at least for some years, have been strangers to.

This air of seriousness, though, by no means detracted from their beauty. On the contrary, it gave it possibly the only charm it wanted.

In a word, the fame of the beauty of the ferryman's daughters was spread wide; and many were the efforts of the young men of Lambeth to get a footing, as suitors, in the ferryman's house; but Master Langdon was not a man to be trifled with.

The ferryman saw that his children possessed the dangerous gift of beauty, and many a weary hour did that knowledge give to him.

With a determination to guard them as well as it was possible so to do, he was seldom away from his home, and he took every opportunity of talking to the girls in the most serious manner.

One thing that a friend had put into the ferryman's head engaged much of his attention, and that was the finding suitable husbands for his two girls.

"You may depend, Langdon," said his friend, "that there is nothing like getting them well married for taking good care of them. A husband looks out sharper than a father can; and so get good husbands for your daughters, and you may leave the rest to chance."

Good husbands, however, were not so easily got for two pretty girls who had no money.

To be sure, there were plenty who would have had them; but, then, unfortunately, Patience and Amy had to be consulted in the matter, and it so turned out that all the steady-going, honest, sober men, that would have suited Langdon, their father, did not at all suit them.

The gallants, too, of the court fluttered about the old dwelling of the ferryman, and more than one fracas had taken place between him and some of the wild, gay bloods of the city, who, attracted by the fame of his daughters' beauty, had come hovering about his house.

Indeed, with all the assurance in the world, some of them had actually tapped at his door, and tried to get by sheer impertinence into his house.

They soon found out, however, that they were mistaken in Langdon, and that he was not the sort of man to be very easily got the better of.

But the fact was, that both Amy and Patience had lovers who would not be said nay to.

The young and gentle Amy was fervently beloved by Robert Lee, the pedlar, who, with his pack, was in the habit of travelling the country round, and of attending all the principal fairs in England.

Some folks would have it that Robert Lee was rich; but such was not the fact. He might have been; but a free and generous spirit, that never heard a tale of distress that it did not try to relieve, pretty effectually prevented him from hoarding any money.

Robert Lee was a young and handsome man, too, and no wonder was it that his many good and noble qualities won upon the heart of Amy so much, that it was a pretty nearly settled thing in her mind that she was to be the pedlar's wife, or die an old maid.

Patience, too, had her admirers.

One of those admirers was no other than Cyprian, the page to Lady Margaret.

The young page, in his progresses down the river, sometimes on his own business, that is to say, to visit his mother, who dwelt at Lambeth, and sometimes on his mistress's, had often seen Patience Langdon, and his young heart was completely taken prisoner by her charms.

But, alas! the course of true love runs not smooth.

A girl of twenty does not usually pay much attention to the amorous sighs of a boy of seventeen or eighteen; and thus was it when one day Cyprian looked over the paling of the garden of the ferry house, when both the sisters were walking there, and declared that he loved Patience better than all the world, they only laughed at him for his pains.

But still Cyprian was a handsome boy, and although Patience laughed at him, she could not somehow quite forget the bright black eyes and the soft tones of the page.

There is hope yet for Master Cyprian.

But Patience has another lover.

There was, not far from her father's cottage, the shop of a cordwainer and matmaker, and this man had an apprentice named Gamiel Gander.

Now Gamiel Gander was a rather strange-looking youth, with a shock of bright-coloured hair like an over-used mop. His sleepy light-gray eyes seemed as if they had never been thoroughly opened; and if we add to this that he was in the habit of, morning, noon and night, indulging an outrageous appetite for what is generally called sweet-stuff, in the shape of lollypops, treacle, brandy-balls, toffee, and sugar-candy, we shall not have presented to the reader the portrait of one who was likely to stand much in the way of Cyprian, the page of the Lady Margaret Lassamour.

Such, then, was fairly the state of affairs at the house of Langdon, the ferryman, on the morning when Martin Lassamour rode forth from Pleasaunce, full of rage against Lady Margaret.

We have seen how he was overtaken by Cyprian, with the apologetical note from the Lady Margaret, and what followed therefrom.

We now, therefore, request the reader's kind attention to the pretty little lawn and garden in front of Langdon's house, in which were walking the two sisters, Patience and Amy Langdon, the fair daughters of the ferryman.

"Well, Amy," said Patience, with a laugh, "I suppose that now the great fair at Lambeth is going to begin, you will soon see a something of your swain."

"My swain, sister? What can you mean?"

"Oh, don't try to play the part of a little prude, now, with me. You know what I mean well enough."

"Indeed, no."

"Indeed, yes, I say."

"Well, but, who do you mean?"

"Oh, this is too bad. You know as

well as I do, that you are all impatience to see him."

"Well, you talk in riddles."

"Do I, though?"

"Of course you do, sister. Come, say at once who you mean."

"Ah, Amy, the sound of his name, then, is so delightful to you, that you want to coax me to utter it, do you?"

"Oh, no—no. I'm sure I don't see anything so very delightful in the name of Robert."

"Oh, then it is Robert? Ha! ha!"

Amy bit her lips with vexation, that she should have been so foolish as to betray herself in such fashion.

"Oh, sister, it is of no use your contradicting the fact," added Patience. The pedler, Robert Lee, loves you, and you are far, very far, indeed, from being indifferent to him."

Amy was silent.

"Come—come," said her sister, placing her arm round her waist, "and where is the harm, I wonder? He is young, and brave, and handsome, I am sure."

"Oh, sister, do you think so?"

"I know so."

"Then you are very kind and good to say it."

"Amy—Amy, you little rogue you! why do you not confide in me? What have I done that you should not trust me? We have no mother, as you know, in whose friendly feeling to confide, and at times our father, although we know well he loves us both, is harsh and stern to us."

"Yes. Oh, yes."

"Who, then, have we to look to but to each other?"

"None !—none !"

"Then confide in me."

"I will. I do, dear Patience, only I was afraid that—that——"

"That what, now?"

"That you would laugh at me."

"Nay, dear Amy, I will not do so, for I love you far too well."

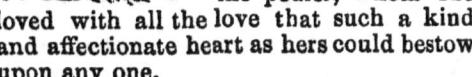

CHAPTER XXII.

WARRENNE DE VOLENCE INTRUDES WHERE HE IS NOT AT ALL WANTED.

QUITE the greatest possible pleasure and relief to Amy Langdon was, to tell the truth, to have somebody to speak to about Robert Lee, the pedler, whom she loved with all the love that such a kind and affectionate heart as hers could bestow upon any one.

When, therefore, she found that her sister Patience was disposed to be so kind and indulgent to her, she poured out to her the whole state of her affections.

"Yes, Patience," she said. "I do love him, for, as you said awhile ago, he is young, and brave, and handsome, and if a maiden cannot love for those qualities, I don't know what she is to love for."

"Nor I either."

"And you approve, then, of Robert Lee?"

"How can I do otherwise?"

"Oh, how kind of you !"

"Not at all. Only I hope that our father will not say those harsh things of Robert Lee that he has said at times."

"Alas ! So do I."

"Well, dear Amy, we will live in hope, for Robert, now that he looks forward to your being his wife, will be able, perhaps, to show our father that he has money, and that doubt has, I believe, been the only fault that could be found with him."

"It is so."

"Then that may vanish."

"It may ; and yet——"

"Yet what? Have you any further cause for fear, dear sister?"

"Oh, no ; no more than that. But then Robert Lee is so generous, and so noble, and so full of high and gentle impulses, that he is not the sort of man to make money only for the sake of money."

"No ; but surely he has other motives?"

"Has he?"

"Or, at least, he ought to have."

"Oh, yes, I understand you."

"Yes, dear sister. If Robert Lee really loves you as you think he does, and as I know you ought to be loved, what stronger motive can he have than the feeling that he is expected to have money before he can make you his, to try and possess himself of it?"

" Why, yes, that is true."

"Of course it is, sister, and you ought to say as much to him."

" I? Impossible."

"Nay, it is not so, and let me tell you, my dear Amy, that this money, which, no doubt, in your little simple heart, you so much despise, is no bad thing after all."

"Oh, yes, sister Patience, I can't help thinking that it is a bad thing."

"Why so?"

"Does it not estrange hearts?—does it not raise the hand of one man against his neighbour?—does it not in every possible way have the effect of making enemies of those who should be, and who would be, friends?"

"True, and yet that is the abuse of money, not the use of it ; and I fear that all your arguments would not be sufficient to induce our father to give his consent to your wedding with Robert Lee, if the pedler cannot show you that he has wherewithal with which to keep a wife and a home."

" Oh, but he has that, sister."

" Indeed, has he ?"

" Yes. He lives himself, you know."

" True."

" Well, that will do, for I can live upon nothing at all, easily."

Patience smiled at her sister, and shook her head.

" My dear Amy," she said, " you know as little of the world as a mere child."

" Well," said Amy, with an arch smile, " how much better able to support a wife do you think a page to a great lady is, than a pedler?"

" Amy?"

" Oh, do not blush, sister, Patience. I know your secret quite well."

" My secret?"

" Yes ; there is a certain youth, with bright black eyes, and a handsome face, who looks over the garden wall."

" At you?"

" Nay, at you !"

" No, no, at you, sister Amy."

" The proof ?"

" Why, as you see—that is—a—I have given him no sort of encouragement, and I hate him."

" Poor fellow !"

" Oh, how provoking you are, Amy. Don't I tell you I hate him?"

" Well, if you hate him, you don't want to say anything to him."

" Certainly not."

" Nor to hear anything about him?"

" Certainly not."

" Nor to write a letter to him?"

" Oh, dear, no."

" Nor to receive one from him that he threw over the wall into the white rose bush, yonder?"

" Oh, sister, where is it—oh, where is it?"

" Ha ! ha ! sister Patience, do not say anything to me about the pedler, honest Robert Lee, for you see I know something about Master Cyprian, the handsome young page of the great lady at Pleasaunce House, on Richmond Hill."

Patience looked vexed and confused, but her sister, who really loved her tenderly, threw her arms around her, and kissing her, said—

" Come, you shall read this letter of the saucy page to me, will you not?"

" Yes, Amy, but it was very wrong of him——"

" Yes, it was."

" To leave a letter in such a public place as a rose-bush in the garden. Why father might have seen it at any moment."

" So I thought."

" Oh, let me go for it."

" No."

" No, say you?"

" I say no, sister, because there is no occasion to go for what I have here. I, too, thought it a very bad place in which to leave a letter, as our father often walks through the garden, so I took possession of it for you, and here it is, dear Patience."

" Oh, Amy !"

" Oh, Patience !"

" Nay, now, do not laugh at me, but give me the letter at once, and let me see what the dear—no, I mean the impudent fellow says."

Amy laughed, as she took from her bosom the page's letter, and handed it to her sister, who, in such a flutter of delight that she found it quite impossible to conceal it, read as follows:—

" ' To the most incomparable and lovely Patience Langdon

" ' Dearest, and best, and loveliest of all that is lovely in this world.' "

" Well, that is very fine, indeed," said Amy.

" Oh, do not interrupt me."

" Well, go on."

" ' To say that I love you, is to say nothing at all, for I want a new language redolent with some very strong and comprehensive words in it, which shall express, to some degree, how very much I love you, my own dear—dear—dear Patience. "

" The deuce !" said Amy.

" Yes, yes."

" Well, go on."

" ' My dearest love, I will look over the garden-wall at the hour of three this day, when I hope to see the fairest flower that ever bloomed within those precincts, which are to me sacred ground.

' 'These few lines are from your own—own—own　　　"'CYPRIAN.'"

"Is that all?" said Amy.

"Yes, that is all. What do you think of it?"

"I don't know."

"Oh, Amy, is not he a love?"

"Well, if you think so——"

"I am—I am!" cried a voice; "I knows as I am! Oh, my Patience!—tol de rol de rido! I love you well, as the old song says—Ah, only look at your own Gamiel Gander!"

With his arms resting on the top of the garden palings, and his exceedingly comic face peering over the top of it, was poor Gamiel Gander, the cordwainer's apprentice.

CHAPTER XXIII.

THE WOLF APPEARS TOO NEAR TO THE FOLD OF THE LAMB.

PATIENCE, when she found herself thus interrupted, would certainly have much rather it had been by the handsome page of the Lady Margaret than by Gamiel Gander, her other admirer, and by far the more troublesome and pertinacious one of the two.

Probably everything that Gamiel Gander said and did was a trouble to Patience, while nothing that Cyprian could say or do was considered to be anything of the sort.

Alas, poor Gamiel!

But Gamiel had a grandmother who was reported to be rich, and as he was her darling, for she thought him decidedly the handsomest youth in all Lambeth, it was supposed that he would inherit the old lady's wealth, when she should be kind enough to walk out of this world.

This was a little circumstance that, in the eyes of Master Langdon, the ferryman, gave Gamiel a decided and powerful advantage over his rival, the page; the sight of whom was gall and wormwood to Langdon.

"Ha—ha!" said Gamiel, as he moved his great stupid-looking head from side to side with his chin resting upon the paling. "Ha—ha! How are you, lovely and accomplished Patience?"

"Now, was ever anybody so troubled with a goose in this world?" said Patience to Amy.

"It is very provoking, sister."

"Ha—ha!" said Gamiel. "'In for a penny in for a pound,' as the old proverb says. I hope I see you well, Miss Patience; why you looks lovelier and more lovelier every day."

"I can't return the compliment," said Patience.

"Oh, can't you?"

"No; for if such a thing were possible, which to be sure it is not, I should say that you look uglier and uglier every day."

"Ha—ha!"

"Oh, you laugh at that, do you?"

"To be sure I do."

"And why, pray?"

"Because I know that it is only your funny way."

"Oh, you are maniacal."

"I know it, Miss Patience, and that's why I love you so much as I do."

What sort of meaning Gamiel put upon the word maniacal, it is hard to say; but it is quite certain that it could not be the ordinary one that the rest of the world put upon it.

"Shall I come over?" he said.

"No—no!"

"Oh, don't say no. The old lady is getting very shaky, indeed, I assure you, and I shall have all she is worth; and won't you be a lady, then, Miss Patience? Oh, my eye! won't you?"

"Sir?"

"Yes, miss. Did you speak to me, miss?"

"I did."

"Go on, then; your voice is so delightful, it sounds to me, do you know, like—like—dear me, what is it like? Oh, I know!"

"What, then?"

"Treacle coming out of a tub."

"You odious wretch!"

"Eh?"

"I say you are an odious wretch! I do not like you—on the contrary, I hate the very sight of you; so go away at once, and don't trouble me any more with your

THE PEDLER CHASTISES DE VOLENCE IN THE FERRYMAN'S GARDEN.

disagreeable passion. Do you understand all that?"

"Oh, dear! I——Murder!"

In the strangest manner possible, Gamiel's head disappeared from the top of the paling, and then a great splash was heard, followed by repeated cries of "Murder!" and then there came the sound as of some one running away at great speed, after which all was still.

The two sisters looked at each other in surprise.

"Dear me, Amy," said Patience, "what can be the meaning of all that, dear?"

"I cannot possible imagine, sister."

"I feel quite alarmed!"

"Nay, dearest Patience," said a soft voice, as the head of Cyprian, the handsome page, appeared, now, above the paling, "be not alarmed—all is well."

"Oh, Cyprian! Is it you?"

"It is, dear one."

"But—but—go away!"

"Do you mean me to go away? I love

you so well that if you really say that I am to go away, I will go and drown myself in the Thames, at once."

"Oh, no—no !"

"There is no danger," said Amy.

"Angel," said the page; "you bid me stay, and my life is saved. How can I do otherwise than devote it to your sweet and gracious service ?"

"But—but——"

"Yes, dear one, say on."

"There was somebody else at the paling only now, and where is he ?"

"I don't know now, dear one ; but only a moment or so since he was in the ditch, on the other side of the way ; and I suppose he has gone home to change his clothes. I think he will be wise to do so."

"Did you commit such violence upon him ?"

"Well, I'm afraid I got hold of his leg, and that I did not let him go again till he was in the ditch ; but I pulled him out again."

"Then, sir, I am offended."

"Mirror of beauty, you can't mean that ?"

"I can—I do mean it."

"Then I die !"

"You must know, sir, that the gentlemen you took hold of by the leg is my suitor, approved of by my father as my husband. His name is Gamiel Gander, and—and I must say that I love him very much."

"At a distance ?" said the page.

"No—no ! Close to me."

"Not after he has been in the ditch ?" Patience laughed in spite of herself.

"Go along," she said—"go along, and don't trouble me any more with your nonsense. I don't want you—I don't like you, so go away as soon as you like."

"Farewell !" said the page. "It was only this morning that my mistress asked me if I would go to some estates she has in the Indies. I thought of you, and said

no ; but I will go now and meet my death in a foreign land ; and when you hear of the sad fate of poor Cyprian, even you will drop a tear to his memory, and say, ' Well, poor youth, he did love me !' Farewell ! farewell ! May Heaven bless you !"

The page suddenly disappeared from the paling.

"Cyprian—Cyprian !" cried Patience. "No—no ! Oh, Cyprian ! do not go ! For my sake !"

"Eh ?" he said, popping his head up over the paling.

"Oh, you wretch !"

"Oh, well ! I thought you called me back. Good-by ! Farewell for ever !"

Down popped his head again.

"No—no !" cried Patience, once more. "No ! I say I do not bid you go. I will try to like you a little."

"That won't do," said the page, from the other side of the paling.

"What won't do ?"

"Liking me a little won't do at all. I must be loved a great deal to satisfy me. Oh, my dear, sweet, amiable and virtuous Patience, why should you only love me a little, when I love you a great deal ?"

"Because—because——"

"What ?"

"I don't know."

"Be comforted," said Amy; "she does love you a good deal, only you must not expect her to say so."

"Then I will take it for granted," said the page, as he popped his head up again. "I have only just time to say how glad I am to see you both looking like twin roses on one stalk, and then I must be off to meet my mistress and her seventh husband, Martin Lassamour, at Putney ; for they are coming down the river for a sail, in the gilded barge that cost such a lot of money. Good-by, dear, dear, Patience ; and good-by to you, too, beautiful and sweet little Amy—good-by to you both, you two ducks !"

CHAPTER XXIV.

DE WARRENNE IS ALIVE TO THE CHARMS OF THE FERRYMAN'S DAUGHTERS.

EALLY in haste was the page, now, for he put his head down from the paling, and was just about to run off at great speed, when Langdon, the

ferryman, who had been brought to the spot by Gamiel Gander, seized him by the cloak, crying out—

"So, my young spark, I have caught you at last, have I ? Poaching, eh ?"

"Ha—ha !" cried Gamiel. "Ecod, he has him now ! Screw his head off, Mas-

THE WIFE OF SEVEN HUSBANDS.

ter Langdon! Oh, the wretch! He is after no good, caterwauling about your garden, I can tell you, Master Langdon."

"Hold your tongue, stupid!"

"Yes—yes! I am a fool, perhaps; but I'm not quite an idiot."

"You are not far off from being one," said Cyprian.

"Come—come, young, sir," said Langdon, "let me ask you a few questions."

"Certainly, sir; go on."

"I am a plain man——"

"Don't mention it, sir. Anybody may see that at a glance, without your saying anything about it ; but, for my part, I beg to assure you that I am never prejudiced against any one by their looks."

"Zounds, Sir Impudence, what do you mean?"

"Why, you said you were a plain man."

"Hark you, master page, I don't want any of your impertinence here. Let me ask you at once, what was your business on my garden wall?"

"Business?"

"Yes."

"Oh, none at all."

"Confound your impertinence! what do you mean by that, eh ?"

"Why, my good sir, it was pleasure, not business, I assure you. I hate the very name of business, and always did. But I don't mean to offend you for all that, so I will say at once, it was to look at the flowers."

"Oh, indeed !"

"Ah, but," said Gamiel, "I heard him call Miss Patience a lovely flower, and a rose, and all sorts of things."

"You be quiet, Gamiel."

"Yes, Master Langdon, but——"

"Hold your tongue, stupid !"

"Well, I——"

"Will you be quiet?"

Gamiel only made a gesture of resignation, and then Langdon said to the page—

"Master page, when you can bring me to look at, with proof that they belong to you, and that they are honestly come by, a couple of hundred gold pieces, you may then, if you like, look over my garden paling at the flowers; but if before that time I catch you at any such sport, I will make you remember it."

"My dear sir, as for that, the only difficulty would be in making me forget it."

"You rascal !"

"Oh—oh, look ! only look ! If there isn't a man and a cow—no, I mean a cow and a man, getting into the ferry-boat, and casting it adrift. Oh—oh !"

"The devil there is," cried Langdon, as he let go the page's cloak in a moment, and ran off to the water's edge. "I'll soon put a stop to that. Hilloa !—hilloa, there, you fellow !"

"All's right," said the page. "Oh, I say, Gamiel Goose?"

"My name ain't Goose, it's Gander."

"Well, it's much the same. My good fellow, do you see that ditch that you have once been in to-day?"

"To be sure I do."

"Then go into it again."

With a dexterous twist of his own foot between both of the feet of Gamiel Gander, Cyprian at once upset him into the ditch again, and then set off at full speed from the place.

"Murder! oh, murder !" cried Gamiel. "Oh, lor !—oh, lor ! Here I am again. In for a penny, in for a pound, as the proverb says."

"And serve you right, too," said Patience, who now, by the aid of a chair, could just peep over the garden paling from the inside.

"Oh—oh ! Here's a nice mess I'm in. It's lucky I hadn't got on my best clothes, that I am going to wear at the fair to-morrow, for if I had, as sure as fate I should have spoilt 'em. Oh, lor—oh, lor ! This is the very worst ditch in all the parish of Lambeth ; and it's quite an out-and-out place for ditches, it is. What a pretty figure I am."

"You always were," said Patience.

"Oh, thank you."

"Will you take my advice, now, if I give it you ?"

"Well, yes, I will."

"Then get the first person you meet who is disposed to do you a good turn, to pump upon you at the nearest pump. That will do you more good now than anything else."

"You don't say so ?"

"I do, indeed."

"Well, I don't know that it's such a very bad idea, after all."

"You may depend it is not."

"I'll go and do it. I shouldn't wonder, now, if I meet some boys, but they will think it quite good fun. I'll just ask 'em, and when I've got my Sunday clothes on, however, to-morrow, I'll come and let you see how I look, Miss Patience."

Off set Gamiel Gander on his expedition to get pumped upon, and the two sisters were laughing at his expense, when Amy suddenly laid her hand upon her sister's arm, saying,—

"Oh, sister—sister, there he is !"

"Who?—Who?"

"The dark man in the cloak who has been here so often before, and who threw a letter into the garden once."

"Yes. I see him."

"Come away from the gate."

The two girls hurried from the gate, but not before a tall dark figure in a cloak had reached it, and without the smallest ceremony unlatched it, and entered the garden.

The sisters paused.

The stranger walked up to them, and with a studied politeness, which sat very ill upon him, however, he made them a low bow.

"Fair ones," he said, "I am in luck's way to-day, I find."

"Our father, sir, is not within," said Amy, "so, if you want to see him, you had better call again."

"Not within!" cried De Volence, for it was in good truth that worthy. "The fact is, my little ladybird, I do not wish to see him."

"Then who, sir, do you wish to see?"

"You."

"Me, sir?"

"Ay, even you, though you look so surprised at it. The fact is, I have landed too often here not to notice that you are beautiful.—I love you. I am rich, and I am noble. Do you comprehend me ?"

"Sir, I have nothing to say to you. Let us come into the house, sister Patience. Surely, even this man's insolence will not be so great as to enable him to pursue us into our father's house."

"Hold!" said De Volence, as he adroitly stepped between them and the house; "you do not evade me quite so easily. I cannot say when the fates may oblige me with such another opportunity as this, so I am quite resolved to make the most of it."

"What would you, sir, with us?"

"Only this much, that I love you, Amy, as I find your name is. You are a sweet and engaging little girl, and I am quite rich enough to make you a capital offer."

"Offer, sir?"

"Yes, of my heart."

"And your hand, sir?" said Patience.

"Oh, that is quite another thing. Girls in your class of life must be satisfied when a nobleman offers you his heart for a time."

"Sir, we hate, loathe, and despise you."

"Indeed !"

"We do, indeed ; and it is only to be lamented that if you are a nobleman you should bring such disgrace upon you order. You are far, very far beneath our contempt."

"I will make you repent those bitter words, girl."

"You cannot."

"Can I not? We will soon see that. But come, now, little one, you have not so bitter a tongue as your sister has. You will come with me at once?"

CHAPTER XXV.

ROBERT LEE COMES OPPORTUNELY TO THE SCENE OF ACTION.

ARTING forward, and passing her, Sir Warrenne de Volence flung his arms round the waist of Amy, and fairly for a moment lifted her off the ground, for he was smarting with rage at the manner in which he had been spoken to by the naturally indignant Patience.

"Help ! oh, help !" she cried.

"It is here at hand !" cried a voice, and in another moment she was snatched from the arms of De Volence, and that atrocious individual was lying on his back on the garden path, half-stunned by a blow on the head from a quarterstaff, which no other than Amy's true lover, Robert Lee, the pedler, had laid upon him with right good will.

Robert had just arrived in time to hear the concluding portion of the dialogue we have recorded as taking place between the villain De Volence and the, as he thought, unprotected sisters ; and at the moment when De Volence considered that nothing would be easier than to carry off Amy to a boat that he had in waiting by the riverside, he, Robert Lee, had made him rather roughly aware of his error.

With a shriek of joy Amy clung round the neck of her lover.

"Saved !—I am saved !" she cried. "It is you, Robert ! Oh, God, yes, it is you !"

"Yes, dear Amy, I am here to protect

you with my life. God be thanked that I was here in time !"

"Oh, yes—yes, dear—dear Robert !"

"Oh, Amy, those words are, indeed, a rich reward for all my love to you."

"What words ?"

"You said dear Robert."

Amy blushed and hid her face on her lover's bosom; but by this time Sir De Volence had so far recovered from the blow on the head he had received to struggle to his feet, and he called out in a voice half-choked and inarticulate with rage—

"Caitiff, you shall die for this !"

"No !" said Robert Lee. "I don't think so. Patience, take Amy from me. There !—So, I am all right."

The pedler grasped the quarterstaff he had with him, and stood upon his guard.

De Volence tore his sword from its sheath, and made a rush at the pedler with the hope of getting within his guard with the quarterstaff, and so by running him through the body putting an end at once to the contest ; but Robert Lee was by far too wary and too good a master of his weapon to permit any such thing.

Stepping back a pace, he whirled the quarterstaff round his head, and then brought it down with such a bang upon the head of his assailant, that De Volence turned fairly round twice, and staggered like a drunken man.

"Come on, sir," said the pedler ; "or have you had quite enough of it ?"

Rage did something towards the recovery of De Volence, and when he faced the pedler again he was more wary in his mode of attack.

His eyes glared like those of some wild animal intent upon the immediate destruction of its prey.

"I know you now, sir," said the pedler, "and I warn you that you had better go off with what you have got already from me. There is not a single swordsman breathing that I should be afraid to encounter with this good quarterstaff in my hands. I warn you, Sir De Volence, that you play a losing game."

"I must wash my hands in your blood, caitiff, before I leave this spot !" cried De Volence.

"Come on, then, and try your fortune."

"Oh, no—no !" cried Amy. "Sister—sister, call for help !"

"Do no such thing," said the pedler. "Let this person and me settle our difference at once, and without any interruption or interference. Come, sir, I am ready."

"To die !" said De Volence, and he made a feint at the head of the pedler

with his sword, and then suddenly stooping almost to the ground, he ran in upon him with the hope of getting under the guard of the quarterstaff.

De Volence was rather disappointed.

Robert Lee, when he spoke of his skill with the weapon he had in his hand, did not in the least exaggerate, and by some means or another, when he least expected it, the extreme end of the quarterstaff came with such a rap against the side of the head of Sir Volence, that the contest was over in a moment, and the villain lay stretched upon the ground without sense or motion.

"That will do," said the pedler.

"Ob, Robert, have you killed him ?" said Amy.

"Oh, dear, no."

"Are you sure of that?" said Patience.

"I think I am. He has a very hard head, I am quite certain. Besides, that last blow was not a very hard one, although with the other it did for him."

"Alas ! there will mischief come of this."

"There may, dear Amy ; and the only way is to give me a husband's right to protect you."

"If I could."

"You can, dear girl, if you will."

"My father will not consent, Robert, I fear ; but you have my consent with all my heart. I cannot refuse my hand to my deliver, and it would be false dealing, now, to pretend, dear Robert, that I do not really and truly love you."

"Oh, Amy," cried Lee, "you do not know how truly happy you make me by those words. Why, we will be the happiest couple in all the world, I'll be bound ; and what do you say to my being this morning nearly twenty pounds the richer than I thought myself before?"

"Indeed, Robert?"

"Yes, dear one, it is so."

"But how can that be?"

"Oh, easily enough ; I will tell you both. You see, it was last Lambeth fair time that I had no money to buy jewellery to sell at the fair, and I consulted Master Martin Lassamour."

"He who has married the rich widow?"

"The same."

"The Lady Margaret, of Pleasaunce House?"

"Yes, that is the lady."

"She has a—a page, I think," said Patience, "of the name of Cyprian?"

"Of that I cannot speak," said the pedler ; "but as I was saying, while I was in the little strait I mention for money, I met with Martin Lassamour."

"And did he aid you?"

"He did."

"But the story goes that he was poor before he wedded the Lady Margaret Shard."

"And so he was; but he had just had a stroke of luck at the gaming-table, to which I am sorry to say he was rather attached, and as I had done him some trifling service, not worth the mentioning, he always if he met me asked me how I got on."

"He is a noble gentleman."

"He is. Well, upon this occasion he asked me as usual how it fared with me, and I told him frankly my wants, when he said to me—

"'See, here are twenty pounds. God knows they were lightly enough come by, but if they are of use to you take them, and take them, too, with this consolation that I did not win them from a poor man, but from a great and rich lord to whom the loss is nothing. You can repay me, you know, when it suits your conscience to do so.'"

"That was kind, indeed," said Amy.

"It was," said Patience. "I almost love him for it."

"And so do I," said Amy; but she said it with such a smile, that Robert Lee did not feel at all jealous upon the subject.

"And did you repay him?" said Patience.

"You shall hear. It so happened that I had to give credit to a good customer, and I had not the means till yesterday of repaying him; but this morning I sought him out and took him the money."

"And what said he?"

"He only laughed, and shook me by the hand, saying as he did so—

"'My good friend, you will accept of the gold as a little present from me, and when you marry, you can buy your wife a trinket with it, for I will take none of it.'"

"How generous!"

"It was. I strove to induce him to take the money; but he would not, and so I am, as I say, twenty pounds the richer than I thought I was. And, oh! my Amy, if I had but one acre of land, and forty pounds per annum, I would make you my wife, and be the happiest man in all England, that I would."

CHAPTER XXVI.

MARTIN LASSAMOUR GETS A LITTLE SUSPICIOUS OF HIS LADY.

 Y far too intent had the little party in the garden of Langdon, the ferryman, been upon their own affairs to pay any attention to Sir Warrenne de Volence, as he lay prostrate on the earth.

It happened, though, that just as Robert Lee was telling his story of the way in which Martin Lassamour had refused to take the twenty pounds back that had been borrowed of him, De Volence recovered sufficiently to be able to look about him.

This partial recovery was but the natural prelude to a more complete one, and finally he rose and staggered out of the garden, making gestures of rage as he went.

The mind of De Volence was in that state of confusion, though, that he left his sword behind him, so that when he was missed by the pedler, Amy at once exclaimed—

"Yes, he is gone; but here is his sword, Robert—the sword which he would fain have buried in your faithful heart."

"Take it within the house, dear Amy,' said the pedler, "and keep it as a trophy of this day's work; and if De Volence should ever, as haply enough he may do, deny having had the share that we all know he had in this business, that sword will be a damning evidence against him."

"It will—it will."

"Then preserve it on that account, and with that idea. And now I must away. Heaven keep you both in its holy keeping, free from all harm!"

"And you too, Robert."

"Amen! Ah! who comes?"

A hasty footstep came up the garden-path, and Langdon, the ferryman, made his appearance in a great heat from the haste he had made to get home, after having taken some passengers across the ferry.

"Zounds!" he said, "I have been on a pretty wild-goose chase."

"Indeed, father?" said Patience.

"Yes; that rascal of a page told me that there was a man and a cow in the ferry-boat, and as my sight is not good at a distance, I had to run all the way to the water's edge to see."

"Indeed ?"

"Yes, indeed, and there was neither a man nor a cow, but a couple of monks and an old woman who wanted to cross the ferry."

"How are you, Langdon ?" said Robert Lee, stepping from behind Patience, where he had screened himself.

"Zounds! who are you ?"

"Robert Lee, the pedler."

"Confound everybody and everything; what do you do here in my garden, I should like to know ?"

"Nothing, sir."

"Nothing and be hanged to you! Be off. I don't want any pedlers nor pages here. Upon my word, my life is a misery to me with these girls. My poor wife made a sad mistake when she spoke about them being a comfort to me in my old age."

"Did she so ?"

"Zounds! yes; far from being a comfort, they are the pest of my existence."

"Oh, father, don't say that," cried Patience.

"He don't mean it," said Amy.

"Zounds! but I do. But you be off, Master Pedler; I don't want you here, at all events—so off with you."

"But, Master Langdon."

"Don't Master Langdon me. I am plain Langdon—nothing in the world but plain Langdon."

"That is quite evident," said the pedler.

"Zounds! you are all in the same story. That was just what the rascally page said to me. Be off with you."

"Farewell, dear Amy!" said the pedler.

"Dear what ?" roared the ferryman. "This before my eyes actually !"

"Langdon," said Lee—"or plain Langdon if you like it better—I am an honest man. I love your daughter Amy, and I don't see the smallest reason on earth to conceal it. I would say 'dear Amy' before all the world, for dear she is to me."

"Zounds! she is dear to me, too."

"Of course she is."

"But I don't mean in your way. I mean in the way of ribbons and dresses. But be off with you; I don't want to have anything more to say to you."

"And why so ?"

"You are poor."

"Well, plain Langdon, if I had an acre of ground of my own, now, and forty pounds a year, what would you say to me?"

"Ah! that would be quite another thing."

"Would it, though ? Would you then give your consent to my union with your daughter Amy ?"

"Zounds! I would."

"Courage, then—courage! I now have something to fight and struggle for in life, and the honest man who with a stout heart and a clear conscience makes up his mind to the accomplishment of an object that is a good one, will be sure to succeed. Good-by, father-in-law, plain Langdon, that is to be."

With these words, the pedler left the garden at a great rate, and was soon out of sight.

"Zounds!" cried Langdon, "if the impudence of some folks don't fairly beat everything in the world. Here is this fellow calling me father-in-law that is to be already. Hilloa! what do you want, stupid ?"

This polite inquiry was addressed to Gamiel Gander, who had just arrived in his Sunday clothes, for which he had been compelled to exchange his suit that had been with him in the ditch.

There can be no doubt in the world but that Gamiel Gander thought himself now a perfect beauty. The only misfortune was, that nobody else agreed with him in that opinion but his old grandmother, Dame Gander; and there was one little circumstance that made her judgment in such matters of not much account or value.

The old lady had been stone-blind for a matter of seven years and more.

That was all.

Now Gamiel, as he had been compelled, so to speak, to put on his Sunday clothes, had come to the ferry-house for the express purpose of exhibiting himself in them to the ferryman's daughters; and all of a sudden to be addressed as an idiot was not flattering.

"Lor, Mr. Langdon," he said, "look at me."

"Well ?"

"Don't you see ?"

"Yes."

"Ah, I thought you would."

"A fool !"

"Oh, lor! well, how sharp you are, to be sure. You don't think so, young ladies, do you ?"

"Oh, yes," cried Patience and Amy, both at once; "oh, yes, we do, and always did."

"Well, I never! that is pleasant. But

do you see these what's-his-names?—Sky blue. Ain't they loves?"

"Be off with you," cried Langdon, "or I'll kick you into the ditch."

"Don't—oh, don't! I've been there twice to day, and know what it is."

"Do you?"

"Yes, I do, Master Langdon; so whatever you do, my dear sir, don't push me in there. But I had a message for you, and I may as well deliver it at once. Dear me, what was it?"

"What was it, do you say? Upon my life you are a pretty fellow to bring a message to any one, I think."

"Oh, yes it was—eh? No, it wasn't."

"Get out, fool! It would be a charity to hang you, that it would."

"Oh, would it? Well, then, Master Langdon, as the old proverb says, ' Charity begins at home,' you can hang yourself first."

"Eh? Well, upon my life that's about

the smartest thing I've ever heard you say yet, Gamiel."

"Oh, is it?"

"Yes; is it original?"

"What do you mean by that?"

"Well, never mind, it was well said; so now go in and get the girls to give you a glass of the old ale. By-the-by, is the old lady getting any worse, eh?"

"Well, she don't seem as if she would last long."

"Don't she, though?"

"Not a bit of it, and then I shall drop in for all her money, Master Langdon, and it's a good thing that, ain't it now?"

"It is. But what noise is that at the ferry?"

"Oh! oh! I forgot. That's it I was told to tell you, to go down there, for the great lady of Pleasaunce House and her young husband were going to stop in their barge. Oh! oh! I forgot."

CHAPTER XXVII.

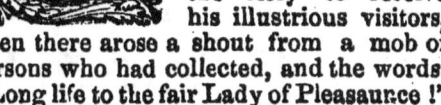

LASSAMOUR PROJECTS A PLAN TO TEST THE CONDUCT OF HIS LADY.

NE withering glance was cast by the ferryman at Gamiel, and then he was about to make a rush down to the ferry to receive his illustrious visitors, when there arose a shout from a mob of persons who had collected, and the words, " Long life to the fair Lady of Pleasaunce !" came fairly upon the air.

"Zounds!" cried the ferryman, "here they are."

"But what do they want here, father?" said Patience.

"Zounds, girl, this is the nearest route to the old church, don't you know? and the gentry have taken it into their heads lately that the old tombs of the monks and the friars of days gone by are worth the looking at."

"But they don't need to come through our garden, father, for all that."

"No, I don't say they do need; but if I can only persuade them it is the best way, don't you think I shall get something by it? To be sure I shall. Leave me alone for looking after the main chance, though I am plain Langdon, the ferryman."

With these words Langdon made off at the top of his speed to welcome his guests,

as he would fain have Lady Margaret and Martin Lassamour to be.

Now it had so happened that the Lady Margaret had expressed a wish to land at Lambeth ferry. Why she so wished she had not thought proper to say; but as it was a harmless enough wish, and Martin Lassamour was on excellent terms with her, he made no sort of objection or inquiry about it, but at once ordered the barge to be put in at the ferry close to the old ferry house.

Master Lamont was still with the party on board the magnificent barge which Lady Margaret had, with such playful tact, repudiated the ownership of, as doubtless the reader will not fail to recollect.

As she landed, Margaret ordered Cyprian, who had joined the party, to throw some small silver coins among the people, and this operation had produced the joyous shouts that had come upon the ears of Langdon and his daughter in the garden.

It was rather a strange thing that the Lady Margaret Lassamour always indulged herself in the luxury of giving *largesse* to the people wherever she went.

Was it that she knew in the inmost recesses of her own mind that she was terribly obnoxious to evil report? and did she adopt this mode of purchasing that popularity and those smiles and cries of the populace

LADY MARGARET SHOWS MARTIN LASSAMOUR THE ANONYMOUS LETTER.

which otherwise might have been turned into shouts of execration and wild accusations against her concerning her deceased six husbands?

It may be so.

The barge was run alongside the little landing-place just as the ferryman reached the spot.

"This way, gentles," he cried. "This is the way to the old church."

"My good fellow," said Lassamour, "we are not going to the old church."

"Never mind, noble sir. This is the nearest way anywhere, and I am plain Langdon, the ferryman, an it please you, noble sir. Will you and your noble lady walk into my garden and rest yourselves awhile?"

"Yes," said Lady Margaret.

"Be it so, then," said Martin Lassamour.

Now the simple fact is, that Lady Margaret had a reason for coming to this place, which will soon be apparent to the reader.

More than once, notwithstanding the

air of cheerfulness that the Lady Margaret had strove to keep up as the little party came down the river in the barge, Martin had thought that he could detect in her face traces of disquietude and emotion.

Any appearance of that sort in his rather mysterious and fair lady-wife was, as the reader may well suppose, calculated to give, even in Martin's situation, considerable uneasiness.

He resolved to make one attempt, even though it were an unsuccessful one, to find out what was amiss.

As they entered the garden of Langdon, finding himself close to her side, and that Master Lamont was a few paces distant from them, quite absorbed in admiration of the pretty little garden, Martin whispered to his lady—

"Margaret!"

She started.

"Yes, Martin."

"You look sad."

"Do I so?"

"You do, indeed; and at times your cheeks flush, and there is a wandering sort of restlessness in your eye. Are you ill?"

"Oh, no—no!"

"By Our Lady, I am glad to hear you say so."

"Are you?"

"Do you doubt me?"

"Oh, no, no, Martin, I would die rather than doubt you; but yet——"

"Yet what?"

"No matter. I promise that before the day is out I will impart to you something."

"Ah, what?"

"You have an enemy!"

"Doubtless. Who is he or she?"

"Patience yet awhile. This is no place for private talk. Here is your young friend, Lamont, advancing towards us."

Lamont had plucked some roses, which, for beauty and fragrance, were perfect rarities, and gallantly handing them to the Lady Margaret, he said—

"I know, lady, that my friend, Martin Lassamour, will not be angry with me for presenting you with a rose."

"Far from it, Lamont," said Lassamour. "On the contrary, every really gentlemanly attention that is ever paid to my wife, I look upon as a compliment to myself."

"You are very good, sir."

"And the remark is a just one," said Lady Margaret, as she took the rose. "I thank you with all my heart, good Master Lamont."

"Ah, by my faith," said Martin, "here are roses though, Lamont, that fade yours, my good friend."

"Indeed?"

The Lady Margaret turned slightly pale as the two daughters of the ferryman now approached the party.

They brought a little table, on which was spread a clean white cloth, and Patience carried with her, with all the grace of her nature, some beautiful strawberries, grown in the garden, and which she placed on the table.

"Fair ladies," said Martin, with a bow, "I have heard much of the flowers of this garden, but no one, it seems to me, was able to say all of them that they demand."

This was too pointed a compliment to escape observation, and both the girls, you may be sure, quite perfectly understood it.

Lamont was rather bashful, so he kept a little in the back ground, but it was quite easy to see that he was enchanted with Patience and her pretty looks.

"By Jove," he said, "she is an angel."

"Sir?" said Lady Margaret.

"Madam!"

"I thought you spoke."

"No, I—that is—did I speak?"

Lady Margaret smiled.

"I think, Master Lamont, that you were so lost in admiration of the beauty of one of these young girls, that you did not know well if you spoke or not."

Lamont blushed up to the eyes.

"Nay," added Lady Margaret, "you are free to admire and to say that you do so."

Lamont bowed.

"It is a great privilege."

"What is a great privilege?" said Martin.

"To be free to admire any pretty face that comes across the gazer's fancy," said Lady Margaret, "as our friend Lamont, who is enamoured, is entirely free to do."

"Hem!"

"All of which means," said Lamont, "that you are not in that condition, Martin Lassamour."

"Oh, I comprehend."

The shadow of a smile passed across the face of Lamont, and the shadow of a frown over that of the Lady Margaret.

She thought that both Lamont and Martin treated the subject rather too lightly, and so she was to some extent displeased just then with both of them.

But Amy now stepped up to the little party, and with a smile and a curtsey, said—

"Will it please you, madam, and you, gentleman, to taste our strawberries?"

"Oh, dear yes, and your tulips, too," said Martin.

"Martin!" said Lady Margaret.

"Yes—I—I didn't say anything."

"'Tis well."

Cyprian was all this time, for he had come into the garden after his lady and her husband, in a perfect agony, for he did not put himself forward for fear of giving offence.

When, however, he saw Patience handing a little plate to Martin Lassamour with the strawberries, and when he saw that there really at one moment was not the space of more than six inches between their very faces, he could control himself no longer, but darting forth, he cried out—

"Allow me to assist—allow me to assist!"

As he did so he gave Patience such a pinch on the arm that she uttered a little shriek, and down went the plate of strawberries on to the lawn.

"Why, you rascal," said Lassamour, "what is the meaning of this?"

"The—a—the meaning?"

"Yes, the meaning! Are you mad all of a sudden?"

CHAPTER XXVIII.

LADY MARGARET EXPLAINS THE CAUSE OF HER DISQUIETUDE TO MARTIN.

THE little group of people in the garden of the ferryman certainly, at this moment, cut rather a ridiculous figure.

Amy Langdon was stuffing the corner of her apron into her mouth to keep herself from laughing.

Patience was looking as confused as possible, for she perfectly understood the real meaning of the extraordinary conduct of the page.

As for poor Cyprian himself, he wished himself anywhere but where he was just then, the bottom of the Thames included.

By the smile that stole over the face of Martin Lassamour it may be presumed that he began to understand the real fact of the case; and as for Lady Margaret and Lamont, they looked on as spectators of the scene. But Lamont would have had great pleasure in boxing the page's ears.

"Upon my life, Cyprian," said Martin, "I must say that, in my opinion, you are a little bit deranged."

"Yes, sir," said Patience, "he always is."

"Oh, you know him?"

"Know him? Oh, dear yes—that is, no."

"Yes—that is, no. Upon my word, my pretty little one, I don't know very well what to make of such an answer as that."

"Nor I," said Lamont.

"Why—you see, sir," said Cyprian, "I—a—and this—a—young girl, sir—You comprehend, sir?"

"Indeed I do not."

"That's it, sir."

"Yes," said Patience, "that is all about it, sir." She added then in a whisper to Cyprian, "Oh, go along, stupid!"

"Stupid?"

"Yes, stupid!"

"Oh!"

Lady Margaret stepped up.

"Well, Martin," she said, "I think we will not intrude for longer upon these good people. It seems to me as if we were rather putting them out of their way."

"As you please, my lady."

"Master Lamont, are you ready and willing to leave this place?"

"Certainly, madam. Confound you!"

Lamont had his eyes so fixed upon Patience that, in retreating in a sidelong sort of way, he came right against Cyprian, and nearly threw him over.

"I beg your pardon, sir," said Cyprian, "for being in your way while you were looking at other people's goods."

"Eh?"

"Other people's goods, sir."

"What do you mean?"

"That young lady is my wife."

"Your wife?"

"Yes, sir."

This was rather a bold assertion on the part of the page, but he was in such a state of desperation by the ardent admiration that Patience excited in the breast of Lamont, that he was inclined to say anything or to do anything that would put a stop to his thinking any further about her.

To an extent he certainly succeeded, for Lamont replied—

"I envy you very much, page; you are the luckiest fellow I know of, in having such a lovely piece of goods that you can call your own."

"Yes, sir."

"Well, I congratulate you!"

"Thank you, sir."

The Lady Margaret laid a piece of gold upon the little table, and said, with a smile—

"Report has not said too much of the beauty of the garden of Master Langdon, the ferryman, or of the beauty of the flowers to be found in it. Farewell! I may, perhaps, some day visit both again. Come, Martin, are you ready?"

"Quite."

She took the arm of Martin, so that he had only time and opportunity to look what probably he would fain have said to the fair daughters of the ferryman.

Lamont tarried a little behind the rest of the party, for, notwithstanding all that Cyprian had told him, he could not keep his eyes off the fair Patience ; but Cyprian kept close to him, and bothered him very much.

Whenever Lamont tried to look at Patience, and to execute an amorous sort of smile, Cyprian was sure to pop his own head in the way, so that the young man felt half inclined to fly at him and knock him down.

The two girls were, as may well be supposed, mightily amused at all this ; and when the party had left the garden, they laughed with glee at it.

On the route to the barge again, Margaret Lassamour was silent, and Martin said to her—

"I still cannot divest myself of the idea that you are unwell."

"Indeed?"

"Such is my notion ; but I beg you will not take my perseverance in such an idea in ill part."

"How can I take anything in ill part from you, Martin?"

"You are too good."

"No—no. I have something to ask of you."

"Of me?"

"Yes ; when you get on board the barge I have a question to ask of you, as well as something to show you, that will a little surprise you. It is a letter. But curb your curiosity. I will soon satisfy you, and, indeed, I brought it with me for the very purpose."

"You surprise me."

"I, too, have been surprised, Martin. But I have received an anonymous letter, which I will confess has given my poor weak woman's heart some little amount of disquietude, and I am in the hope that you will be able to come to some sort of correct guess as to the unknown hand that penned it."

"Show it to me."

"Soon. Well, Cyprian, what is it?"

The page, with his cap in his hand, stood bowing to his master as if he had something to say, and as he so bowed, he put on the most doleful sort of face that any one could possibly extemporise on the spur of a moment.

"Why, good gracious, Cyprian, what is the matter?" said Lassamour.

"Oh, my noble lady—oh, worshipful sir —oh !"

"What is it?" said Lady Margaret.

"Yes, Cyprian, speak out. What is it?"

"Oh—oh—oh !"

"Well, is that all?"

"No, worshipful sir ; but the only relation I have in the world is my poor old mother."

"Well?"

"Oh, noble, sir, she was taken very ill last night, and not able to leave her bed, and I have made bold to hope that you and my dear lady will let me have leave of absence from your noble service for to-day, to go and see her."

"Poor Cyprian !" said Lady Margaret.

"Filial and admirable Cyprian !" said Lassamour.

"He weeps."

"He does, indeed."

"I—I—may have the leave ?"

"Yes," said Lady Margaret.

"Hold !" said Martin.

Cyprian looked perplexed.

"If, my good Cyprian," added Martin, "your gentle and excellent mistress were to give you leave to swallow the barge, I should say do it, provided the reason why she gave you that leave was correctly known to her. But I can inform her and you both, Cyprian, that you have been cruelly hoaxed."

"Hoaked !" said Cyprian.

"Hoaked !" said Lady Margaret.

"Yes. I suppose, Cyprian, some one told you of the severe indisposition of your mother."

"Yes, noble sir."

"Then I can tell you, whoever it was has been playing with your feelings."

"Sir?"

"Yes, for I saw an old lady this morning at Pleasaunce House, who was pointed out to me as your mother, and I gave her a gold piece ; and I must say she looked in excellent health, and she said that that scapegrace, her son, Cyprian, was hiding from her in the great hall."

Cyprian looked very much staggered.

"Is this so?" said Lady Margaret to Martin, who could not keep from laughing as he spoke, and so led the lady to conclude that it was just possible he was joking.

"Indeed it is so."

"Truly now?"

"Most truly."

"Cyprian, who gave you license to act thus?"

"I—a—my lady—if a—the old lady was at Pleasaunce House this morning, why then I must have been misinformed."

"Undoubtedly," said Martin Lassamour; "so follow us, Cyprian, if you please. Ah, how delighted you must be."

"Delighted?"

"Yes, to be sure, to find out that the old lady is quite well."

"Oh—yes—yes."

"Don't he look delighted, Margaret?"

The Lady Margaret shook her head reprovingly at Cyprian for his attempted deceit, and with a groan the page found there was no resource but to follow his master.

No doubt Master Cyprian thought to have got instant leave to absent himself, and acting upon such leave, he would no more have thought of his poor old mother than he would have thought of Noah; but he would have hastened back to the ferryman's garden, with the hope of getting some further talk with the fair Patience.

But love proposes, and fate disposes, so the page found himself in a very short time on board the barge again.

"And now," said Martin Lassamour, as he led the Lady Margaret into the saloon of the barge, "and now, where is this anonymous letter of which you spoke?"

"It is here."

She took it from her bosom.

Martin Lassamour hastily opened it, and read as follows:—

"FAIR LADY,—There are those in the world who, although they may not be in any way personally affected by the villanies and treacheries of particular individuals, still feel that they scarcely do their duty if they do not warn others of theirs.

"I am one of those.

"Therefore, fair lady, look well to Martin Lassamour, your husband, for Simon Langdon, the ferryman, has a fair daughter.—This from—   "A FRIEND."

Martin looked up in the face of his lady.

"And this disquieted you?" he said.

"Will you think meanly of me if I confess that it did?"

"No; jealousy is one of those feelings which lie at the bottom of all hearts; but I will mark the villain who wrote this note to you!"

CHAPTER XXIX.

BRINGS DE VOLENCE AGAIN UPON THE SCENE OF ACTION.

"H, Martin," said Lady Margaret, "I said that before I would show you this letter, I had a question to put to you; but I forgot it, and placed the letter in your hands first, in mistake."

"Never mind that. Propose you question now."

"I will. But will you promise me, upon your word of honour as a gentleman, that you will answer it truly?"

"I do."

"Then had you before to-day any sort of acquaintance with either of the really fair daughters of Langdon, the ferryman?"

"Never!"

"I am satisfied."

"Why, Margaret, is it possible——"

"Possible that what?"

"That this expedition to the ferry was for the purpose of watching my conduct at the house?"

"No—no."

"I am glad to hear you say no to that."

"No, Martin, it was not with any such object; but it was to see if what I had heard from time to time of the beauty of the daughters of the ferryman were true."

"And you found it—"

"Quite true. They are both very lovely girls, and your young friend, Lamont, is, I think, of the same opinion."

"Ah, yes, no doubt. And now, Margaret, that you mention Lamont, it puts me in mind of something that may possibly enable me to come at the author of this anonymous letter you have shown to me. Where is he?"

"On the deck."

"Cyprian!"

"Yes, worshipful sir."

"Request of my good friend, Lamont, that, if not better engaged, he will favour us with his good company."

"Yes, sir."

In a few moments Lamont was in the saloon of the barge, and Martin, turning to him, said—

"I think I gave you back that challenge that you received from a certain party?"

"You did."

"Have you it about you?"

"Yes, it is here."

"Then give it to me. Now, Margaret, compare the hand-writing of this note with that of the anonymous one you have received, and which, I regret, has given you any disquietude, and see if you can observe any similarity between them."

Lady Margaret took the two notes and compared them, and then she at once exclaimed—

"The writing is identical!"

"Then turn over the page of this one and you will see who it is that has tried to awaken your fears."

"The villain, De Volence !"

"Just so."

"Oh, Martin, I know the reason of it, too !"

"So do I. He was a disappointed suitor for your hand, was he not?"

"He was."

"Then he is, of course, my implacable foe; and he is the implacable foe of Lamont, because Lamont saved me from assassination from him, that is all. Now you comprehend all about it?"

"I do, indeed. But the challenge?" said Lady Margaret.

"You would ask what shall be done with it?"

"I would."

"Nothing but what has been done. I have written an answer."

"And that answer?"

"Is to the effect that I consider the quarrel entirely my own, and that I will meet it as such on the first convenient opportunity; which means, the first time I can meet this De Volence in such a situation as to force him to fight me fairly."

"Oh, Martin, you will be careful of yourself for my sake, will you not?"

"In good truth I will."

"If you please, madam, there is a small boat making for the barge, and a man is waving his hand as if to intimate that he has a something to say."

"Bid the rowers pause," said the lady.

The barge instantly became stationary, and the man in the boat turned out to be no other than Robert Lee, the pedler, who, upon getting permission so to do, clambered up the side of the barge, and desired speech of Martin Lassamour.

"This is a good fellow, Margaret, and a great friend of mine; so, by your leave, I will see him."

"Oh, yes, yes."

"Well, Robert, what would you say?"

"My good sir, and worshipful patron, I come to crave your noble advice in a matter of difficulty."

"What is it, man?"

"I will tell all, from first to last."

The pedler then acquainted Martin and his lady, and Master Lamont, with the fact of his half kind of betrothal to Amy, the elder daughter of Langdon, the ferryman; and how Langdon himself had so far countenanced his addresses to his daughter as to make his consent only contingent upon his acquisition of an acre of ground, and forty pounds per annum of his own. Then he told how, upon calling to see his loved one, he had found her actually in the arms of De Volence, and how the contest had taken place between them, ending in the discomfiture of De Volence.

The pedler concluded by saying—

"Now, worshipful sir, and you, noble lady, I know well that De Volence is a man of family, and that he has got friends, and I fear that he will adopt some kind of revenge against me, that will prevent me from communicating to any one some sad condition in which I may be placed, so I thought it but a proper and prudent step, provided your honour would listen to me, to tell you all about it at once."

"You did quite right."

"Quite," said Lady Margaret. "It is impossible you could have adopted a more prudent step."

The pedler looked gratified.

"Yes, my good fellow," said Martin, "you may depend upon my protection to the utmost extent. I know this De Volence as a scoundrel, and as a man who will not scruple at anything for vengeance. He is a coward, so as regards any fresh attack from him you are now quite safe."

"Yes, noble sir. It is not that I fear."

"Certainly not, for you have shown that you can take you own part well with your quarterstaff."

"Well," said the pedler, "I may say that I can manage to do that; but he may hatch up some plot against me, and so be my ruin in some way."

"Heed him not; I will keep an eye upon his movements, and if you should get involved in any trouble of any sort, send at once to me, and I shall know what to think of it."

"Yes," said Lady Margaret; "and we will at once aid you."

"I do not know how to thank you sufficiently."

"Do not name it. Be of good cheer, my good friend, and all will go well; I myself have sufficient of a quarrel with the rascal De Volence that may, perhaps, in its results put a stop to his pranks for ever."

"Indeed, noble sir?"

"Yes; the first time I meet him I have to put a question or two to him at the point of my sword."

"Heaven give your worship the victory."

"Amen! I think there is not much doubt of that. You may now go your way in peace, good pedler."

The Lady Margaret, who was ever beneficent, took a gold bracelet from her wrist, and presenting it to the pedler, said—

"Give this to your bride upon her wedding day."

"Oh, my good lady, it is too much."

"Nay, it is not. It will help you to the object of your wishes; and should you find yourself near to the achievement of them, I am in the possession of the land and the money Langdon requires in a son-in-law. Come to me again, and the deficiency may possibly be made up."

The pedler was deeply affected at the great generosity on the part of the lady, and he left the barge and dropped astern of it in his little boat, by far too much affected for speech.

"That is a shrewd and hardy fellow," said Martin.

"He is, Martin. I pray that De Volence may not succeed in doing him a mischief."

"The rascal will try for it. By heavens, I would have given something to see the fight between them in the garden. How De Volence must have looked as the quarterstaff rang on his head."

Lady Margaret smiled.

And now, after a little thought, Lassamour sat down and wrote the following note to De Volence—

"VILLAIN!—If you are not as cowardly as you are base, stir not abroad without your rapier, for, by the heavens above us, so soon as you and I meet I will exact such an account of you as will make you pray that you had never been born to become the anonymous slanderer of the fair fame of others.   "MARTIN LASSAMOUR."

"Cyprian," cried Martin.

"Yes, sir."

"You will take this note. You see its superscription?"

"To Sir Warrenne De Volence," read Cyprian. "Yes, noble sir, I know the man."

"'Tis well; you will land now at the next quay, and it will be your duty to find him as soon as possible and deliver this to him with your own hands into his."

"I will do it."

"Be it so; and now, Lady Margaret, you will be so good as to let Cyprian be landed as soon as possible; my mind will be somewhat more at ease as regards this rascal De Volence."

Lady Margaret gave the necessary order, and the page was soon put on shore, and the moment he was so he cut a great caper of delight, exclaiming—

"Bravo—bravo! If the job don't last me all day it will be a wonder indeed. I will run off at once, in the first place, to the ferry, and see Patience. Oh, how lovely she is."

Placing the letter in the bosom of his doublet the page soon forgot all about it in his eagerness to get to the ferryman's garden.

The amorous looks that Lamont had cast upon the fair Patience had enraged Cyprian dreadfully, and he could only hope that from the lips of the girl herself he might be able to get some consolation in the shape of an assurance that he was preferred.

It was with this view that, quite panting and out of breath, he reached the paling of the garden, and clambered up it and looked over.

Alas! the garden was empty.

"A plague take it," he said, "they are in the house. Never mind: faint heart never won fair lady yet, so I'll just clamber over at once, and try and get a few minutes' talk with the sweet, delightful Patience. Oh, what a love she is!"

CHAPTER XXX.

GAMIEL GANDER GETS INTO FRESH DIFFICULTIES.

ERTAINLY the page, Cyprian, was very much to blame indeed in neglecting the business that he was sent upon by his indulgent master, Martin Lassamour, for the purpose of going in pursuit of his own pleasure.

Perhaps he bore Lassamour something of a grudge for the affair as regarded his old mother. At all events, he seemed to make up his mind very quickly to letting the letter that his master had given him for Sir Warrenne De Volence wait his leisure.

Hurried away, then, by the violence of his passion for the fair Patience, the page got over the garden paling and lit exactly in the middle of a bed of tulips, upon the beauty of which Simon Langdon the ferryman prided himself not a little.

"Hilloa!" said Cyprian, "if old Langdon had only been in the garden now, and seen me make such havoc of his tulips, there would have been a pretty row. Oh, you duck!"

This last exclamation was addressed to Patience, who made her appearance in the garden at this moment, looking as innocent and as totally unconscious of the presence of the page as though she really had not seen him from one of the windows, and really watched him climb over the wall.

Now, in order to keep up appearances, Patience gave quite a nice little scream; but it was by no means so loud as to alarm the neighbourhood, and, in point of fact, it is very doubtful if it was loud enough to alarm any one at all.

"Oh, go away—go away !"

"Away?"

"Yes, go at once. I feel as if I should faint."

Of course, upon this, it was quite impossible that Cyprian should do anything but very gallantly assist Patience in keeping her feet; and in order to do that, it was necessary to place his arm round her waist.

It was a sad necessity, but we are bound to say, as faithful historians, that he did not shrink from it.

"Oh, Patience," he said, "you know how I love you."

"No, I don't."

"Well, but——"

"That makes at least twenty."

"Oh, dear no," said Cyprian, kissing her again and again, "it is not half the number, I assure you."

"Then I won't have any more."

"But you told me I might take twenty."

"No, I didn't."

"Oh—oh, I appeal to—to all universal nature."

"Go along with you, I didn't say any such thing. Why, I said you had given me twenty kisses, not that you might do so."

"Well, that is all the same."

"Is it, indeed? Now I tell you what, Mr. Page : if my father were to come home all of a sudden and catch you here, he would take your life."

"Ah, what a happiness !"

"A happiness?"

"Yes, to die for you."

"Oh, don't say that, I beg of you. I would much rather that—that——"

"I would live for you?"

"No, I didn't say that, either. But how could you think of jumping among the tulips ?"

"Oh, that's nothing."

"Is it nothing ! I can assure you, Mr. Cyprian, that when father sees them all broken down, he won't know what to think."

"Yes, he will. He will think it has been some strange cat."

"On two legs."

Cyprian laughed.

"But now, Patience, that you have confessed to loving me to distraction——"

"What?"

"To loving me to such distraction——"

"Well, I never ! The impudence of some people ! Why I never said I loved you at all."

"Oh !—oh !"

"Go along, do. The fact is, I rather hate you."

"Well, that comes to the same thing."

"Does it, though? But be off with you, I don't want you here. I don't like you, and I won't have you for a sweetheart of mine. You are not at all good looking, so go away do, and I don't care what becomes of you. There, now."

LANGDON, THE FERRYMAN, FINDING GAMIEL GANDER IN THE FLOUR BIN.

"Then I can easily die."

"Die !"

"To be sure, when my time comes ; but you may depend not one moment before, my dear, pretty Patience."

"Oh, Cyprian, Cyprian !"

"What—what?"

"I can see father coming !"

"The devil !"

"Yes—that is—no. Get over the wall."

"I can't in time."

"No more you can. Come this way into the house. Oh, how foolish of you to come here ; but you will be murdered, that's for certain, and then I shall have the consolation of getting rid of you for good. This way—this way."

She ran on before him, and Cyprian following her closely, found himself for the first time in the ferryman's house.

The first person they met now was Amy, who seeing Cyprian, cried out—

"Oh, Patience, what is this?"

"A—a page, sister."

"Yes," said Cyprian, "here I am. Love, all powerful, has pushed me over the garden wall."

"Oh, you wretched boy."

"Thank you."

"Don't talk to him, sister," said Patience. "Here is father coming, and there will be murder done, if we do not hide him in the house somewhere. Oh, I am in such a flutter, I don't know what to do."

"Father coming?"

"Yes—yes."

"Are you sure?"

"Oh, don't go on in that way, I beg of you, sister, don't. I shall go out of my mind. I don't like him at all, as you know, but I don't want to have his blood on my conscience."

"This way," said Amy, who had more presence of mind than her sister, "this way. Get in there."

She opened a large cupboard, and Cyprian, just as he was peeping into it to see what sort of a place it was, was all at once pushed into it head over heels by the two girls, and he fell right into a great basket full of hay.

They were not a moment too soon in so disposing of Cyprian, for the ferryman came at a rapid pace up the garden walk.

The moment Langdon got to the door of his house he cast an angry glance at the two girls in silence.

"Dear me, father, is that you?" said Patience.

"It is me."

"Well, I thought you had gone to Little Britain."

"Little fiddlestick."

"Well, you said you were going there."

"So I did, but you see—ha—ha! I have come back."

"Yes, father."

"Would you like anything to eat?" said Amy.

"Yes."

"What, father?"

"A page."

"A what?"

"A little whipper-snapper of a page, and be hanged to him! That's what I should like to eat. Ha!"

"Really, we don't understand you."

"Oh, don't you? Well, then, I'll try to make you. There was a boy met me as I was going along, and he says to me,' 'Are you Langdon, the ferryman?' says he. 'Yes,' says I. 'Oh, then,' says he, 'there is a fellow just got over your garden paling,' says he. 'He is a sort of a page, says he. 'Oh, has he?' says I; so on I came at a good pace, and here I am. Ha!"

Patience felt ready to faint.

"And did you find him?" said Amy.

"No; but I found all the tulips smashed."

"You don't say so?"

"Yes, I do; and a bit of the top of the paling pulled off, too. Oh, if I catch him, by the Lord I wouldn't be in his skin. Where is he?"

"Who?"

"The page."

"The page?"

"Don't go on repeating my words, girl. Where the devil is that little piece of mischief, Cyprian, the page to Lady Margaret Lassamour. Where is he, I say?"

"Well, father, if you really want to know, perhaps it will be better to ask some one else than your own daughter, who cannot be very well supposed to have Mistress Lassamour's page in her thimble-case."

"Oh, indeed; you are witty over it. But—ah, we shall see—ah, we shall see. Come, now, we shall see. There now, the door is fast, I rather think, and I mean to have a thorough search of the house, and I'll begin at the top of it and come right down in a regular sort of way till I get to this room. What do you say to that?"

"Nothing, father."

"Well, we shall see—we shall see."

The ferryman, with a look of great anger and ferocity, slipped up stairs to commence his search.

"Oh, Amy, he is lost," said Patience.

"No—no. He must escape."

"Yes, I'm d—d if I mustn't!" said Cyprian, popping out of the cupboard. "Excuse me, ladies, for the strong expression, but—Oh, the devil!"

"In—in."

They thought that Langdon was coming down the stairs again, but such turned out not to be the case, so Cyprian popped out again, saying as he did so—

"Open the front door, and give me a fair start."

"We cannot. He has taken the key."

"The deuce you can't."

"No—no, you had better get up the chimney."

"Up the chimney! No hang it, I won't do that. I say, though, couldn't you let me out at one of the windows?"

"Oh, look—look, sister, who is that?" suddenly said Patience, pointing through one of the windows right across the garden.

Amy looked, and so did Cyprian, and there they saw the round, comical-looking face of Gamiel Gander just peeping over the top of the paling.

"I have it," cried Amy. "I have it; be quiet, both of you. I have a scheme that will, I think, answer yet."

CHAPTER XXXI.

THE FERRYMAN IS DECEIVED, NOTWITHSTANDING ALL HIS PRECAUTIONS.

 MY opened the casement, and although it was rather high from the ground, and rather narrow to get through, she, with great agility, surmounted those difficulties, and was in the garden in a moment.

"What is she about?" said Cyprian.

"I don't know. Oh, what shall I do?"

"Come into the cupboard."

"Go along, I won't! It is you who have brought all this mischief and misery upon me, you wretched page. Oh, how I ought to hate you!"

"But you can't."

"I can't, I own it; and now that you are at the point of death——"

"The point of what?"

"Of death—I don't mind saying to you that I did like you a little. Of course you will be found out, and then there will be an end of you; but it is all your own fault for coming here at all. I never told you to come."

"Oh, how kind," said Cyprian. "But I don't intend to die easy."

"You had better."

"No, I won't. Hand me that spit that is by the side of the fire-place; it is a good length and will keep your sweet father off, I rather think."

"Oh, you wretched boy! you don't mean to say you would take his life, do you, and leave me an orphan?"

"I'd much rather take his life than he should take mine; and as for leaving you an orphan, I intend to adopt you, you sweet little baby."

"Oh! oh!"

"What's the matter?"

"There's somebody coming."

"The devil!"

Cyprian popped into the cupboard again, and Patience began to exert herself at the spinningwheel at such a rate that the thread kept curling every moment dreadfully.

The somebody coming was Amy from the garden, but she was not coming alone, for, to the surprise of Patience and the delight of Cyprian, she brought no less a personage than Gamiel Gander with her.

Now, in order to understand how Amy managed this, we must follow her into the garden after her escape from the room by the window.

She ran to the side of the paling, over the top of which Gamiel Gander's face appeared, and said to him—

"Oh, is that you?"

Now, there was not much in this, but it served to commence with, and Gamiel at once replied that it was him.

"Well," said Amy, "I tell you what is, Gamiel, you are in love with my sister Patience."

"Oh, crikey, ain't I?"

"And you have hitherto found that she has disregarded your protestations?"

"Oh, lor, yes!"

"But I like everybody to have a fair chance, and as father has gone to Little Britain—"

"I know it—I know it!"

"Well, then, I think that you might say it over all you have got to say to Patience, and see if you cannot melt her obdurate heart in your favour; for, to tell the truth, you are very good-looking just now."

"Am I, though?"

"You are, indeed; and I, for one, beg to say that I am very glad to see you; so get over the wall and come into the house at once."

"Oh, lor, yes! Well, I a—am so very much obliged—Dear me, Miss Amy, you is a girl of ten thousand, you is!—Well, I do hope as I shall have you for a wife-in-law—no, dear me, I mean a sister-in-law."

"Come, if you are coming."

"I'm a-coming—I'm a-coming!—Don't hurry a fellow with his best what's-his-names on, and ever so many nails on the top of the palings. Oh! oh! oh! oh!"

"Good gracious, don't make that noise!"

"It's one of 'em."

"One of what?"

"The nails."

"Well, never mind."

"Never mind?—oh, it's all very well to say never mind, but if you felt it you wouldn't say that, I'll be bound—Oh, lor! oh, lor! Well, I'm a-coming! It's torn a hole, though, in the best thingumies, I declare it has, and a pretty figure I shall look."

"Oh, be quick !"

"Yes, it's all very well to say, ' oh, be quick.' You ain't a-top of two dozen of rather jagged nails, Miss Amy."

Finally, though, Gamiel did manage to get into the garden, and then Amy plucked a tulip and gave to him, saying—

"Accept this for my sake."

"Oh, thank you. I—ah—upon my life—but I cannot marry you both, you know, and I have promised myself to Patience."

"Oh, don't mistake me. I have no wish to shake your allegiance to her in the least, for I am engaged, as you know quite well, to Robert Lee, the pedler. It was only out of good feeling that I asked you to take this tulip, and put it into your jacket."

"Oh, well, I'll do that, then."

"Now follow me."

"Yes, that I will. Well, after all, gals is rum creatures."

"What?"

"Gals, I was a-saying, is rum creatures. Now, after all her laughing at me, and her making fun of me, who would have thought that she really had an *infection* for me after all?"

"Ah, who, indeed !"

"Yes, and she always used, a year or two ago, to laugh when the boys called me all sorts of names."

"She did."

"And they used to pelt me, you know, and then she used to laugh, too, and now she loves her Gander."

"Ah, very odd, is it not?"

"It were—it were !"

"Now, quick, in with you !"

"Eh?"

"In at this window."

"This window ?"

"Yes, to be sure."

"Well, but is the door of the blessed house gone to Little Britain too, that we can't get in at it in the ordinary way?"

"No, Gamiel, but father has locked the door and taken the key with him. Now you comprehend?"

"Oh, ah," said Gamiel, placing his finger by the side of his nose, "I see."

"Of course you do."

"Safe bind safe find—eh?"

"To be sure; so in with you."

"After you, miss, if you pleases. There ain't no nails here, but there has been a few. After you, if you please."

Amy sprang into the room through the window in a moment, and then, by the aid of Patience, Gamiel was got into the apartment, although it was really no easy job to get him into the rather narrow casement.

"There now," said Amy; "are you content now?"

"Oh, yes, yes. Oh, Patience, you lily of the valley ! In for a penny, in for a pound. Let me embrace you, and call you my own—own——"

"Hush !" said Amy.

"Hush !" said Patience.

They both threw themselves into rather startling attitudes of profound attention, to the great alarm of Gamiel, who looked from one to the other with his eyes gradually opening wider and wider.

"Wot is it—wot is it?"

"Hush !—hush !"

"I am a hushing. Wot is it about !"

"Our father !"

"Oh, lor !"

"With the pistols——"

"The what !"

"The pistols he went to Little Britain on purpose to buy, and he said that if he ever found anybody of a he kind in the house with us, he would blow his brains out, and fling him into the river by the side of the ferry, with the old grindstone that is now in the garden tied round his neck to keep him down."

"Oh, no !—oh, no ! I'm a he !—I'm a he !"

"No !"

"I am—I am. Grandmother says I am."

"Then you are doomed."

"Damned?"

"No, doomed. How dare you swear here, you wretched, lost, and miserable individual?"

"Oh, save me, save me !"

"Ah, I have it," said Amy.

"No ?"

"Yes, I have; open the flour bin."

"The who?"

"The flour bin. There, get in, Gamiel. It is the last place in which our father will think of looking—get in. Oh, get in, and when he is gone again we will let you out."

"Oh, but——"

"Your life is in danger. The flour won't hurt you. There you are; don't speak, don't breathe."

"I won't."

"Don't sneeze."

"A-chew !—a-chew ! I won't."

Bang went down the lid of the flour bin, and down stairs at once rushed Langdon, with fury in his looks.

"What was that?" he cried; "I heard a noise."

The girls laughed.

"I heard a noise, I say. What was it? I'll sacrifice that little wretch if I find him here. Oh, I didn't go to Little Britain for nothing. No, no: but I'll be revenged —I'll be revenged !"

"Father," said Amy, approaching him, and speaking in a low tone, "will you forgive us if we tell you all?"

"Forgive you? Ah !"

"Yes, father. The fact is—Come, now, don't look so cross with us. The fact is you are misinformed."

"Oh, dear, no. I'd like to know how anybody could misinform me as regards some one getting right over my garden paling."

"Oh, that was correct enough."

"It was, was it?"

"Yes; but you were misinformed regarding the individual, and if you will forgive us, father, we will make you a snarer in the joke, for it is nothing else, and tell you all about it. You will not be angry with us, dear father, when you know all."

CHAPTER XXXII.

POOR GAMIEL IS MADE TO SUFFER FOR OTHER FOLKS' SINS.

SHAKING his head, Langdon said—

"I don't know that," but still evidently softened by this appeal to his better nature; "I don't know that."

"Oh, yes, father, you do."

"Well, well, we will hear all about it first. I won't make any promises on the subject, for fear I should be wrong. Come, come, tell me all about it."

"We will trust to you, father."

"You had better."

"Well, then, you must know," said Amy, "that that stupid Gamiel Gander has always been trying to get into the house when you are not at home ; and to-day, hearing by some means, for he has very long ears, indeed, that you were gone to Little Britain, what must he do but climb up the paling and look over into the tulip bed."

"Ah—the rascal !"

"Yes, father; so just to punish him, and out of sport to play some trick upon him, we let him come into the house."

"You did?"

"We did, father."

"Oh, but that won't do. The boy that told me some one was here, quite clearly and distinctly said it was a page."

"The boy might make a mistake."

"Well, I don't mean to say but that may be just possible, but the only thing that would convince me of it would be the evidence of my own eyes. If Gamiel Gander is the man, where is he?"

"Oh, father—oh !"

"What now? What the deuce are you laughing at? Confound you both! what is there to giggle at in that sort of way, I should like to know?"

"He—he is—he is in——"

"In what? Were?"

"The great flour bin !"

"The devil he is!—Why you don't mean that, do you? Gamiel Gander in the flour bin now?'

"Just so, father. There he is. When he heard that you were coming, he was in such a fright that there was only the chimney and the flour bin in his mind to choose between, and as he preferred flour to soot, why then he is in the latter, father; and now, as you can't suppose that we are either of us in love with Gamiel Gander, you will see that it is only a joke."

"Well," said Langdon, trying to control his laughter, "perhaps it is; but I don't like such jokes, for all that."

"Then we won't do it again."

"Mind you don't. Of course, having such a fool as Gamiel Gander in the house is a very different affair to having a smart young page here, who, no doubt, is up to all sorts and kinds of wickedness in the world. But—I—I—Ha! ha! I'll have some amusement with him myself.'

With this Simon Langdon went at once and sat down on the flour bin, and roared out, in a voice of thunder—

"I tell you what is, girls, I have come home with the determination to take the life of anything in the shape of a man that I find on the premises, and I am going to sit here all the day, ay, and all the night too, till you confess if any one is hidden in the house."

How poor Gamiel shook at this.

And to be sure Cyprian did not feel very comfortable, for the fact was, that the conversation between the father and the daughters had been carried on in so low a tone by the latter that he did not very well know what was going on.

No doubt the girls enjoyed, too, the idea of the page being in a little perplexity.

"Ha! ha!" cried Langdon, in a still more furious voice. "Ha! ha! I seem as if I could wash my hands in somebody's blood to-day!"

"Dear me, father," cried Amy, "what for?"

"For nothing at all."

"Well, that is too bad."

"Too bad do you call it?—Too good, you mean! Oh, my children, do you know I have had a sort of a—a hope."

"Oh, of what?"

"I'll tell you, as we are alone, but you must not let it go any further."

"Oh, no—no."

"Well, I am always getting wet feet down at the ferry, and I have heard say that nothing is so good to make your boots thoroughly waterproof, as to grease them with human fat."

"Oh, how horrid!"

"So I don't mind, now that I am in the bosom of my family, saying that if I find any fat sort of person here in my absence, one of my inducements for killing him will be that."

"Oh, how dreadful!"

"I'm as done as a cooked goose," thought Gamiel Gander.

"What the deuce is the meaning of all this?" thought Cyprian; "I am not very fat, goodness knows!"

"Hem!" said Langdon. "By-the-bye, I have ordered a stone of flour."

"Flour!"

"Yes, flour; what the deuce makes you both turn as white as a sheet for at that—Eh?"

"Oh—a—nothing! I—a—thought—"

"What?"

"That we really had plenty of flour."

"Plenty of flour, stuff! Do you call this plenty of flour, you little jade, you?"

As he spoke, Langdon, who had thought he had carried that part of the joke far enough, suddenly sprang off the flour bin and opened the lid, when, with a howl of fear and agony of spirit, up rose Gamiel Gander, covered with flour from his head to his heels.

"Murder! murder!" he shouted. "No—no!—Oh, don't. I won't be made into grease for anybody's boots! Murder! I am fat, but I can't help it. Murder! help! I won't come here any more! Murder!"

"You rascal!"

"Yes, I know it."

"You villain!"

"I know that, too. Ha! ha! You will catch me in a hurry."

Gamiel sprang out of the flour bin, and seeing the door of the cottage partially open, he bolted out of it, and across the garden, and rolled over the palings with such frightful rapidity, that even Langdon was too much astonished at such unwonted activity on the part of Gamiel to follow him.

As for the two girls, they were almost convulsed with laughter.

Langdon could not help indulging in a laugh himself, but at length he said—

"Well, well, girls, let there be an end of this. I don't like these sort of jokes, though; there has been enough of this to make a cat laugh. I will own I'm glad, though, to find it turn out so harmlessly, and if I meet the boy again who told me it was Martin Lassamour's page that was here, I'll make him remember me for some time to come."

"Do, father, it was so very wrong."

"It was so, the young scoundrel. But now let there, I say, be an end of this."

"Oh, yes—yes."

"Very well. I am now going to the ferry, and shall be back by dinner time. Why, what's this? A tulip lying on the floor."

"Gamiel Gander dropped it."

"Ah, the rascal, not content with knocking over many of my choice tulips, he was actually trying to carry some away with him."

"Oh, father, you surely would not have me marry such a goose as he?" said little Patience, with a very afflicted air.

"Pho—pho! You don't know what you are talking about, girl. He will have money. His old grandfather is rich."

"Yes; but——"

"Listen girl. I know you are looking after that page. Let him show me a couple of hundred gold pieces and he may come and get into the flour bin and be quite welcome. Ha—ha!"

Simon Langdon thought this rather brilliant, so out he went on very good terms with himself indeed.

The moment the girls made sure that his back was turned they ran to the old cupboard and opened it, and called to Cyprian—

"Come out—come out; it's all right."

"Oh, is it though? Well, I'm glad to hear that; but what a row there has been to be sure, and the floor is all over flour."

"Yes, wasn't it droll?"

"What I heard of it was; but dear—dear Patience, did I really hear your father say that there was no hope for me unless I showed him two hundred gold pieces?"

"He did."

"Then I'll—I'll——"

"Oh, what?"

"Go on the highway."

"You go on the highway? You are too little."

"No, Patience, I am not. It is the spirit that makes the man; but I tell you what I will do if you don't approve of that plan, I'll run away with you at once, and we will live in some cottage on water-cresses and penny loaves."

Patience looked pensive.

"What do you think of that scheme?"

"I don't know, Cyprian, but with you——"

"Ah, yes."

"Rubbish!" cried Amy; "you would soon get tired of that sort of fare both of you, so don't talk nonsense. The only plan is to wait till better times come. There will be some sort of change soon, I daresay, and in the meantime you be off, Mr. Cyprian, for if father were but really to find you here after what has happened he would never forgive either of us."

"He would not, indeed," said Patience, "so do go."

"Then I will tear myself away."

"Yes, do. Oh—oh—oh!"

"Good gracious, what is it?"

"Father's in the garden."

"The devil! Where shall I get?"

"In the flour-bin."

"No."

"Yes, it's the best place; he won't think of looking there again. In with you—in with you at once."

Just as Langdon with rather a scowl upon his brow appeared on the threshold of his door again, Cyprian was crammed into the flour-bin, and the lid closed down upon him.

Cyprian felt anything but happy.

For the space of about half a minute or thereabouts the ferryman glared all round him, and then bending a searching glance upon the two girls, he said—

"I don't feel quite sure, but——"

"Oh, but what, father?"

"If I did feel quite sure that I had been tricked after all, I'd make an example of you both, that I would."

"Tricked, father?"

"Yes, tricked, father. I have met the boy again who told me about the page, and after I had given him a couple of good boxes on the ears for telling lies, he assured me that whoever it was that did climb into the garden had a cap and a feather, and a slashed velvet jerkin, and a dagger hanging by a guilt chain."

"Oh, is it possible?"

"Yes, it is possible, and I'll have a good look about me, too, to see if it is probable as well as possible; I suspect I am done, and if I am, woe be to you all."

CHAPTER XXXIII.

CYPRIAN DELIVERS THE LETTER TO SIR WARRENNE DE VOLENCE.

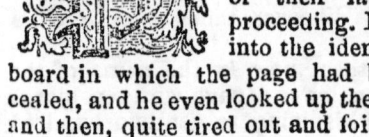PATIENCE and Amy, to be sure, were rather in a fright while this new search, on the part of their father, was proceeding. He looked into the identical cupboard in which the page had been concealed, and he even looked up the chimney, and then, quite tired out and foiled, he sat down upon the flour-bin.

But he never thought of looking there again.

"I don't know what to think," he said, and then starting up in a rage he put on his hat and fiercely left the house.

"Ha—ha!" said Cyprian, looking out of the flour-bin.

"Oh, get out and be off, do."

"Yes, but how long do you think it will take you both to brush me?"

"To what?"

"To brush me, and get all the flour out of my clothes."

"Oh," said Patience, "this is better than a brush," and she with a little cane began to strike away at the page, so that the flour rose in clouds all about him.

"Murder ! don't do that ; that is a little too vigorous and effective, my dear Patience ; but just let me get rid of as much of the flour as I can, and then I really will be off after I have given you both fifty kisses each."

"Both !" cried Patience. "Did you say both ?"

"Yes. You don't want the whole hundred to yourself, do you ? Oh, what greediness is that to be sure !"

Patience held up the little cane threateningly to him, and Cyprian took good care to keep out of her reach. The fact was, he had two reasons now for wishing to go. The fact was he was rather afraid of the return of the ferryman, and that the result of the whole affair would be his instant discovery; and the second was that he began to be apprehensive that his long delay in the delivering of the letter to Sir Warrenne de Volence would come out to his master in some way.

"I will be off at once, dear girls," he said. "May Cupid bless you both, and may you live to be a hundred years old, each of you, and continue all the time as lovely as you are now."

"Oh, thank you," said Amy. "After that, now, the sooner you go the better, I can tell you."

"And so can I," said Patience, "and you are not wanted here any more."

"Till the next time," said the page.

He left the house now, but Patience of course, with a view of seeing that he fairly did go away, saw him to the palings, and there was then a great many sounds so amazingly like kissing, that if it was not such, it certainly was the very best imitation that could possibly be conceived.

Without any further accident, then, Cyprian got away, and after feeling if he had the letter all safe, and being satisfied, without taking it out of his vest, that there it was, he set off for Westminster, in order to make some inquiries about De Volence.

The shortest way of the page was by Langdon's ferry, and with all the unblushing assurance in the world he went to it.

The moment he got there he cried out,

"D—n it, Master Langdon, I have met with such an adventure."

"Oh, have you ?"

"Yes. I was coming quickly round a corner, when who should I meet but that fool Gamiel Gander, and he could not stop himself, and I could not stop myself, so right into my arms he flew, and look at me."

"Humph !"

"Look at me, I say."

"I see you."

"All over flour."

"Yes, I see. Oh, plague take him. He has been in my flour bin."

"In what ?"

"My flour bin. I thought that somebody else might be in the house, but it turned out to be him."

"Did it, indeed, father-in-law ?"

"Father in what ?"

"In-law."

"Then don't call me father-in-law. What the deuce do you mean by that, I should like to know ? Father-in-law indeed !"

"Why, you are the father of Patience."

"D——n it, I would need to be the essence of patience to put up with all the worry and the trouble I have about those girls."

"Now I tell you what it is, Langdon, that was a very clever thing you have just said; so now as you have got ready your boat, pull me—for heaven's sake be quick—over the Thames, for I have a most important letter to deliver from my master to De Volence."

"What, Sir Warrenne ?"

"The same."

"Mayhap, then, I can tell you where to find him."

"You will very much oblige me, I can assure you, if you can."

"Then there has been a couple of fellows—ill-looking knaves enough—across the ferry, and I overheard them whispering the one to the other that they had to meet Sir Warrenne de Volence at the Abbey."

"Ah ?"

"Yes. It's not above an hour ago that they met, and if you want him, it's like enough that there you will find him, Master Page."

"Many thanks."

"But I tell you what, now. Don't let me catch you about my house, for I won't have it. If you can come to me and hold out your hand with——"

"Oh, I know, I know—two hundred gold pieces."

"Yes."

"You said that before, you know, so I know all about that ; but my very good father-in-law, you don't want me to go and rob our Abbey, do you ?"

"No. Whoever thought of such a thing ?"

"Well then, how in the name of the what's-his-name is a page with ten marks a year and his living, to get two hundred gold pieces ?

"Ha ! ha !"

"Ha ! ha ! what do you mean by that ?"

"Only that I don't expect you to get

CYPRIAN DELIVERS THE LETTER TO DE VOLENCE.

hem, that's all, and so you only waste your time by looking after my girls, I can tell you, and you put yourself in danger too. So be warned in time, good Master Cyprian, and don't let me see your baby face over my palings again. Ha! ha!"

Cyprian, as the rest of the passengers in the ferry-boat, laughed at this, would say no more, but putting on a look of great disgust, and as much dignity as he possibly could, he did not speak again, but when the boat reached the landing he sprung on the shore and set off at full speed.

The distance to Westminster Abbey was but short, and Cyprian soon found himself at the entrance to it, amid the swarm of idlers that used to make the part now called Poets' Corner, a kind of waiting place at that period. He walked into the Abbey and began to look about him for Sir Warrenne de Volence, but for some time he could not see him. At length he saw three figures in the recesses of one of the cloisters, and one of them looked so like De Volence that the page looked very closely at him.

It was, indeed, Sir Warrenne, who, seeing Cyprian advancing leisurely towards him, dashed forward in a passion, saying—

"You scoundrel! how dare you come prying into the affairs of a gentleman? Were it not that we are beneath the roof we are, I would wring your neck for you!"

"Thank you, sir," said Cyprian, with mock civility and respect; "but I did not look at your worship without a motive."

"A motive, knave! what motive?"

"I have a letter for you, if you be Sir Warrenne de Volence."

"Yes, my name is De Volence. From whom is the letter?"

"My master."

"And your master?"

"Is Martin Lassamour."

De Volence bit his lips.

"So, so," he said, "you are his page, are you? Give me the letter, boy, and wait until I have read it. It may be that I have some message to send to your master in reply to it."

De Volence tore open the letter, and his sallow complexion got yellower and yellower as he read it. Turning with a furious gesture to the page, he said—

"Caitiff! tell your master that I spit at him and defy him!"

"Very good, sir."

"Tell him my foot shall spurn him when I see him! Tell him—ha! ha!—that I wish him joy of his six-times-a-widow! Ha! ha!—tell him——"

"My son," said a monk, who was passing, and who paused to hear the loud tone of the enraged De Volence; "my son, this is no place to brawl in."

"Psha!—I—I— Well, well I have done. Off with you, boy! the sight of you is disagreeable to me, since you are the servant of one whom I hate and despise. Tell him that, too—tell him that, too!"

"Very good, sir," said Cyprian, with the most provoking coolness in the world, as he hurried away from the spot.

De Volence looked after him almost foaming with rage, and then he turned on his heel and sought the other two men with whom he had been conversing. The two men deserve some little description.

It would certainly have been among the impossibilities of London to have found two such thorough-looking blackguards as these two fellows. Not much of their attire could be seen, for they were wrapped up in very faded brown cloaks, and they hid as much of their faces as they could by their slouched hats, which, in defiance of the cathedral, they had put on; but still there was no mistaking the fact that they were men who were of the very worst grade, in point of morals.

We shall soon see what sort of companionship De Volence and those two rascals had together.

The taller of the two men was named Glass, and the shorter went by the nickname of Tabby, by which he was always addressed.

When De Volence went back to them, they winked at each other in glee to see how much he was disturbed in his mind, and Glass said to him in affected tones of condolence and commiseration—

"Good my lord, what is amiss now with things in general? Did that little whipper-snapper of a page offend you, my good lord?"

"Yes, to the soul."

"Shall we after him and trounce him for it?"

"No—no. It don't matter—it don't matter."

"As you please, noble sir; but we feel for your honour as we do for our own, and our own is quite unimpeachable—hem!"

"Oh, quite," said Tabby; "quite."

"Well, Tabby, I said as it was."

"I know you did, and didn't I back you out in it? Don't I always back you out in all your lies?"

"Hold your row, will you?"

"Hold your own."

"Gentlemen," said De Volence, "it strikes me, that if you are going to amuse yourselves by quarrelling with each other, that I may as well conclude our interview, and find some others to do the work I thought of paying you both so well to perform."

This speech brought the two rascals to reason, and Glass at once, with a scrape of his foot, and a low bow, said—

"Noble sir, we won't say another word in the quarrelling way; but my mate, Tabby, is so very provoking."

"Well, so are you," said Tabby; "but that don't matter a bit, noble sir. We will attend to your instructions, and put off any little matter as between ourselves till a more fitting time and place."

"Do so; and now walk with me down here further into the dim obscure of the cloisters, for I have something for your private ear."

CHAPTER XXXIV.

DE VOLENCE HIRES THE TWO ASSASSINS TO RID HIM OF HIS ENEMIES.

LASS and Tabby, two rascals as they were, knew perfectly well that it was some piece of quiet villany that De Volence wished to consult them about, and so they followed him cheerfully enough.

Well they knew that they would be capitally paid for what they were about, and so they congratulated themselves upon the prospect of acquiring cash sufficient to live for a considerable time in the wild riot and disorder which they alone delighted in.

The days of which we write were Roman Catholic ones, and the old Abbey of Westminster resounded with the chant of the Latin prayer from the lips of the priests. In common, too, with all cathedrals and churches, the abbey was a sanctuary.

That is to say, it was a refuge from the consequences of crime.

A man might commit a murder about the purlieus of the church, and if he could but reach the abbey he was safe.

The Holy Church threw her protecting shield over the blackest of evils.

The very place that a man stained with crime, and with no thought of repentance for that crime, from which he should have flown, was the very place to which he flew: namely, the church.

Hence was it that about the cloisters of Westminster Abbey might always be seen the ferocious countenances of branded criminals; and about the dim old chapels of the place where saints reposed, or were supposed to repose, you might encounter the lurking step of the assassin.

The reason why those two men, Glass and Tabby, as they called themselves, were in the abbey at the time we found them there is, that an atrocious murder had been committed at the back of Whitehall, and, somehow, public opinion said it was they who did it.

Hence, then, was it that if any one required an unscrupulous ruffian to do any deed of blood, he was pretty sure to be found in one of the sanctuaries.

With this brief explanation, we will follow De Volence and the honourable Masters Glass and Tabby.

At all events, they were to the full as honourable as their rascally employer.

De Volence may be considered now to have quite made up his mind to the death of Martin Lassamour as the only way by which he could hope to get rid of a bold and dangerous foe.

Little cared he how that was done, so that it was done, and that too most effectually and surely.

Glass and Tabby had now but one source of disquietude, and that was regarding what they should charge De Volence for what he expected of them in the shape of good service in the assassinating line.

It was quite easy for them to guess the sort of work that was expected of them.

That they were generally anything but wrong in, for they judged of it by the customer. What could such a man, then, as De Volence want with two cutthroats but their aid to commit a murder?

The employer, then, of these two vagabonds walked on till he got to a very retired corner of the old cloisters, and then he paused.

Glass and Tabby were by his side in a few seconds, and with every appearance of intense interest they awaited his communication.

"Be silent and discreet," said De Volence.

"Ay, ay, my good master, we will be that," said Tabby. "None more so."

"To be sure," said Glass, "for though I say it perhaps that shouldn't, considering I may be accused of being a little partial to him, there ain't such a rogue unhung in the good City of Westminster as my friend Tabby."

"Oh, you flatterer!" said Tabby.

"No, no."

"Well, gentlemen," said De Volence, when you have done with your little playful compliments to each other, you will perhaps have the goodness to attend to me."

"With pleasure, noble sir."

"Yes, with pleasure."

"'Tis well. You know one Martin Lassamour by sight?"

"We do!"

"That is well!"

"Yes, and what is more, we know his fair lady by sight, too," said Glass. "By the Lord, what an eye she has."

"I believe you," said Tabby.

"Peace," said De Volence; "I want not to hear of her—it is of Lassamour himself I would speak."

"Yes, noble sir."

"That boy whom you saw even now, and who, as you noticed, brought a message that chafed my soul, was his page. Yes, he came from him."

"Did he so, noble sir?" said Glass, with a wink at Tabby; "what a shame!"

"Oh, lor, yes," said Tabby.

Now the two rascals knew perfectly well that the page belonged to Lassamour, or, to speak more correctly, we might say to his wife, for they were familiar with the colour of the livery of the fair lady.

"'Tis well, indeed, that I did not plunge my rapier into his heart," muttered De Volence.

"It is so, noble sir," said Tabby.

"Ah," said Glass, "and no doubt his nobleness would have done so, but for the place he is in, and his respect for the church."

"True—true."

"I guess that much, noble sir."

"Well, then, my good friends, as I have let the page go in peace, I feel all the less inclined to let the master do so!—You comprehend me?"

"To be sure."

"I would have revenge."

"To be sure."

"A deep—a bloody revenge."

"To be sure."

"And you will aid me in the procuring of it? You will aid me, I know."

"We will."

"If I make it worth your while to do so—eh?"

"Exactly."

"You must live as well as other folks."

"In course."

"Then it is agreed, with the exception of the price, and I shall have my revenge."

"Yes, good sir," said Glass, "it is agreed, and your revenge you shall have. Lord bless me, and the saints be good to us all, if that same capital old poetical passion, revenge, is not the best I know of."

"It is," said Tabby.

"In fact," added Glass, assuming quite a look of philosophy, "I don't know what some gentlemen of our little profession in London would do without it. But as you say, noble sir, the price is the thing to settle."

"To be sure," said Tabby.

"Well, the job will be easy," whispered De Volence, as at the same time he glanced round him, to make sure that there were no listeners.

"Hem! We don't know that," said Glass.

"In course not," said Tabby.

"But I tell you it will. I know it, and I ought to know it, for I know the man well. I have studied him, and my curses be upon him."

"But how do you make out that the job will be easy, noble sir? We know him a little."

"Ah! You do?"

"We do. And what we do know of him leads us in rather a different opinion. He is young, active, and strong, and such a master of his weapon as few can boast to be in London."

"And yet he is," said De Volence, "so weak, so—so confiding, so callous, and so unsuspicious, that a child might plant a dagger in his heart."

"Humph!"

"Well, what say you?"

"There is something in that, and so, to cut the question short, we will do the little job for two hundred crowns, and not a farthing less."

"Two hundred?"

"Ay, noble sir, and cheap, too. One hundred down, according to the usual way of doing such matters of business, and the other hundred when the deed is done."

"Be it so."

"Agreed, then?"

"You promise me it shall be done?"

"Honour!"

"Oh, honour!"

Both Glass and Tabby placed their hands on the region where, if they had hearts at all, they might be supposed to be, and bowed.

"Then here is the money in gold. It is in less compass, but it will be as well for you."

"Better, noble sir."

"Be it so, then; and mind, I can give you no aid. You must find out for yourselves a fitting time, and a fitting place, but I pray you to be quick about it; and the sooner you get the deed done, the sooner will you finger the other hundred crowns."

"All right, noble sir. It will be done, you may rest assured."

"I will rest assured, and when that is done, I have another job for you."

CHAPTER XXXV.

MARTIN LASSAMOUR MAKES AN AWKWARD DISCOVERY.

O doubt the other job that De Volence had for the pair of cut-throats consisted in the assassination of young Lamont.

This was a savoury mode of getting rid of his foes, but it was a costly one.

Indeed, if De Volence had not very recently effected a mortgage of certain estates to the Jews for a sum of ready money, he could not by any means have afforded so expensive a luxury as the employment of a couple of bravoes.

Even to rid himself of such an enemy as Martin Lassamour, it would have been very much beyond his means indeed.

But as it was, De Volence had some ready money, so, like everybody so situated, he began to spend it in the way that would afford to him the greatest amount of gratification.

But we will now leave De Volence and the two villains he had employed to commit murder, in order to follow Martin Lassamour's proceedings in an adventure that promised to have for both him and Margaret, his fair lady, very important results.

Passing over, then, some incidents of a trivial nature, which do not call for our special attention, we will at once conduct the reader to that same apartment in Pleasaunce House, where Martin had slept on the sofa on the night when he had come home so late.

It was the state bed-chamber of the house.

It was, too, in that same room that Lassamour had had the strange and fearful dream, which appeared to shadow forth the fate of the six husbands that the Lady Margaret had had before she placed her hand in his, and acknowledged him as the seventh.

But in those days a state bed-chamber was a something more in reality than a mere sleeping room.

The house in which Lassamour and his fair lady resided had been built in that age, when it was customary to receive visits, both of business and of ceremony, in the chambers devoted to repose.

This was a custom which, along with many more bad, lazy, and not altogether decent ones, had been imported from France.

It is one that soon went out of use, as it could not for very long hold its way in a country where there is so much manly good sense as in England.

But the custom, while it did last, had had the effect of causing very great outlay upon the state bed-chambers of the houses of the nobility of the land, and other wealthy people.

Hence, then, long after it had ceased to be the fashion for ladies and gentlemen to hold a sort of levee before they were up, the state chamber was in use in the day time as a reception-room.

When, too, it was not intended to make use of it for repose, it was common enough to sit in it till the time for retiring came, which was then very much earlier than modern notions make it.

Now it had happened that Lamont had dined with Martin Lassamour, and that Lady Margaret had retired very early in the evening, complaining of fatigue and indisposition.

Lamont, then, and Martin Lassamour sat alone drinking their rich wine in the state bed-chamber.

They had been talking about very many subjects, and among the rest about De Volence, and the bold and bad career that he was known to have carried on for some years; and the old rich wine sparkled in their cups, and they warmed towards each other in friendly feeling.

Now there was one subject among all the others which they spoke upon which both thought much about, but which by common consent they avoided.

The one avoided it because it was anything but an agreeable one.

That was Martin Lassamour.

The other avoided it out of delicate feeling to his friend and host.

That was young Lamont.

But what was this subject of such special careful avoidance?

It was the marriage of Martin Lassamour to the Lady Margaret, the widow of six husbands.

Now Martin, under ordinary circumstances, would not have hesitated to have said to himself—

"Nothing in the world shall ever tempt me to make mortal man a depository of my thoughts and feelings regarding Margaret, and my union with her."

But man proposes and Heaven disposes, and so Martin, after draining a cup of old canary, looked hard at the ingenuous countenance of Lamont, and bethought him that it would be a great relief to him to have some one to whom he could talk freely of all his cares, and all his many anxieties.

Lamont, too, was rather silent, for by the glance he had taken at the countenance of his friend, he had seen that his mind was occupied.

At length, with a sudden start, Lassamour cried out to the young man—

"You don't drink, Lamont."

"Oh, yes—yes."

"Nay, you are shy of the old wine."

"Not I, I assure you."

"By our lady, but I think you are; and yet I will be bound that there is not a headache in a barrel of it."

"Think you not?"

"There ought not to be."

Lamont smiled, as he said—

"Perhaps that depends more upon the strength of the head, than upon either the goodness or the age of the wine, my dear friend."

"It may a little."

"A great deal, I am sure. Now, my brain is as yet not inured to the bottle, and I am afraid that if I ventured upon anything like what you perchance could take with impunity, I should be but poor company on the morrow."

"Well, I will not press you to more than one more tankard."

"Here goes, then, for it. In truth, Lassamour, it is rare old wine."

"It is—it is."

"And it merits all the good things you can say of it. I'll warrant, now, it has been in the cellars of Pleasaunce House for many a long year."

"Yes—yes."

"How long?"

"Faith, I can't tell you. I am but young here myself; and in good truth there is much in the old mansion that I know nought of."

"Indeed?"

"Yes, Lamont. I don't suppose that for a master of such a house as this, there is one living who knows less of it than I."

"I am surprised."

"Are you, though?"

"In truth I am. It is such a rare old place, with such a world of nooks and corners and crevices, of all sorts and descriptions, that were I the happy possessor of it, I should never rest till I had been everywhere in it, and had it all as plainly writ down in my brain as if it were on a map."

"Ah !"

"You sigh?"

"I do sigh."

"Surely you are happy?"

"Happy?"

Lamont gave quiet a start of surprise at the tone in which his friend echoed that word. It was quiet clear that if ever the word happy was misapplied in this world, it was in the case of Martin Lassamour.

Young Lamont felt that this was the case, and he was sorry that he had touched upon so tender a theme.

The silence that ensued for a few moments was very painful to both of them.

At length Martin Lassamour hastily poured out for himself a tumbler of wine, and then pushing the flask to Lamont, he said—

"My friend, I cannot keep longer pent up in may heart what is panting for utterance there. You, I believe, love me in all sincerity of heart and purpose, and so I will say to you what I would say to no other man in life. What do you think of the Lady Margaret, my dear friend?"

CHAPTER XXXVI.

LAMONT GIVES LASSAMOUR GOOD ADVICE.

OF all the embarrassing questions which it was in the power of one man to put to another, certainly this one wh'ch Lassamour had just propounded to Lamont was about the most so.

No wonder that the young man stared

at his host in mute surprise and embarrassment.

"Come, my friend," added Lassamour, "the ice is broken, now, and I feel all the better for it."

"My dear friend, I—I——"

"Nay, why do you hesitate?"

"I know not what to say,"

"Lamont, I can feel for the awkward situation in which you find yourself at the present time ; but when I tell you that it is absolutely necessary that I should submit to another mind what is now weighing upon mine own, I am certain that you will not refuse me your friendly sympathy."

"By no means will I refuse it."

"The fact is," added Lassamour, with a faint and feeble attempt to smile, "when we feel that we owe a man one great obligation, we are very apt to think that we may as well owe him another or two."

"Nay, do not speak of that."

"But it is true."

"My best services in all sort of ways, either with head or hand, are at your disposal, Lassamour."

"I am sure of it."

"You may, indeed, be so."

"Well, then, what do you think of my wife?"

"What do I think of the Lady Margaret?"

"Ay, even so."

"That she is a right loyal and noble lady, abounding in each grace of mind and person."

"Ay, it seems so."

"Seems, only?"

"Yes, Lamont, seems. You know that she is——"

"What?"

"The wife of seven husbands."

"Yes. That is known to all the world."

"It is ; but did you never ask yourself this question—'What became of the other six?'"

Lamont was silent.

"Your silence is an answer in the affirmative."

"I may not deny it. You will not be offended with me for so admitting it?"

"Offended? Oh, no. It is who am forcing this conversation upon you, Lamont ; and, therefore, nothing can offend me in it, but that which I know I would not look for from you."

"And what is that?"

"Insincerity."

"You are right, Lassamour—you are right. As I am a living man, I will reply to you as I think."

"Then tell me, what do you think of the strange circumstance that one woman should have six husbands in succession?"

"I think that—that——"

"Well?"

"It is so strange as to be within the bounds of possibility that all has been fair and well ; but I think that that is all; and now much do I grieve that I have had this to say to you, Martin Lassamour."

Lassamour sighed deeply.

"Do not grieve at it," he said, in a low, husky voice. "I have said it to myself a thousand times."

"It would force itself upon you?"

"It would, and it has."

"But yet you should bethink you that you are like a man who has some sore point, and who is not content, for fear that there should be some place in it that his most curious gaze cannot detect."

"It may be so."

"It is so, my friend."

"Oh, if I could but find ease of mind !"

"You will find it if you seek. Let me beg of you to banish all this suspense from your mind. It will be time enough, if ever that time should come, and Heaven forfend you from it, to be unhappy when you have positive cause."

"You do not know all."

"Do I not?"

"No. Listen to me, Lamont, and I will tell you just what has happened to me since I have been the husband of this seeming fair dame."

"I will listen; and yet——"

"Yet you will say that you would as soon not be the depositary of such secrets."

"No—no, I did not mean that. What I meant was, that I feared your imagination did much to unnerve you."

"Well—well, you shall judge of that too."

Martin Lassamour now gave to Lamont a brief outline of all that had taken place with relation to his going to London on the night when he had got into the quarrel with De Volence, together with the very strange dream that he had had afterwards in that very room.

Lamont listened with attention.

There was much in the strange tale to make it attractive to a young and eager fancy, and at its conclusion the young man could not help casting a strangely curious glance around the chamber that had been the scene of such strange and unearthly presences.

"Hem !" he said; "then you saw them?"

"I did."

"In this very chamber?"

"Even so."

"It is strange indeed. I have heard and read of many a strange, eventful story, but never one like this."

"You may be well surprised, Lamont—you may well shudder even at the recital; but what must your feelings be in comparison to mine, who actually saw the visions?"

"What, indeed."

"You feel that?"

"I do—I do; and yet——"

"What would you say?"

"You slept. It was but a dream after all, Lassamour, and the fancy does play such tricks with the judgment, that one may well cast off along with its trammels when we awaken all its fears."

"Listen. I will surprise you further."

"Can you?"

"Ay, you may well doubt that, but listen; I can in a strange fashion confirm the dream."

"Confirm the dream? I do not take your meaning well and fairly, Lassamour."

"I will explain to you. Before I wedded this Lady Margaret, I knew but the name of one of her husbands. That was the sixth, namely, Sir Thomas Shard. The names and the said positions of the others I knew not. I might have known them easily enough, but I purposely shunned making the inquiry."

"It was as well to do so."

"Yes. But since this dream, if it was so, in which they all appeared to me, I wrote down their names as they had told them to me in the vision, and then I made the inquiry."

"Ah!"

"The names were all correct!"

Lamont looked very grave.

"What say you to that?"

"I is more than strange, Lassamour, I must needs admit to you."

"It is so. And now, my friend, what am I to think? What am I to do in this case? I am very unhappy, Lamont, I feel that notwithstanding all its brilliant advantages, this marriage has been an ill one for me. My youth and manhood are blighted by it, and I may some day, when I least expect it, make way for an eighth husband."

"Ah!"

"What is that?"

They both sprang to their feet.

A deep hollow groan had sounded in the room, and by them both hearing it at the same moment the idea that it could be a delusion of the senses was quite out of the question.

Lassamour half drew his sword.

"You heard it, Lamont?"

"I did."

"A groan?"

"Even so."

They looked at each other in dismay. All was still in the chamber, now. The silence indeed was so intense, that it had something awful and painful about it. Lamont was very pale.

"What may this portend?" he gasped.

"I know not."

"It is truly fearful. Let us have more light, Lassamour. There is much of this large room in deep gloom. Let us, if you please, have more light."

CHAPTER XXXVII.

ONE OF THE MYSTERIES OF THE STATE CHAMBER IS DISCOVERED.

YOUNG LAMONT felt so oppressed, that he went to the window, and flung one of the casements open.

A rush of cool air into the room was very welcome indeed to them both.

Martin Lassamour drew a long breath.

"Lamont?"

"Yes, my friend."

"What am I to think? What am I to do? Am I indeed, and in truth, surrounded by the agents of an invisible world? Am I the sport of the spectres of those six men who have before me held the position I now occupy? Oh, tell me?"

"Cheer yourself."

"That is not possible."

"Yes, my dear friend Lassamour, all things are possible to a courageous spirit. I implore you not to allow your better reason to be led away by what you see, and by what you suppose you hear in this

MARTIN LASSAMOUR'S SEARCH.

place. Your fancy is in such a disordered state that you see nothing as it really is."

"Think you so?"

"Yes; but——"

"Hush! some one comes."

Cyprian made his appearance in the apartment, and, with tones of respect, inquired if anything were wanting.

"I did not call," said Lassamour, coldly.

"Did you not, sir?"

"Certainly not."

"It is very odd."

"What is odd?"

"I was passing the door even now, and a voice so like to yours that I did not for a moment doubt it, called out to me 'Cyprian—Cyprian!'"

Lamont and Lassamour exchanged glances.

"Are you jesting, sir?" said Lassamour.

"On my soul, no, sir."

"I did not call you."

"Then, sir, it is the more strange; and

I fear that—that, after all, I shall not be able to——"

"To what? Why do you look around you in this strange way? What ails you, boy?"

"Oh, sir, you are my lord and master, and I have seen enough of you to know that you are a noble and an honourable gentleman. I have been for some time, too, in the service of your noble lady, but yet I fear that I must leave you, if I go to a much meaner service, or to the wars!"

"Go to the wars?"

"Yes, noble sir. I am not very big, but still, it is likely enough that I may do some good."

"But why go at all, Cyprian?"

"I—I—don't—know."

"You do know."

"Oh, sir, do not ask me!"

"Cyprian," said Lassamour, in a kind voice, after a pause, "attend to me. I think you are a good and a kind lad, for I have studied all sorts and conditions of people, and there is a something in your face that I rather like, and it tells the story of the heart generally, too, which is not a very bad sign either."

Cyprian blushed like a girl.

"Ah, I liked you, then, boy," added Lassamour. "Did you think me blind when I saw you at the Lambeth Ferry-house? No—no."

"Oh, sir!"

"Tush, boy! Never be ashamed of falling in love with a rosy cheek, a pair of bright eyes and pouting lips. It is an old fashion, Cyprian."

"Oh, my good master, I do love her."

"I know it; but——"

"But what, noble sir?"

"I was going to say something, Cyprian, that now I will leave unsaid, and substitute a question."

"I will answer you anything, sir."

"Do you like me and my service sufficiently to be made a confidant of?"

"A—confidant?"

"Yes, you know what that means. Do you feel that if I took you into my confidence you could keep that confidence I ask, and serve me to the best of your ability, Cyprian?"

"Yes, sir—if——"

"If what?"

"If, in serving you, I do no wrong or injustice to my Mistress Margaret, sir; for she has been liberal and kind to me."

"Cyprian, I like your answer."

"It came from my heart, sir."

"I am sure it did. But, Cyprian, if you should find out one of two things by being a confidential friend to me, that is, the entire innocence and nobleness of your mistress, or her guilt, would that suit you?"

"Yes, sir. Being innocent, I should feel that I ought to love and serve her well; but if there be guilt at her door, why, then, I am serving a very devil!"

"You are right;—and you consent?"

"I do, sir."

Lassamour rose, and taking his cross-hilted sword, he held it up before the face of Cyprian, saying—

"Swear, by all your hopes of bliss in the world to come, and peace and calm happiness in this world, that you will not betray the confidence I now place in you."

"I swear."

"In the name of Heaven."

"In the name of Heaven; and may I never know what it is to call my dear little Patience mine, if I betray you, sir, by word, or by look, or by act."

"That is a fast oath," said Lamont.

"It is, indeed," said Lassamour. "And now, Cyprian, that you have sworn it, I swear to you in my turn, that I will do all in my power to make Patience yours, and I will bestow upon you on your wedding-day one hundred pounds in gold."

"Oh, gracious! Then she is mine!"

"Indeed?"

"Yes; that old villain, Langdon, her father, only sets her down at forty pounds."

"Then you have won her, indeed. But now, Cyprian, I will have no disguise, with you, and you must have none with me. I —I—want to—to ask you——"

"Oh, I know, sir."

"You do?"

"Oh, yes. Sir Thomas Shard wanted to ask me the same thing, but I did not like him. He was a sot, and he did not go the way to work to win the heart of any one to love him. You want to ask, sir, I presume, if I can tell you anything more than all the world knows of the fate of the other six?"

Lassamour nodded.

"Then, sir, I can't; but, sir, on the night that your worship came home after you had been to London, when you were rather late——"

"The first time?"

"Yes, sir. I was crossing the old picture gallery where the frames all hang with their faces to the wall——"

"Stop!"

"Yes, sir."

"Cyprian, although I am the master of this house, I have never seen that gallery."

"Indeed, sir!"

"No, nor any pictures with their faces to the wall. What pictures are they?"

"Oh, sir, they are the portraits of the other six."

"What?"

"Of the other six husbands, sir; and yours is in progress."

"Mine?"

"Yes, sir."

"Now, Cyprian, you are romancing, for I have never so much as been asked to sit to any portrait painter, or sat to one in all my life."

"It's all as one for that, sir. My lady has it nearly done. She paints as well as any of them, I can tell you, sir; and she has such a way, that she does bit by bit to the portrait till she gets it to her liking; and she is doing a little to yours every day; and when it is finished, it will be hung up along with the others."

"You surprise me."

"Yes, sir, no doubt of that; and when you are gone, it will have its face turned to the wall."

"When I am what?"

"Gone, you know, sir—in the family vault, you know—dead."

"The devil!"

"Oh, yes, sir, it will. I saw her turn Sir Thomas Shard's to the wall, and I heard her say, 'That is over at last!'"

CHAPTER XXXVIII.

THE MYSTERIES OF PLEASAUNCE HOUSE DEEPEN IN INTENSITY.

CYPRIAN told this in such a way that there was a *naïve* simplicity about it; and it carried with it the impress of truth.

No wonder that Lamont and Lassamour looked at each other in amazement.

"But, my good boy," said Lassamour, "you speak of my going, as you call it, as of a thing all but settled."

"Yes, sir."

"Yes? But I don't mean to go."

"Well, sir, I don't suppose that any of the others meant to go if they could have helped it; but still, you know, sir, they went for all that."

"They did."

"But you were about," said Lamont, "to tell us something of this picture gallery, or something that happened to you there, were you not, Cyprian?"

"Yes, sir."

"Then let us hear it."

"Well, then," said Cyprian, "I may say that that was just what put it into my head that I should have to leave the place, and it was this. I was passing along in the kind of half-dark, caused by the moonlight coming through a painted window, when I saw advancing towards me, a strange mass of something."

"What?—what?"

"It looked like a moving cloud; but as it came nearer, I saw faces and forms, and hand-in-hand there come no less than six people."

"Six?"

"Yes, sir."

"The husbands, by Heaven!"

"They were so. I was half-dead with fright, and I propped myself, so to speak, up against the wall to let them pass, and they all six floated past, hand-in-hand, until they were lost in the shadow and the gloom at the farther end of the gallery."

"This is strange indeed."

"But," said Lamont, "how do you know this?"

"Why, sir, I had often peeped at the portraits turned with their faces to the wall. I dare say if they had not been so turned, I should not have cared to take a glance at any of them; but being so partially hidden, they attracted my curiosity."

"Yes—yes?"

"And so I often looked at them, until I knew each face quite well."

"This is passing strange."

"And you are sure of this, Cyprian?" said Lassamour. "You are not deceiving me?"

"No, sir."

"You had not taken a cup of wine too much for your young brain, had you, boy?"

"Oh, no, sir—no. They were all in the house that night, I will swear to it, for good or for ill."

"Yes," gasped Lassamour. "I saw them."

"You, sir?"

"I did, boy."

"Then, sir, I don't wonder at your being rather unhappy when you come to consider that there is no knowing how soon you may be hand-in-hand with the others. Oh, sir, I sometimes think that my lady has the art of killing by looking at one ; and when she bends her glance at me of late, it has seemed to say—'Cyprian, you are living too long !' "

"Fear nothing, boy."

"But I can't help it."

"Nay, all will yet be well."

"I pray that it may be so, sir."

"Hark you, Cyprian: your fair mistress is either the most unfortunate and innocent of women in all the world, or she is the most guilty."

"Yes, oh, yes."

"I pray to Heaven she may be the former, but I have hideous doubts. Tell me, Cyprian, what means, or what opportunity, can my friend here or myself take for thoroughly exploring this mansion?"

"And particularly for a thorough examination of this room," said Lamont.

"Yes, yes."

"Why, the only way," said Cyprian, "will be for you both to say that you will ride to London and be back by midnight. Then you must go no further than a mile or less down the road, and leave your horses at the old Maypole Inn."

"Ah, I see."

"You can then both of you walk back, and I will let you in by the garden gate. Lady Margaret will have gone to rest, no doubt, or if not to rest, she will be shut up in her own little chamber, and you can then go all about the house as you please."

"But we run the risk of falling in the way of some of the household."

"Oh, no. There is but one out of the whole lot who will venture after nightfall, if they can possibly help it, out of the old kitchen."

"And who is that one?"

"My lady's maid, Loon, as they call her. I don't like her at all ; and if there is any secret at all to tell, she knows of it."

"I have noted the woman," said Lassamour; "she has an evil countenance. The chance, then, of meeting her is worst of all, as she would at once report it to her lady."

"She would, sir, if you did meet her; but that will you not, for the Lady Margaret, when she retires for the night, ever has her in the adjoining chamber, ready to come to her at a moment's notice."

"Ah! Is it so?"

"Yes. She dreams."

"The Lady Margaret, you mean?"

"I do. And once I heard Loon mutter to herself—'Curse her dreams ; she might still them as I do mine with strong waters.' "

"That speaks volumes," said Lamont.

"It does, indeed. But what say you, my friend. Will you embark in this adventure with me?"

"I will, indeed."

"With all your heart?"

"Ay, with all my heart."

"And you, Cyprian?"

"Yes, sir With all my heart, too."

"Then, Cyprian, it shall be done just as you propose it. So, do you go to Lady Margaret, and tell her from me, that I think of riding forth to London with my friend Lamont, and bring me word what she says to it."

"I will, sir."

Cyprian left the state bed-chamber, and was absent about ten minutes.

When he came back, both Lamont and Lassamour eagerly questioned him about what Lady Margaret had said.

"I told her, sir, and she said—'Commend me to my good lord and husband, and give him this,' whereupon she took this embroidered purse from a small drawer in a cabinet, and here it is."

"The same amount I had before," said Lassamour. "Did you say I should be back by midnight?"

"I did."

"And to that, what was her reply?"

"Not a word. But she smiled in her strange way."

"She doubts it."

"Then she will be in the wrong for once," said Lamont, "seeing that we shall be back long before that time. And let us go at once, Lassamour. For all that you and Cyprian have told me of your lady, sits like a very nightmare on my soul."

"And I," said Lassamour, mournfully, "what must I feel?"

"I am sorry for you."

"Well, Lamont, I have ever lived in this world upon the philosophical notion of making the very best of my bad bargain."

"It is well to do so."

"And of never regretting that which is beyond our own control, my friend."

"Yes, Lassamour, it is easy enough when the heart is free from storms, and when nothing is occurring to vex the temper, to be a philosopher; but, the worst of it is, that philosophy never is found in a man's company when he really and truly wants it."

"There is much in that, Lamont."

"I am sure there is, for I have tried it many a time and oft myself."

"I will not say that I, too, have not gathered some such an idea from my own experience, too; but come what may, we will carry out this adventure that we have set ourselves upon to-night."

CHAPTER XXXIX.

LADY MARGARET SUSPECTS SOME MISCHIEF.

ITH all his opinions regarding the little good that philosophy was calculated to do a man at a push, young Lamont set about aiding his friend Lassamour with all his heart and soul.

It is very doubtful, though, if without the active assistance of Cyprian they could have at all, with any hope of success, have carried out their plan.

The Lady Margaret was accomplished and prudent. No doubt many circumstances in her past career had made her so, and it is probable that she relied upon Cyprian to tell her if anything took place of an unusual character in the mansion.

We do not mean to say that Cyprian was a spy of the Lady Margaret's, or that there was any understanding between him and his lady that he should act in that capacity; but still she might have expected that he would bring her news.

This feeling on the part of Lady Margaret, no doubt arose from this fact.

Cyprian had entered her service when he was a mere boy, and she had, to some extent, flattered and indulged him, so that while he remained a mere boy he saw in her nothing but a most kind and indulgent mistress.

At that age, too, Cyprian was not at all likely to trouble his head either with the actions or the notions of the Lady Margaret except just those that concerned him.

A boy of twelve years of age was not likely to indulge in any abstuse reflections as to whether her husbands went out of the world naturally or not."

But time, the great author of all changes, was soon to alter all this.

Cyprian grew from a mere handsome boy into a good-looking young man.

This change was likely enough to be all but unnoticed by the Lady Margaret. We do not readily perceive those revolu-tions and slow alterations that the hand of time makes in persons with whom we are in daily connection.

The young man began to think.

No wonder then that, although still retaining much affection for his mistress, he should feel very much horrified at the suspicions that crossed his brain regarding her conduct.

If she were guilty of what the world did not in any sort of way scruple to impute to her, then a greater wretch than she certainly did not exist beneath the canopy of Heaven.

If she were innocent, then a more unfortunate being had never been the sport of a wayward destiny.

Tortured between these suppositions, no wonder was it that Cyprian eagerly enough seized the very first opportunity that presented itself of trying to come to some conclusion with regard to the subject.

Hence, then, it was, from motives in all respects rather unaccountable than otherwise, that he joined as he had done Lassamour heart and hand in his efforts to penetrate the mystery of his lady's strange and most eventful life.

Cyprian promised to be on the alert to let his master and young Lamont into the premises by the garden gate, when they should return from their very short ride down the road to London.

Everything, then, appeared to be quite favourable for the little enterprise, which, by a possibility, might have many important results indeed.

To be sure, Cyprian felt a little nervous; and as he followed Lassamour and Lamont to the great gate where their two horses were standing, he whispered to his master—

"Honoured sir, there is one part of the subject that we have none of us said a word about, but which yet I trust has not escaped your thoughts."

"What is that, Cyprian?"

"I don't like to mention it."

"Nay, out with it."

"You will forgive me?"

"Surely yes."

"Then in addition to everything else that folks say of the Lady Margaret, they don't scruple to call her a witch."

"Indeed!"

"Yes, and they say that it is in consequence of her dealings with the devil that she has been able to get rid of her six husbands so oddly."

"Oh, they say that, do they?" asked Lassamour.

"They do, and if it be so——"

"Well?"

"Why, we are all in a pretty mess, for she will find out what we are about to-night, and we shall none of us be in life by to-morrow morning."

"Make your mind quite easy upon that score, my good Cyprian."

"You do not think it, sir?"

"I do not; or if the Lady Margaret has communion with devils, they are in the likeness of her own passions."

"Even so," said Lamont.

Cyprian was a little strengthened in his spirits by the manner in which Lamont and Lassamour disposed of the notion of Lady Margaret's possible supernatural powers, for he had himself, upon more than one occasion, been inclined to believe in them than otherwise, and it is hardly to be wondered at, considering all things, that he should do so.

That was an age in which the devil was considered to busy himself much more with human affairs than he does now.

Probably, by the increase of civilisation and population, he finds his hands so full of business that comes to him without any trouble upon his own part, that he does not think it worth his while to go soliciting custom.

This is the only explanation we can give of the fact of the total disappearance of the devil in this world.

The night was a very beautiful one on which Lassamour and his young friend, Lamont, went forth with an intention of so soon returning to the mansion.

In fact, when they were both fairly mounted and on the road, Lassamour said to Lamont, with a smile—

"Now, upon my faith, Lamont, this is about as fair a night for a ride as can be, and were it not that we are engaged otherwise, how I should enjoy it."

"Well, you can give up the inquiry at home for this night, if it so please you."

"No—no! Oh, no!"

"I think it would be well not."

"I am sure it is well not; and, besides, I will not, now that I have so fast sworn Cyprian to my service and to keep faith with me, break it with him."

They rode on, then, till they came to the inn that Cyprian had mentioned, and they drew rein at its old ivy-covered porch.

"What ho! House!" cried Lassamour.

There was a great rush to the door of the hostel, for a glass had let them see who it was, and the husband of the rich Lady of Pleasaunce was not to be kept in waiting any longer than possible.

The landlord himself appeared at the side of Martin's horse, and with a low bow, inquired his honour's pleasure.

"Simply," said Lassamour, "that you take charge of these two horses ti I call or send for them."

"Certainly, noble sir."

"And you must not say that you have them in your stable."

"Certainly not, noble sir!"

"That will do. You will see that I know well how to reward good and faithful service."

"Of that we have no doubt, your honour."

Martin and Lamont at once dismounted, and left their steeds to the care of the landlord and his assistants, and then they turned their steps again towards Pleasaunce House.

The soft balmy stillness in the air made it truly refreshing; not a breath of wind of more account than a zephyr was blowing, and the stars looked down from nearly a cloudless sky in countless myriads.

The perfume of early flowers, and of the sweet-scented May with which the hedges were loaded, gave a soft sweetness to the air that was truly delicious.

Lassamour and Lamont, as if by one accord, paused on a little eminence to look about them.

"This is a fair scene," said Lamont.

"It is, indeed."

"Do you see the Thames yonder, like a silver thread, winding among the trees?"

"I do. Who would suppose now to look at the quiet and the beauty of such a scene as this, that there was anything like the wickedness that there really is in this great world of ours, Lamont?"

CHAPTER XL.

LAMONT AND LASSAMOUR ARE IN SOME DANGER.

ARTIN LASSA-MOUR'S thought has, from the beginning of the world, we suppose, struck very many people, both gentle and simple, and it will continue to strike very many more.

Incongruities of all kinds easily suggest themselves.

"Come on, Lassamour," said Lamont. "I must confess that my mind is so full of all that I have heard from you and from others of your lady, that I long to get back to the mansion."

"This way, then."

Lassamour led Lamont by rather a near cut across a meadow to the confines of the garden of Pleasaunce House, and paused at the little gate at which Cyprian was to be to admit them.

"Cyprian!" said Lassamour, in a low tone, as he tapped with the hilt of his dagger at the gate.

The gate was opened.

"I am here, noble sir," said Cyprian. "You have been long in coming."

"We did linger a little on the road."

"Is all as we left it at the mansion?" asked Lamont.

"Yes, sir. Everything seems to be going on much as usual, and yet——"

"Yet what, boy?" cried Lassamour.

"I do tremble a little lest, after all, my lady should be a witch, and so able to find us all out."

"Pho! Be at ease on that score, boy."

"You think I may, sir?"

"Of a surety you may."

"Then I will at least strive to be so."

"Do so, and you will find that striving is one half the battle. And now lead the way, Cyprian, for I dare say you are better acquainted with all these garden paths than I am."

"I know them well, sir."

"No doubt."

Cyprian led the way, but he did not lead them by the nearest route to the wing of the mansion at which he intended to effect an entrance. On the contrary, he was compelled to take them by such a route that their figures would be concealed from any one who might be looking from any of the windows of the mansion.

Upon so fine a night, it was possible enough that some one, even possibly the Lady Margaret herself, might be looking from a casement.

It was, therefore, but an act of ordinary prudence on the part of the page to conduct Lassamour and his friend by the more indirect route he did.

But the distance, after all, take it in what direction they might, was not great, so that they were soon at the house.

"Stop, noble sir," said Cyprian, "I am thinking that if we could effect an entrance by one of the windows of the yellow banqueting room, it will be better than opening any door."

"It will, Cyprian."

"What room is that?" said Lamont.

"Of a truth I know not," replied Lassamour. "Is not this the north wing of the mansion, Cyprian?"

"It is, sir."

"Then it is a portion of it that is all new and strange to me, for I have never been in it."

The page led them now on to a kind of terrace that was raised about six feet from the level of a lawn below it, and from which there opened some six or eight windows, all connecting with the yellow banqueting hall he had made mention of.

Cyprian knew very well what he was about. There was one of those windows that he knew was ready to open at a touch, for he had often gone in and out of it himself upon occasional absences from the mansion, with the knowledge of which he had not wished to trouble the household.

"This way," said Cyprian. "The floor of the room is about half-a-foot below the window-sill."

They both stepped into the room after Cyprian, and he then closed the window with all convenient speed.

"You know the old house well, Cyprian," said Lassamour.

"Of a truth I do, sir."

"I am glad of it, for it enables you to be a far better guide to us than you otherwise could be."

"And I, sir, am glad of it for that very object. Now, sir, will you go to the long gallery where all the portraits are put?"

"Yes, be it so."

"I am curious to see them," said Lamont.

"And I, too," said Lassamour; "so lead on, Cyprian, with what speed you may; and after that we will proceed to the state bed-chamber, and leave no corner of it unexplored."

Cyprian now lit a small piece of wax taper that he had with him, and which cast about them all a faint and star-like radiance; but it was, at all events, sufficient to banish absolute darkness, and it prevented them from encountering any of the furniture of the room they were in, or from making any noise by stumbling upon the stairs they soon had to ascend.

It was the roof of the banqueting-room they were now in that attracted the attention of Lassamour the most.

On that roof was painted, with very great art, some sort of fabulous dragon, or monster, half-crocodile, half-snake, who held, or seemed to hold in its mouth the gilt chain from which depended a large chandelier.

"That is a strange device," said Lassamour, to Lamont. "Have you noticed it?"

"I have, indeed. How the eyes glitter."

"Yes—yes."

"Ah," said Cyprian, "everybody says that, and I don't suppose that there is a servant in the whole household who would for any consideration venture here alone at night; and I must say that for a long time those glittering eyes, that never seemed to grow dim, affected me, till I found out what they were in reality."

"And what are they?"

"Pieces of stained glass, sir, only, cunningly let in at the proper places, so that they really do seem like ferocious eyes, as they catch the reflection of anything that passes them on the floor below."

"It is so."

Cyprian opened a tall door in the wall of the room and passed out, holding his little taper-light in his hand, and as high as he could, so as to give as much of the benefit of it as possible to Lassamour and Lamont.

Immediately outside this door of the yellow banqueting-room they found themselves in a long, narrow passage, and at the far end of it was a flight of narrow stairs.

These stairs led to the picture-gallery.

As they proceeded along the passage, Lassamour more than once started, as their shadows were reflected on to the wall at his side.

"You start," said Lamont, in a whisper; "saw you aught?"

"No—no; and yet——"

"Yet what?"

"Look there!"

"Where?" said Cyprian, and he shaded the light with his disengaged hand.

A considerable distance in advance of them they all saw a something that looked like a shadowy figure of a dim, gray-like colour.

"Good God!" gasped Cyprian, "what is it?"

"Ah, you see it?"

"Yes—yes."

"Then it is no delusion."

Lassamour drew his rapier, and dashed forward at full speed after the figure.

He reached the spot where he had felt quite certain it must have stood, but it was gone. Whether it had vanished into thin air, or had been a being of flesh and blood like himself, and had managed, from its intimate knowledge of the locality, to escape through some secret door, it was not in his power to say.

When he was joined by Lamont and Cyprian he was looking about him with his drawn sword in his grasp.

"It is gone," he said.

"The Lord be good to us!" said Cyprian; "I am glad of it."

"That am not I."

"But, noble sir, what is the use of running after ghosts, and all those kind of people?"

"I don't know, Cyprian, exactly, if this was a ghost."

"Oh, sir, what else could it be?"

"That I cannot say; but it is very strange. Does this staircase lead at once to the picture-gallery?"

"It does."

"And where does that passage to the left go to?"

"It winds round this wing of the mansion, and leads then to the servants' hall."

"Well, Cyprian, we will ascend to the gallery, now, if you will lead the way."

"Yes, noble sir."

Cyprian was evidently in a fright, and was not a little glad to get out of the passage in which so very suspicious an object had shown itself.

He ran up the stairs with avidity.

"Hold! not so fast."

Cyprian paused, and held the light behind him, and in a few moments the whole party were on the landing at the head of the stairs.

A large oaken door faced them, on the panels of which were deeply engraven the arms of the Lady Margaret, the heraldic portion being very richly gilt.

LADY MARGARET'S WAITING WOMAN, LOON.

CHAPTER XLI.

LADY MARGARET AND HER MAID HAVE A DISAGREEMENT.

OMETHING was taking place in the chamber of the Lady Margaret, which is well worth the attending to, while all this was going on, calculated to rather disturb the peace and the serenity of the lady.

Incidental mention has been made of her own and confidential waiting-woman, Loon, as she was named, and it is of her we have to speak.

When Cyprian had brought the message

to the Lady Margaret, that Lassamour intended to go with Lamont to London, a cloud had gathered upon her brow.

But she had made a great effort, and had sent back the gracious answer we have duly recorded.

She then sat upon a low devotional chair, and with her head resting upon her arm, she seemed to give herself up to thought.

Those thoughts, whatever they were, were soon disturbed by the approach of Loon, the waiting-woman.

Lady Margaret looked up.

"Oh, it is you?"

"Yes, my lady."

"I don't require your services to-night. You may retire to your own room."

Loon was silent, but she did not retire as she had been ordered.

After a few moments, Lady Margaret looked at her in some surprise, and said—

"Did you hear me?"

"I did, my lady."

"Then go."

"I have something to say."

"Ah!"

"Yes, my lady. I have been with you now for five years, come midsummer."

"Well?"

"You never trusted me, but I have eyes and ears, my lady."

For a moment a deathlike paleness came over the face of Lady Margaret, but it was only for a moment, and by a great effort she recovered her composure, and with an appearance of great calmness, she said—

"Well?"

"And so, my lady, I am now tired of service, and I think of leaving you and going to reside at my birth-place, where everybody will be glad to see me."

"Are you sure of that?"

"Yes, my lady."

"How so?"

"Because they will soon find that I am rich."

"Rich?"

"Yes, my lady, for I am quite sure you will send me away from you rich, rather than that I should choose to gossip about what has for five years taken place in this old house, my lady."

"Ah!"

"You comprehend me?"

"I do."

"Very good, my lady; I'm quite sure you will never miss a very large sum to ensure the continued silence of one who has served you well."

Lady Margaret turned slowly upon her chair, and looked the waiting-woman full in the face. Loon shrunk from that calm,

bloodless kind of look. She cowed before it as one might before the glare of a serpent.

"Yes, Loon," said Lady Margaret, "I do understand you: for five years you have been my attendant."

"Yes, my lady."

"And during that time I have loaded you with all sorts of favours and comforts."

"I don't complain of the service, but——"

"But what?"

"When one has a secret one has a right to sell it for what it will fetch, and it is worth more to you than to any one else except one."

"One?"

"Yes, my lady."

"And that one?"

"Is Martin Lassamour."

"Wretch! Viper!"

"Oh, my lady, it is of no use to abuse me about it. That will do no good. I say I have eyes and ears, and I have seen six coffins go out of this house. No, five: what am I saying? Only five, for you were a widow when I came to you, if you recollect, madam."

"Peace!"

"Well, my lady, how much am I to have? that is the question. What will you give?"

Lady Margaret seemed to be seized with a sudden spasm, and then she smiled, as she said—

"Loon, what do you fancy you have got to tell?"

"Fancy, my lady?"

"Yes, fancy."

"Hem! Well, my lady, I did not expect you would have asked that of me."

"But I do ask it."

"Well, then, my lady, I think that I could say something about the deaths of your husbands."

"Indeed?"

"Yes, my lady."

"What?"

Lady Margaret smiled so as she spoke that Loon did not know what on earth to make of it. To tell the truth, she felt much more alarmed at being met in that way than as if her lady had flown into the most violent access of rage.

"Go on, Loon."

"My lady, I—I——"

"Speak out. Why do you pause? Are your thoughts regarding me of too monstrous a character for you to dare to give utterance to them?"

Loon was abashed and silent. The enormous amount of effrontery in her mistress got the better, for a time, of even her spirit, and that was, in good truth, none of the mildest or the weakest in the world.

The Lady Margaret had all the power that an educated mind has ever over an uneducated one, and, besides, she had long schooled herself to withstand pretty well any such quailings of conscience.

But Loon, although she might for a time be cowed by the audacity of her mistress, was not likely to remain for long in such a position.

Of one thing she felt certain.

That one thing was that for the future Pleasaunce House was no place for her.

This was the thought that gave her boldness to speak further.

"My lady," she said, "I did not think that you would have driven me to say this much, but——"

"Hush!"

"You understand me, then?"

"I do, Loon. You suspect, and that, too, upon better grounds than the great world without, that some, if not all, of my husbands may have come by their death by means that—that——"

A convulsive shudder came over the frame of the Lady Margaret.

Loon was alarmed.

"Enough, madam," she cried. "There is neither occasion for you nor for me to pursue this subject further. Let it rest; it is quite enough that we comprehend each other."

Lady Margaret by a great effort recovered, and then, as she slightly bowed her head, she said—

"We do—we do."

"And, therefore, you will have no reluctance to pay me?"

"You wish me to secure your silence?"

"I do, madam."

"Is that generous?"

Loon gave her head a toss, and then she answered—

"I don't know, my lady, what you call generous or not; but you know very well that four out of your six husbands were men of very large fortunes, and that you have all they were worth."

"That is true."

"To be sure, the last one was, as I know, a poor gentleman."

"That is true."

"But then, my lady, with your means you could afford to begin to please your fancy a little."

"Just so."

"As I mean to do with my means."

"Just so."

"Well, my lady, I am glad to see that you view the matter in so reasonable a light as you now do."

"Yes, Loon, I plainly see now that I must secure your silence. I am not very well to-night. Can you get me a cup of wine?"

"Oh, yes, surely, my lady."

Loan left the room.

The moment she was gone Lady Margaret sprang to her feet, and went to a small cabinet that was in a corner of the apartment.

By the aid of a little silver key that she had round her neck tied to a piece of ribbon, she opened the cabinet in a moment.

Within the door of it there appeared a number of very small drawers. Lady Margaret opened one of them, in which were several small bottles, each standing upright.

CHAPTER XLII.

THE SILENCE OF THE WAITING-MAID IS SECURED.

ONE of the bottles that was in this drawer, after a glance, Lady Margaret took out and placed it beside her.

From a shelf, then, she took down a tall glass, such as were beginning to be used in the houses of the wealthy instead of silver cups.

Opening, then, the little phial, she placed her forefinger on the top of it and tilted it up so that her finger was just damped with a perfectly limpid and pale-looking liquid that was in it.

Carefully, then, Lady Margaret anointed the edge of the glass with the damp that was upon her finger.

But she took care that the anointing was confined to about one third of the circumference of the rim, and she was guided by a kind of pattern on the glass where to begin and where to leave off.

With great quickness, then, she wiped her finger dry and replaced the bottle in the little drawer, and locked up the cabinet again, but she left the anointed glass standing quite carelessly as if left there by a servant upon a side table.

In another moment the Lady Margaret was in the seat again, and in very much the same attitude that she had been in when Loon left her to fetch for her a cup of wine.

It was well for Lady Margaret that she had been tolerably quick about what she did, for she soon heard the footsteps of her maid returning.

"Yes," she muttered, "she must be silenced. She brings it on herself. Not all the gold that ever was coined will bribe her to silence so effectually as I intend to do."

Loon entered the room.

She carried on a silver salver a small goblet of the same metal full of wine.

"Are you better, my lady?" she said, with hypocritical tenderness of tone and manner.

"Yes, Loon."

"Thank Heaven for that, madam."

"Do you really wish me better?"

"Oh, dear, yes, madam. He! he!"

"Why do you laugh?"

"I could not afford to lose you, madam, I was going to say. There is no one more interested in you than I am."

"That is true."

"To be sure, madam."

"Well, Loon, you are sincere with me, at all events. What wine is this?"

"Canary, madam."

"Ah, then, you must get a glass for it. I cannot drink it from silver, good Lonn, and you know that well enough if you had given it a moment's thought."

"Nay, it was Malmsey that I thought you could not drink from a cup."

"Canary, I say!—Canary, likewise."

"I will get a glass."

"Do—yet stay; is that one on yonder table?"

"It is."

"Fetch it hither, Loon; it will do if it be clean—look into it—is it clean?"

"Quite so, my lady."

"Then it will spare you trouble. This will do quite well. I suppose it has been used, but if so it is by myself, so it don't matter."

Loon was glad enough to save herself the trouble of fetching a glass, so she took the one from the side table and handed it to Lady Margaret, who at once poured the wine from the silver cup into it; taking care, though, not to touch the edge of the glass with it, or to fill it.

Guided, then, by the pattern of the glass, she drank from the portion of the rim of it that was not anointed with the pale liquid from the little bottle in the cabinet.

Then she placed the wine before her.

"Loon," she said, "this is the last evening you and I must spend together, I think."

"I think so, too, my lady; and yet—"

"What?"

"I should be sorry to inconvenience you, and will wait until the morrow, if you think you can then send for another tire-woman, my lady."

"No, Loon, you must go."

"Be it so, madam."

"After what has passed between us there is no remedy for it, Loon, and go you must."

Lady Margaret drank again from the glass.

"When we have settled with each other, madam, I am quite ready to go."

"That is true. Sit you down, Loon. You have been at times kind to me, and always faithful."

"Always, madam; and so now I claim my reward."

"Or you would be faithful no longer?"

"It would be very hard, madam, to expect me to keep you secrets for nothing."

"It would. Sit down—sit down."

Loon took a seat opposite to her mistress, who, with her fair white hand upon the stem of the wine glass, said, in a low tone—

"Loon, how much, now, do you expect?"

"I hardly like to say."

"Nay, do say."

Lady Margaret drank again.

"This wine is superb."

Loon licked her lips.

"Come," added Lady Margaret, "as we are about to part, and as even now I no longer consider you as in my service, you shall drink with me. This tall glass holds more wine than it is at all prudent for either you or I to drink at once."

As she spoke, Lady Margaret pushed the glass on the little table that was between them to Loon.

She took it at once, and drank from the rim that had been anointed.

The eyes of Lady Margaret blazed for a moment like hot coals.

"It is fine wine," said Loon; "and—yet——"

"Yet what?"

"If I did not know that it was the old Canary——"

"Well—if you did not?"

"I should say it had rather a strange taste with it."

"Imagination, my good Loon, imagination. I tasted nothing strange in it."

"Then it must be fancy."

"Quite so."

"And, besides, I fetched it myself."

"You did."

"And you drank first."

"I did."

Loon drew a long breath.

"Why, my good woman, what on earth is the matter with you? I hope you have put nothing into the wine?"

"I?"

"Yes, you!—Who else could?"

"Oh, no, no!—I put nothing in it, and I am quite sure, madam, that you put nothing in it."

"That is true."

"But will you not drink again?"

"With all my heart."

As Loon had placed the glass again on the table, the side of the rim that was uncontaminated by the presence of the liquor from the little bottle, remained next to her, so that the Lady Margaret could take it up and drink as she had done before with impunity.

Loon looked relieved, and smiled.

"It must have been fancy," she said.

"Nothing else, I assure you. The wine tastes to me quite as usual, Loon. But, now, let us to business;—how much money as a reward will satisfy you?"

"I think, my lady, that you will not object to the clear sum of one thousand pounds."

"Well, it is little enough in all conscience to purchase your secrecy."

"If you think so, madam, nothing can be much easier than to receive it."

"That is true, too."

Loon suddenly placed her hand upon her brow, and looked rather pale.

"What is amiss?" said her lady.

"Amiss, madam?"

"Yes, amiss. What is it?"

"Heaven help me!"

"Amen! It is to be sincerely hoped, my good Loon, that Heaven will help all of us; but really you look just now, if the truth must be told, anything but well."

Loon shuddered.

A strange mocking and terrible smile came across the face of Lady Margaret as she saw the rapid change of colour in the face of the waiting maid. Twice or thrice the wretched woman tried to speak, but her voice failed her, and she could only utter a deep groan.

"Loon," said the Lady Margaret, "why do you not speak? What is the matter?"

"The matter?"

"Yes, my good Loon. It really seems to me as if you had lost all power to do other than repeat my words. How is it with you? Come, now, make an effort to speak to me in an intelligible manner."

CHAPTER XLIII.

LADY MARGARET DISPOSES OF THE DEAD BODY OF HER WAITING MAID.

COMING death was pretty plainly written in the glance Loon cast at Lady Margaret.

"Murder!" she now gasped. "Murder!"

"Murder, say you?"

"Oh, God! yes, I am poisoned! I know it!—I feel it burning and tearing at my vitals.—Poisoned! Oh, Heaven! what a dreadful death is this!"

Lady Margaret rose and approached Loon. She stood quite close to her, and she looked in her face, as she said—

"It is true. You are poisoned. You have just about two minutes more to live. Fool! fool! I say. Did you think to measure your small wits with mine?"

"Save me! Oh, save me!"

"Ha! Save you? For what?"

"To repent."

"Of what?"

"Of—of all and everything, and oh! most of all of dreaming of leaving you, or of opposing you. Oh, God! I declare there is a fire raging in my heart!"

"Of course there is," said Lady Margaret—"of course there is. I have taken care of that, poor fool that you are. And so you do indeed repent at last?"

"I do—I do! Mercy! Help!"

Loon rose, and staggered towards the

door, but the Lady Margaret flew at her like the fiend she was, and clutching her by the back of the neck, she held her down on a couch by main force.

"Wretch!" she said. "Did you think that I should release such as you with what you know, and even have the remotest thought of allowing you to leave me? Fool! Idiot! You bring your death upon yourself. The tool rebelled against the hand that wielded it, and the hand breaks it."

Loon uttered a strange gurgling, choking kind of cry, and then a shiver ran through all her limbs, and after that all was still.

The Lady Margaret took her hand from the neck of her late attendant. Loon was dead.

"So much for one obstacle—so much for one danger past away," she said; "and now for the disposal of the body. By good fortune I have the means of doing that."

Lady Margaret went to one of the walls of her room, on which hung a portrait of some saint, with a halo of glory round his head.

This saint, too, was in the dress of a palmer from the Holy Land, and he wore a scollop-shell upon the border of his robes.

Lady Margaret pressed the lower portion of the scollop-shell with her finger, and in a moment a tall narrow door, the whole length and width of the panel, sprung open.

Immediately beyond this door in the wall there appeared complete darkness, as if it were the mouth of some very dreary cavern.

But the Lady Margaret knew perfectly well where that secret passage led to.

Yet she listened attentively to hear if any sound came from the narrow passage. What sound could she expect to hear?

A strange moaning came upon the still air: she knew what that was well. She had heard it before, for the wind found an entrance to that place with ease; and as it rushed up a narrow staircase it moaned and whistled, and at times when the night was boisterous without, it howled like a living thing.

"It is the wind," she said. "I know the sound well. I have heard it, and trembled at it, when I knew not what it was, and I had not the courage of despair that now nerves my soul."

At these words she clasped her hands for a moment over her face, and a tremor passed through her frame.

She was deathly pale when she took her hands away from before her face.

"I am one," she said, "who has embarked in such a stormy sea, that it is better to go on seeking even the unknown shores of another world, even with all its terrors, than to try to put back to where I came from."

She now lighted a small hand-lamp, and after carefully bolting and otherwise securing her chamber-door against even the possibility of intrusion, she cast one glance at the dead body of the waiting-maid, and then passed through the aperture in the wall of her room.

The passage in which Lady Margaret now trod was a very narrow one, and she held the light very carefully so as to guide her footsteps onwards, and it was well that she did so, for at a distance of about twenty feet from the panel-door there appeared a deep spiral staircase made of iron.

This staircase descended apparently for a considerable distance, for the light from the hand-lamp that the Lady Margaret had with her was not sufficient to penetrate to the foot of it.

Again now she listened attentively.

Again too she made up her mind that the only noise she heard was the moaning and the sighing of the wind up the spiral of the iron staircase.

"All is well," she said.

The Lady Margaret then slowly and carefully descended the stairs.

As she went, more apparently from some old habit than from any real necessity for so doing, she counted the steps.

From one to thirty she so counted, and then she reached the foot of them.

Then she paused again, and listened.

The air that sighed and moaned about the place caused the flame of the little hand-lamp at times to dash about as though it would on the moment be extinguished.

But it was not so.

And now turning sharply to her right, the Lady Margaret looked upwards to the wall before her, and placed the lamp upon a small iron bracket that was there.

This iron bracket was only just within her reach, and when she had placed the lamp upon it, the light no longer darted and flitted about, but appeared to be, by the secure and the steady way in which it now burnt, to be no longer within the influence of the draughts that had before disturbed it.

Lady Margaret then placed her hand upon a curious shaped piece of iron or steel, at a portion of the wall just below where she had placed the lamp.

A little pressure released a spring fastening, and a door, very similar in size and shape to that which opened from her chamber at the top of the spiral staircase, now exhibited itself.

By the rush of cold air that came through the doorway, one would have imagined that this door opened unto the open air.

But such was not wholly the case.

It opened into a gloomy, desolate, and ruinous conservatory, that stood close to one of the wings of Pleasaunce House.

This conservatory had for long been suffered to go to decay, and the tall trees in its immediate neighbourhood had been allowed to grow unchecked, and in some places overspread it by their luxuriant foliage and branches.

The glass roof of the conservatory itself had suffered much from tempest and from accident, so that all the winds of Heaven, let them blow from which quarter they might, found their way into the place.

Lady Margaret passed through the doorway, but she did so very carefully, for it was actually a portion of the back part of a niche in the wall, in which stood a statue of a wood nymph.

So, in going through the secret door, she had to be careful to avoid the statue.

She stood in the conservatory, and again listened, apparently with more anxiety than before.

But throughout the whole place, and all the adjacent grounds of Pleasaunce House, there did not seem to be the slightest indication of moving life.

"'Tis well," she said.

There was a dim and partial kind of light in the conservatory, engendered by the moonlight, as it forced its soft and gentle rays even into that well-shrouded spot.

Lady Margaret crept slowly along the floor, which was paved with slabs of marble, till she came to one in the centre of which there was an iron ring.

This slab of stone was of much lesser dimensions than any of the others.

This iron ring was sunk in the surface of the stone, so that it should lie flat, and be no impediment to any one who might be walking in the conservatory; and much dust and many decayed leaves lay about it, so much so, indeed, as nearly to cover it up.

In fact, but that the Lady Margaret knew perfectly well where to feel for the iron ring, it is not at all likely that she would have seen it.

But she soon felt it with her hands, and clearing away with busy fingers the dirt and the decayed leaves that had collected about the stone, and the hollow in which the ring lay, she laid hold of it in both hands.

It required all the strength of Lady Margaret to lift the stone; but she knew that she could do it.

She had raised it before that night.

In the course of about half a minute she had lifted the stone, and placed it on one side close to the gloomy-looking and absolutely dark aperture that it covered.

She did not now pause one moment to take any glance within the black opening disclosed in the floor of the summer-house or conservatory, which the removal of the stone disclosed, but with a rather hurried step she hastened away.

Passing through the door in the wall behind the statue, she left it open, and taking the lamp from the bracket on which she had placed it, she rather hurriedly ascended the spiral iron staircase to her own chamber.

CHAPTER XLIV.

MARTIN AND HIS FRIEND PURSUE THEIR RESEARCHES AT PLEASAUNCE.

E must now leave the truly unfeeling, criminal Lady Margaret for a brief space, in order to follow the proceedings of her husband, Martin Lassamour, and his young friend Lamont, in their researches through the wing of Pleasaunce House which was so much neglected, and of which they knew so little.

It will be remembered that they had completely gained over the young page, Cyprian, to their cause.

They had, on pretence of going to London, fully succeeded in lulling the active suspicions of the Lady Margaret, so that for once her cleverness was at fault; and there is no sort of doubt but that she considered she had Pleasaunce House all to herself on that night.

This state of fancied security; though, would hardly have taken place but for the one circumstance, that Loon and her lady no longer acted harmoniously together.

There can be no sort of doubt in the world but that if Loon had been going on just as usual in the confidential service of the Lady Margaret, she would, by her peeping and prying about the mansion, have soon found out that something was amiss in it.

She would probably, indeed, have discovered what was going on, or something like it, and so the position of Martin Lassamour and his friend Lamont, as well as that of Cyprian the page, might have been very much altered for the worse ; but such was not the case.

Not only had the misunderstanding between Loon and her lady at once so much occupied the mind of the Lady Margaret that she had no time, no wish to think of anything else than the best and safest mode of putting her quondam maid out of the way, but it at once got rid in the household of the only person who was at all likely to interfere with the proceedings of Martin Lassamour and those who were with him.

From the moment that Loon had made up her mind to retire from business, so to speak, she had done nothing in the way of service for the Lady Margaret.

Her death then so soon followed that both she and her wicked and imperious mistress were entirely occupied the one with the other.

Thus, then, a field of action was open by the recent accidental combination of circumstances for Lassamour, such as could hardly have been hoped for.

Passing, then, many little circumstances of no importance, we find Martin and Lamont and Cyprian in the long picture-gallery of Pleasaunce House.

There was something in the stillness that reigned in that portion of the mansion at once solemn and awful.

It had the same effect on them that being in a church has upon ordinary minds; that is to say, it induced a soft and stealthy mode of walking, and a whispering style of speech.

How strange it is that man, from his own skill and ingenuity, will pile up bricks and mortar and stone, and then be half afraid to speak aloud in the space he has so enclosed!

But such is the case.

They all three stood still for some few moments, and looked about them in silence.

The light that Cyprian carried was anything but sufficient to illumine that long gallery, so that the effect of the distance going off as it did far away into dim obscurity, was very vague and mysterious.

There were the portraits, too, upon the wall, with their faces all turned to it, and Martin Lassamour, with a shudder, thought to himself—

"Will mine, indeed, ever find a place among these, and so be turned to the wall out of sight?"

Cyprian made a faint kind of attempt to be courageous.

"Well, noble sir," he said, "here we are, you see."

"Yes, Cyprian."

"And a gloomy place it is," said young Lamont.

"Well, sir, for that matter I am fain to confess it is; but do you still see the portraits with their faces to the wall, as I told you?"

"We do," said Martin.

"And are they really," said Lamont, "the portraits of the six husbands of the Lady Margaret?"

"They are, sir."

"How strange."

"It is, indeed, sir."

"More than strange," said Martin.

"But, my good lad," added Lamont, "do you mean to tell us that they have all been painted by the Lady Margaret?"

"To the best of my belief, yes, sir."

"And," said Martin, with rather a faint smile, "she is painting mine, is she not?"

"She is, sir."

"A bad sign, that, Lamont."

"Upon my life," said Lamont, "I don't know what to think of it. Her conduct quite staggers me. To sit with her—to talk with her, and to see her at the ordinary duties of social life, one would say that she was a right loyal and noble lady."

"Even so," sighed Martin.

"And yet——"

"Yes, my good friend, and yet?"

"That is it," said Cyprian. "Yet, you would say, sirs, what an odd thing it is that she should have so many husbands is it not?"

"It is, indeed."

"It is something more than odd," said Lamont; "but I should like, now that we are here, if you have no sort of objection, Lassamour, to the sight of the likenesses of your predecessors, to have a good look at some of them."

"We will look at all of them," said Martin.

"Be it so, then."

"Come, Master Cyprian, I will help you to turn their faces to the light again."

"Nay, sir, I can manage by myself easily enough to do that," said the page. "You see, sirs, that they are hung from strong brass hooks close to the roof, with thick cords, so that there is but little difficulty in turning them either way."

Cyprian at once illustrated what he said by turning one of the portraits with ease.

"The light!" cried Lassamour; "the light! Hold it a little higher, good Cyprian, that I may see the face well. That will do, boy, that will do."

Cyprian, after a moment or two, was able to hold the light so that it cast its rays as much as it very well could upon the face of the picture.

Both Lamont and Martin Lassamour looked upon it with deep and absorbing interest.

Lassamour's paramount feeling was this:—

"Shall I," he said to himself, "or shall I not discover in the portraits the likenesses of the persons who came to me in my strange and terrible dream in the state chamber?"

The awful presentiments of that dream are, we dare say, quite fresh in the minds of the readers of this most eventful history.

One glance at the portrait that the light of Cyprian's lamp fell upon, set the question at rest at once.

Martin Lassamour knew the face at once.

It was one of those he had seen in his dream or vision, whichever it was.

Martin drew a long breath.

"This is terrible," he said.

"Terrible, my good master ?" said Cyprian.

"Yes, boy, yes. But heed it not. You comprehend well what I mean, my friend, Lamont ?"

"I do. You recognise this face ?"

"Yes—yes !"

"Lord bless you, sir," said Cyprian, "that must be some mistake, I should think, with all deference."

"No, boy—no."

"But this was my lady's first husband, you see, gentlemen."

"I know it."

"Do you, though, sir ?"

"I do. Go on, boy—go on, we will see them all. It may be that I may know them all."

Cyprian looked rather surprised at this style of remark from Lassamour; but he went to the next portrait without saying anything about it, and at once turned it.

Again the light then fell upon features well implanted in the memory of Martin Lassamour.

"It is quite needless for us to pursue an investigation of the curious adventure. Let it suffice that as Cyprian, the page, turned each of the portraits, each was so recognised by Lassamour.

They came to the last one.

"No more," said Cyprian; "that is all."

"And enough, too," said Lamont, with a perceptible shudder. "I don't at all wonder at her turning the faces of the portraits to the wall."

"Nor do I," said Martin.

"Why, the sight of them all, if she came through the gallery, would kill her."

"She never dare come through the gallery, though," said Cyprian; "and I should say that it is some years now since she was in this part of the mansion at all."

"No doubt of that."

"Indeed, she don't at all like any mention to be made of this gallery or its contents. But there are other rooms further on which, I assure you, have been shut up for quite a length of time."

"We will see them, boy."

"But how is this," said Lamont; "one of the portraits will not lie flat to the wall ?"

"Ah ! neither will it. Look, Cyprian. It quite projects at the side."

"It does, indeed."

"And why so, boy ?"

"I don't know, sir ; but we will soon see. I will hold it up if you will be so good as to look behind it."

They were all three pretty well occupied now ; for the young page held up the picture, Lamont held the light, and Martin Lassamour carefully looked behind the picture to see what was the nature of the obstruction to its lying flat on the wall.

He was not long in finding it out.

"Ah ! here is a discovery."

"A discovery ! What ?"

"There is a door here."

"Good Lord ! is there ?" said Cyprian, as he let fall the picture in his fright, and nearly hit Lassamour on the head with it.

"How can you be so clumsy ?" said Martin ; "raise it again."

"Would it not be better to take it down ?" suggested Lamont.

"Yes—yes !"

Martin took a knife from his pocket and cut the cord of the frame.

CHAPTER XLV.

ANOTHER OF LADY MARGARET'S VICTIMS COMES TO LIGHT.

THE moment the cord that held the picture to the brass hook in the roof of the gallery was cut, down fell the picture with a sullen sound to the floor.

Martin Lassamour and his friend started.

"That noise may well alarm the house," he said.

"Nay, that it won't," said Cyprian. "It would take a much louder noise than that, noble sir, to reach the ears of any one in the other portion of the mansion."

"It may be so."

"And if it did reach their ears," added the page, "it would only render our being uninterrupted here only the more certain."

"Think you so ?"

"Oh, yes, I know it. The fact is, they will have it that this whole wing is haunted, and so every sound that they might hear from it could but be considered as a sort of a confirmation of that supposed fact."

"True—true !"

"Yes," said Lamont, "that is reasonable enough."

"It is, sirs, as I think."

"You are quite right, my good boy Cyprian, after all," said Martin.

"I should be sorry to deceive you, sir."

"I trust you entirely."

"Well," said Lamont, "shall we now see what we can do, now that we have fairly got rid of the picture, in the way of finding out what mystery there is behind it ?"

The wall now underwent at their hands a very searching kind of investigation.

It appeared that there was a door evidently in it, but so artfully made that it might not be noticed by any merely casual observer.

Indeed if it had been closed fast there can be no doubt but that, even without the picture as a shield to it, it would very easily escape all observation.

But by some means or another it had warped a little, so that the two ends of it were a little projecting from the ordinary level.

That circumstance decided the fact of its existence at once.

"It is a door," said Martin.

"No doubt of that," added Lamont.

"Yes," said Cyprian, "but it seems to be quite fast."

As he spoke he inserted the blade of his dagger in the crevice left between the edge of the door and the wall, and made an effort to move it, but it resisted.

It was quite clear that the portion of the door that was made fast was in the centre of the side edge of it that was to their right hands as they faced it.

But it was not at all likely that the fastening should be of a character to resist much force brought to bear against it.

Martin Lassamour was not the sort of man to pause long over any obstacle, and he said—

"Give me your dagger, Cyprian."

"Yes, sir."

Cyprian handed him the dagger.

By then working it in the crevice right up to the latch of it, Martin succeeded in bringing the very thickest point of the blade into operation.

With one jerk, then, that he gave it aside it was tolerably clear that he must either break the blade of the dagger or at once overcome the fastening of the door.

The latter was the result.

With a sharp crack the door in the wall burst open.

The moment it did so they all three started back, as well they might, for a bundle of something that looked very awful rolled out through the opening at their feet.

This bundle, as it fell on to the floor of the gallery, and as the rays of the light from the lamp gleamed on it, too awfully decided what it was.

It was a dead body in a state of decay of the most horrible character!

The rich dress which it had worn was stained and faded. The body itself was a mass of horrible corruption. The flesh of the face had quite fallen away, and the hands appeared to have been lost entirely.

No doubt as the flesh of the hands had rotted it had rotted with it the cartilages of the bones, and they had one by one fallen off.

A terrible odour, as if a charnel-house had suddenly been opened, came upon the senses of Martin Lassamour and his friends.

No wonder that they all started back with horror, and that it was some few moments before either of the three could find a tongue in which to speak of the terrible sight before them.

It was the page whose fears first urged him to speak.

"Oh, my good master," he cried, "let us fly from this place ; I did not expect—indeed I did not expect to find such a thing as this here."

"Hush, Cyprian—hush !" said Lassamour.

"But it is too horrible."

"It is horrible, boy."

"It is, indeed," said Lamont; "and yet why should we fear it? It is but a spectacle that we must all present, although probably to no mortal eye."

Cyprian kept going further and further off with the light in his hand, so that Martin and his friend Lamont ran a chance of soon being left in the dark altogether.

This was not a pleasant idea with such a sight before them, and Lassamour called to the boy—

"Hold, Sir Page—hold !"

"Yes, sir, I—I——"

"Come hither."

"Is it the light you want, noble sir?"

"Yes—yes."

"Then there it is," said Cyprian, as he placed it on the floor, and then darted back a pace or two. "There it is, noble sir. I beg you will not think me disrespectful or unmindful of your service, but the fact is I cannot make up my mind to come any nearer to the horrible object for the life of me."

"You are cowardly."

"No, no, sir. Show me a foe in flesh and blood, and I will fight for you to the last; but—but—this—oh, horrible!"

"The boy is young," said Lamont. "I pray you urge him not, my friend—his feelings are those of nature."

"Be it so, then," said Lassamour. "But by my troth, Cyprian, I did think there was sterner stuff in you."

"No, my lord, there is not, indeed."

"So I see."

Martin himself now took the light, and although he felt, certainly, some repugnance to doing so, he approached the dead body.

"Come, Lamont," he said, "I would fain find out, if it were possible so to do, who this was in life."

"And I, too."

They both approached so near to the body that, as Martin held the light close over it, they could see that the dress in which it was must have been of the finest character.

By all that they could perceive the apparel had been of velvet, with either gold or richly gilt buttons on it; but owing to the state of the face, they could come to no sort of conclusion as to the age of the person.

"I fear," said Martin, "we shall gain no ntelligence from this mass of decay."

"I fear not."

"Yet, what is that?"

"What, Lassamour?"

"A folded paper seems to be but half-concealed in the pocket of the vest. Do you not see it?"

"I do."

"It may enlighten us."

"Yes, but—but——"

Lamont shuddered.

"I comprehend you. You would say, what hand can bring its will to be stretched forth to take it?"

"It is my thought."

"I have a mode, though, that may save that horrible and that most sad disagreeable. Take the light."

"Yes, yes."

Martin Lassamour drew his sword, and very carefully with the point of it ripped the pocket, through the half decayed exterior of which the paper showed itself plainly."

A folded paper fell from it.

"Now, I think," said Lassamour, as he drew the folded paper towards him, with the point of his sword, "we may, surely, avail ourselves of what information this paper may chance to give to us."

"Oh, yes, yes; now we may."

Martin lifted the paper from the floor.

It must be confessed that, although he, perhaps, did not show to any great extent that it was so, yet that it was, in truth, only by a very great effort and command over his nerves that even Martin Lassamour could pick up that note.

Its association with the dead imparted to it rather a horrible character.

It was damp with exhalations from the dead body, and Martin, at the moment that he held it in his hand, blessed his stars that he had on a pair of thick riding gloves.

"Bring hither the light, Lamont."

"Yes, and we may as well read this paper if there be anything to read upon it, at a greater distance from its once former owner."

"True—true."

They walked on along the gallery in the direction of which Cyprian was standing.

"Have you found anything, my good sir?"

"Yes, Cyprian. You can hold the light, now, while Lamont and I read this paper."

"Yes, sir—yes. Will you be so good, too, as to utter the words aloud as you read them, that your poor servant may be a partaker of what news they contain?"

"Yes, Cyprian, I will."

CHAPTER XLVI.

THE MYSTERIOUS PAPER REVEALS ANOTHER TRAGEDY AT PLEASAUNCE.

ARTIN LASSA-MOUR'S hand shook as he held the paper, and well it might, for he was, after all, but a young man, and this strange sort of communion with the dead was just the sort of thing, above all others, to affect his imagination.

The writing had grown old and faded, and yellow; and in some places it had suffered so much from contact with the decaying body, in the vicinity of which it had so long lain, that here and there a word was altogether gone.

Still Martin Lassamour, amid the breathless attention of those who were listening to him, managed to read as follows:—

"Norfolk House, Strand.

"If these few lines should come into the possession of any one—that one, be he or she whom they may, will be pleased at once to come to the conclusion that I am murdered.

"This paper will be by me immediately destroyed if I leave Pleasaunce House, so that then it can lead no one astray; but if I do not lose it in life, why, then, it remains in my clothing as a proof of foul play.

"I have that faith in murder coming to light, that I believe sooner or later this paper will reach the hands of some one who can and who will take steps to avenge the foul deed by which I am done to death.

"My brother, Sir Archibald Renton, had married the Lady Margaret, the fair and rich mistress of Pleasaunce House at Richmond, as it is called.

"Last week he mysteriously died.

"I brought with me a learned physician to examine the body, but he could only say that the death was very mysterious, and that he could not account for it in any way; so I have been compelled, this day, to let my poor brother be buried in peace.

"My visit, however, to Pleasaunce House has been for the purpose of trying to engage the Lady Margaret in such talk, as might condemn her out of her own mouth, if possible.

"She may try to take my life if she should find me dangerous; but if she does, this paper will tell that I came to Pleasaunce House, and that there I must have been murdered.

"Avenge me, and save others from the same fate!

"That is the prayer of

"CHARLES RENTON."

This very strange document had a date upon it which threw the writing of it back for the space of six years.

When he had concluded reading it, Martin Lassamour let it drop from his hands.

He looked at Lamont, and Lamont looked at him, and Cyprian looked at them both.

"Good God!" said Lamont.

"This is conclusive, then," said Lassamour.

"Let us all fly," cried Cyprian.

"No, boy—no. Not yet."

"But we are all in danger!"

"Stop a bit. Of the guilt of the Lady Margaret in this matter, there is, unhappily, but too strong a presumption. All I can say now is that it has put me at once and thoroughly upon my guard."

"Yes," said Lamont, "and you must be specially careful now, my dear friend, that poison does not do its work with you."

"I will, indeed."

"Oh, dear—oh, dear!" said Cyprian. "I am for us all three getting out of the house as quickly as possible."

"No—no! The danger is not so imminent as that."

"It is—it is, good sirs. There is Loon, the waiting-woman of my lady. She is a sort of spy upon everybody in the mansion. I dread her more than I do any one else."

"But she is not on our track, my good Cyprian."

"I don't know that, sir."

Of course Cyprian had no idea just then of the fate that had overtaken Loon.

If the page had but known that the waiting-woman was no more, he would, indeed, and in truth, have rejoiced greatly on that fact.

"Come—come!" said Martin Lassamour. "This is a very awful discovery that we have made, and I quite dread what a still further search may disclose to us in this house; but yet it is quite necessary that we should take cool and calm counsel with each other."

"It is so," said Lamont.

"It is—it is."

"Oh, sir," said Cyprian, and he quite trembled as he spoke, "let me beg and implore of you to be so good as to grant me one favour."

"What is it, boy ?"

"It is that—that——"

"Come—come, speak out."

"That you will be pleased to consider the dreadful discovery you have now made as enough for one night, and that you will take some other opportunity than this present one of resuming the search in this wing of the house."

Cyprian was evidently in such a state of agitation while he made this request, that Lamont glanced at Lassamour, and said in a low voice—

"I think, my good friend, that if it be, as I think it is, important that we should have Master Cyprian's guidance and aid in the exploration of this portion of Pleasaunce House, it will be quite necessary to put it off for the present."

"Oh, yes, yes," said Cyprian, "I beg to say that I am quite willing, of course, to be of all the assistance in the world, but I really am so cut up at what has happened to-day, or rather to-night, that I feel I shall run the chance of fainting away if I don't soon see the open air."

"Be it so, then," said Lassamour.

"A thousand thanks, noble sir."

"It is well decided," said Lamont.

"But hark you, Cyprian," said Lassamour, in a deep and solemn tone of voice, "it concerns your own life, as well as ours, that you should place such a guard upon your expressions and your feelings, that the Lady Margaret should not entertain the slightest suspicion that you know aught criminal to her safety."

"Oh, trust me for that, sir."

"Are you sure you can so comport yourself ?"

"Quite—quite."

"For if not, it would be easier and safer for you to leave the mansion at once."

"No, noble sir, I would rather stay."

"Be it so."

"At least while you stay; and yet——"

"You want to go ?"

"I do, indeed; and if I could but induce you to go, I should be glad indeed."

"It is my mission, and my duty to stay, Cyprian. I have a feeling that Heaven has put upon me the duty of unmasking this female fiend, and of solving the dreadful mystery of the deaths of all my predecessors."

"It must be so, sir."

All this time that Cyprian spoke, though, he took good care to be getting nearer and nearer still to the door of the great gallery, and as he carried the light, Lassamour and his friend Lamont had really not much choice but to go after him.

It was an immense relief to poor Cyprian when they had descended to the room below, in which there was the strange dragon painted on the roof.

"Now," he said, with a long breath, "I feel a little easier."

"And if the truth must be told," said Lamont, "so do I, my good friend, Cyprian."

"And I," said Lassamour.

"Well, sirs," said Cyprian, "I am right glad to hear you both say that much, for it makes my own fears appear to me to be not quite so ridiculous, you know, as they otherwise would. I like to be a coward in good company."

Lassamour smiled faintly.

They now all three made their way into the open air as soon as possible.

The moonlight was resting very sweetly upon trees, and flowers, and lawn, and there was a sweet and delicate calmness in the air that was excessively grateful to the senses.

"Ah, this is a change, indeed," said Lamont."

"It is—it is."

"And greatly for the better, too, I should say," replied Cyprian, as if the words had been addressed to him.

At this instant there came the baying of trumpets on the night air at some distance in the direction of the high-road.

Lassamour started.

"What is that?" he said.

"Trumpets, I take it," said Lamont. "There must be some soldiers passing."

"Oh, dear no," said Cyprian, "I can guess what it is."

"What is it?"

"Why, Lambeth Fair begins to-morrow, and I will warrant that those trumpets belong to some of the mummers and the mountebanks who will be at that place of merriment in full force.

"It may be so."

"Ah, dear me !" sighed Cyprian, "I know one pretty girl who will be there."

CHAPTER XLVII.

LADY MARGARET FINALLY DISPOSES OF HER WAITING MAID.

PON the night air the trumpets sounded again clearly and shrilly, and the martial tune that they played moved the heart of Lassamour.

"Oh, would that I had continued in the wild and adventurous life of a soldier that once I led," he cried, "rather than have cooped myself up in this place with such a bride!"

"It would have been better," said Lamont.

"Oh, yes, my young friend; but the time of my free action will come again."

"I think it will."

"And when it does I shall take a last look at Pleasaunce, and never hope to see it again. Cyprian?"

"Yes, my good lord."

"You will be my page, I am sure, instead of a lady's?"

"For a time, yes, noble sir."

"Only for a time?"

"Why, sir, I can't always be a page, you know; and even now—(here Cyprian stood on his tip-toes)—even now I find that I am getting a trifle too tall for a page."

"It is true, Cyprian; you are indeed."

"I am quite afraid you think so, sir."

"I do think so."

"And so do I," said Lamont. "But if your lord goes to the wars, Cyprian, you can go as his squire, if not as his page."

"Yes, so he can."

"Why a—" said Cyprian, "I—a—The truth is——."

"What?"

"You see, a married man——"

"A what?"

"A married man, I think, has nothing to do with the wars; and he ought, in my opinion, to stay at home and take care of his wife and his expected babies."

"Ha! ha!"

"Yes, sir; you may laugh, but it's a fact."

"My good Cyprian, I believe it is to be a fact. You are going to wed the fair daughter of Langdon, the ferryman?"

"Ah, I hope so."

"And I have promised you certain aid, so be assured, Cyprian, that I will keep my word."

"Of that I do feel quite assured, my noble master; and I intend to take the sweet little creature, with your good leave, to Lambeth Fair to-morrow."

"You may."

"A thousand thanks. But I will be home early in case you should want me, or the Lady Margaret inquire for me."

"Ah, yes, Cyprian, that is well thought of. Mind you, for the present, you must make no kind of difference in your services to the Lady Margaret."

"It might be fatal to him if he did," said Lamont.

"Trust me for that," said Cyprian; "I know my own danger too well to tamper with it, good sir; and I will in all respects so comport myself to the Lady Margaret, that she shall see no change in me."

"You will do well. And now, Cyprian, we will not trouble you further to-night, but should Lamont and I determine upon any particular course of action, you shall be no stranger to it."

"Thanks, noble sir."

Cyprian went into the mansion by another entrance, and his master, with Lamont, walked to the inn at which they had left their horses.

When they got there and had mounted, the clock of a little church in the immediate neighbourhood struck the hour of nine.

Lassamour counted the strokes.

"Lamont," he said, "let us breathe our steeds a little by a gentle ride."

"Be it so."

"For my part, I feel just at this time as if the air of Pleasaunce House would choke me."

"It is a frightful place."

"On—on, then, to the road to London, my good friend, even if we go not so far as there."

It was not very likely that Lassamour and Lamont would go on the road to London without reaching the city; but we must leave them for the present, in order to return to Pleasaunce, and follow out the adventures of the Lady Margaret with her waiting woman, the poisoned Loon.

It will be recollected that the Lady Margaret had made ample preparations for the disposal of the dead body of the poisoned maid, but that she had not actually disposed of her.

After thus opening the sort of hole in the floor of the greenhouse, Lady Margaret, leaving all doors open behind her on her route, hurried up stairs—up the iron spiral stairs to her own chamber again.

There lay the dead body of the maid.

"Ah," said Lady Margaret, "that busy tongue and plotting brain is still enough now!"

She went then to the door of her chamber and opened it, and then slipping out into the vestibule that lay beyond it, she listened intently for any sound that might be stirring in the house.

There was none.

"Pleasaunce is still enough," she said; "Lassamour and that new friend of his, whom I like not, for I have caught him glancing too curiously at me, are at their cups at the tavern in London by this time. Well, be it so!—Yes, be it so! We shall soon see what that will come to."

She closed the door again, and carefully locked it.

The Lady Margaret, in good truth, need not have been anything so particular about the fastening of the room door, for there was not a living soul in the mansion who was at all likely to intrude upon her.

But she was one of those persons who like to make assurance doubly sure.

There are very many evil disposed persons—persons with wicked and depraved hearts enough to commit a murder—but out of all that number, there is not, perhaps, the smallest per centage of them that, without trembling, would approach or touch the corpse from which they had just hurried the breath of life.

But Lady Margaret was in good truth, and it is to the credit of human nature that she was so, an exception to all general rules.

She had no fears.

She might have said with Lady Macbeth—

"It is the eye of childhood fears a painted devil. The sleeping and the dead are but as pictures."

Certain it is, she either had no feeling of dread for the corpse she had produced, so to speak, or she did in a most strange and marvellous manner succeed in keeping such a feeling most completely under her control.

She approached the corpse of Loon.

"Come," she said, "dead piece of nature's workmanship, I must prepare to dispose of you."

She dragged the corpse to the little panelled door of her room.

"Much I fear me," she muttered to herself, "that there is no sort of poison but will leave its taint so clinging to the corpse that has been done to death by it, that a cunning chemist might detect the act."

In these few words might be found the motives of the Lady Margaret in taking such pains to get rid of the dead body of her waiting-maid.

And in those few words, too, may be found abundant reason to conclude that it was not by poison that she had disposed of her six husbands.

The whole of them had been left to the examination of all their friends and relations, so that she certainly had, in their destruction, adopted some plan that gave her no uneasiness with regard to its discovery.

After getting the corpse of the waiting-maid to the little secret door in the wall, Lady Margaret herself stepped over it, or rather we may say that she actually stepped upon it in her path, and herself passed through the panelled door very fast.

She then stooped, and seizing the body by the shoulders, began to drag it after her.

That was, no doubt, her easiest mode of getting it along.

But hardly had she got half way through the doorway, when there came a distinct tap upon the upper panel of her chamber door.

Even the boldest self-control of the Lady Margaret was startled at this sound, and small wonder was it that it was so when we come to think of what she was about.

She let the dead body drop at her feet, and uttered a short cry of alarm, and then she said,—

"Hush! oh, hush! What is that?"

The tap at the door came again.

Lady Margaret shook now for a moment or two like an autumn leaf in the gale of wind that is to dash it to the earth.

But a very short time sufficed to enable her to recover from this state of alarm.

"Courage! courage!" she said.

In a moment she dragged the body right through the doorway, and then she stepped on, and over it, again into her room.

With a sharp snap of the spring that held it, she shut the secret panel in the wall.

The tap came again at the door.

Pale as death, partly from rage, and partly from apprehension, Lady Margaret called out,—

"Who is there? Who knocks?"

There was no reply.

"Who knocks?" she said again.

Still no answer.

Lady Margaret strode to the door, and flung it open.

CHAPTER XLVIII.

CONSCIENCE BEGINS IT'S WORK WITH THE LADY MARGARET.

 O the intense surprise, and somewhat too the consternation, at that moment, of the murderess, there was no one at her chamber door when she went and opened it to see.

Lady Margaret trembled excessively.

"What is this?" she said, "what can this be? Am I at last, after all that I have seen and done, after all that I have gone through, to be made the fool of my senses?"

She closed the door, and replaced a night bell upon it.

Never had the mind of Lady Margaret been in such a state of alarm as it now was. Her colour went and came in a manner that ashamed even herself, for she said that she felt that it did so.

She tottered to a chair, as she gasped out the words,—

"What if it should, indeed, turn out to be true that the spirits of the dead have power to visit this world for the torment of those against whom even their purer minds may cherish a world of torment and revenge. What if it be true that the time will come when I shall never be alone."

This idea was torture.

"No—no!" she cried, impatiently. "Of all things that I have hitherto fought up against, and conquered, superstition has been my most ready foe. I will fight with it again, and I will conquer it again."

She sprang to her feet.

"What was that?"

A low mysterious tapping at her door again.

A faintness came over the Lady Margaret, and for a moment or two it seemed to her as if every sense but that of hearing had deserted her.

That one, though, being the one through which she had already achieved so much terror, appeared to be preternaturally acute.

The tapping came again.

Aroused now by despair, she flew to the door, and moving the night bell by a single touch of her hand, she sprang out into the corridor beyond.

"Who is there?" she cried. "Who is there?"

All was still.

"Speak, devil! fiend! Human tongue or ghostly one, I say speak to me!"

A loud ringing laugh ran through the corridor, but she could see nothing; and she staggered back to her room again.

"I think," she said, "that I am mad, or that my time has come."

The condition of mind of this terribly guilty woman was now one of the most painful and agonising description.

She sat upon a low devotional chair for some time, and with her hands clasped over her face, she rocked her body to and fro, uttering deep groans.

It was quite impossible that anything human could go through such an excess of emotion as that, without leaving the visible marks of its passage upon the face.

So was it with the Lady Margaret.

When at length this storm of her guilty soul wore itself out, and when she rose to her feet, the look that was upon her face was truly appalling. She seemed in that quarter of an hour, for it evidently was not more, to have lived ten years.

But she did not trust herself to look at her own face, although a mirror was close at hand in which she might have done so.

She went to her chamber door again, to be sure that it was fast, and having ascertained that it was so, she spoke in a low, earnest, half choking tone of voice—

"It must be done—it must be done! To be now left undone, were worse than to be never have begun. It must be done, and done at once, too."

She alluded, as her actions quickly enough showed, to the disposal of the dead body of the waiting woman in the place that she had so duly disguised and prepared for it.

She opened the little door that lead, now, to the secret staircase, and there was the body of the waiting woman just as she had left it. She again trod upon the insensible form as she passed over it, and descended a few steps of the spiral staircase.

It had been the intention of the Lady Margaret to drag it after her, as being preferable to the trouble of attempting to carry it.

But when she got in a position so to do she altered her mind.

She came rapidly back, and then pushing the body to the verge of the first stair, she said—

"Go—go!"

She toppled it over at once, and it went with a deadening fall the whole flight of the spiral staircase.

This was certainly an easier mode of sending the body down to the foot of the staircase than either pulling, or pushing, or carrying it.

But how few are those who would have done as the Lady Margaret did?

Even she, callous and cruel as she was, when she heard the dull, heavy blow with which the body came upon the stone flags at the foot of the staircase—even she, we say, gave a shudder.

But she followed it.

She felt now all the necessity, if she would have any safety or any impunity from the consequences of the act she had committed, she must at once dispose of that horrible, bruised, maimed, and poisoned witness against her.

To drag the body, now, through the secret door in the wall of the summer-house, and to place it over the very brink of the opening in the floor of it, was but the work now of another minute.

With one push she toppled the dead body head foremost through the little square opening in the floor of the summer-house.

It was gone.

Heaven only knows where it went; but after it had gone some few seconds, there came up through the opening a faint noise, like a splash of distant—very far distant water.

Then all was still.

The Lady Margaret replaced the stone.

She gathered together some dried and some decayed leaves and other matter, and spread them over the edge of it, where it joined to the other stones with which the greenhouse was formed, and so she took away the appearance of the stone she had lifted having been disturbed.

She felt a sensation of relief when this was done. At all events, she considered that burdensome object was disposed of, and could no longer, by any likelihood, if not by any possibility be evidence against her.

The night was now getting far advanced, and the Lady Margaret crept silently back to her own chamber, full of strange thoughts.

She carefully closed both the secret doors—the one at the foot of the secret staircase, and the one at the head of it, and then she raked together the embers of the fire that were upon the hearth, and then she sat down to think.

Yes, that bold, bad woman, dared to think.

Oh, what strange and terrible thoughts must they have been that found a home in such a brain as that!

After a time she rose and took a small light, and trimmed it carefully.

"Yes," she said, "yes, I will go now and look at them all. I will see that they are, at all events, undisturbed; and then, as I cannot sleep, I will look at his portrait."

She passed out of her own room with the lamp in her hand, and made her way slowly but surely to the portrait gallery.

As she crossed the threshold a dimness came over the flame of the little lamp that she carried.

The Lady Margaret shook like one in an ague fit, and then she, with a shriek, fell to the ground.

A tall figure glided past her, and then another, and then another, until seven had so passed her, and as they so passed on, they each pointed a shadowy finger at her.

They were the shades of the seven husbands that had preceded Martin Lassamour as lords of the fair estates of Pleasuance, and of the fair lady who had so much to bestow.

The cry of the Lady Margaret was loud enough to reach the ears of the domestics in the old kitchen of the place.

With appalled looks they sprang to their feet—that is to say, some half-dozen of them, who had sat up long beyond the proper hour for retiring to rest, just to sip some more of the old ale, and to listen to the ghost stories, which one of their number had a very peculiar and amiable tact in telling.

"The Lord preserve us!" cried one; "what was that?"

They all looked thunderstruck.

"Did you hear it?"

"Yes—yes."

"What was it?"

"A scream."

"Yes; but from what lips?"

"No mortal's, you may be sure."

"Then let us all go to-bed at once, for the love of Heaven, and pay no sort of attention to it."

CHAPTER XLIX.

THE FAIR AT LAMBETH MARSHES PROGRESSES WELL.

IN order to revert to better people, we gladly leave the gloomy precincts of Pleasuance House to gayer scenes. It will be recollected that on the following morning was to be the commencement of the old fair of Lambeth, and it is to those of our *dramatis personæ* who will be at that ancient merry making that we now conduct the reader's attention.

And first, of the fair itself.

The spot on which the fair used to be held is now covered with houses of very questionable respectability, and with manufactories of very questionable odour.

At the period of which we write, though, Lambeth was by no means the low pestiferous neighbourhood it now is.

To be sure, in consequence of lying low, and being so closely contiguous to the Thames as it was, it was always liable to be flooded at intervals, and so had not by any manner of means a good character in a sanitary point of view; but still in the summer time of the year, and in general dry seasons, there were very many sweet spots about old Lambeth.

It was upon rather an extensive district, called the marshes, owing to the fact that it, of all others, was most liable to the overflowing of the Thames, that the fair was held.

This fair was looked forward to all over the country as a source of feasting, and jollity, and merriment, to young and old. Of course, as it is ever the case in England, drunkenness formed the staple commodity at the meeting; for, strange to say, it seems impossible that the lower orders in England can get together for any purpose without a strong inducement to intoxication in its worst forms.

The fair then covered an area of some twenty-five acres of ground, and upon that space was to be found every description of amusement so popular at such gatherings, and which are too well known to our readers to need our detailing.

There was one feature, though, at the old English fairs which then existed, and which we are very sorry indeed to see exists no longer.

We allude to dancing.

Then it was considered as a main part of the amusement of the young to tread a measure in some of the old country dances.

Now it is quite out of the question to get up a real dance at a fair.

With these few brief remarks, then, we will leave the reader to imagine that on the morning immediately succeeding that eventful night at Pleasaunce, the old fair of Lambeth began in all its glory.

It will be found that the events of this fair had a very great effect upon the fortunes of those persons in whom we are interested.

In the first place, we will now introduce the reader to the crypt of our Ladye Chapel at Southwark, where at a very early hour of the morning, indeed, three persons might have been seen conversing together.

They have only just met.

The one who seemed to be alone in his own interests, and to be conversing with the other two leant his back against a tomb, and so wrapped himself up in his cloak, that it was next thing to impossible to see anything whatever of his countenance.

The other two were by no manner of means so particular; but stood in all the swagger of their faded and dusty finery, exposed to the gaze of any one who might come that way.

But these two persons who kept such open looks to the world did so more in appearance than reality.

They were, in good truth, both of them completely disguised.

One of them had covered his complexion with a kind of mask, that completely altered its colour.

The other wore a patch over one eye, and a false beard and a false moustache.

We may inform the reader, though, with whom it is not necessary to have any secrets, that these two ruffians were none other than Glass and Tabby, the two rascals who had been employed by Sir Warrene De Volence to assassinate his foe, Martin Lassamour.

After this, it is almost unnecessary to say that the personage in the cloak who was leaning against the tomb was no other than our old and anything but esteemed acquaintance, De Volence himself.

"Well, noble sir," said Tabby, "here are we as big as life, and twice as natural. What would your nobleness have with us? Ha! Here are——"

"Silence!"

"Oh!"

"Silence, I say! Do you take this for the common room of a tavern, that you brawl away in it as you seem to please?"

"Well, I—a——"

"His honour is quite right," said Gloss. "Hold your row, Tabby, do. I'm greatly ashamed of you."

"Body o' me! what for?"

"What for?"

"Yes, what for?"

"Oh, for everything."

"Then I——"

"Hark you, gentlemen," said De Volence, with such an emphasis upon the word "gentlemen," that it was much more insulting than as if it had given place to any terms of ordinary abuse—"Hark you, gentlemen. I told you to meet me here to give you further instructions, for the sake of giving them in a place where we were not likely to be disturbed; but if you prefer your own conclusion to mine, please to say so, and I leave you to yourselves at once."

"Oh, no, noble sir; quite the reverse."

"Quite—quite."

"Very well; then attend to me."

"But, after all," said Tabby, "I have always heard that this was anything but a quiet place, this chapel of our ladye; for it used to be full of all sorts of saints and sinners."

"But not lately."

"Indeed, sir?"

"No, not lately."

"And why, noble sir, is it that they come no more, as they used to do, to such a well-known shrine?"

"It is unsafe."

"Unsafe?"

"Even so."

"How—how?"

"A portion of the roof has fallen in, and the saints don't at all wish to go to Heaven a bit sooner than they can possibly help; so they stay away, in case the remainder should come down."

"The devil!"

"Where is he?"

"Noble sir, I didn't mean he was here."

"Oh!"

"I only just said the devil in a common sort of way. But, noble sir, don't you think that if the roof of the chapel is unsafe for those saints you speak of, it may be so for us'"

"Yes, if——"

"Oh, it is no,t then?"

"Not as I think. The portion of the roof that fell was, no doubt, unsafe, and acted as a drag upon the remainder; but being down, I take it, the place is now secure enough."

"Ah, it may be so."

"And now to business."

"Noble sir," said Glass, in his oiliest tones. "the little job is not done."

"So I find."

"But, noble sir, it will be done."

"So I hope to find."

"It is as good as done; but the fact is, noble sir, although we have hung upon his very footsteps, it has so turned out that we have never been able to take him at a disadvantage, or to drag him to any spot where, with any chance of safety, the deed may be done."

"That's it," said Tabby.

"Just so, noble sir. It has ever happened that there was either some obstruction present, or some obstruction sure to be present, before the blow could be struck."

"Well, be it so."

"It is so, noble sir, we assure you."

"I take your words for it, and need for more. I am not so unreasonable a man as to suppose, for one half moment, that such a job can be done at any hour or place appointed like any ordinary piece of business. I leave it to you both to get it out of hand as soon as time, and place, and opportunity will permit you."

"We will, indeed."

"And," growled Tabby, "it's quite a pleasure to do a little bit of business for such a nice gentleman as you are."

"Oh, you flatter me.,'

"Not at all—oh, not at all."

"Well, be it so. And now the reason why I sent to you both to meet me here was not to chide you for delay, or to know why the delay had arisen. I had faith in your wish and desire to do the business as speedily as possible."

"Yes, my noble sir."

"Hold your row," said Glass. "The gentleman has got another little job for us, I can see, by the corner of his eye."

"I have."

"Bravo! bravo! We will do your honour's work well for you."

CHAPTER L.

DE VOLENCE THREATENS THE PEACE OF THE FAIR AMY.

E VOLENCE was now silent for a few moments; but when he spoke again, it was with a suppressed bitterness of tone and manner that showed how much his passion was interested in this new scheme.

Tabby and Glass could not very well comprehend that silence, and the former cried out at length—

"Noble sir, you may depend upon us in any sort of emergency. Fire and fury, noble sir! I say you may depend upon us. Blood and thunder, noble sir! I say, that——"

"Silence!" cried De Volence.

He paced the aisle of the old church to and fro for some seconds, and then pausing, he said—

"The little affair in which I wish to engage you both now is one that will require courage and caution of no ordinary character. I almost dread that you are not the men to carry it out."

"Not the men?"

"No, I fear me not."

"Fire and fury, noble sir! only tell us what it is, and you will see it done in a twinkling. Is it to pull the king's nose? Is it to ——"

"Pshaw! Listen to me."

"With all our ears."

"Do you know the old ferry at Lambeth?"

"We do."

"Do you know Langdon, the ferryman?"

"Ay, truly," said Glass; "and I know that he has two of the sweetest cherry-cheeked, blue eyed girls that ever a sinner looked upon. I know that they are so much alike in beauty, that I would long ago have taken one of them to myself, only I did not know which to choose."

"You?"

"Ay, my master, even I."

"Ha! ha! Well—well, it matters not. There is one of the girls goes by the name of Amy."

"She does."

"Well, then, do you think that for a good hundred gold pieces it would be possible to place her in a house that I can point out to you on one of the arches of London Bridge?"

Tabby whistled profoundly.

Glass rubbed his nose with the hilt of his dagger.

It was quite evident that the two rascals were rather discomfited at this proposal on the part of the villanous De Volence.

"You cannot do it?" he cried.

"Nay, my good master," said Tabby, "we did not say that we could not do it; only we felt that—that, in a way of speaking, you see, it was——"

"Rather troublesome?" put in Glass.

"Exactly."

"Because, you see, noble sir, that same Langdon, the ferryman, is a most powerful knave with the quarter-staff; and so, you see——"

"Oh, you are afraid of the ferryman? Now, I tell you that you will not at all encounter him. I have certain intelligence that the two girls will go to the fair to-day."

"You have, noble sir?"

"I have, indeed; and upon that certain intelligence you may rely."

"Of course—of course; but does your honour think that your honour may not by a possibility be deceived in this matter?'

"No. The girls have two lovers, curses on them!"

"Amen!" said Tabby. "Why don't you say 'Amen!' Glass, when our noble friend De Volence curses somebody?"

"Well, I do. Amen!"

"The one," added De Volence, "is a rascal by name Robert Lee."

"Ah! the pedler?"

"The same."

"Humph! I hope——"

"What do you hope?"

"That when I lay hands on any pretty little minion of his he may not be by, that is all."

"Well, the other girl has a lover, too, or rather two lovers, for I have taken some pains to make myself acquainted with all this affair. One is Cyprian, a young page to the Lady Margaret La samour, and the other is a booby boy, by name Gamiel Gander."

"Ha! ha! We know him."

"That is well. Now, hark you. It is likely enough that at the fair the pedler will be by far too much engaged with his wares to attend to his sweetheart; but she will be there for all that. The sisters, too, will keep together, and Cyprian the young page, if by force or fraud he can get away from Pleasaunce House, will be there too."

"Good."

"That would not be good, for they must be separated in some way; and how to do that I will leave entirely to your good genius; but seize the girl and carry her away in safety, and my life on it it will be the best night's work you ever did."

"We will make pretty sure of that, noble sir; but whither are we to carry her?"

"On the third arch of London Bridge there is a house with a green canopy."

"We know it."

"Go there with her, and tap thrice at the door, and when any one appears at it, say, 'One—two—three!' and just push the girl in, and leave the place then as soon as you can. I shall consider that to be good service done to me."

"It is as good as done, noble sir. You may consider it as good as done."

"And the gold pieces?" said Glass.

"Call upon me at my lodgings in the Temple on the morrow, and they are yours."

"Be it so.'

"And now as for this Martin Lassamour?"

"Oh, be easy about him, your honour—be quite easy about him, we beg of you. You will hear the last of him to-day. We have a plan upon foot, you may depend upon it, that will settle that little portion of the business. When we have disposed of the girl, we shall dispose of him."

"Be it so. I hope that I may trust you both to the execution of this matter?"

"You may, noble sir—you may, indeed. It is all as good as done."

De Volence inclined his head, and then with a grim smile he stalked out of the church.

Tabby and Glass remained for a few minutes in deep and anxious consultation together in the aisle, and then Tabby said, in a low tone—

"Come on; she will write the letter, you may depend upon it, and so we shall have Lassamour in our power, and put an end to that job."

They both left the church, and at about a stone's throw from it they separated, and agreed to meet again in an hour at a tavern near to Milbank.

Tabby went on alone, now, through a labyrinth of very low and dirty streets, close to the marshes, until he fairly stopped at a miserable house, the outer door of which had long since disappeared.

The house was from top to bottom in the occupation of the very poorest of people, and the staircase was almost blocked with all sorts of abominations.

No one paid the least attention to Tabby as he ascended to the top of this mansion of squalor and wretchedness.

He paused at a door on the topmost landing, and then listened intently.

There was no sound from within.

"Curse her!" he muttered; "she has never gone out, surely; or is she dead at last?"

He pushed the door open, and entered a miserable attic, destitute of almost every furniture. On a miserable bed, made of the most dilapidated of mattresses laid upon the floor, lay a woman, apparently in a deep sleep

"Oh," said Tabby, "there she is."

He paused, and resting his chin upon his hand, he looked at the miserable, attenuated, squalid form before him in silence for some time.

Then he spoke in a low tone.

"Well, it's a queer world we live in. Who would think, now, to look at her, that she had once been a duke's leman, and about as pretty a piece of womankind as you would wish to see in a summer's day? Ah!"

The philosophy of Tabby was a feeling that was not likely to last very long.

"Hilloa!" he cried, in a loud voice.

The poor creature on the mattress awoke with a scream of affright.

"Hilloa! Don't you know me?" said Tabby.

"Know you?"

"Yes. I'm Tabby. Come, my lass, I've a job for you."

"For me?"

"Yes. You are quite a scholar, you know, in your way, and you have gained many a crown for writing a love letter from some Simple simon to his sweetheart before to-day, or I know nothing about it."

CHAPTER LI.

SHOWS THAT IN THE FALLEN THERE IS SOME VIRTUE YET LEFT.

PON hearing these words from Tabby, the wretched creature raised herself upon her arm, and looked intently at him.

"A crown, did you say?"

"Ay, old girl. A silver crown.'

"Oh, yes, yes, I will do it."

"Then up with you, and sit at this table, that don't, I see, boast of too many legs; and mind you do it well. Come, now, set about it."

"Paper—I have no paper. I have a pen and some ink. No one would give a tester for them. You must go and buy paper."

"Confound it! so I suppose I must."

Tabby ran down the stairs, and made his way to a stationer's that was near, and bought several sheets of paper, with which he returned to the abode of the poor wretch who was to write a letter for him, since it was very far, indeed, beyond the powers of Tabby himself to do such a feat.

When he was gone, the poor woman had risen from her squalid couch, and made a faint attempt to put her room in order, so that it evidently did not present so wretched an appearance quite as it had done.

She had lit a few sticks in the chimney, and there was a fitful sort of blaze going and coming at intervals. It was, in truth, an apology for a fire.

"Why, how now, Doll," said Tabby, with a sneer that he did not affect to conceal, "you look quite sweet, now, that you do."

"Do I?"

"Yes, to be sure. Why, I'm half inclined to make you an offer of my hand and fortune. Ha! ha!"

"You?"

"Yes, me."

"You forget that I am not at every ruffian's disposal who chooses to say such things."

"Ruffians?"

"Yes, ruffian, and cursed thief."

"Have a care, Doll. I know that you have a sharp tonge when you like to set it wagging, but I have as sharp a dagger; and if I have much more of that sort of thing, I'll earn the name you give me."

"You?" cried the woman, as in a moment she produced a small stiletto from some portion of her dress where it was concealed. "I defy you, villain! I defy you utterly and entirely. Write your letter yourself."

"Nay—nay!"

"Off with you!"

"But, good Doll, there is the crown. Only look at it, now. A good silver crown as ever was, you see. Come—come; why, it will buy you half a score of comforts. You must."

"God! yes, it will."

"Then let us be friends."

"No—no!"

"You must."

"I won't be friends; but I will write the letter. You can dictate it to me. Now—go on."

"Well—a—I—a—Hem!"

"Go on."

"On? Oh—a—well—'Pon honour, now, what an odd thing it is that I can't think of how to begin it. You see, Mistress Doll, it is to come from a young girl to a gentleman that she has fallen in love with, and she wants him to meet her at eleven to-night, by the old cross on the Lambeth marshes, in the bridle road through the wood. Do you know it?"

"I do."

"Then the poor girl, you see, wants him to meet her there, and of course he will."

"Likely enough."

"Oh, yes. Ha! ha! When did a pretty girl ever write to a rich young gallant to meet her in a wood, and he refuse—eh?"

"I don't know."

"Well—well; now, from what I have told you, you know just the sort of letter to write, you see. Write it sweet, and tender, and modest. Ha! ha!"

The wretched woman drew the paper towards her, and wrote for some few moments, and then she read to Tabby what she had written.

"Noble sir,—This comes from one who loves you, and who has much to say to you, if you will meet her at eleven this night by the old stone cross on the bridle path across the marshes. Oh, noble sir, I am a young maiden, and it is hard to love and not say so. Why did I ever see you? But I can write no more. Oh, come—come!"

"Will that do?" said Doll.

"Capital! Oh, Lord, what a thing it is to have a bad pen. Why, Doll, you are a perfect genius. Ha! ha! that will bring him. It would stir up a toad to love. Ha! ha! It is better than good."

"Well?"

"I say well."

"But the name?"

"The—a—the name?"

"Yes, the name of the girl. Do you think that this gallant to whom you are about to send this epistle is a conjurer, that he can find out who speaks to him in it?"

"By Jove, I—a—didn't think of that Doll?"

"What now?"

"You will be secret?"

"As the grave."

"Well—well, put down 'Amy Langdon' at the foot of the letter."

"Amy Langdon?"

"Yes, that's the girl's name."

"It is down. But——"

"But what!"

DE VOLENCE WATCHING HIS EMISSARIES.

"Don't you know that the grist of a lady's letter is ever in the postcript?"

"Oh, is it?"

"It is so."

"Then pop one down."

"I will."

"Let it be to the purpose."

"You shall read it for yourself, Tabl ̇

"I! Lord bless you, while they were educating me when I was a small boy, do you know, they quite forgot the reading. They taught me everything that a gentle-man ought to know; but reading slipped their memory altogether."

"And writing, too."

"Why, a—yes, and you may say writing, too. But you can read it to me the same, you know, as you write the letter."

"True; I can, and will."

Doll, as she was called, now wrote the following postcript to the letter—

"P.S.—The above letter is a gross and wicked forgery, and he to whom it is addressed is advised to be very careful what credence he gives to it, as it may possibly cost him his life to obey the mandate."

"Come, now, read it," said Tabby.

The woman read pointedly as follows—

"P.S.—It is a sad thing for a maiden to have to declare her love, but then what can she do ? Come, my love, come, and you will have no cause to repent your kindness to one who is rather young and pretty."

"Will that do ?"

"Oh," cried Tabby, "you are a treasure. Give me the letter."

"Stop. I will fold it and tie it with a skein of silk for you, and it will look well."

"Do so—do so."

"And I must address it."

"To be sure."

"Well ?"

"Eh ?"

"I say well. To whom is it to be addressed ?"

"Oh, ah,—to be sure. Well, I suppose, Doll, I must just trust you about it. You can address it to ' The worshipful Master Martin Lassamour, of Pleasaunce House, Richmond.' "

"Very well. There it is."

"Thanks—thanks, you are quite a rarity, you are, and I feel very much for you. There is the crown, and now good day to you, Doll."

Tabby caught up the letter, and hastened off with it, quite convinced in his own mind that he had possession of an epistle that would have the effect of causing Martin Lassamour to fall into the snares that were there laid for his assassination.

Tabby was so elated with what he considered his brilliant success in the matter that he did not wait to carry the letter to Glass, but finding a messenger, he at once despatched it to Martin Lassamour, at Pleasaunce House.

What sort of effect it was likely to have upon that personage the reader may imagine.

Tabby then went on to the tavern at Milbank at which he had agreed to meet Glass, and when there he slapped his comrade upon the shoulder, saying—

"It's all right, my boy—it's all right. We shall have ample time to settle the affair of the girl, and then we can earn the money for the despatch of our other little affair before night. For once in a way I have managed well."

CHAPTER LII.

GAMIEL GANDER IS OF GOOD SERVICE TO PATIENCE AND AMY.

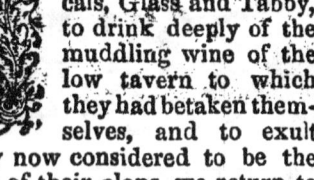 EAVING the two rascals, Glass and Tabby, to drink deeply of the muddling wine of the low tavern to which they had betaken themselves, and to exult over what they now considered to be the certain success of their plans, we return to Pleasaunce House.

The morning dawned upon the old house and grounds, and found Lady Margaret still up and about.

She had not pressed her couch that night ; but at an early hour she was found in a state of half insensibility on the verge of the corridor where hung the pictures.

She had made no reply to the questions of the servants, but merely had contented herself with rejecting the proposition to send for a medical man, saying that she was quite well.

Her looks quite sufficiently belied any such assertion as that in a moment.

But the servants could do nothing but obey her, and they retired to their own hall to hold deep and solemn conferences, by the aid of old ale, upon the state of affairs at Pleasaunce.

There was no small share of wonder, too, in the household, with regard to what had become of the waiting woman.

The implacability of this individual, however, was so great, that notwithstanding all the servants were full of conjectures about her, not one cared to take the least trouble to look after her.

Then thus we see how, in consequence of having no human heart in all the household with a kindly feeling towards her, this wretched woman went even to death without further inquiry.

The servants, in good truth, were only

too glad, as the day advanced, to miss her unceremonious and abusive tongue.

About the hour of breakfast the Lady Margaret, who to her own regret, had been left alone, rang her bell.

It was answered by one of the female servants of the mansion.

"Did you ring, madam?"

"Yes. Where is——"

Lady Margaret appeared to have a great difficulty in pronouncing the name, but, after a pause, she did succeed in saying,——

"Where is Loon?"

"We don't know, my Lady."

"Not know?"

"No, my lady. She has not been seen this morning, at all."

"It is very strange."

"Yes, my lady."

"Well, I cannot account for it. You will attend upon me, as she is absent."

"Yes, my lady."

This was all the remark that the Lady Margaret made about Loon, and the young woman who was then summoned to attend upon her in the absence of that individual, said nothing more upon the subject, for, in good truth, she cared not whether Loon made an appearance again or not.

In the course of another half hour Lady Margaret was up and dressed for the day, and she did not look as if anything very particular had happened to her."

She always had a cold, pale, stately kind of spirit. It is possible enough that the servants were right in thinking that she looked just a little paler than usual, but that was all."

And so she descended into one of the stately rooms of the mansion, where a good old-fashioned breakfast was laid.

One glance round the room let her see that it was vacant.

She took her seat in a chair covered with brocade, and in a low, soft tone, she spoke to the serving man, who stood by the beauffet, in the corner of the apartment.

"Samuel?"

"Yes, my lady."

"Inform your master that the breakfast waits.

"Yes, my lady."

The lady Margaret turned and looked sternly at him, and then she added—

"If you know he is in the house."

"Ye—e—s, my lady."

"Samuel."

"I—I—Oh, Lord, my lady, don't be angry, but you see, my Lady, Master and the young gentleman, Lamont, has only just come home."

"Only just come home?"

"That is all, my lady."

A sort of spasm for a moment appeared to shake the frame of Lady Margaret, and then she said, with an affectation of calmness.

"Well. Tell him the breakfast waits."

"Yes, madam."

The servant left the room, and then Lady Margaret clutched, with convulsive force, the arms of the chair on which she sat, and muttered between her clenched teeth,—

"So! It has come to this at last, has it. From home all night. What am I to think of that? From home all night. Well—well, be still my heart, or it will break; I will hold my peace. I do not brawl, and creep, and riot, as many wives do upon the doubt of the faithfulness of their spouses, but I act—and woe be to him when I do so act—but yet I will dissemble. We shall see. Yes, we shall see. This may be the last day of the existence of Martin Lassamour."

She heard the door of the apartment open, and she saw Martin, closely followed by his young friend, Lamont, enter the room.

A sickly smile lit up the face of the Lady Margaret, as she said—

"I give you good morning, good lord, and you, too, fair sir."

"You do me an honour," said Lamont, with a bow; but he took care to take a seat as far off from the lady as possible.

Martin Lassamour flung himself into a chair as, with an assumption of gaiety he was far, very far, indeed, from feeling, he said—

"And a fair good morrow to the Lady Margaret. Does all go well with you?"

"All."

"Then all is well. Come, Lamont, to breakfast, my good friend, with what appetite you may."

"Samuel?" said the lady.

"Yes, my lady."

"Bid our page, Cyprian, attend us."

"Oh, Cyprian," said Martin. "By my faith, I think he will hardly be found in Pleasaunce."

"Indeed?"

"No. I gave the young rascal leave to go to Lambeth fair to-day."

A shade passed over the face of the Lady Margaret.

"Nay, wife, I grieve that I sent him from you, if you want the lad; but, you see, he is deep in love with Patience Langdon, one of the fair daughters of the ferryman of Lambeth, and so to refuse the boy seemed little short of absolute cruelty.

I could not find it in my heart to do so; so I let him go, and told him I would stand between him and your anger."

Lady Margaret smiled.

"You did well, Martin," she said. "I have no anger to stand between me and the boy. I should myself have given him the leave he asked you for had he asked me; and I rather feel hurt that he should have doubted that little fact."

"Well, well, forgive him, poor boy."

"I do with all my heart."

At this moment one of the serving men came into the room with a silver salver in his hand, upon which was a letter, tied round with green silk, and he approached Martin Lassamour with it.

"For me?"

"Yes, noble sir."

Martin Lassamour took the letter, and with a knife that was upon the breakfast table, he cut the silk that bound it, and hastily opened it.

His countenance changed the moment he read the signature at the foot of the epistle.

This was the very letter which Tabby had got the poor woman whom he called Doll to write for him, and which bore the signature of Amy Langdon.

Now, as Martin Lassamour glanced at this signature, his eye naturally fell upon the postscript of the letter first, and then to his surprise he read the few words which, as the reader is aware, contained a flat contradiction of everything that went before it.

The look of surprise deepened upon the face of Lassamour.

CHAPTER LIII.

JEALOUSY FURTHER INFLUENCES THE PASSIONS OF LADY MARGARET.

THIS look of bewilderment and surprise upon the face of Martin Lassamour was translated by the Lady Margaret to be one of pleased confusion. She was just near enough to see that the address of the letter was in a female hand.

Such a conviction, combined with the fact of his absence all the night from Pleasaunce House, added fuel to the flames of jealousy which already had found a home in her breast.

Her colour went and came, and then she became more deadly pale than before.

Martin Lassamour read the letter through, and then turning to Lamont, he said—

"I beg pardon, sir, for this seeming, but quite unintentional disrespect to you, and you, too, Margaret; but—but—this letter——"

"Distracts you?" said Margaret.

"It does, on my soul."

"May I counsel you upon it?"

"Yes—that is—no——"

"What am I to think of this seeming contradiction, Martin? Why do you look so strangely at me?"

Martin Lassamour sprang to his feet.

"By the Lord!" he cried, "I can play this part no longer. My friend, Lamont, follow me."

Lamont rose, too.

"Lassamour—Lassamour!" he cried, be calm. I pray you to be calm, my friend."

"I cannot—I dare not. It is not in nature that I should be calm. Bear with me; but I am almost mad. Margaret, farewell for a time."

Martin Lassamour sprang from the room.

Lamont hesitated for a moment; and then, with a low bow to the Lady Margaret, he followed his friend.

Lady Margaret had arisen upon this outburst of feeling that came from Martin Lassamour, and now that she was alone again, she sank into her chair with a deep groan.

"God! what does all this mean?" she said, "What is it? What does he suspect? What does he know?"

"Hem!" said Samuel, who was at the beauffet. The young man thought it only prudent and right to let his mistress know that some one was there.

Lady Margaret started.

"Who is that?"

"Only me, my lady."

"Who? who? Oh, Samuel?"

"Yes, my lady."

"What did I say?"

"What—did—your ladyship say?"

"Yes."

"Now, my lady?"

"Now."

"Oh, you only said that—that—'What could it all mean?'"

"Was that all?"

"Yes, my lady; but—but——"

"Come hither. I can see by the look of your eye that you have a something to say, if you could make up your mind to say it. What is it? I am liberal."

The Lady Margaret took out her purse.

"Oh, my lady," said Samuel, whose eyes glistened again at the sight of the coin he saw through the interstices of the silken network of the purse—"Oh, my lady, upon my life I don't like to see a noble lady—and though I say it, perhaps, who should not — a beautiful lady like yourself slighted."

"Slighted?"

"Yes, my lady — I — a — was—close behind master when he opened the letter."

"Ah!"

"Yes, my lady."

"I comprehend you; and your eyes were open?"

"They were, my lady."

"And you saw——"

"The name that was at the foot of it, my lady."

"Samuel?"

"Yes, my lady."

"Here are half a dozen gold pieces."

"Gold?"

"Yes, gold. Take them. Be cautious, be discreet, and your fortune is made. What, now, was it you saw at the foot of the letter your master and my husband has just read?"

Samuel cleared his voice to a whisper, and he shook in every limb, as he replied—

"It was—it—it was—Oh, my lady, I'm afraid."

"Of what?"

"Of doing all sorts of mischief. Of—of making such a row as never was known; but the truth is the truth, and we ought to speak it, and shun the devil."

"The name?"

"Then—then, my lady, it was Amy Langdon!"

The Lady Margaret gave a short scream, and bit her lips till the blood came.

"Murder!" cried Samuel.

"Silence!" she said. "On your life, silence! Samuel?"

"Y—e—s, my lady."

"If you breathe one word of this to any mortal ear, you will die the death of a dog. From this time forth, mark me, you must be as silent about this affair as the grave."

She rose with an appearance of perfect calmness, and left the breakfast-room.

"Oh, Lord! oh, Lord!" said Samuel, fanning himself with the table napkin he had in his hand; "I don't know very well whether I am on my head or on my heels. What a terrible situation I am in! Oh, how I do wish I had said nothing about it! Die the death of a dog! Oh, Lord! I wonder what her notions of the death of a dog are now? I am a fool—I am more than a fool. What had I to do with the letter or the name of the person at the foot of it? Oh, dear! oh, dear! nothing, and here I am threatened with some horrid end that some dog came to. Oh! oh!"

No doubt Samuel considered, and with good reason, too, that he was rather on the horns of a dilemma than otherwise.

If he kept the counsel of the Lady Margaret, he ran a great risk of getting into rather serious mischief with Martin Lassamour.

If he told Martin Lassamour, at this juncture, all he had to tell, he ran the risk of punishment from him for overlooking the letter in the first instance, and likewise of the revenge that the Lady Margaret might inflict upon him for betraying her in the second.

Samuel's philosophy was hardly sufficient to show him the way out of this perplexity.

But we must leave him to find out, as best he may, the course that he should pursue, while we attend to more important affairs than any that can possibly concern him.

There now really did seem to be a something closely approaching to the proclamation of open war in the mansion between Martin Lassamour and his fair lady.

The manner in which he had left the breakfast room, after the receipt of the letter forged in the name of Amy Langdon, at once confirmed everything that the jealous mind of Lady Margaret could possibly suggest.

But in reality, his so leaving had been from the impossibility he felt of longer preserving even the exterior of affection for a woman whom he began to believe was really, and without a doubt, stained with the most obnoxious crimes.

When Lady Margaret reached her own apartment she clenched her hands, and stamped with her feet, and uttered short screams of rage and despair for a few moments. That was the very transport of wild passion.

Its more concentrated and dangerous frenzy remained to come.

After giving vent, then, in some degree to the storm of angry feelings that raged in her soul, she sat upon a low chair, and with her hands clasped over her face, she rocked to and fro in apparently a state of hopeless misery.

But she was thinking.

She was deeply thinking.

But what was the character of the wild thoughts that now found a home in her heart?

Revenge!

Yes, that one word, with all its terrible significations found a home in both heart and brain.

Revenge!

Oh, fatal word to human passions—to human hopes, to human subordination. It was that one word, surely conceived by some evil genius, if not by the arch spirit of all evil, that found a home now in the diabolical bosom of the mistress of the fair lands and stately mansion of Pleasaunce.

"Yes," she said, "I will be revenged! They shall all die!—I will be the destroyer! They shall, in the pangs of death, taste a something of the bitterness of spirit which has scorched up my heart like a burnt skull."

She rose and paced her room.

"Yes—yes, Amy Langdon shall die; but first I will grasp at the revenge that lies within my reach. Martin Lassamour, when you lie down again to rest in Pleasaunce House, it will be a rest that will last you until you awake in another world, if there be another world."

CHAPTER LIV.

GAMIEL GANDER SEEMS TO BE QUITE A THRIVING WOOER.

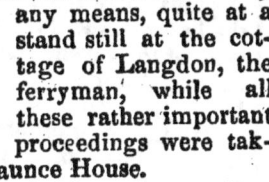 ATTERS were not, by any means, quite at a stand still at the cottage of Langdon, the ferryman, while all these rather important proceedings were taking place at Pleasaunce House.

The neighbours of this rather uncomfortable and ill-tempered person, had given him divers hints concerning the visits of the young page to his house and garden, and daughters, in his absence.

A long conversation, too, with Gamiel Gander had made him have very serious doubts as to whether he really had got at the truth with regard to the adventure of the flour bin.

In fact, Langdon began to get very uneasy, indeed, and he felt all the alarm that a man with two daughters might very well feel, upon the conviction that they had, in good truth, arrived at the age of *in*discretion.

On the morning of the commencement of Lambeth Fair, the ferryman was unusually gloomy and discontented with his house—his breakfast—his daughters—and, in fact, with everything and everybody.

"Dear me, father," said Patience, as she saw her father shaking his head dubiously, "what is the matter?"

"Humph!"

"Is the ale sour?"

"No."

"The cakes over-baked or under-baked?"

"No."

"The brawn too salt?"

"No."

"Then whatever is the matter? You look so dull, and so serious : and this, too, is the first day of Lambeth Fair. Heigho! all the world will be there, and there will be such sights to see, and such dancing on the grass, and such pageants, and such—"

"Silence, girl. Bah! you are mad."

"Mad?"

"Yes, all women are mad whenever there is a fair, or a merrymaking, or anything of that sort toward. You are mad, both of you, for though Amy says nothing, I can see by her looks that she is like old Bowyer's parrot, she only thinks the more."

"Of what, father?"

"Humph! I am a miserable man."

"You?"

"Yes, me! who but me? Have I not two daughters, and is not that enough to make a man miserable? What else, I should like to know, could possibly be required for such a purpose—eh? Answer me that?"

"Father, we don't know what you mean."

"Then I'll tell you. Amy attend to me."

"Yes, father?"

"There is that Robert Lee, the pedler. Oh, you need not put on such a face, I can tell you, and blush like a pæony in May. Come, girl, I want to see you well married, and rid of. A husband can and will look sharp after you, but I can't."

"Oh, father!"

"Oh, daughter! What now?"

"You give your consent?"

"I do."

"Oh, how can I thank you? You are so good and kind to me——"

"Yes, gammon!"

"Oh, no, no."

"But I say it is gammon. I will tell you why I am so good and kind, because it happens to jump just with your humour. If it did not, I should be quite a—a brute—a kind of blue-beard—an ogre!"

"Nay, but——"

"But me no buts—I know it. Oh, it's no use trying to deny it. I tell you I know it, girl; but that Lee has written to me a letter. Where is it?—oh, here."

"A letter?"

"Yes, girl."

"About—about——"

"You, of course."

"Oh, father——"

"Oh, it's all very well to say 'Oh;' but he tell's me that he has explained all his affairs to young Martin Lassamour, he who married the rich widow, and he says that he is in a fair way, in the course of so short a time that he may say he has it in possession, of being master of an acre of good ground, and in possession of such a sum of money that he can keep a wife well and capitally, and—humph!"

"And what, father?"

"Me, too."

"You?"

"Yes, to be sure. Now, girls, listen to me. I don't intend, and I don't feel disposed to work at the ferry all my days, I can tell you. Now you both want to get married—don't deny it—you do. Well, that's settled; but I'll be hanged if anybody has either of you except on one condition."

"And that?"

"That is they make up to me a clear income of forty pounds a year. There, you have it."

"To you, father?"

"Yes, to me, daughter. What then? Do you think I am to get nothing by it, eh? I say that if you, Amy, marry Robert Lee, he shall pay me forty pounds a year for doing so; and when you, Patience, marry, why your husband shall pay twenty of the forty, and that will let Robert Lee off of one half of the price he has to pay for you; and those are my terms, and I don't intend to move from them, no not so much as an inch."

"Father," said Amy, with a heightened colour, "is this generous?—is it even just?"

"I don't care. I tell you, girls, it's my will, and just or generous, it shall be done."

Patience began to cry.

"Silence, I say!"

"Yes—oh, yes, father."

"Father," said Amy, "does Robert know of this?"

"Perhaps he does, and perhaps he does not."

"Then he does not?"

"Well, never mind that. He will know of it, you may take your oath, and that pretty soon. A man, with an acre of ground, and a good sum in ready money, and youth and health to work, can afford it, so there is an end of that; and if he thinks he can't afford it, why, he can leave it alone, and there is an end, too, of that. Ha! ha?"

"Father, I——"

"Amy—Amy!" cried Patience, "oh do not."

Amy turned from her father, and walked to the window. The warning, now, of her sister had stopped her from saying a something that might have produced a violent quarrel between her and her father.

But there had been no watching the expression of her face, or the tone of her voice. Langdon had seen very well that the finer feelings of his daughter revolted against the coarse and selfish proposition which had been made by him; but he was glad that Patience interfered; for, after all, he did not want an altercation with his children.

Perhaps he felt in his inmost heart how utterly and completely indefencible his selfish proposition really was.

"Well," he said, "now you understand all about it; "so you can make the best of it. Hilloa! what's this? I say, what is all this?"

Smash! went a pane of glass of the little lattice window, and an arrow, blunt, it is true, but still an arrow, fell at once to the floor.

It needed but a glance to see that, tied to the arrow, was a piece of written paper in the form of a note.

"Ha! ha! Hawks abroad," said the ferryman.

He made a dart at the arrow, but Patience was beforehand with him, and seizing it in an instant, she fled with it up the narrow staircase to her own room on the upper story of the cottage.

"Fire and fury!" cried Langdon; "This before my own eyes! A thousand devils! do you think, girl, that I am going to put up with this? Come down, you little slut. Come down, I say, or I will fetch you in a way you won't like, I take it."

Amy appeared.

"Oh, I hate him," she said. "Why did he send a note to me?"

"Eh? Who?"

"Gamiel Gander."

"Gamiel Gander?"

"Yes, father."

"Do you mean to tell me that it was he who shot the arrow, and that the note comes from him?"

"Take it."

Patience handed to her father a note, folded just as the one round the arrow had been. The ferryman opened it on the moment, and read as follows:—

"Ducks of deers and darling Patience—

"This comes, hoping from your own Gamiel Gander that you will go to the fair with him. Granny has made her will, and left me eighty pounds a year and the old house, and all the plate, and two feather-beds. Think of that. Oh—oh—oh, come to the arms of your own—own—own!"   "GAMIEL GANDER."

CHAPTER LV.

GAMIEL GANDER IS USEFUL, IF NOT AT ALL ORNAMENTAL.

WITH a dubious-looking face Langdon read this letter, and then he scratched his chin, and said—

"Oh! ah!"

"Yes," said Patience, "there it is."

"Bother me, though, what induced the knave to send it through the window on an arrow?"

"Ah, that was his folly."

"His folly?"

"Yes, father."

"And his skill, too. Why, who on earth, now, would, to look at him, have thought for one moment that he could handle a bow at all?"

"Oh, any fool can do that."

"Can they?"

"Yes, father; but you are not angry with such a goose as this Gander, surely?"

"No, daughter, I am not; but I shall be angry with such a goose as you if you do not mate yourself with this Gander, I can tell you. Why, he is rich—he is really and positively rich."

"Rich, father?"

"Yes. His old grandame is quite a wealthy woman. Hark, ye, Patience, I am now quite decided. You shall be the wife of Gamiel Gander, and then my mind will be quite at ease. I shall give up, that is, I shall sell the good-will of the ferry, and retire upon my forty pounds a year."

"Oh, but father——"

"Silence!"

"I—I——"

"Silence, I say. Is the girl mad? Why, there are two good things in your marrying him."

"And what are they, father?"

"Money, and a fool. I tell you what it is, girls. If you are wise, you will marry a fool, for then you can guide him as you like, and if the fool has but money, why then you are to be envied, indeed, for you step into quite a snug inheritance, where, if you marry a man with wit, and with judgment, he will soon let you know that you are the weaker vessel."

"But he is so ugly, father."

"Ugly is as ugly does. My mind is made up about it, so there is an end of that, and look you, haughty Patience, I don't want to say anything that will make you at all uncomfortable, but this much I will say, that if I catch any saucy page here—mark me well—I say any saucy page, I will wring his neck!"

"Oh! oh!"

"Ah, it will be 'oh,' then!"

THE ATTACK UPON SIR RALPH SHARD.

"Bravo! bravo! father-in-law, Langdon, that is to be," cried the voice of Gamiel Gander, as that individual appeared at the door of the cottage. "Bravo! and the sooner you do it, the better."

"Ah, Gamiel!"

"Yes, here we are. In for a penny, in for a pound, as the saying is."

"How dost thee, boy?"

"Oh, all right. A little hungry or so, that's all. But look at me! look at me!"

"Is it possible?"

"Ah! it is, sky blue, ain't it, and fits like a miracle."

Gamiel Gander was attired in a suit of blue, of a very light colour, and he turned round several times, so that the ferryman and his fair daughters should have a capital opportunity of seeing all the beauties of his figure.

"There," he cried, "there is a fit for you. I daren't sit down, though, for fear of the consequences. The what's-his-names are rather tight, you see, and they might go. But in for a penny, in for a pound, as I say; there wasn't no sort of time to get 'em altered.''

"Why, good gracious, they are tight."

"Yes, father-in-law, Langdon, that used to was, they is, rather, you may say that. I never felt so jammed up, in a way of speaking, behind before."

"Ha! ha!"

"Yes, it's all very well to laugh; but what do you think of me, lovely young ladies?"

The two girls laughed.

"Ah, well, that does one good now. What is your opinion, dear little Patience, of my figure?"

"Oh, I can have but one opinion."

"And what's that?"

"Why, that you look like a goose at all times; but that in your present suit you look like the same goose trussed for roasting!"

"Really, now, you don't?"

"I do."

"And you, Miss Amy?"

"I think so, too."

"Well, I never! but it's all the same to me. Of course, it ain't every day you see such a figure as mine; and my old granny says I am just the thing, and quite elegant. To be sure, she is partial; but that don't make much difference."

"Well—well," said Langdon, "I can guess what all this finery is about."

"No?"

"Yes, I can."

"Well, if you ain't a conjurer if you do. What now?"

"Well, to go to the fair."

"Well, I never!"

"And you want me to let Patience go with you?"

"Did you ever!"

"But first, Master Gander, let me tell you one thing, that I won't have my windows broken by your amorous tricks."

"Eh?"

"I say, I won't have my windows broken by your amorous tricks.'

"Oh, Lord! what do you mean? My amorous tricks, sir? Father-in-law, how can you say such things? I'm quite ashamed of you, I am."

"Come—come, Master Gander, you are not such a fool as you look."

"No. Ain't I, though?"

"Oh, yes, father, he is," said Patience.

"Silence, girl!"

"Oh, thank you, Miss Patience, for taking of my part. It's very kind of you."

"Why, they are only laughing at you,

Gamiel. But the next time you want to send a letter to my daughters, don't shoot it through the window."

"Don't shoot it?"

"Yes, don't shoot an arrow through the window."

"Don't shoot the window through an arrow? I'll be hung, father-in-law, if I know what you are talking about. 'In for a penny, in for a pound,' as the saying is; what do you mean?"

"Oh, Gamiel," said Patience, "how can you?"

"What?"

"Oh! oh!"

"Eh? Oh, sir, what have I done?"

"I'm ashamed of you, I am, indeed."

"So am I," said Amy.

"What—what? They haven't really given way, have they?" exclaimed Gamiel, feeling very anxious about his rather tight wearing apparel.

"Tell me, once for all," said the ferryman; "did you or did you not shoot an arrow through the casement with a billet attached to it?"

"Oh! oh!"

"Did you, or did you not? By the lord, I begin to smell a rat."

"Do you, though? Puss! puss! puss!"

"You rascal!"

"Oh, father," said Patience, "let me speak to him. I will make him confess it. Gamiel, come here."

"Yes, dear Patience. Oh, my eye! she asks me to come here. Oh! oh!"

"Sit down!"

"No — no. Anything but that. I daren't."

"Well, well, never mind them. Gamiel, Gamiel?"—Patience here decreased her voice to a whisper—"Gamiel, do you want me to go to the fair with you?"

"I does! I does!"

"Hush! Agree, then, and say yes to whatever father says to you. He has had a drop this morning."

"You don't say so?"

"I do."

"Then I will."

"Come—come," cried the ferryman, "none of that. I don't like all that whispering, and billing, and cooing, before my face. I will have an answer. Did you not shoot an arrow this morning?"

"To be sure," said Gamiel.

"Oh! and through this window?"

"To be sure."

"With a letter to Patience?"

"To be sure."

"Then why the devil did you deny

it before, you blue looking donkey, you?"

"He was afraid I might be angry with him, poor fellow," said Patience, "that was all; and I do think he is quite to be commended for it, instead of blamed. I'll go with him to the fair if I cannot go without, and Amy will come with us, for I won't go alone for fear of what the neighbours should think."

"Well—well," said Langdon, "be off with you, and I give you joy, Gamiel, of your grandmother's will. Ha! ha! She has made a man of you."

CHAPTER LVI.

CYPRIAN STEALS A MARCH UPON GAMIEL GANDER.

ERY easily explained is the mystery of the arrow, and the letter attached to it.

It was from a small cross-bow that it was the good pleasure of the page, Cyprian, to carry at his back when he had on what he considered his holiday attire.

Fearing, and in fact knowing very well that anything in the shape of a request upon his part to old Langdon for the company of his dear Patience to the fair would meet with a refusal, and that anything but a courteous one, too, the young page had revolved in his mind deeply how to manage to secure her dear and delightful company notwithstanding.

Chance had befriended him.

Hovering about the neighbourhood, he chanced to pass the cottage of old Dame Gander, the worthy Gamiel's grandmother, and hearing the sound of voices within, Cyprian had placed his ear to the key-hole, and heard what passed.

Gamiel was getting with great difficulty into the blue suit of clothes which was so very much too tight for him, and the old woman, in deep and profound admiration of what she considered to be his manifold graces, was aiding and assisting him to the utmost of her ability.

"Ah, my dear Gamiel," she mumbled, "you will turn the heads of all the damsels at Lambeth fair, that you will."

"Oh, yes, granny," said Gamiel Gander, who, with his old grandmother, was quite a great man; "of course I shall."

"Yes, my love, you will."

"Oh, yes, I always do. There's Patience and Amy, the ferryman's two daughters, they are quite a fighting and pulling each other's hair out by the handfulls, about me."

"Sure?"

"Yes, granny, it's a fact. But how do I look now?"

"Oh, so smart and nice."

"Do I, though?"

"You do, my love; but oh, take care of your precious life when you go to the fair, for when it is found out, as of course, my beauty, it will soon be, that all the young girls are in love with you, why you know, that the young men will want to murder you."

"Oh, leave me alone for that, granny I'll take care of myself. But oh, granny oh, granny?"

"What, my love?"

"How much are you going to give me to take to the fair with me?"

"My duck, here is a bag with a matter of three pounds in silver groats i   "

"Oh! oh!"

"Yes, my darling; and you shall bring your poor old granny home a fairing."

"That I will. Three pounds in silver groats; well that is something. Why there won't be many at the fair, I should say, that will have so much as that to lay out?"

"No, my duck; but as you are to have all I possess in the world, for who could I give it to one half so beautiful as yourself, I thought I might as well make you happy at the fair."

"Well, that's right enough, granny."

"But now tell me, my sweet love, how do you get on with the ferryman's daughter? I should think she ought to be comfortably off, my dear?"

"No doubt of it; and the fact is, granny, that I loves her, and she loves me to distraction."

At this boast on the part of Gamiel Gander, Cyprian felt so enraged that he had half a mind to break open the cottage door and give Gamiel Gander such a drubbing that he would be quite incapable of going to the fair.

But a moment's reflection let the young page see how absurd it was of him to be either angry or jealous of such a person; so he listened still to what the old woman had to say to her hopeful grandson.

"Yes," added Gamiel, "she doats upon me."

"Of course, my love. I don't see how she could, very well, having eyes in her head, do otherwise."

"No, no; but the other one, you see, granny, doats upon me, too."

"Oh, dear."

"And so they are ready to cut each other's throats about me, and it's no easy matter, granny, to hold one's way with them both; but I sent a letter to Patience last night."

"Did you, my dear. Oh, what a thing it is to be a scholard."

"Yes—yes."

"And what did she reply, my dear?"

"Nothing, as yet. Poor little thing, she is all of a flutter, I daresay, to reply to it. But come, granny, be quick and put me all to rights, for I am going off to the ferryman's cottage, to ask her to go to the fair with me, and the day is getting on."

"Yes—yes, my love."

The old woman, who was half blind, bustled about to get her beloved Gamiel to rights, as he called it. She still looked upon him as a little boy, whom it would be very wrong to send out of the house without active superintendance in the dressing, washing, and combing; but at length the old lady, having but just caught a slight idea that Gamiel looked very blue in his new suit, and very fat, felt satisfied.

"Go, my dear, go," she said; "and oh, take care of your precious life, do."

"I will—I will."

"Recollect your poor old granny."

"Yes, yes."

"I should come to a premature end if I were to lose you."

"All's right. I'm off."

"And—and Gamiel, my dear?"

"Well, what?"

"I would not, after all, be in any great hurry to promise marriage to Patience Langdon."

"No?"

"No, my dear."

"Why not?"

"Because who knows, but that with your beauty you may attract the eyes of some great and grand lady about the court? Some countess or other grand lady, who may want you for herself."

"Well, there is something in that."

"There is, my dear; so be careful of yourself, do, and don't be in a hurry to throw yourself away upon anybody. Hem, if Patience Langdon—hem! is so fond of you—why—a—a—hem!"

"What do you mean by hem?"

"Well, well, my dear, of course young gallants will be young gallants, and if she is so fond of you, as no doubt she is, why all I have to say is—he! he! he! Oh, I shall die of this cough some day."

"But what do you mean, granny?"

"Why, that you must not slight a young lady's favours, that's all, Gamiel."

"Oh, I begin to see."

"Of course you do."

"You think that—that if she will have love, and from me, too, I may as well—eh?"

"Yes, my duck."

"Oh! ah!"

"Now, by all the saints!" said Cyprian, "if I am not half, and something more, too, than half, inclined to set light to this abominable old devil's house, and burn her in it."

But Cyprian bethought him of what Gamiel had said about taking Patience to the fair, and in the midst of his rage at him and his unscrupulous old witch of a grandmother, who would have sacrificed anybody to the pride of thinking Gamiel was quite a gallant seducer, he saw that he might get Patience with him at the fair through the very means, which at a first glance, seemed as if they would effectually put a stop to such a proceeding.

"Let him take her to the fair," said Cyprian, "and if I don't take her from him, I'm a Dutchman, that's all."

But Cyprian knew perfectly well that Patience, under no circumstances, unless she were convinced that there was an object in it pleasing to him, Cyprian, would go to the fair with Gamiel Gander.

So he had to set about devising some plan of letting her know what he meant to do.

Upon a slip of paper he hastily wrote the following words:—

"My own dear, dear Patience.—Go to the fair with that donkey on two legs, Gamiel Gander. It is the only way in which you can go to the fair with me. I will soon rid you of him, and then have the joy of your society for the rest of the day, as my good lord, Martin Lassamour, has given me leave. Ever and for ever, my own dear Patience, your true lover,
                                "CYPRIAN."

Now it was easy enough to write such a

note as this, but it was not so easy to get it delivered safely. However, at the risk of all consequences the page fastened the little billet to an arrow, and, as we have seen, sent it through the window.

How Patience contrived to substitute Gamiel's note for the one Cyprian sent her, and so deceive her father, is already known to the reader, who has no doubt followed her up stairs.

CHAPTER LVII.

MARTIN LASSAMOUR CONSULTS WITH ROBERT LEE, THE PEDLER.

 YPRIAN must have had a tolerable idea of the tact and the cleverness of Patience, to chance a letter to her through the lattice window of her father's cottage.

To be sure we must acquit him of a portion of this seeming indiscretion, for he could not know, or even think, that the ferryman was at home.

The hour at which Langdon was wont to repair to his duties at the ferry had come, and Cyprian had no possible reason to suppose that he was in the house at such a time.

Nor would Langdon have been there but for the fact that he had the conversation we have recorded the principal portion of, with his two daughters, concerning their settling in life.

Such a conversation was very interesting to Langdon, inasmuch as it combined the forty pounds a year for which, in plain language, he was willing to sell his two daughters, and hence was it that he had let such a discourse delay him so long at home, that he had been a witness to the arrival of the billet of Cyprian, attached to the arrow from his good cross-bow.

The reader is aware, though, how cleverly Patience managed the whole affair, and how she carried out the advice of the page, so far as to consent to go with Gamiel Gander to the fair.

It is only then necessary to say that Patience went with the full assurance that Cyprian would adopt some mode of rescuing her from Gamiel Gander, and that Amy went with the hope of falling in with Robert Lee, the pedler.

How they both sped upon this affair we shall soon see ; but it would have been an amusing sight to notice the two young girls leaving their father's cottage with Gamiel Gander.

"Dears, my loves of dears," said Gamiel, "one of you shall walk on one side of me, and the other on the other."

"Oh dear, no," said Patience.

"No ?"

"Certainly not. You must go on a few paces before, good Gamiel."

"Before ?"

"Yes. How can you clear a way for us, and how can we see how nice and round, and plump you look in your new clothes, if you do not?"

"Oh, well, there is everything in that."

"Everything ?"

"Well, in for a penny, in for a pound. Here we go, then, and woe be to everybody—I mean, any small boy that dares to come in the way, or to look saucily at either of you."

In this way, then, on they went, feeling that their state was

"All the more gracious,"

that they had succeeded in avoiding actually walking side by side with such a gallant as Gamiel Gander.

On the route, then, to the fair in this fashion, and laughing heartily at the little rotund figure of their courier as he stalked on about half a dozen paces in advance of them, we must leave the two fair sisters, while we take a glance at what Martin Lassamour is about.

Upon leaving the breakfast-room so very abruptly, Lassamour made his way at once with speed to the stables of Pleasaunce House, in order to procure his horse, for he felt that he could not remain another hour beneath the same roof with the Lady Margaret.

"My horse ! my horse !" he cried. "I will away to London."

Before his steed could be got ready for him, he was joined by his friend, Lamont.

"Oh, Lassamour," said Lamont, "control your feelings, let me beg of you. Be calm—be calm."

"Calm?"

"Yes, my friend. Hush! You know not who may be a spy upon your every word and every look in this house."

"That is true."

"Then profit by the truth, and do not say a word that may be reported to your detriment to the Lady Margaret.'

"You are right, Lamont—you are right. But I can't stay here. The very atmosphere of this house is death to me. Come away with me at once."

"Away with you I will go at once, of course. But whither?"

"I know not."

"You know not?"

"No, Lamont. All I can say is, let me go anywhere, so that it is from here."

A servant approached.

"Two horses, my good master?" he said.

"Yes—yes. My friend here rides forth with me."

The two steeds were speedily at the disposal of Lassamour and his friend, and they both mounted.

Lsssamour turned his eyes towards the terraces and the turrets of Pleasaunce House, and waving his hand, he said, with a shudder—

"Farewell!"

They both trotted from the gate, and then Lamont said, with an air of concern—

"Lassamour, you do not surely mean to say that you bid farewell for ever to Pleasaunce?"

"I hope so."

"Then again let me say, 'Whither go you?'"

"I scarcely know; and yet I have a duty to perform, which must be performed at once. I have to seek out Robert Lee, the pedler, and to show him this letter. Look at it carefully, Lamont, and tell me your opinion of it."

Lamont did look at the letter carefully, and, to tell the truth, it puzzled him, since the postscript was in the same hand as the letter itself. That it boded danger to Lassamour, and that she whose name was appended to it had no hand in its composition, he could well enough believe; but beyond that all was vague conjecture.

"Well," said Lassamour, "what say you?"

"In good truth, my dear friend, I know not what to say, except that it would be the very height of imprudence to keep the appointment made here."

"Except in force?"

"Ay, that, indeed."

"Well, we will think of all that,

though. I feel certain that there is some fearful plotting at work, and I feel certain that it is from the seething and revengeful brain of Sir Warrene De Volence that it all proceeds. I will at once, now, seek Robert Lee, and from his shrewd, good sense, I will hope to get some further insight into this iniquitous proceeding."

"But know you where to find him?"

"I do. He will assuredly be at the fair at Lambeth—his vocation will carry him there to-day, so there will be no sort of difficulty in lighting upon him. Let us trot onwards to Lambeth marshes, my good friend. I feel as if things were now coming to a crisis with me at Pleasaunce House, for, of the terrible guilt of the Lady Margaret, I think both you and I have so much evidence that it would be flying in the face of all probability to doubt it."

"I fear so, too."

"On—on, then. There is a Providence above us which, be well assured, will ordain all things for the best."

They now put their horses to speed, and were very soon close to the outskirts of the fair. The first peculiar indication of its presence that they saw was a bear chained to a stake, and amusing a crowd of curious and idle spectators by various gambols, which the unwieldy creature seemed to go through with perfect ease.

Further on they came upon a troop of morrice dancers, who were preparing a spot of smooth turf for their festive entertainment.

Booths, shows, and all kinds of necessaries now came upon their view; but they could see nothing for a time of Robert Lee.

At length Lassamour called to a boy, who was listlessly wandering through the fair with longing eyes.

"Hilloa, my lad!"

"Yes, master," said the boy, taking hold of the reins of Lassamour's horse, for he naturally fancied that he was called to hold the animal.

"Nay, I only want to ask a question of you, my lad; but I will reward you if you answer it, far more better than as if you took care of my steed for an hour."

"I will try to answer it, noble sir."

"Know you, then, if Robert Lee, the pedler, has a stand in the fair?"

"Oh, yes, right well."

"Can you guide me to him?"

"With ease, noble sir, if you will follow me."

"Lead on, then, in God's name."

The boy ran on before, and Lassamour and Lamont followed him for about a quarter of a mile, till they came to a row of booths, in one of which the boy pointed, saying—

"That, sir, is Master Robert Lee's."·

"'Tis well ; there is your reward. Get thee a fairing."

Lassamour gave the boy so much more money than he expected, that he ran off with screams and shouts of delight.

Lassamour smiled.

"Lamont," he said, "how easy it is to make a happy heart. Here I have given this boy but a trifle of money, and he is more joyful than any emperor on his throne."

"Even so. It is the extent of the craving that is everything."

CHAPTER LVIII.

THE PLOT THICKENS ABOUT THE FAIR AMY LANGDON.

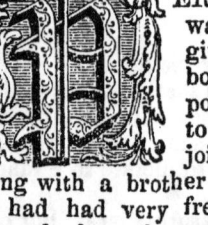ERFECTLY correct was the information given by the boy. The booth that had been pointed out did belong to Robert Lee ; but jointly he had taken it along with a brother pedler, with whom he had had very frequent dealings, and whom he knew he could trust.

This, as it turned out, was a very fortunate connection for Robert Lee.

Lassamour dismounted at once, and Lamont held the bridle of his horse for him while he entered the tent.

"Ah, my good lord," cried Robert Lee, advancing towards him, "your presence gladdens my heart."

"I come to seek you, Lee."

The grave face of Lassamour at once let the pedler know that it was on no light errand that Lassamour came ; he turned pale, and clasped his hands, pronouncing at once, as though with the divination of soul, the name—

"Amy—Amy Langdon !"

"You are as good as a conjurer, Robert Lee," said Lassamour, "for it is of her I come to speak."

"Of—of Amy?"

"Even so."

"Oh, God help me now ! Good sir, do not tell me all at once, lest it kill me !"

"Look man !—courage ! I have nothing to tell that can hurt thee."

"Nothing?"

"Nothing in the world. For all I know the fair Amy, whom Heaven preserve, is snug and safe in her own chamber."

"Heaven be praised. You did alarm me, though, noble sir, for look you here,

about ten minutes since, this paper was thrust into my hands by a girl, who then ran off as if the very devil was behind her."

The paper which Robert Lee placed in the hands of Lassamour, had on it the following words,—

"Robert Lee,"—

"If you love Amy Langdon, leave merry making and trafficing at Lambeth Fair, and look to her safety."

"This is strange," said Lassamour.

"And alarming !"

"It is—it is."

"Well, noble sir. You would not have found me here in five minutes more, for I was just arranging with my friend and partner, here, Master John Brown, than whom a more honest man don't live, to look after all my stock, and I was going fast back to the Ferry House."

"Stop a bit, Lee. I can give you further material for thought, though no further positive information. Read this before you go."

The gallant Martin Lassamour placed in the hands of Robert Lee the mysterious letter, with its still more mysterious postscript, and let him read it through.

"Good God!" exclaimed Lee. "What can it all mean?"

"Danger !"

"Yes, no doubt—no doubt. You do not—oh, noble sir, you cannot——"

"What?"

"Suppose for one moment that my Amy wrote the letter?"

"Certainly not."

"I thank you from my heart for that."

"I never did, Robert, suppose it for one half minute. I believe her to be what she looks to be, a being full of action and kindly feeling, and truth, and honour. But it is quite clear from all this, that there is something on foot that concerns you, and me, and her."

"Oh, yes—yes. What shall I do?"

"Permit me to advise you. I should say do as you were about to do, so far as regards the leaving your goods to the care of your partner, and then go if you like to the Ferry House; but let me hope that you will permit me to take upon myself, from this day, the task of watching over the safety of Amy Langdon."

"You, noble sir?"

"Yes, along with my young friend, Lamont, here. I will take good care to watch that no one comes near her, and you can trust to our honour."

"As I trust in honour, sir. But—but——"

"What would you say?"

"That I think I ought myself to be near her."

"Be it so, if you like. But it is in my mind, not only enough to foil this iniquity, be it what it may, that is about to be attempted, but I want to find out who is the instigator, and who the instruments of it."

"Surely, many."

"Then I and my friend, Lamont, wanted to get disguises in one of the Play House Booths, which we can hire from the Mimics for a trifle for the day, and so, without ourselves being known, we can hover about her, should she come to the fair, as in all likelihood she will."

"Oh, yes, she will."

"You know that?"

"I think it. She told me she would manage to come to the fair, to see me, if possible, and to those who truly love, I think that all things are possible."

"You are an earnest lover, Robert Lee. But come, now, you may as well adopt a disguise along with us, and come with us on our errand."

"With joy, sir."

"Then be it so. Are you ready?"

"Quite—quite. Brown, my friend?"

"Ay, Master Lee."

"Look well to the wares."

"Trust me for that."

"I do—I do."

Robert Lee reached from a corner his trusty quarter staff, which in his hands, who knew so well how to use it, it was in truth a most formidable weapon, and then he sallied forth from his booth, along with Martin Lassamour. They soon found an hotel, on the outskirts of the fair, where they could let their two horses remain quietly till they were wanted again, and then they looked about for one of the travelling theatrical caravans at which they might hire disguises for the day, a thing very easily done.

The great anxiety that had taken possession of the mind of Robert Lee, found so much expression in his face, that Lassamour could not avoid speaking to him concerning it.

"Courage," he said. "You may safely, I think, depend upon it, that all will yet be well. Do you not know that to be fore-warned is to be fore-armed?"

"Yes, yes, I know all that, noble sir; but yet——"

"Yet, you would say, that you are full of fears."

"For that dear girl, who is all the world to me, I do admit I am."

"Banish them."

"Ah, how?"

"By resolution."

Robert Lee shook his head.

"What is there in that same resolution," he said, "that is not part and parcel of ones own mind and soul. What the heart and the head agree to dictate to a man, he does."

"Well, there is truth there; but come on. Here is a tragedy about to be played in this travelling caravan, and I doubt not but they will be easily enough able to accommodate us with cloaks and masks."

They all three now entered the caravan belonging to a travelling company of mimics, and for a trifling payment, and a sum left by Martin Lassamour as a security for the due return of the things, they procured disguises.

These disguises consisted of three ample cloaks, and three half visors.

It was very much the custom for the high and the noble, at that period, to frequent the many meetings of the community in such disguises.

That was a time of day when dress set up the most effectual barrier between the different orders of society.

It was not as now, when a clerk or a shop-boy can, if he has the money or the credit at command to do so, don as good garments as any nobleman in the land.

At that time he possibly dared not do so, for there were laws to prevent him.

Thus, then, in order to prevent them from being known, the nobility, and others of rank, and station, and wealth, generally, at public places, where they did not wish to be known, wore the half-mask, or visor, as it was called.

Thus disguised, Martin Lassamour felt that, at all events, he might very well defy

CYPRIAN AT THE FEET OF PATIENCE.

the scrutiny or recognition of any one who did not happen to be remarkably familiar with him.

"Behold, now," said Lassamour, suddenly to the pedler, "Heaven aids us !"

"How?　How, my good lord?"

"Look to your left."

There sure enough was Amy Langdon, with her sister Patience, and Gamiel Gander close to them with his hand deep in the bag that held the silver groats his grandmother had given him.　He had

that half-manical look sitting upon his face — that assumed simplicity, which with some with much more shrewd sense than Gamiel Gander had possessed had become a growing habit not easily got rid of.

"'Tis she !"

"Yes, Lee, and you see she is safe and well."

"Heaven be thanked, she is so."

"Hush ! be wary.　Do not let her recognise you yet."

CHAPTER LIX.

DETAILS WHAT TOOK PLACE AT LAMBETH FAIR.

IF he had consulted merely the dictates of his own heart, the pedler would have ran forward to Amy, to tell her that she was in some possible danger, and that he and his friends were there to protect her.

But the grasp of Martin Lassamour detained him, or he would have done so.

"What would you do?"

"Go to the dear girl and tell her——"

"What ?"

"That she would be protected."

"Nay, what is the need?"

"The—a—need?"

"Yes, good Master Robert Lee. You should recollect that the dear girl does not know that she is in any danger as yet."

"True—true."

"And, therefore, my good friend, what is the good of alarming her at all about it. Come, come, you must let those who are cooler headed than you can possibly be yourself in this matter, be the judges in it."

"I will—I will."

"Recollect what I told you awhile ago, my good friend. It is not only necessary to protect her from all wrong; but it is necessary likewise to find out who it is that threatens it."

"Oh, yes, yes."

"You will be guided, then, entirely by me in this matter?"

"I will—I will."

"You do well. Now I promise you that we will keep by you, and that you and I, and my young friend, Lamont, here, will together form such a body-guard to your Amy, that she shall be quite safe."

"I am content. But yet——"

"Yet what?"

"I should like to know if she came here with any idea of danger. It is possible that she may have something to say to me herself."

"She may. Will you let me find that out?"

"Yes, noble sir, if you will."

"She will not know me, while one breath of your voice would be certain to betray you to her. I will seek a word or two with her, or what say you to this plan— Suppose I ask her to trust to me for your sake, Robert Lee, and accept of my arm in the fair? My fate, to-day, appears to be in some mysterious way bound up in hers."

"As you think best, noble sir."

"Nay," said Lamont, "there is that idiot of a boy, in the ridiculous blue dress, with her.

"His name is Gander. But yet, noble Master Lassamour, if you are with her, or I, or your friend here, it seems to me that you will fail in discovering if any danger threatens her, for the danger to a young girl is sure to come from some cowardly heart, and if that cowardly heart sees that she is with any one, it will shrink away."

"Yes, and hide its head."

"You speak my thoughts, noble sir."

"And I think so, too, good Robert. Let her be, then, and let her run the risk of being apparently in danger, while in reality she is in none at all, for we will all three keep together and watch over her safety with vigilance."

While they were thus speaking, Gamiel Gander and the two sisters approached the spot on which they stood.

"In for a penny, in for a pound," said Gamiel, as he took out some money from his bag. "Now, my dears, what shall I buy you?"

"Nothing," said Amy.

"Nothing—eh? Did you say nothing?"

"I did."

"Oh, but come, don't say that. Charming and delightful little Patience, what shall it be?"

"A fool's cap."

"Eh?"

"A fool's cap."

"Oh, a—a fools——Oh, you don't mean it?"

"Yes ; and you can wear it, you know, and then folks will see at a glance what you are."

"Ha ! ha ! upon my word you be quite a wit—you be, indeed. But come, now, don't say such things to your own Gammy."

"My own what?"

"Oh, that's only my funny way of man-ing myself. Gammy, I call myself, for Gamiel, you know."

"Oh, yes; but not the fun of it," said Patience. "Oh! oh! oh!"

"Dear me, what is the matter? In for a penny, in for a pound, what is amiss?" Cyprian stood before the group.

The page gave a meaning look to Gamiel Gander, and another to Patience. Patience smiled, but Gamiel shrunk back, saying—

"Hilloa! hilloa! I know you. Come, come, young fellow, no impudence—no impertinence!"

"So," said Cyprian, "it has come to this."

"What?"

"To this."

"To what?"

"That you have taken my sweetheart away from me."

"Well, you may say I have, if you like, though, to tell the truth, she was my sweetheart before she was yours, Mr. What's-your-name."

"Was she, really?"

"Yes; I knew her when she wore little frocks, and small whats-his-names, and used to roll on the grass before old Langdon's cottage, and——Oh! oh!"

"Take that," said Patience, as she saluted Gamiel Gander with such a box on the ears that he saw sparks for several minutes.

"Oh! oh!—oh lor! well, who would have thought it?"

"Perhaps you will mind what you are saying another time, stupid."

"Yes, I will; but what was I a saying? No, no, I ain't a-going to say it again, I ain't. I didn't mean it—I didn't. But as for you, Mr. Page, you had best be jogging. We don't want you, you see, so be off. Be off!"

"Well," said Cyprian, "of course my heart is nearly broke."

"Oh, is it?"

"Yes, Mr. Gander; "you are such a lady's man, you are. Why, you look just like——"

"What?"

"An over-stuffed pincushion in that suit of clothes, that you do."

"None of your *odorous* expressions, sir. Be off with you, will you?"

"Well, I suppose I must. Oh, Patience! Patience!"

"I am glad to hear that you are going to have patience," said Gamiel, "so be off."

"But, oh—oh! Let me part friends with this last love of mine. My heart is breaking all the night, and cracking all the day. But in yonder tent, ye Gods, they sell such charming curds and whey."

"Eh?"

"Curds and whey."

"In for a penny, in for a pound. Ha! ha! If I have an inkling—ha! ha!—it's —it's for curds and whey."

"Is it?"

"Yes, yes; oh lord! it is. I say, girls, suppose we have some to begin with— eh?"

The page looked expressively at Patience, and she said—

"Well, I don't mind. We will follow you, Gamiel Gander, so go on."

"And won't you part with me in good fellowship," said the page, "and treat me to some?"

"Well, I dont mind a pennyworth, if you will go off, then, at once, and never let me see your face again?"

"You shall be obeyed, sir. But wait a minute. I'll just step into the booth, by this slit in the canvass, and see if they have got any left."

The page darted into the tent by a private entrance, and the good woman and her daughter, who kept it, uttered two screams at the intrusion.

"Stop," whispered Cyprian, pointing to an immense broad tub of curds and whey "what is that worth?"

"Worth?"

"Yes, the whole of it?"

"A golden angel, as I'm a sinner."

"There is the full value of it, then; and now, there is a stupid fellow in blue, who wants to seduce a young maid, and I want to souse him in this. May I?"

"With all my heart."

"And serve him right, too," said the daughter. "I know what being seduced is."

CHAPTER LX.

GAMIEL GANDER GETS MORE CURDS AND WHEY THAN HE WANTS.

OLD your tongue, Nancy," said the curds and whey woman, "what do you mean. Bring him in here, my good young sir, and you may souse him in it with pleasure. Oh, Nancy, I am quite ashamed of you. Stop a bit.'"

The woman installed the tub of curds and whey just to within the opening of the tent at which Cyprian had come, and then she said—

"There, sir, if you only bring him here, in he goes in a moment, and nobody the wiser."

"True, all's right, and you can sell it all the same, you know, afterwards."

"So I can."

"Nobody will be the wiser."

"Not a soul. Thank you, sir."

"You are as welcome as flowers in May, my good woman. I'll soon bring the rascal."

"Do so—do so."

Cyprian left the tent, quite delighted with the result, and the complete success of his stratagem. The moment he re-appeared to Amy and Patience, and Gamiel Gander, the latter cried out to him—

"Come, now, Mr. Page, tell the truth, and shame the devil. Do they really sell curds and whey there?"

"They do."

"You are quite sure?"

"As sure as fate."

"Well, I don't know about that; but let me tell you, Mr. Page, that a bargain is a bargain."

"What do you mean?"

"Why, that if I pay for the curds and whey, you will not be hanging about the garden of my father-in-law what is to be, Langdon, the ferryman."

"Oh, honour!"

"Well—well, I will see about it, then. In for a penny, in for a pound, as the saying goes. Come along, Miss Patience Gander that is to be—come along. Oh, how I do love you—I mean, curds and whey—that is, no—I mean you. This is the way, is it?"

"No—no!" said Cyprian.

"Yes; there is the front of the booth."

"Yes, my good Gander; but the good woman told me that she kept some specially fine and cool, and covered up from the common view of people who came to the fair, and that if we came in by this way we should be served some from that."

"No?"

"She did."

"Did she, though?"

"Even so. This way—this way. It may likely enough cost a groat more; but when a handsome young spark, you know, like you, is with his sweetheart, what does he care about a groat more or less?"

"Nothing at all."

"Of course not."

"I tell you what it is, Mr. Page, I begin to think you are quite a sensible little fellow."

"Oh, no—no!"

"Yes, I do, though."

"Praise from a Gander," said Cyprian, with a low bow, "is praise, indeed."

The two sisters, while this conversation was going on between Cyprian and Gamiel Gander, were almost in the agonies of suffocation by the dreadful efforts they were forced to make, from time to time, to control their laughter.

They all now made their way to the tent.

"In with you," said Gamiel—"in with you all."

"After you," said Cyprian.

"After me?"

"Yes; the good woman wanted to know if it was the handsome fat youth in sky-blue that was coming."

"Did she, though?"

"Yes, and I said it was, and then she said you should have so much that you would cry out that you had had too much."

"Did she? She don't know me."

Gamiel Gander thrust his head through the little slit in the canvass of the tent, calling out as he did so—

"Curds and whey!"

"Here you are," said Cyprian, as he at once then laid hold of Gamiel by the collar of his jerkin, and as much of his tight small clothes as he could possibly get a grasp of, and with one throw sent him head foremost into the tent.

There was a scream and a splash, and poor Gamiel found himself with his head at the bottom of the large tub of curds and whey, and his legs sticking up in the air, wildly kicking for release.

"Off we go!" said Cyprian to the two sisters.

Taking, then, one arm of each, away the page flew with them both, closely followed by Lassamour, and Lamont, and Robert Lee.

Alas, poor Gamiel Gander!

The tub upset, and he rolled out of it, with curds and whey down his throat—down his breast—down his back—in his hair, and, in fact, half drowned in an ocan of curds and whey.

The woman who, although she had been well paid by Cyprian for the whole tubful of the precious liquid, had been calculating upon yet retailing it, notwithstanding the immersion of Gamiel in it, and she was so provoked to see it all upset, that she chose quite to consider herself robbed, and so she set upon poor Gamiel with a good stout stick.

"Oh, you rogue!—oh, you rascal!" she cried. "Is this the way you try to take the bread out of the mouth of a poor widow? Take that — and that — and that!"

"Murder!" cried Gamiel.

"Oh, you seducer!" cried the daughter. "Oh, you vile seducer!"

The cries of Gamiel, the lamentations and shrieks of the woman, and the general *meleè*, brought a crowd of people into the tent.

Gamiel was secured and lifted on to his feet, and the deplorable spectacle he presented caused a roar of laughter.

"Hold him fast!" cried the woman. "Hold the villain fast! He has ruined me!"

"And he wanted to ruin me, too," said the daughter.

"All my curds and whey spoilt."

"And my virtue in danger," cried the daughter.

"Oh! oh! Murder!" shouted Gamiel.

"Come, come," said a man, collaring poor Gamiel, "the least you can do is to pay the poor woman for her curds and whey."

"But I haven't had any."

"Not had any? Why, you seem to have had no end of it. There are twenty quart's worth hanging about you."

"Oh! oh!"

The mob roared and laughed at this still more, and pretty Gamiel had to pay a sum that reduced his bag of groats by one half.

When this was accomplished, a sturdy-looking man stepped up, crying—

"Come—come, I won't see a young gentleman imposed upon; what is the matter here?"

"Somebody poked me in," said Gamiel. "It was that villain of a page, and now he has gone off with my sweetheart and wife that is to be."

"Indeed?"

"Yes, my good sir. His name is Cyprian, and he is the page of the Lady Margaret, the great dame that lives at Pleasaunce House. Oh, I am all over curds and whey. I'm half dead, and I shall catch my death of cold."

"So you will. Oh, the rascal; but come this way, my dear sir, and I will find him out, and cudgel him for you."

"You will?"

"Honour!"

"Then I'm main obliged to you. If you will only cudgel him for me, I'll I'll——"

"What?"

"Treat you to a flagon of mulled sherry."

"Then it is as good as done. Ah, there he is—there he is! Ah—ah!"

"Where?—where?"

"There. Stay where you are. I'm after him!"

The burly-looking man ran off; but, alas! he took with him the bag containing Gamiel's money; so that the disappointed youth, in addition to having too much curds and whey, had lost his sweetheart and his groats.

Alas, poor Gamiel Gander!

CHAPTER LXI.

LADY MARGARET LASSAMOUR ADOPTS A BAD PLAN.

HILE all this was going on at Lambeth fair, whither it will be seen that the principal persons connected with our tale have already arrived, the Lady Margaret was at Pleasaunce House a prey to a thousand distracting passions.

The idea that Martin Lassamour was actually carrying on an intrigue with Amy Langdon had taken firm possession of her mind.

The name of Amy to the letter that he had read while at the breakfast-table appeared to be confirmation so strong, that there was no longer room for doubt.

His agitated behaviour, then, and his strange departure from the mansion, all tended to confirm her in the opinion.

She sat like a statue in her own room with her hands clasped.

"Yes," she said, "it is over now. All doubt—all sort of hesitation—all weakness is now past. He dies; and yet I loved him best of all, and thought that it was possible he might not give me cause to kill him. But that chance is past: he dies! There only wanted this. Drunkenness, and that species of unfaithfulness which I could only lay down in my own mind as an innate principle, or want of principle, I might have borne with; but this is too much. He dies."

She rang her bell.

To the female servant that appeared, she said—

"Send Samuel to me."

The trembling Samuel, who so bitterly repented that he had had anything to do with the affair, was soon in her presence.

"Samuel?"

"Yes, my good lady."

"Your master has gone hence?"

"Yes, my lady."

"Do you know in which direction?"

"Lambeth Fair, my lady."

"Ah!"

"Oh! oh! Don't——"

"Don't what, idiot?"

"Don't look so at a poor fellow, my lady. I am very sorry, I am, indeed."

"For what?"

"For—for saying anything——"

"Sorry for doing a good mistress a service? No, Samuel, never be sorry for that. You were my servant long before the shadow of Martin Lassamour darkened the door of Pleasaunce House. There is gold for you. Tremble not—there is nothing with you to be sorry for."

"Thank you, my lady. But yet——"

"Say on."

"It may be nothing."

"Nothing?"

"No, my lady. The letter may have come on some very innocent errand, my lady."

Lady Margaret looked at him with an air of deep abstraction.

"An innocent errand, said you?"

"Yes, my lady."

A strange, wild-looking smile hovered upon her lips for a moment, and then she repeated the words:—

"An innocent errand? Go, Samuel, I have nothing further to say to you—go."

"Yes, my lady; but——"

"Go, I say!—minion! go!"

Samuel hurried from the room in a fright at his lady's vehemence and rage.

Lady Margaret was again alone. She shuddered as she sat in that room, which was to her, now, full of fearful associations.

"Yes," she said, at length, "I will trust to nothing now but the evidence of my own senses. I will make assurance doubly sure. I will go at once to this fair, and if Martin Lassamour be, indeed, there, and in dalliance with this light o' love wench, his doom is sealed."

Having come to this resolve, the Lady Margaret set about at once carrying it into execution.

Opening a cabinet that was in the room, she took out of it the complete costume of a monk. A wig, too, which had the tonsure clearly defined upon it, she produced from the same receptacle.

When she had carefully combed back all her long hair, and placed this wig upon her head, it would have been quite impossible, even for those who knew her the most intimately, to have any idea of her identity.

The disguise of the features under that new aspect was complete.

The priest's robe that she then put on was a favourable disguise, and then having placed sandals on her feet, she felt that she was in all respects fully equipped for the adventures she sought.

"Yes," she said, "it shall be so. I shall soon discern if he be there, and if she be with him. I have but to preserve the outward serenity of soul necessary to my disguise, and all will be well."

She passed out of her room, through the secret door in the wall that led to the greenhouse, beneath the floor of which she had disposed of the murdered body of her waiting maid.

It required some amount of courage to do this; but the Lady Margaret was, indeed, composed of "impenetrable stuff."

She had a mind to do things that, to a weaker spirit, would have been destruction.

With sundry and passing glances towards the spot where the opening was in the floor of the greenhouse, she walked through the little building, and gained the garden.

From there it was quite easy to reach one of the private doors in the park wall, to which she had a key, and having passed through it, she was in the open country.

"Now we shall see," she said.

She placed the hood of the monk's cloak further over her face, and took her route slowly and carefully towards Lambeth.

From the care with which the Lady Margaret went on with her disguise, one might very well be led to the conclusion that it was by no means the first time she had worn it.

Heaven only knows what wild and wayward adventures the strange and insane spirit of that bold, bad woman may have involved her in. It is more than probable that in that very friar's habit she had been from home on occasions when she had not so much at stake as at present.

But be this as it may, it is foreign to our present story, and we will but follow her to Lambeth fair.

The route she took betrayed a very intimate acquaintance with the whole neighbourhood, and she was soon within hearing of the many sounds that made up the bustle of the fair.

Little did Martin Lassamour think that, of all people in the world, his wife would be at such a scene, and so disguised that even he would not know her.

In the course of another quarter of an hour the Lady Margaret was actually within the precincts of the old fair at Lambeth.

There she was quite safe from anything in the shape of attracting attention; for amid the motley crowd, there were persons in all sorts of costumes, and of every variety.

There were monks, friars, soldiers, lacqueys, and, in fact, every imaginable class of persons, each sufficiently indicated, as was then the usage of the age, by the dress he wore.

Amid such an assemblage, the Lady Margaret was perfectly safe, and in that perfection of her disguise she had such abundant faith that, far from shunning any one who might know her, she looked about with no small anxiety for any one whom she could recognise.

Of course, her grand object was to see Martin Lassamour, and her great expectation was to see him in company with the ferryman's fair daughter.

Perhaps it would be a very great disappointment to her jealous eye if she did not see him in such company.

But the Lady Margaret was not doomed to such a disappointment, if, in good sooth, it would have been one; for by such a combination of circumstances as could hardly be looked for, she saw enough at the fair to add fuel, indeed, to her jealous rage and despair.

CHAPTER LXII.

DETAILS PROCEEDINGS AT THE FAIR OF LAMBETH.

 OW, while all this was going on, and while Martin Lassamour and his young friend, Lamont, and the pedler, Robert Lee, in their disguises were following the track of the ferryman's two fair daughters, as they both ran off with the page, Cyprian, after the maledictions of Gamiel Gander, the darker and sterner personage of our story was not idle.

Sir Warrene De Volence was at the fair, disguised and masked.

The two rascals, Glass and Tabby, were there, too, in very different dresses to those they usually wore, and they were concocting some plan by which they might lay hold of Amy Langdon, and carry her to the old house on London bridge, which had been mentioned to them by De Volence.

The day was yet young; so as regarded the assassination of Martin Lassamour the two rascals gave themselves no concern.

They did not dream of the possibility of his suspecting anything wrong or treacherous in the letter that had been sent to him with the name of Amy Langdon to it, and they considered his appearance on the lonely spot indicated in that letter at the hour, too, therein appointed, as a fact all but certain.

With such a feeling, then, they gave their whole attention to the first job they considered they had to do, namely, the abduction of Amy.

Rather in the shadow of a range of booths, not far from the tent in which Gamiel Gander had met with such a misadventure, they stood and conversed in whispers together.

"Glass," said Tabby, "do you really think this girl will come to the fair?"

"To be sure I do."

"Well—well, I hope so."

"Why, you see, Tabby, a lover to a girl is like a loadstone."

"As how?"

"Wh, you stupid, it attracts her, always provided she is as true as steel to him."

"Ha! Why, you are coming out strong, now. I had no sort of an idea you had half that amount of wit."

"Oh, hadn't you?"

"Not I."

"Ah, you don't know me yet."

"So it seems. Hush!"

"What's the row?"

"Do you see that fellow in the mask, and the old grey cloak?"

"Yes."

"And do you know him?"

"No; and yet there is a something about his walk that—that—Ah, yes, it is our own man."

"De Volence?"

"Yes, to be sure. I know him now. Shall we speak to him?"

"It's perhaps as well. He may be ooking for us."

Tabby stalked up close to De Volence, and whispered in his ear—

"Governor?"

De Volence started.

"It's only me."

"Tabby?"

"Yes."

"Is it done?"

"Done, noble sir?"

"Yes, yes."

"What done?"

"The girl taken off. Is she safe?"

"Lord bless you, worshipful sir, here is me, and there is poor Glass, both of us as dry as dust, and we have not seen her yet."

"Not seen her?"

"No, noble sir."

"Why, I saw both her and her sister at the further end of the fair only five minutes ago, along with the page, Cyprian."

"Did you, though?"

"Yes; and here you two are here doing no service at all. Curses on you both! what do you mean by it?"

"Time and patience, noble sir—time and patience."

"Go to the devil!"

"In good time, noble sir—in good time. It's all right, I can tell you, noble sir; it's all right, and we shall have her in our hands in no time now. You say you saw her with her sister?"

"Yes."

"And that little whipper-snapper of a page, Cyprian?"

"Yes, I told you."

"Good."

"Good for him, possibly, if he liked it, and good for her; but not for me. In a word, have you, or have you not made any arrangements for carrying her off?"

"Plenty."

"What are they, then."

"Just these. Down close to the clump of trees, and, in fact, right in among 'em, I should say, we have got a sedan chair in waiting, and a man in it, an old friend of ours, who is taking care of it."

"Well?"

"Well, then, he will wait till the girl comes and pops her nice little head into it, and then he lays hold of the nice little head, and in he pulls her, and pops a gag in her mouth before she can give one squall, and then Tabby and Glass, your two good friends, trot her off to London Bridge.

"But how to get her there?"

"I will whisper in her ear that the pedler is waiting for her."

"Ah!"

"Yes, that will do it."

"Do you think she will be so deceived?"

"Lord bless you, yes, noble sir; the moment a girl hears the name of her lover she is like a pig with a nose ring and a

AMY LANGDON.

cord through it, on she comes as orderly as possible. They are cunning enough in other matters; but when once they give their hearts to a man, he or his very name can lead them anywhere."

"You are quite a philosopher."

"I is."

"But this man who is with the sedan chair. Can you trust him?"

"With untold gold."

"Indeed."

"Yes; and he'd never stop to count it, but walk off with it just as it was. But put your noble mind at rest about him. We know him, and he daren't play false to us, any more than he dare go up to old Newgate prison, and say to the man at the gate, 'Here I am.' Oh, it's all right, noble sir, you may depend."

"Well, I leave it to you."

"You may, safely."

"And then of Martin Lassamour, what do you say of him?"

"Hooked!"

"Not dead?"

"No, but fairly hooked. The barbed hook is in his gills. He will be at an appointed spot, where he will die. Are you satisfied with that?"

"I am. Do not seem to know me, and it is well that we come no more together. See that all is ready for me at the old house on the bridge."

"We will."

De Volence, with a nod of satisfaction, at once walked off, leaving the two ruffians to carry out their infamous designs in the best way they could.

The information that the sisters, Amy and Patience, were in the fair, now set Tabby and Glass on their mettle, and they commenced a rigorous search for them.

Suddenly, upon turning the corner of a number of caravans, they came upon them both, along with Cyprian, who was rather liberally spending his money upon them.

They were both looking rather anxious, for Amy could not see her lover, Robert Lee, and Patience had some fear, lest Gamiel Gander should run to her father, and bring him to the fair, to see her with Cyprian, the young page.

"Come, come," said Cyprian, "you look both of you, as dull as possible. Dear Patience, are you not happy?"

"Not very, Cyprian."

"And yet I am here."

"Ah, Cyprian, I ought to be happy, I know, while you are here, but I dread the malice of that Gamiel Gander."

"I only wish I had twisted his neck for him," said Cyprian, "instead of only leaving him in a but of curds and whey with the woman and her daughter."

"That would have been worse."

"Do you think so?"

"Oh, yes—yes. As for Amy, here, she too, is a little unhappy, for she can't imagine what has become of Robert Lee."

"Oh, if I were but sure he was safe," said Amy, "I would be quite content; but while I know he has such an enemy as De Volence, I may well feel ill at ease not to find him at the fair."

"Never fear," said Cyprian, "all will be well."

"Do you see that monk," suddenly said Amy, "how he seems to dog our footsteps and how he fixes his gaze upon us."

"Where?"

"Yonder. There he is."

"Ah, yes. Confound the fellow, I see him. Well, I suppose we must not quarrel with him for looking. A cat may look at a king, and so a monk may look at a pretty girl, but I don't like him, for all that."

"Nor I, and it seems to me——"

"What, dear?"

"That there is something about his expression of face that I have seen before. It is very strange, but the more I look, the more I think so."

CHAPTER LXIII.

EVENTS THICKEN AT LAMBETH FAIR.

PON the supposition of Patience, that the features of the monk were not quite strange to her, Cyprian, himself, took a keener look than he had done before.

"Upon my life," he said, "I, too, have a dreamy sort of recollection of the face."

The monk, upon seeing that the eyes of the party were fixed upon him, passed them at a slow step.

As he did so he said,—

"Benedicitie my children. Be merry, but, be wise!"

"Thanks, holy sir," said Cyprian, "we will."

The monk passed on.

This monk was no other than the Lady Margaret Lassamour, and it spoke volumes for her disguise, and for her power of simulation, when we find that familiar as Cyprian must have been with her every look, and every tone, he knew her not.

"He is gone," said Amy.

"Yes," said Patience, "and a good riddance."

"So say I," said Cyprian, "my blood appeared to curdle in my my veins as I spoke. On my faith, I don't like him at all."

"Nor do we."

"But as respects the curdling of your blood, Cyprian," said Patience with a smile, "that is owing to your thoughts running upon the curds and whey that you sent Gamiel Gander into."

Cyprian smiled too.

"No doubt," he said, "no doubt. But a plague take it, we seem to attract universal attention."

"How?—how?"

"Don't you see those three masked gallants there, looking at us all as if they would devour us with their gaze?"

"Oh yes."

"Come away—come away, then. This way. No doubt they are some of the bad ones from the court, come to the fair like wolves, to see whom they can devour."

"Well, Cyprian, you must not drag one so," said Patience; "you may depend they won't devour us."

"I'll take good care they don't."

At this moment a man stepped up to Amy, and in a low tone he said—

"Fair lady, am I right or wrong. I am a poor serving man out of place, and some one has given me a half-groat to do him a service."

"Be off with you, will you?" said Cyprian.

"Noble sir," replied Tabby, for he was the man, "I will at once, if this fair lady will tell me her name is not Langdon."

"Langdon? yes," said Amy, "that is my name. Who sent you to me?"

"One master Lee."

"Ah! Robert Lee?"

"The pedler."

"Yes, yes; it is, then, to me his message is, if you have one from him."

"I have. He sends this."

The pretended messenger handed a little billet to the poor girl, on which was written:—

"MY AMY,—The bearer of this is, I daresay, no better than he should be, but he can and will bring you to me. Follow him, and alone, for there is danger.

"Your own—ROBERT LEE."

"Yes—yes, at once," said Amy.

"At once, what, dear sister?" said Patience. "What is all this about?"

"Read this."

Patience did read it, and Cyprian, although he was not wanted to do so, took it for granted that he might, too, so he peeped over her arm at it."

In a moment or two they were both possessed of the contents of the mysterious little billet, and then Patience said—

"Oh, Amy, I fear."

"What?"

"Treachery."

"No, no; that is impossible. Treachery and Robert Lee hold no converse together."

"Certainly not; but how can you be sure that this is not a base attempt of some one else?"

"Ah, you terrify me!"

"I am terrified at my own thought. Oh, Cyprian, what do you think of all this."

"It looks surpicious; but I will question the messenger. Come here, fellow."

"Yes, noble sir."

"From whom got you this billet?"

"From Master Robert Lee, the pedler."

"And where is he?"

"In a little thicket of trees not very far off."

"What manner of man is he?"

"Tall, and strong, and handsome, and he wore a blue jerkin, with silver points. He clasped his hands together, after he had given me this note, and I heard him say—'If she comes not I am lost.' But I was paid my half-groat, so it don't matter to me. I bid you good-day."

Tabby affected to be walking away; but Amy cried out to him at once.

"Stop! stop!"

He, with apparent reluctance, returned.

"I will go with you."

"As you please, fair lady."

"We will all go," said Patience.

"As you please."

"Nay, nay," said Amy. "Let me go alone. He says I must go alone, or it will be fatal, or something of the sort. Wait for me here, and I will go alone. We cannot tell what may have happened, or what is going to happen."

"An it please you," said Tabby, "I think something has happened to good master Lee, for there is blood upon his arm."

"Blood?"

"I saw it, though he tried to hide it."

"I no longer hesitate. Lead on at once, and I will follow you. As for you, dear sister, and you, Cyprian, fear nothing for me. I am quite convinced that it is Robert who sends for me, and so you may be sure he would not send for me to danger. Keep near about this spot, that I may find you easily upon my return."

"We will," said Patience, woefully.

"Oh, be quick," said Cyprian, "for I feel in doubt as to whether I am doing right or not."

"Doubt nothing, but wait for me. Now, sir, I am ready to follow you at once."

"This way, then."

Tabby walked slowly off, exulting in

the success of his stratagem, and followed by Amy Langdon.

But there were other eyes upon the whole proceeding besides those of the persons most closely concerned in it.

From a small hiding-place, close to the canvass of one of the tents, Martin Lassamour, and Lamont, and Robert Lee had seen the whole proceeding, although they were not sufficiently near at hand to hear a word that had passed.

They had seen, though, the note given and read—they had seen the impassioned gesture of Amy, and the doubtful and distressed look of the page and of Patience, and from all that they guessed that something was amiss.

"What is all this?" said Lassamour.

"I know not, my lord," said Robert Lee; "but this I know, that I will not lose sight of Amy."

"Nay—nay, let me advise."

"I shall go mad if she ventures from the fair, with that ruffian, to fall perchance, into the hands of De Volence."

"My good friend, you are not fit to carry out this affair. I ask you, as a personal favour, to trust it to me."

"To you?"

"Yes, to me. I am calm and cool, and you know that I can and will fight if needs be. Can you not take my word?"

"Yes, for anything."

"Then it is far better for you to stay here with Lamont. I will follow Amy and that man. If it be some plot against her liberty you would, by all likelihood, be known were you to dog her footsteps, while I shall not."

"It is true."

"You had better let him go," said Lamont.

"Go, then, dear sir, in the name of God; but it is a hard thing to remain idle here when one whom we love is in possible danger. My feelings are all against your going instead of me; but my judgment is convinced that it is better you should do so."

"That will do," said Lassamour; "you may depend upon me giving a good account of this adventure."

As he spoke, he gathered his cloak still closer around him, and started off in the path that Amy, following the rascal Tabby, had taken.

There was not much space between them; but it was the great object of Lassamour to avoid being seen, or suspected of following; so he took every possible precaution to that effect.

He not only wanted to secure Amy from the consequences of any villany that might be on foot against her; but he wanted to find out precisely of what the villany consisted, and who were its agents.

Now Tabby thought he had done a very clever thing, so long as he had stopped the page and Patience from following or coming with Amy; and as he went, he cast his eye now and then in the direction they had been left, to see that no after thought induced them to follow.

He never looked at all in the direction in which he was slowly but surely being dogged by Martin Lassamour.

"Have we far to go?" said Amy.

"No, fair lady, not far."

"Lead on quickly."

"At what pace you please, fair one."

Tabby quickened his pace, which suited him all the better; and if Amy could but have caught a glance at his face, which he took good care she should not, she would in a moment have seen by the look of guilty exultation it wore that he was not the indifferent and scantily paid messenger he affected to be.

CHAPTER LXIV.

TABBY AND HIS FRIENDS FIND PERIL INSTEAD OF PROFIT.

 ERY true was the remark of the nefarious Tabby to De Volence, to the effect that when a woman truly loves, her judgment is smothered.

The full and entire truth of such a proposition was, indeed, shown in the case of Amy Langdon; for we have seen that even the name of Robert Lee had been to her a spell that had induced a course of action decidedly adverse to all prudence.

For its sake she left her sister—she left

Cyprian, who, she knew well, would to the extent of his ability protect her, and she followed through the mazes of the fair a perfect stranger.

There was much, too, about the general appearance of Tabby to have warranted suspicion of his good faith; but the forged letter that he had brought had so far stultified the faculties of Amy, that she could think of nothing but that Robert Lee wanted her to come to him, and that he was in some possible danger from those which she, by the faith of her pure love, might save him.

Yes, that was the idea.

That was the idea with which this young girl followed the rascal who was about to endeavour to betray her to a fate far, very far worse than death.

But Heaven had ordained it otherwise.

Little did Mr. Tabby imagine that there was a champion of Amy's close at hand, with his eye upon every movement, and that champion was such an one as Martin Lassamour.

Able and willing, both, it is not possible, with the sole exception of Robert Lee, that such another defender could have been found in all the fair as the hero of our story.

Martin was one of the most powerful young men of his age. His skill with his sword was so well known, that his name alone would have so terrified Tabby that, if he had had it only whispered to him that he, Lasssmour, was on the look-out to oppose him, he would have fled in precipitation from the further prosecution of his nefarious plan against the person, the honour, and the happiness of Amy Langdon.

But the rascal had not the remotest idea that he was watched by any such formidable foe, and on he went.

Amy called to him again.

"Stop! stop!"

"Yes, my lady."

"I am doubtful of your faith. Whither are you leading me now?"

"Faith! I am leading you to him who sent me."

"Robert Lee?"

"Even so."

"But we are leaving the fair?"

"Yes, 'Even so,' is all I can say again to that, fair one."

"And we are approaching yonder trees, are we not?"

"Yes. There you will find him."

As Tabby spoke, he pointed to a clump of trees, within the shade of which he had stationed the man with the sedan chair.

Now, this very action of Tabby's, which he intended should have the effect of letting Amy see that they had not very far to go, and so facilitating his progress with her to the place of rendezvous, where Glass and the other rascal were waiting, acted quite in the contrary way from this, indeed.

It had so happened that Martin Lassamour was just beginning to feel the difficulty of following Tabby and Amy Langdon across a rather open space of ground, without making it obvious, so as to put mistake out of the question, that he was upon their track.

This action, though, of Tabby's aided him at once and effectually.

It let him know that the little clump of trees was the place of destination, and it at once convinced him that no attempt upon the life or the liberty of Amy Langdon would be made till they should reach there.

It was rather a hazardous thing to do, lose sight of her even for a moment; but Lassamour felt so convinced that it was within the umbrageous shadow of the little clump of trees that he should find a solution of the mystery, that he did not hesitate what to do.

By taking somewhat of a circuit round some large caravans belonging to the vendors at the fair, he knew that he should reach the clump of trees in another direction.

To feel the possibility of doing this, and to set about it was the work of a moment.

Time was never more active and swift than Martin Lassamour.

With a speed, then, and a precision that set failure at defiance, he ran the round-about way to the little copse.

At the pace Amy Langdon was proceeding, he felt perfectly sure that he should reach it before she and Tabby had decreased the distance one half, and he was not disappointed.

Before any one could, looking at the actual distance, have supposed it possible for him to do so, Martin Lassamour plunged into the wood.

The very first thing he did was to see a sedan-chair, without any bearers, standing in a very strange manner, all alone, in a little cleared space in the wood.

The object struck Martin as being rather suspicious; but his suspicion was very much increased by seeing a head, adorned with a very rough beard, and a huge swaggering pair of moustaches, project from the sedan, while a voice cried out—

"Hilloa, is that you?"

"Yes," said Lassamour, at a venture.

"Have you got the girl? I'm tired of waiting, damme. Why don't you bring her along, and stop her squalling?"

This put the whole affair beyond any question, and Lassamour's action was sufficiently indicative of the fact that he had made up his mind about it.

Drawing his rapier, he cried—

"Hold still, my friend, and I will make short of you. I will pin you like a cock-chafer to the inside of the sedan."

"Oh lord, no!—Murder!—Oh, don't! Mercy!"

Lassamour made a dash at the chair with his drawn sword, and passing it through the panel next to him, he just inserted about half-a-dozen inches of it into the carcass of the rascal within, as he rolled out at the other side, and then with a roar of pain fled as fast as his legs could carry him.

"So far, so good," said Lassamour. "One is disposed of, and I think my best plan will be to take his place."

With this Martin Lassamour stepped into the sedan, and closed the doors as they had been before.

Hardly had he done so when some one came running up to the spot, and called out—

"What's the row?"

This was Glass.

Now Glass ought, according to his arrangement with his friend, Tabby, to have been with the sedan chair; but he had been so anxious to see if Tabby was successful in bearing Amy Langdon to her destination, that he had crept to the edge of the wood next to the fair, to watch for his coming.

As Lassamour had reached the little clump of trees from another direction, Glass had not seen anything of him.

It was the roar that the rascal, who was to receive Amy in the sedan, made at the touch of Lassamour's rapier, that had come upon the ears of Glass, and caused him to come back, with his prudent enough inquiry of—

"What is the row?"

The first impulse of Lassamour was to sally out and attack Glass; but upon second thoughts, it struck him he might get some information from him; so with a full recollection of the surly tone of the rascal he had dislodged from the sedan-chair, he said—

"Oh, nothing's the row."

"Then what did you bawl out in that way for?"

"I'm tired of waiting."

"Now, curse you, ain't you paid?"

"Yes."

"Well, then, be quiet."

"What's to be done with the girl when you get her?"

"You are to gag her, but don't smother her; and don't you be taking no liberties on no account, or you will have De Volence about your ears, and you will have a nice ride with her to the house."

"What house?"

"On the bridge."

"What bridge?"

"Old London, to be sure. Why, Tabby told me he had told you about it."

"So he had; but I have such a head piece, I forget things so devilish quick, damme."

"Ha! ha!" laughed Glass; "that is all the better."

CHAPTER LXV.

TABBY MEETS WITH A LITTLE SURPRISE.

UT all this passed with very great rapidity, so much so, indeed, that it was all done with by the time Tabby and Amy Langdon reached the clump of trees in which was the sedan-chair.

"I will go no further," said Amy.

"Thank God," thought Lassamour, "I am right. That is her voice."

"I will go no further."

"No further, pretty one," said Tabby, who, now that he had got her so far, would rather she got into the sedan-chair, but yet felt that he had her pretty secure from all interruption in case she would not. "No further did you say?"

"I did."

"Oh, why?"

"It matters not why. I will go no further till I see Robert Lee."

"Oh, the pedler?"

"Yes. I will go no further till I see or hear from him. Where is he?"

"Close at hand, miss."

"Where is close at hand?"

"Hush—his life——"

"His life?"

"Is in danger."

"No! no!"

"If you speak too loud——"

Amy felt faint at heart, and her voice decreased to a whisper, as she said—

"Robert Lee's life in danger if I speak too loud! What do you mean by that?"

"Just what I say, pretty one. He has a foe."

"He has."

"You know that?"

"I do—I do. It is——"

"Ah, you can name the foe?"

"I can. It the false and cowardly De Volence."

"It is."

"My heart told me that it was so; but tell me, only tell me now, how I can aid him."

Tabby, with a slight smile, saw that Glass had taken care to get between Amy and the route back to the fair, so he said—

"Why, I will tell you. The fact is, he is wounded."

"Oh, God!"

"Wounded rather badly."

"He is murdered!"

"No, not that, whatever he may be; but wounded he is, and no sort of mistake, and he is——"

"Where, oh! where?"

"In that sedan chair."

"Oh, why did you not tell me this at once. He may even be within sound of my voice, and thinks it cruel of me not to come to him. Wounded and unable even to call his own Amy to him. Robert—Robert, I come to you!"

"Ha!" laughed Tabby, "she nibbles now, and it's all right."

Amy rushed beside the sedan-chair.

All the finer feeling of this young girl's nature were awakened by the supposed danger, and possibly the death of him whom she loved.

Every feeling of worldly caution was at once, and as completely forgotten, as if there had been no necessity in the world for the restriction of any such feelings.

"Robert!" she cried, again, "oh, Robert, speak to me if you are, indeed, able."

There came no sound from the interior of the sedan-chair.

"He's inside," said Tabby.

"Here?—here?"

"Oh yes. The door will open with a touch."

Amy did not hesitate. Had the rascal that Tabby and Glass thought they had left there, been there, indeed, the fate of poor Amy would have been sealed, and Heaven only knows what might have been the consequences.

But as it was, a warm and a sincere friend was there instead of the ruffian Tabby fully expected was waiting for her.

With eager haste Amy opened the door of the sedan-chair. The moment she did so, Martin Lassamour spoke in low, quick accents.

"Fear nothing," he said; "all is well with Robert Lee. Come into the sedan, and you will be out of harm's way. I am the friend of Robert Lee—Martin Lassamour is my name. Do you not know me?"

"Yes, oh yes!"

"Then with that knowledge you know that you can trust me."

"Yes, I can—I can."

"Seem, then, to be pulled violently into the chair, while I get out at the other side."

Amy was too much surprised and bewildered to attempt to ask for, or to form in her mind any explanation of what she heard, but with a faith which was by no means misplaced, she at once conformed to the wishes of Martin Lassamour.

Taking hold of her by the hand, he seemed to force her into the sedan-chair, as he got out of it on the other side.

"Pull the door close," he said.

"Yes, yes."

Amy in another moment was within the chair, and Martin Lassamour, although hidden by it from the sight of Tabby and Glass, was out of it.

"Ha!" cried Tabby, as he ran up with Glass at his heels, "that is capital. Well, done!—well done!"

"And quietly done, too," said Glass.

"Yes, capitally."

"I said quietly."

"I know you did. Let's carry them off."

"I hope he isn't a-choking of her."

"Oh, no—no. Trust him for that."

"Yes," said Martin Lassamour, as he stepped out from behind the sedan chair with his drawn rapier in his hand, "and you may both trust me to punish your odious rascality."

Certainly, if an apparition had suddenly started up from the ground and interfered between them and their prey, Tabby and Glass could not possibly have been more astounded than they were at the unexpected appearance of one who seemed so well prepared to do battle with them.

They both staggered back as though they had received some sudden shock.

"Murder!" cried Tabby.

"The devil!" said Glass.

"Villains!" cried Lassamour, as he sprang towards them. "Take the reward of your crimes!"

He wounded Tabby; but before he could follow up his attack, or touch Glass at all, they started off at a magnificent pace, yelling with affright, and Tabby in particular, howling with the pain of a wound in his shoulder that the rapier's point had given him.

Lassamour pursued them for some distance; but the idea struck him that he was leaving Amy alone in the wood.

He could not tell but that the rascals whom he had discomfited might possibly have some confederates, and this supposition caused him to pause on the instant.

He felt that it was a far higher duty to stay by Amy and defend her against all possible danger, than to pursue the two discomfited ruffians.

To feel a sense of duty of this description was to Martin Lassamour but the instigating power of action consonant with it.

He turned, at once, and sought the little

wod again at as great speed as he had just left it.

But Glass and Tabby were not destined to get off quite so easily as it seemed out of the adventure; for it so happened that the anxiety of Lamont and Robert Lee, the pedler, had induced them to follow as closely in the track of Amy as they dared to do without exciting observation.

These two, then, saw Glass and Tabby rushing off with evident affright, and they saw Lassamour following them for some distance.

"Ah," said Lamont, "our friend has hunted the game; do you not see?"

"I do, indeed."

Robert Lee ran on till he felt certain that the two rascals must pass him, and then, just as they were about to pass him, he, with his quarter-staff, dealt Glass such a blow across the back, that he sent him headlong into a ditch; and before Tabby could get out of the way, he recovered the command of the staff, and hit him a rap on the side of the head with it that sent him roaring to the ground.

"I think that will do," said Robert Lee.

"It will, indeed," said Lamont. "But come on, now, and let us seek Lassamour."

"Yes—yes, and Amy."

"And Amy, as you say; but you may depend upon it, my good friend, that she is quite safe."

"I pray Heaven it may be so."

"You may make up your mind to it, Master Pedler."

CHAPTER LXVI.

AMY IS RESTORED TO THE CARE OF HER LOVER.

EASILY may it be imagined how all these rapid movements must have both puzzled and alarmed Amy Langdon, shut up in a sedan chair as she was.

Indeed, but for her faith in Martin Lassamour, as one who with heart and hand would willingly befriend her lover, Robert Lee, she must have suffered by far too great an amount of anxiety to have enabled her to wait as she did his return.

But he had told her there to remain; so she felt bound to do so.

If for no other reason than for fear of deranging some plan of proceedings of which she knew nothing, she felt that she ought to take the request to stay in the sedan chair as an order.

Suffering, then, such an amount of anxiety as may be much more readily imagined than by any possibility described, the poor girl listened, with all her attention fearfully and mentally excited, to catch the slightest sound that might inform her of what in reality was going on.

She heard the cries of the retreating Tabby and Glass—she heard the quick tramp of the footsteps of Martin Lassamour as he pursued them, and then all was still.

But this painful stillness did not last for long. The sudden thought that had arrested Lassamour in his pursuit of the two scoundrels, Tabby and Glass, soon brought him back to the spot.

To fling open the door of the sedan was then, with him, the work of a moment.

"Alight, Miss Langdon," he said; "you are quite safe."

With a feeling of joy that she could find no appropriate language to express, Amy welcomed the sight of Martin Lassamour again, for she felt certain, although how was to her a complete mystery, that he had saved her from some very great peril

She was pale with agitation; and as he helped her from the sedan chair, Lassamour thought she had never looked so fair.

But such a thought was an innocent one. He did not by it commit any disloyalty to the friendship he professed for the pedler.

It is true that Martin Lassamour had been something of a libertine; but in all his actions there had still been such a sense of honour as had even prevented him from falling into the usual errors of his class.

He felt that he could tell himself that Amy Langdon was fair, and yet preserve his good faith to Robert Lee uncontaminated.

And the half smile that now crossed the face of Lassamour did more to assure the young girl of her safety than any words he could have used.

"You have saved me," she said.

"In good faith I suppose I have; and yet from what I hardly know."

"Nor I. What can be the meaning of this attempt to cajole me from my friends?"

"I am afraid there is but one man who would think that it would be well for him to attempt such a deed."

"Ah, yes, I know that man."

"You can name him, doubtless."

"I can—I can."

"And, if I mistake not, our fancies go in the same direction. You are thinking, as I am, of the bold and the bad Sir Warrene De Volence."

"Yes, for there is no other man who could or who would dare to make such an attempt upon your liberty. But fear nothing now. His rascally myrmidons are thoroughly defeated, and all is well."

"Yes, you have saved me."

"Nay, I did but little, after all. But do you not see who is coming?"

"Who?—oh, who?"

"More danger!"

The smile with which Martin Lassamour spoke was quite sufficient to assure Amy that the danger was of a very doubtful order, indeed, if danger it was at all, and she felt no terrors in consequence.

But in the course of another moment she saw who it was that approached.

Robert Lee, with the young Lamont but a few paces behind him, were hastening to the spot where stood the sedan.

"Ah, yes," she cried, "'tis he!"

"Robert Lee?"

"Yes—yes. He will thank you for me, noble sir."

"Nay, put not, I pray you, such a task upon him, for it is needless. If you do, I shall be at once compelled to fly from this spot, and that I do not wish to do, for I think that it is necessary to have some consultation with him about other matters."

"Then I will say nothing."

"You will oblige me so far. I rely greatly upon the sound sense, and the high courage of Robert Lee."

The flush of satisfied pride with which Amy Langdon heard these words sufficiently testified to the depth of her love for the pedler.

But further conversation was now put a stop to by the arrival of Robert Lee himself, who flew towards Amy at once, crying—

"Oh, Amy—Amy, you are safe?"

"Yes—yes, thanks to this gentleman."

"He has, indeed, done much to bind our hearts to him for ever. Oh, noble sir, what shall I say to you to prove to you, or to attempt even to prove to you that I am really grateful?"

"Nothing, my good friend—nothing; but let us now consult what is to be done with this rascal, Sir Warrene De Volence, who is, no doubt, at the bottom of all this mischief."

"Oh, if I get him but within reach of my quarter-staff," said the pedler, "I will put it beyond all question what can be done with him."

"You had better, my good friend, leave him to me," said Martin Lassamour. "I will find some means of bringing him to an account for all his misdeeds; and now that Amy is preserved from this attack of to-day, I would fain commit her to your care, Robert Lee, and recommend that you lose not sight of her till you have placed her in safety in her father's house."

"That shall be my care."

"Yes," said Amy; "but in the first place find my dear sister, Patience."

"She is with young Cyprian, the page, in the fair."

"I know it, Robert. Cyprian loves her."

"And she?" said Lassamour, with a smile.

Amy shook her head.

"I must not tell tales out of school," she said.

The tone in which she spoke, though, was quite a sufficient answer in the affirmative to the question of Martin Lassamour, who then said—

"I have made it my duty, as well as my pleasure, to see that both you and your sister are well bestowed, Miss Langdon; but I grieve to think that it is a feeling which can go by no other name than selfishness in your father's heart that stands in the way of your happiness."

Amy was silent; but she sighed deeply in acknowledgment of the truth of what Lassamour said.

In fact, had he characterised the feeling that had been displayed by Langdon, the ferryman, in very much stronger language than he did, it would have been but the truth in the matter.

"But," said Robert Lee, "Amy and I intend to be quite happy, despite all the selfishness in the world."

"Yes, oh yes; and yet——"

"Yet what, dear one?"

"It is very, very sad for our father to hold such a position, so adverse to the one that he ought to hold, is it not?"

"It is, love."

"Well, it cannot be helped," said Lassamour. "These things will happen; but I will take good care that the objection of Langdon shall vanish."

"To me you have already done all that the kindest and best friend could do," said Robert Lee.

"Mention it not; but do you go home now, Amy, and take your sister home with you; and when you see your father, tell him that Cyprian, the page of Martin Lassamour, is rich enough to do all that he requires."

"Oh, sir, how can I say what my heart would fain dictate to my lips?"

"Hush! Cyprian already knows of my feeling towards him, and all will yet be well. Can you, do you think, Robert Lee, meet me this evening at eight of the clock, at the porch of Lambeth church?"

"If the church porch stand for me to be at it, I will be there."

"Enough."

Martin Lassamour held out his hand, and cordially shook hands with Robert Lee and Amy, and then they separated, Martin Lassamour taking Lamont with him.

Robert Lee, with a fair clutch of his quarter-staff, strode on to the fair again with his Amy. He feared none with her by his side.

CHAPTER LXVII.

THE PLOT THICKENS, AND VILLANY RECEIVES ANOTHER BLOW.

 T was with pride and pleasure both that Robert Lee, the pedler, walked back to the fair of Lambeth from the little copse where the adventure with the sedan chair had taken place.

His Amy was with him!

This adventure, with all its concomitant circumstances, had had the effect of binding their hearts closer to each other.

Mutual dependance and mutual danger will ever bind together more and more closely those who truly love.

The danger of disunion is in prosperity, not in the storms of adversity.

Mean spirits will not be able to withstand the many shocks of adverse fortune; but it is a characteristic of the truly noble heart that under the storm clouds of adverse fate, even, they are the more united.

"And so, dear Amy," said Robert Lee, "you came to the fair to see me?"

"I did, indeed, Robert."

"And can you suppose that I had any thought but what was connected with you and your dear image! Ah, no. I felt that I should see you; but I did not imagine that there was danger dogging your footsteps."

"There was danger, Robert, but along with the danger, you see, came the aid."

"Yes—oh, yes."

"Yes, noble and gallant friend, Martin Lassamour, soon put them to flight, who would have dragged me from you."

"I owe him life service in return, and much I fear, Amy, that the villain, De Volence, means him no good."

"Robert?"

"Yes, Amy."

"You know that you are dear to me. You know that without you, love, I would not wish to live."

"Oh, Amy."

"But yet, Robert, I charge you, even by that love that you have for me, and that I have for you, that you look to the safety of this noble gentleman."

"I will, indeed."

"Even to the exceeding peril and danger of your own life, I charge you to do so."

"You are a noble girl, Amy."

"Nay, what is life without the honour that gives to it all its grace, and all its dignity?"

"Nothing, Amy, nothing."

"Then you think with me, Robert."

"I do, indeed."

"And I am proud of you, that you do so."

"Amy, I have to meet him, as you know, at eight o'clock this evening, by the porch of old Lambeth Church, and believe me, that man never went to do good service to a fellow man with better heart than I go to that meeting."

"Heaven guard you."

"Amen, for that, Amy."

"And I, too, say Amen!"

"Life is very dear to me, now."

"And to me, Robert."

"Yes, dear Amy, we love and bless—we have much to live for."

"Ah, there is, Patience."

"And Cyprian, as I live."

Patience and Cyprian now saw Robert Lee and Amy rapidly approaching, and Patience holding out her hand to the pedler, said—

"Why, Robert Lee, what on earth could you mean by alarming us all so, and Amy in particular."

"I alarm you, fair Patience."

"Yes, indeed, by sending that horrid-looking man for Amy."

"And with whom," said Cyprian, "I have been reproaching myself, ever since, that I let her go alone."

"You was not to blame," said Amy. "But the worst trouble is, that that horrid-looking man would have led me to a fate that I dread to think upon."

"No?"

"It is so, indeed."

Cyprian drew forth the light ornamental rapier he wore by his side, and stamping his foot upon the ground, he said,—

"Now where is the rascal. By all the saints I will make him bite the dust."

"He has bit both dust and mud, I think," said Robert Lee, with a smile, your valiant master, Cyprian, put him and two others to flight."

"He did?"

"Even so."

"Then the good lord be with my valiant master, always, for he is in truth a noble gentleman."

"In that we all agree."

"Oh, there is some mystery in all this," said Patience. "Pray have pity on me, and tell me all, dear Amy?"

"Ah, and on me, too," said Cyprian.

Upon this, Amy related all that happened, and as some of it was new to Robert Lee, as well as to the others, he, too, listened with great and absorbing interest to it.

Amy concluded by saying—

"There, now, you know all about, and where I should have been now, but for Martin Lassamour, Heaven only knows."

"The villains!" cried Cyprian.

"Oh," said Patience, "I could kill them myself."

"Heed them not, now," said Robert Lee. "I rather think that two of them will have, for some time to come, a very lively recollection of my quarter staff; but the day wears on apace, and it is the advice of Martin Lassamour that you go home."

"Home be it, then," said Patience. "You look pale and fagged, dear Amy."

"I am sick at heart, Patience, and would fain be home."

"And what is to become of me," said Cyprian.

"I will tell you as we go along," replied the pedler. "I am charged with a message, on your account, to Langdon, the—a—the—a—worthy father of these fair ones."

"Hem!" said Cyprian.

It was quite clear that in his use of the word "worthy," in connexion with Langdon, the ferryman, Robert Lee was very much more influenced by his love for the daughter than respect, if he had any at all, for the father.

But Amy looked her thanks.

They now all went their way from the fair towards the cottage of the ferryman, and Cyprian, managing to get close to Robert Lee, said—

"I pray you, good friend, tell me of the message you bear to our inestimable blue beard of a father-in-law, that I hope sincerely is to be."

"I will."

"What is it?"

"It is, that he should keep his eye well on the movements of a certain page."

"The devil!"

"Yes, he intimated that that page was the very devil!"

"Oh, that opinion and that message from him will ruin me for ever with Langdon."

"You don't say so?"

"Yes—yes, it will, indeed. Alas! I am undone, and he promised, too, that he would say all he could for me, and in fact that he would befriend me to the utmost of his power, and his power to do so is only by any possibility limited by his will."

"Well, that is a pity."

"I am lost!"

"Are you, though?"

"Yes—yes. Patience?"

"Well?"

"Oh, what do you think?"

"I never think."

"You don't?"

"No, Master Cyprian, I leave others to do that for me; and if you had any gallantry at all, you, at least, would take that trouble off my shoulders and not bother me with any more."

"Well, but here is Robert Lee going to tell your father, from Martin Lassamour, all sorts of bad things of me."

"Yes," said Robert Lee, in answer to an appealing look from Patience, who opened her pretty eyes very wide, indeed, upon the occasion—"yes; and among others, I have to tell him that he, Martin Lassamour, intends to take good care that all pecuniary disabilities on the part of Master Cyprian to marrying you shall be done away with."

"What?" cried Cyprian.

"Yes, that is a part and parcel of the message."

"You don't say so?"

"I do."

"Then I am the happiest of pages."

Oh, my dear little Patience, it is all settled."

"What is settled?"

"Why, that you are to be Mistress Cyprian."

"Indeed, that is like your impudence."

"Like—my—impudence?"

"Yes."

"Well, but don't you love—that is to say, didn't you—no, I mean, won't you?"

"I don't, I didn't, and I won't. There, now, all your three questions are answered in a breath."

Amy laughed.

"Don't believe her, Cyprian. She is bound to do one of two things, I can tell you."

"And what are they?"

"You are bound either to marry Gamiel Gander——"

"Oh! oh!"

"Or Cyprian."

"Then I endure my fate."

"Do so," said Cyprian, as he threw his arms around Patience, and gave her a kiss, for which he received such a deliberate little box on the ear that he was quite delighted with it, and cried out,

"Do it again!—do it again!"

CHAPTER LXVIII.

MARTIN LASSAMOUR MEETS AN OLD ACQUAINTANCE.

OW we will leave the two couple of lovers to their own desires, and to amuse themselves as best they may, while we follow the fortunes of Martin Lassamour.

He did not see, nor did Amy see that, while Lee and she were conversing together in the little copse where the sedan chair was, just previous to the arrival of Lee and Lassamour at that spot, that a friar had appeared from behind one of the trees.

That friar was the disguised Lady Margaret Lassamour, who had followed Lassamour himself to that spot; but not closely enough to comprehend really what took him there.

Nor did she get close enough to hear one word of what was said.

She trusted to her eyes; and seeing should not in all cases be believed.

That it should not is sufficiently exemplified by the fact that from what the Lady Margaret Lassamour saw, she made up her mind that she had ample confirmation of the fact, or the presumed and supposed fact, that Martin Lassamour was engaged in an intrigue with Amy Langdon.

She saw Amy leaning upon his arm—she saw the look of half affright, half joy, upon the face of the young girl.

She saw the flush of excitement upon the face of Martin Lassamour, and so she put her own interpretation upon all these signs. She called them love; whereas the reader is well aware there was nothing of the sort in the minds of either of the parties.

Turning rapidly, Lady Margaret sought her way from the fair towards her own house.

"He dies to-night!" were the first words that passed her lips.

The threaded route that the Lady Margaret could take to Pleasaunce House from the little copse was by the ferry of Langdon.

When she reached the boat no one was ready to cross the water in that direction, for it was away from the fair, and Langdon was waiting for customers.

"To your boat," said the Lady Margaret, assuming, as she could really very successfully, the tone of a man. "To your boat, Sir Ferryman."

"It's all very well, Sir Friar," replied Langdon, "to say to your boat; but think you your pay will pay me for crossing the river?"

"Quick! quick!"

The Lady Margaret sprang into the boat.

"Oh, you may wait there, if you like."

"Wait? Why wait, knave?"

"Knave me no knave, Sir Friar; but I don't intend to cross the river till my boat is full."

"Ah!"

"Yes, ah, indeed."

"And how many does your boat hold?"

"Twelve, if you must know."

"There is twelvepence, then."

"Truly welcomed it is."

"There is the way. Now take me across."

"Oh, if that is the game, well and good. Twelvepence for one person is as good to me as for twelve."

"It is. Then go on, good fellow."

"Free and easy. Save you, good friar, I am going on as quickly as I well can with you."

"Save you, my son," said the mock-friar, with an air of pretended sanctity.

"Thanks, holy sir; mayhap you go on some errand of life or death, since you are in such haste?"

"I do."

"Ah, I thought so."

"Of death!"

"Indeed. I pray, then, for the poor soul."

"Amen!"

The ferryman connected all this with the idea that the friar was bound to some dying man, to shrive him; but the Lady Margaret put a signification of a very different character upon the words she used.

"Yes," she said to herself, in a low tone, "he dies to-night!"

In the course of another hour the Lady Margaret was in Pleasaunce House, and there she shut herself up in her own room, to brood alone over the awful resolve which she had taken, to add, that night, Martin Lassamour to the already frightful list of her victims.

"He dies! he dies!" she cried, vehemently.

She paced her room for more than an hour with disordered steps.

Then she approached an easel, on which was the still unfinished portrait of Lassamour.

Tearing off the cloth that covered it, she stood regarding it for some minutes in silence,"

Then she spoke in a strange, calm voice—

"It is like him; but it wants the finish. It shall be done yet before midnight."

She hastily set down to the work, and from memory, for she was really a good artist, she now put the few finishing touches to the portrait of the man whom she had made up her mind to murder.

It was a strange fancy of the Lady Margaret that she would have the portraits of all her husbands before she consigned them to the tomb.

For more than four hours she toiled at the picture, and then she had brought it as near to a state of perfection as she cared to have it.

"It is done," she said.

She rang the bell that communicated from her room to the servants' hall.

It will be borne in mind that none of the household had been aware even of her absence from Pleasaunce House, for she had returned to it by the same secret route by which she had left it, so that the ringing of the bell, although no agreeable sound, did not take them by surprise.

Samuel felt that it was his special duty to answer the summons, and as no one appeared to the smallest extent inclined to dispute the honour with him, he went to the apartment of his mistress.

"Did you ring, my lady?"

"I did."

"Ye—e—s, my lady."

"Samuel?"

"Yes, my lady. At your ladyship's service."

"Idiot, why do you tremble?"

"Tremble, my lady?"

"Yes; why so?"

"Do I tremble? Oh, ah—tremble!—yes—I—a—do. Ha! ha! I have got a severe cold."

"Indeed?"

"Yes, my lady. The house, your ladyship sees, is a—that is—rather, you see, full of draughts, and I have caught a cold. I always tremble, my lady, when I have a cold."

"Be it so."

"As your ladyship pleases."

"You see this portrait?"

"Yes, my lady. Oh! oh!"

"What now?"

"It is the very moral——"

"Of who?"

"My master."

"So you think it like him?"

"Oh, yes, my lady; and I'm sure master will be quite delighted with it when he sees it. I suppose, my lady, it is intended as some delicate little compliment to him. Perhaps the good gentleman's birth-day is near at hand, my lady?"

"No."

"Well, then, your ladyships——, but be it which way it may, I am quite sure that—"

"Silence!"

"Yes, my lady."

"You will take this portrait and hang it up in the hall, or rather the long gallery, where the other paintings hang."

"Yes, my lady."

"You will be careful that it is in its proper place directly after the last one that hangs there. I am glad this portrait is finished, for life is uncertain."

"Yes, my lady; and—and——"

"What?"

"Nothing, my lady."

Samuel took the portrait in his arms, and he was only too happy to get out of the room with it, for there was, as he thought, and thought rightly, too, something inexpressibly awful in the looks of his mistress.

Instead of going to the gallery with the picture, the bewildered and terrified Samuel flew direct with it to the servants' hall and rushing in, he cried—

"Here's another!—here's another!"

This exclamation upon the part of Samuel, combined with the fact that his feet tripped over something, and caused him to fall with a terrible riot on the floor, with the portrait in his hand, had such an effect upon the nervous system of the servants that they burst into one simultaneous scream.

One, indeed, made an effort to get up the chimney.

The cook flew to a large copper that was in the scullery, and actually got into it.

In fact it took a good half-hour before anything like equanimity was restored in the servants' hall of Pleasaunce.

But we must now attend to Martin Lassamour, who, as we have announced, met with an old acquaintance.

CHAPTER LXIX.

THE MURDERESS IS ENCOMPASSED IN THE TOILS.

YET, notwithstanding that Martin Lassamour had got so well through with the adventure in which Amy Langdon was concerned, it will be in the recollection of the reader that the mysterious letter that had been sent to him with Amy's signature, was still in want of clearing up.

Knowing well, as he did, that it did not come from Amy at all, and connecting all the circumstances that had already taken place at the fair, he could come to no other conclusion than that the attack upon the liberty of Amy was materially connected with the same train of circumstances that had produced that letter to him.

Indeed, it was no extravagant supposition, and one not at all unnatural—as the reader well knows, with the truth—for him to conclude that the rascals whose machinations he had defeated in the copse, were those who were associated in the plot against his own life.

That it was his life that was sought, there could be now no reasonable doubt.

Hence, then, was it, that Martin Lassamour had determined upon holding a consultation with his two friends, the pedler and young Lamont, as to what had better be done in the case.

But before that occasion for consultation actually arrived, Martin Lassamour, by accident found an ally in all his proceedings that he did not think of, or in any way expect.

It will probably be in the recollection of the reader, that upon the occasion of the marriage of Martin Lassamour with the Lady Margaret, he had, at the church-door, been cautioned by a gentleman by the name of Sir Ralph Shard.

This gentleman had announced himself as the uncle of Lady Margaret's last husband, Sir Thomas Shard, and had volunteered a n advice and warning to Martin Lassamour.

Now Martin, at that time, did not, and could not bring himself to believe in the guilt of the fair lady of Pleasaunce, and so he had not only rejected the warning of Sir Ralph Shard, but he had spoken rather haughtily and defiantly to that gentleman for offering it.

Many a hour since, though, Martin Lassamour had thought much more favourably of the old gentleman, and he had felt that disagreeable impression on his mind which haunts us all when we fancy we have been guilty of an injustice.

It so happened, now, that as Martin Lassamour and Lamont walked through the fair, still in their disguises, after parting from Amy and her sister, they heard a cry for help.

"What is that?" said Lamont.

"It was a shout for aid. This way."

Lassamour sprang towards the spot, and when he turned the corner of some trees, he saw no less than four ruffianly-looking men, armed with knives, about to make a rush upon one person, who had wrapped his cloak around his arm, and had a rapier in his hand only.

"Thieves!—thieves!" cried the gentleman with the rapier; "thieves! Come on, you rascals. If one honest man is not a match for four thieves, the devil is in it. Come on."

"We will make the odds a little more even," said Lassamour, as he drew his rapier, and dashed forward to the rescue.

Lamont did the same.

The four thieves, for such they were, no sooner saw that two men had come to the rescue, than they fled with such speed that it was quite out of the question to try to follow them.

"Bravo!" cried the gentleman who had been attacked. "I warrant the rascals would not run into action half so fast as they run out of it."

"You may swear to that, sir," said Lassamour.

"Are you hurt, sir?" said Lamont.

"No, by the Lord, no! I took care of that. The knaves must have seen my purse, as I took it out in the fair to purchase a toy for a child, whose longing eyes were fixed upon it, but who lacked the means for it."

"No doubt, sir."

"Gentlemen, I give you my thanks; and if you should ever come near my farmhouse, and ask for Sir Ralph Shard, he will give you a welcome."

"Sir Ralph Shard?" said Lassamour.

"Ay, sir."

"Then—then you——"

"I what, sir?"

"You are the uncle of the late Sir Thomas Shard, who—who was the——"

"The sixth husband of the Lady Margaret, of Pleasaunce House, you would say?"

"Yes—yes."

"You are right, sir; my murdered nephew was the sixth victim of that lady. The Lord help the pig-headed fool who is the seventh!"

"Sir?"

"I say the Lord help him."

"Amen!"

"Well, amen! I bear no malice; but would you think it now, gentlemen, I came all the way up from Gloucestershire to warn that fellow, and I caught him at the very church door, and did warn him?"

"You did, sir?"

"Ay, did I; but what do you think I got for my pains in doing so?"

"Hard words," said Lassamour, "and a threat to be called out for it."

"True, by all the saints."

"But," added Lassamour, taking off his mask and bowing, "the pig-headed fellow knows better now, and begs to apologize to Sir Ralph Shard for what he said at that meeting by the church door."

"The devil!"

"No, Sir Ralph, not the devil; but poor Martin Lassamour, who feels and acknowledges the truth of the warning you gave to him, and all the kindness that dictated it, now stands before you."

The old baronet seized his hand, and gave it such a squeeze, that Martin was compelled to make quite a wry face over it.

"Body o' me," cried Sir Ralph, "don't say another word about it."

"Can you forgive me, sir?"

"With all my heart; but it must be mutual. Can you, and will you forgive me for saying what I did just now of you?"

"Oh, yes, Sir Ralph, I deserved it; while what I said to you was wholly undeserved. But we will say no more about it, if it please you."

"With all my heart, Martin Lassamour; and I beg now to say that when I

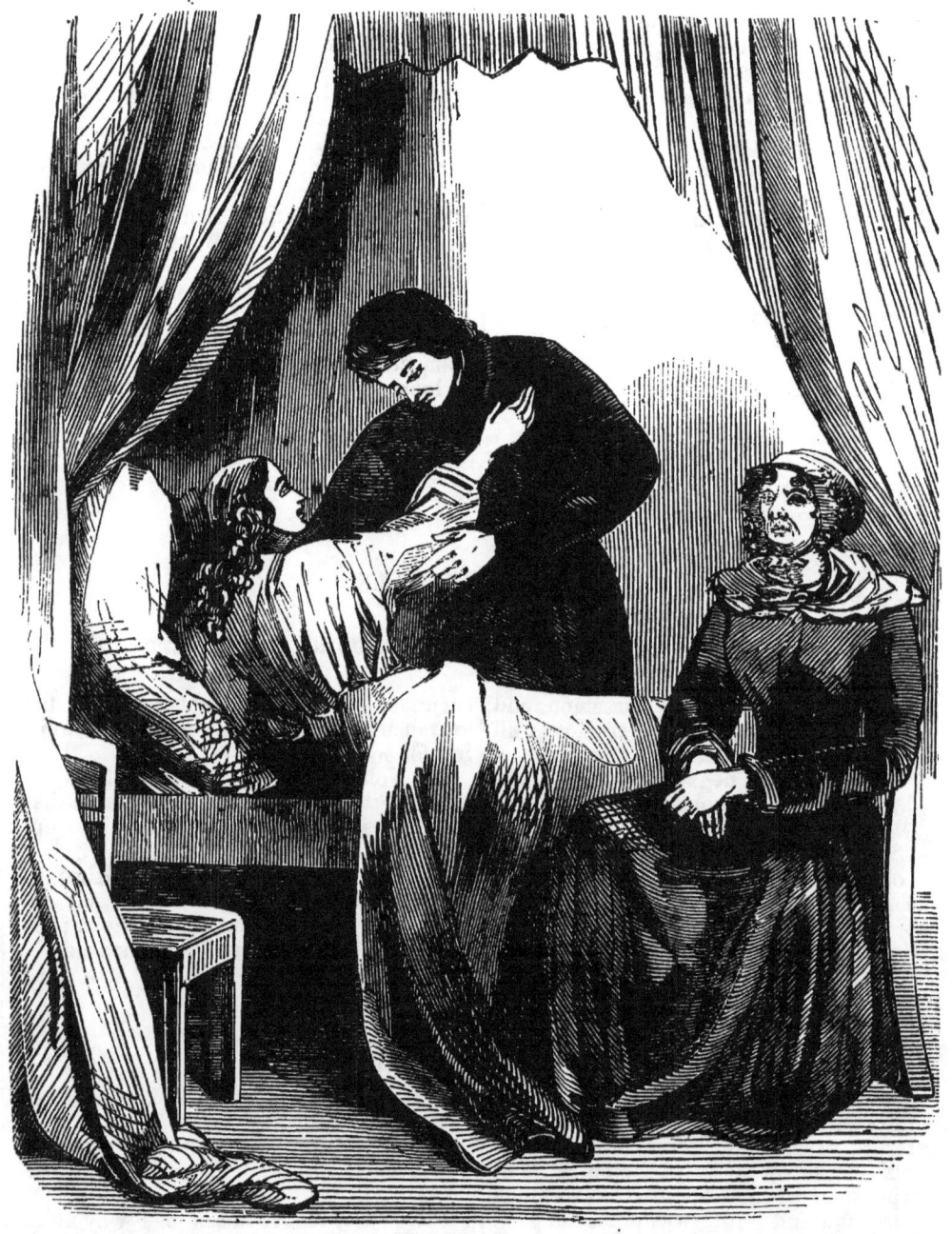

give my right hand, I give my heart, and that you may depend upon me as a true friend to the death."

"I am sure of that."

"You may be so; but who is with you?"

Lamont had taken off his mask, and Martin introduced him to the old man, who received him with the greatest cordiality, and then he cried—

"Upon my word, and by all the saints, Martin Lessemour, I do think that there is more in this meeting of ours than meets the eye."

"There is, Sir Ralph. I never was more in want of some calm judgment—some clear head and true heart to advise with me than now."

"Hem! well, I'm afraid——"

"Ot what, sir?"

"That I don't answer all these considerations; but now, mind, make a confidant of me, and we will see what can be done. But I can guess your trouble."

"No doubt of that."

"You have found out something that is not very pleasant concerning the fair dame of Pleasaunce House."

"I have, indeed."

"Ah, I thought so."

"I have found out much, Sir Ralph, and I suspect much more, which time I fear will confirm."

The old man shook his head.

"A bad one! a bad one, master Lassamour," he said, "you may be sure. Why, if all the world were to say to me that my nephew, Sir Thomas, came by his end fairly I wouldn't believe it."

"Nor I."

"He was murdered, sir."

"I fear it."

"And I am sure of it. And you, too, will soon."

"Not if I can help it."

"And," said Lamont, "my friend here is forewarned, and to be so, you know, Sir Ralph, is to be forearmed."

"Well—well, it is so."

"Yes," said Lassamour, "I am, indeed, forewarned, and I hope that your time and inclination both serve you to aid and to hear me in what I have to say to you."

"Both! both! Egad, you know I am a bachelor, and quite at your service; but I am most truly athirst; so let us in somewhere, and have a cup of wine, and a long talk over your affairs, Martin Lassamour."

CHAPTER XLXX.

DE VOLENCE BEGINS TO SUSPECT THINGS ARE GOING WRONG WITH HIM.

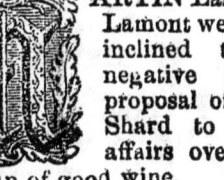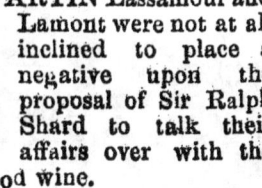

ARTIN Lassamour and Lamont were not at all inclined to place a negative upon the proposal of Sir Ralph Shard to talk their affairs over with the aid of a cup of good wine.

So, while they are arranging what is best to be done in the present position of affairs, we may just as well take a very brief and cursory glance at our old acquaintance, Sir Warrene De Volence.

De Volence, then, had too much on hand that day of Lambeth Fair to absent himself from it altogether.

In several disguises—changing one for another at different times, in order the better to assure the secrecy of his movements—he hovered about the outskirts of the piece of ground upon which so much reckless fun and jollity was proceeding.

He knew well that Tabby and Glass would do all in their power to carry out his nefarious designs, and yet he much dreaded their failure.

Hence was it that he was full of anxiety to know how matters progressed.

De Volence was not very long ere he came by some information; although, for his peace of mind the real truth is, he had much better have been without it.

As he passed a booth, in which liquor of the commoner sort was sold, he was rather surprised to see Tabby standing at the entrance of it, apparently in anxious waiting for some one's arrival.

De Volence had on a half mask.

From the glance of non-recognition that Tabby gave him, he saw that he was not known.

But it did not suit De Volence to remain unknown to the base tools he employed to work out his nefarious purposes; so approaching Tabby, he said—

"What is amiss?"

"Oh, noble sir, it's you, is it?"

"Yes."

"Well, everything."

"No?"

"Yes, though, it is. Here is poor Glass in rather a bad way."

"A bad way?"

"Even so, sir."

"Drunk?"

"No—no, that is not a bad way at all for him, for he is used to it; but I rather think his head is a little gone, owing to a tap he has had upon it from that confounded knave, the pedler,"

"Robert Lee?"

"The same."

"Curses on him!"

"Ah, so say I; but it's not much use cursing a fellow with a quarter-staff such as his, and with such hands to use it with. His is the worst curse upon any one he chooses to give a salute with it."

"I intend to have his life."

"Would that you had intended it before this day. But I was looking for a leech I sent for to look at Glass, for I feel rather afraid he is very bad."

"Then what has been done?"

"Nothing."

"The girl?"

"Has escaped. It was as well managed as anything could be, when, all of a sudden, from where the Lord only knows, up starts this fellow, Martin Lassamour, with a drawn sword in his hand, and he commences such an assault upon me and Glass, that we found it the best way to run for our lives, and we should have got well off, but who should we meet, then, but Robert Lee with his infernal quarter-staff."

De Volence stamped with rage.

"That Martin Lassamour," he said, "is born to be my fate—my absolute ruin. Oh, that I could crush him! but he shall be crushed, Tabby. You will do that deed?"

"Ay, if I can."

"Well—well; now mark what I say."

"I will."

"Do but make sure of the death of Martin Lassamour, and for that deed I will give you as much as you were to have had, both for it and the abduction of the girl."

"Good."

"When he is no more, we will again see to the safe stowing away in some secure place of this pretty piece of virginity."

"Good."

"Now, you understand me, Tabby?"

"Oh, yes, your honour, I will say that for you, and of you, that it is not at all difficult to understand you."

"Then you will see to it'?"

"I will, you may be sure. It is a matter of business; and if poor Glass gets better, he will do what he can to help me; but I'm afeard for him."

"Oh, pho! a tap on the head won't kill."

"It depends a little upon the strength of it."

"True—true."

"I think it is true, indeed."

"Well—well, take this purse. There is gold in it, and do all you can for your comrade; but let me depend upon your active and energetic proceedings in the case of Martin Lassamour."

"You may depend upon that."

"Be it so."

De Volence sauntered away, for he had no idea of venting any true or pretended sympathy upon Glass; and, in fact, in his own mind, he considered that if he was wounded past being able to aid in his nefarious and villanous schemes, the sooner he was dead the better.

The idea, indeed, did just cross his mind of suggesting as much to Tabby; but he thought then that, perhaps, it was better not, lest Tabby should think that a similar suggestion might be made to some one concerning him on some other and similar occasion.

But still De Volence hovered about the fair, for the idea was in his mind that it might be possible to do Martin Lassamour an ill turn at unawares if he should chance to have a good opportunity.

And now, while the villains, De Volence and Tabby had been having this little conversation together, Martin Lassamour, and Lamont, and Sir Ralph Shard, had found out a tavern, and called for some sherry, which was a wine then getting much into fashion.

Without more ado, then, Lassamour communicated freely to Sir Ralph Shard all that he had to say about the Lady Margaret.

He likewise informed him of the letter he had received in the name of Amy Langdon, and showed it to him.

The old baronet listened with great attention to all this, and then he said—

"Now hark you, Martin Lassamour, I don't at all pretend that I can see further into a mill-stone than my neighbours can, but I think I can give you some good advice."

"I am sure it will be good from you, Sir Ralph Shard."

"Well you can judge of it when you hear t."

"We are all attention."

"My nephew, Sir Thomas Shard, soon got into such a state of mind about his wife, that he used to leave Pleasaunce House and go to a tavern."

"As I have done."

"Just so; and the Lady Margaret was wont to smile upon him, and encourage him to do so."

"Yes; and she gave him plenty of gold to spend——"

"Ah!"

"And she told him to be home always by midnight, and that if he did that, and came home sober, she would never question him as to where he had been."

"She did the same by me."

"Well, he did not get home by midnight, nor sober; so one morning he was found dead."

"So I have heard."

"Now I have a plan."

"Let me hear it, by all means."

"Martin Lassamour, it is but right and proper that the innocence or the guilt of the Lady Margaret should be at once, and as clearly established as possible."

"Yes, yes."

"I hope, then, that you are quite prepared to go any lengths, my young friend, for such an object, and that no foolish scruples, or tenderness for such a woman, will sway you in the matter."

"Never!—never! If she be the guilty thing she seems to be, how can I hold her otherwise than in abhorrence?"

"True; then I advise this. The present Sheriff of London is a cousin of mine, and I say, let us go to him, and arrange that he, with such force as may be considered requisite, be admitted, this very night, by you, into Pleasaunce House, and that he and they be hidden in the state bed-chamber which, from all I hear of it, has many facilities for such a purpose."

"It has."

"Good. Then do you go home at two in the morning, pretending to be a little the worse for wine, and lie down on a couch and see what comes of it."

Martin shuddered.

"You don't like it?"

"No; but I will do it, so help me, Heaven!"

"It is a bargain, then?"

"It is; and I thank you for the trouble you take in this matter, Sir Ralph Shard, let what may come of it. But what about this letter."

"Oh, I should say, be on the spot with force, and crush the rascals in the meshes of their own snare."

"Yes," said Lamont, that is the way to act."

"Be it so, then," said Lassamour, rising. "Let us go to the sheriff at once, and possess him of all the facts of this strange affair."

CHAPTER LXXI.

DE VOLENCE, IN SEEKING VENGEANCE, FINDS HIS DEATH.

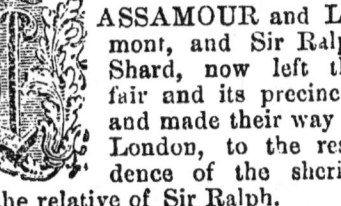ASSAMOUR and Lamont, and Sir Ralph Shard, now left the fair and its precincts, and made their way to London, to the residence of the sheriff, who was the relative of Sir Ralph.

The Sheriff resided at St. Margaret's Hill, in which locality, although now so sternly devoted to the purposes of commerce, there were then some very good and stately houses.

The announcement of the name of Sir Ralph Shard, soon procured admittance, and in the course of an hour's converse, with which we need not trouble the reader, the sheriff was put in possession of all the circumstances of the position of Martin Lassamour.

The most ready aid was promptly promised.

"Believe me, gentlemen," said the sheriff, "that the singular life and career of the Lady Margaret, of Pleasaunce House, the wife of seven husbands, as she is commonly called, has not escaped the consideration of the authorities; but it has been found, hitherto, impossible to take any step in the matter, just for want of the sort of co-operation which now you come to offer to me."

"Then it is all settled?" said Sir Ralph.

"It is, my good friend."

"And as for the meeting to-night, at twelve o'clock, between my young friend Lassamour, and the writer of this letter, purporting to come from Miss Langdon?"

"Let him so dispose of the six good men and true, that I shall now place under your orders, that whoever comes to that meeting shall be arrested."

"That will do."

"And as for myself, Martin Lassamour, I will meet you at your garden-gate of Pleasaunce House, at the hour of one."

"Do so, sir. I will, if I live, be there."

"We will all be there," said Sir Ralph.

"I think you say," added the sheriff, "that you can introduce us secretly to the house?"

"Yes, easily. My page, Cyprian, shall be in waiting for us, and he will manage all that well."

"Be it so."

The sheriff then wrote upon a scrap of paper the names of six of his men, and told Martin Lassamour to hand it to a person he would find in the hall of the residence, where the men so named would be found, and placed under his orders.

All this was done, so that Lassamour, and Lamont, and Sir Ralph, soon found themselves at the head of such a force, that any assassins that might be in the pay of such a man as De Volence could have no chance against them.

The day was so far advanced that it left no leisure for any action between that time and the hour when Lassamour had promised to meet Robert Lee at old Lambeth Church.

He stated this to Sir Ralph, who said—

"Well, we will all stay at some tavern till it is time to go to the appointed place of meeting in the forged letter, and we can easily send some one to bring the good pedler to us."

"If I could but find my page, Cyprian," said Lassamour, "he would do that message well."

"Can you not send for him?"

"Alas, no; I know not where he is."

"I will hazard a guess," said Lamont.

"Where, then?"

"At the house of Langdon, the ferry-man."

"It is like enough. I will chance sending for him there, then, at once, by one of the sheriff's men-at-arms."

"Do so," said Sir Ralph.

Lassamour sent a note to Cyprian, desiring him to come at once to him at the tavern, where he and his friends were staying; and as the page was really at Langdon's cottage, he came back with the sheriff's man, and soon appeared before his master.

"I am here, noble sir."

"'Tis well, Cyprian. How have you left the ferryman's fair daughters?"

"Oh, quite well, master."

"I rejoice to hear it. And now, Cyprian, I must claim your services for some hours to come."

"My life is yours, noble sir."

Lassamour then gave him directions to go and meet Robert Lee, and bring him to the tavern, so that he might join them in all that was to be done on that eventful night.

So well did the page perform his mission, that Lee, the pedler, was soon added to the party at the tavern, and all was explained to him.

Behold, then, at the tavern, Lassamour —Lamont—Sir Ralph Shard—Robert Lee—and Cyprian, all ready to start to the place of rendezvous appointed in the letter, purporting to be from Amy.

And while all this was going on, De Volence had made up his mind to go personally to the spot, to the aid of Tabby and the rascals whom he now intended to get to aid him to murder Martin Lassamour.

And the Lady Margaret sat in her own room at Pleasaunce, planning the death of her husband.

Such was the state of affairs, on that most eventful evening, of all concerned

Little did the villain, De Volence, expect that his designs against the peace and the life of the brave, but immaculate, Martin Lassamour, were so well known as, indeed, they were to that individual.

If he had had but the least idea of such a thing, he would soon have taken good care to place a considerable space between himself and London.

But with all his cleverness, he had fallen into the snare he had laid for others, and what could he expect but the most disastrous consequences to result therefrom?

Who will pity him?

No one.

The little party that Martin Lassamour had with him now, were in the highest spirits, for they one and all made quite sure of getting a tolerably easy victory over the rascally De Volence.

As for Cyprian, he seemed to be so near to the accomplishment of his dearest wishes, that he was full of life and joy.

The reader by this time is well aware that the love Cyprian felt for the amiable, and gentle, and fair Patience, was as sincere as it was great, and that there was nothing in all the world the page would not do, in an honourable way, to advance his suit with that young and beautiful girl.

Her conduct from first to last, since he had been acquainted with her, had all been such as to greatly add to his affection for her.

Nor was Patience, in her gentle and timid, and quiet way, one whit less attached to the handsome young page than he was to her.

Indeed they were a pair very well matched, and their union seemed to be, when it should take place, just one of those calculated to bring abundant happiness to both of the parties.

Before Martin Lassamour had taken so much interest in Cyprian's little love affair, and before he had made the promise to the page of the pecuniary assistance, which would have the effect speedily of banishing all the scruples of the miserly and selfish old Langdon to the match, the page had felt much attached to Lassamour.

There was a something about the frank and chivalrous bearing of Martin, that had attracted the regards of the youth towards him ; but the generous way in which he had offered to smoothen the road to his own happiness with Patience, had for ever fixed him in the affections of Cyprian.

It is not at all too much to say that the young and ardent Cyprian would have risked his life at any moment to serve Martin Lassamour.

Young Lamont, too, was actuated by the same feelings.

Taking, then, all things into consideration, the party that was about to meet the assassins that De Volence counted upon as quite certain to carry out and accomplish the object of the death of Martin Lassamour, was such an one as he might well have dreaded to meet.

But all this time the guilty De Volence was wrapped up, so to speak, in fancied security.

He sat in an obscure tavern, not far from our Ladye's Chapel at Southwark, waiting anxiously for the time to come which he fondly hoped would get him rid of his foe.

"Yes," he said, as he paced the confines of a rather narrow room in which he sat. "Yes! This night Martin Lassamour dies, and then I have nothing to fear further from him. I will then put only just such a price upon the head of that young Lamont, and the page, Cyprian, as will induce my bravos to kill them both, and then who shall hinder me from doing as I please ?"

This was quite a delightful prospect to the villain, De Volence, who panted and thirsted after revenge.

There can be no doubt in the world but that his definition of doing as he pleased was to do no end of mischief ; but well it is to be able to reflect that his power to do it is of so limited and evanescent a character as we know that it is in reality.

But time and tide wait for no man, and the hour was speedily coming at which the conflict, if that could be called one in which the force now was to be greatly on the side of might, was to take place in the narrow path through the shrubbery, where it had been resolved to murder Martin Lassamour.

And we have said that while all this was going on, the Lady Margaret sat in her chamber at Pleasaunce House, resolving in her mind the murder, that night, of her seventh husband.

Yes, she, not knowing of the snare that was laid for that seventh husband without —not knowing of the gallant friends he had to save him from that snare—not knowing that her own doom was all but fixed—she sat in her chamber as though she was the arbiter of life or of death, resolving in her mind his destruction.

The guilt of this bold, bad woman, is no secret now.

That she had murdered — foully and certainly murdered all her husbands, there can be no sort of doubt in the world.

That not one of them had died a natural death we are now so well aware that it is quite needless to waste any argument upon it.

No doubt these six murders had impressed her with the idea that in the perpetration of such deeds, she had some special sort of immunity which rendered it only just necessary that she should, for her own part, determine that the deed should be done, and there was an end of it.

The many escapes from detection, and from the hands of justice that she must have had during her career had endowed her with that sort of feeling that a soldier has who has been in very many battles, and not hurt.

She had began to think herself charmed against the consequences even of committing the terrible crime of murder.

CHAPTER LXXII.

LADY MARGARET MAKES A FEW LITTLE PREPARATIONS.

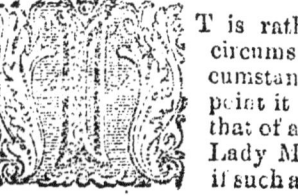 T is rather a strange circumstance, but circumstances seem to point it out as a fact, that of all her husbands Lady Margaret loved, if such a term can be at all applied to the feelings of such a woman Martin Lassamour the best.

Yes, his chivalrous spirit had certainly created a feeling in her mind that none of her former six spouses had done.

This may be accounted for in a variety of ways, we think.

In the first place, Martin Lassamour was some years younger than the Lady Margaret.

Her first youth had passed completely away, and she looked upon so young and gallant a cavalier as Martin, as paying her a very great, and to a woman, a very acceptable compliment, by wedding her at all.

This was, no doubt, the basis of those feelings that she had in his favour.

Then again, he was decidedly very good looking, and that, no doubt, had a good deal to say in the matter.

Taking it, therefore, on the whole, it was with more anguish of soul, and deep regret, that she set about trying to compass his death, than had at all possessed her upon the occasions when she had murdered her other husbands.

And, indeed, but that all her woman's mad jealousy was aroused by the fact that she had been foolish enough to believe his supposed affection for one or both of the ferryman's daughters, she would have hesitated much at his murder.

Not for the neglect with which she might have been treated—not for the inebriety with which he might return from his visits to London, would she have taken the life of Martin Lassamour.

But when the demon, jealousy, once took possession of her soul, it was her master, and turned her in any direction that it pleased.

And so, amid the gathering gloom, she sat in her own chamber at Pleasaunce House, considering the fate of Martin Lassamour.

That is, she was considering of the mode of causing his death, not of whether he died or not.

That she had already determined.

On a chair, not far from the one on which she sat, lay the disguise she had worn at the fair when she had watched him, and, as she thought, gathered such information as to confirm her in the opinion that he had made, or was about to make the fair Amy Langdon his victim.

"Yes," she said, "he dies—he dies!"

A shudder passed over the frame of that wildly revengeful woman.

"He dies!" she said, again. "Ay, if he had ten lives, he dies! I have said it, and I never yet said that of mortal being but the act was sure to follow quickly upon the saying.

The night got darker.

She started as she glanced around her, and saw that the objects in her room were getting mixed up with their own shadows.

"The time is coming," she said. "The time is coming. It shall be done to-night, and done safely."

She rose, and trimmed the fire in her room herself, but she found that there was not wood enough to last the night.

She touched a bell, and one of the servants who had been appointed to attend upon her, in the, as she said "unaccountable" absence of Loon, answered the summons.

"Sarah," said Lady Lassamour, "is not the night a chilly one?"

"I think it is, my lady, for the time of the year," was the reply.

"Ay, I thought so. You will bring some wood to this chamber."

"Yes, my lady."

The attendant departed on the errand, and Lady Margaret, while she was gone, opened a cabinet in the room, and took from it a dress of black velvet.

She placed the dress aside, though, so that the attendant should not see it.

Sarah came back with wood.

"Will these two blocks, my lady, suffice, think you?"

"Yes."

"Very good, my lady."

"Place them near to the log on the hearth, that they may dry."

"Yes, my lady."

"And see that a good and cheerful fire be made up in the state bed-chamber, for your master will sleep there to-night."

"Yes, my lady."

"Ay," muttered Lady Margaret. "He will sleep there, to-night, the sleep that knows no waking, or I am very much deceived."

"Did you speak, my lady?"

"No. You may go."

"Shall you want anything done to-night, my lady?"

"No. And yet——"

The attendant lingered.

"See that a flask of rare old wine from Spain be placed for your master in the state bed-chamber."

"Yes, my lady."

"Place it at once, and then you may retire for the night, I shall require no further service of you till the dawn."

"Good night, my lady."

"Good night."

"Pleasant dreams, my lady."

"Begone!"

The attendant departed in all haste, for the tone in which Lady Margaret had said "Begone" in, was, to tell the truth, anything but a pleasant one.

After the attendant had left her, Lady Margaret continued standing in the very centre of the room, in the same attitude, and then she said in a low, deep tone of voice—

"Pleasant dreams? Pleasant dreams she wishes me? Did she mean that? Oh, God, what a mockery! Pleasant dreams to me! No—no, I shall never have pleasant dreams again!"

She sank into a chair, and wrung her hands for a few moments, and swayed to and fro as if she would have wept, but not a tear came from her eyes. That fount of feeling had been dry for many a long day."

"I cannot weep," she then said, "my eyebolts burn and throb as they would burst, but I never weep more, never—never!"

"This is very terrible!"

She rose, now, from her seat, and looked, comparatively, quite calm and composed, and set about doing something with the old fashioned velvet dress she had taken from the cabinet.

It was a very costly dress, indeed, with a rich train to it.

Yards and yards of what, at that time, was a very much more expensive article than it is now, Genoa velvet, had been used in the making of that dress.

But utterly regardless of all the mischief that she did to it, the Lady Margaret cut and slashed about the skirt of it with a poniard that she took from her bosom.

The reason of this conduct was soon quite apparent.

The dress was so long and heavy, that in order to ensure its falling into good and graceful folds, there were sewn into the skirt of it, at intervals, little pullets of lead, the weight of which gave it the necessary fall.

It was to extract these little pullets that the Lady Margaret now so heedlessly cut and slashed the velvet dress about.

One by one she took them out of the little places made for their reception, and placed them on the table before her.

When she had got six of these, she rose, and carefully put the dress away again in the cabinet, arranging it as though it had not been touched by any one.

"That will suffice," she said

The expression upon her face, now, was so truly awful, that any one who could have seen it, would have at once come to the conclusion that some great crime was in progress in that woman's mind.

She seemed to have some sort of an idea herself that she had something of a strange aspect about her, for she walked to a dressing-glass and gazed at herself in it.

There was only the fire light for her to see by, but she lit a lamp.

Then she took a long look at her own features in the glass.

She shuddered, as well she might. Upon former occasions, when some such deed as that which she now contemplated, was resting, like an awful shadow, upon her soul, she had so looked at herself; but never before had her face worn such an expression as it now wore.

"This is my last act," she said. "When this is done, I will bid adieu to this house, and to everything that will remind me of the fact, and I will leave England for ever."

It seemed to be some sort of a relief to the Lady Margaret to have come to this decision.

She glanced about her in rather a strange fashion, though, and she lifted up and looked at several things in her chamber, as if for the last time.

And still the night deepened around her; but she did not notice it now that she had lit a lamp, but a glance at a time piece told her the hour.

"Ten," she said. "It is ten, now, and in about two hours more there is little doubt but the deed is done."

CHAPTER LXXIII.

TABBY AND DE VOLENCE ARRANGE MATTERS TO THEIR SATISFACTION.

 CONFERENCE ensued at the hour of ten between De Volence and his accomplice, Tabby.

At that time De Volence was pacing the aisle of the chapel of Our Ladye.

In monkish days, and when catholicism was upon the length and breadth of the land, the churches were never closed.

Day and night lamps burnt at the various shrines, and when the conscience or the piety of any person suggested the propriety or the relief of a prayer beneath a consecrated roof, that roof was always to be got under.

It is very different now.

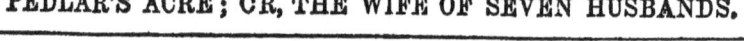

GAMIEL GANDER'S DIFFICULTY;

The church belongs to the parson, now, and to the churchwarden—the parish clerk, and the beadle ; and you have no business in it except on the Sunday, and at the stated times which they particularly term the hours for divine worship.

No doubt the proud parson, and churchwarden, and beadle and parish clerk think the church a very nice place if they are not bothered and bustled by the congregation ; but even with that little drawback, religion is the best trade going in this country.

We must confess, though, albeit far from professing or loving catholics, we like the idea of the open church, night and day.

It is true that it becomes a very much abused privilege.

It is true that in catholic countries the church is the place for assignations of all sorts ; but still the proof of the abuse of a good thing is no real argument against the use of it.

In the present instance, for example, the rascally De Volence made use of the church of Our Ladye, at Southwark, for the purpose of meeting assassins in.

He walked to and fro in the aisle for so long that a monk noticed him at last, and passing him, said, in solemn tones—

"Heaven save you, my son."

"Amen, holy sir."

"Seek you aught ?"

"No, holy father."

"A confession ?"

"Not so, holy sir ; but if you know of any deserving way of bestowing this noble or two, you will do me much grace."

De Volence placed a couple of gold coins in the hands of the monk.

"Ah, my son, you are a true son of the holy church."

"I am, indeed."

"Benedicite !"

The monk clapped the money in a leathern pouch that he had by his side, and was off in a moment from the aisle.

"Now that rascal," said De Volence, looking after him, "is as well aware that I paid him to go as if I had said it in so many words quite plainly."

This was no doubt the fact.

De Volence was now getting not a little hasty and impatient at the non arrival of Tabby ; but he was soon gratified by the appearance of that personage, accompanied by a couple of very ill-looking fellows, indeed.

De Volence held up his finger, and Tabby followed him into the darkest part of a cloister.

"Well ?"

"Oh, noble sir, its a gone goose with—with our poor Glass."

"Is it ?"

"Yes. He's cooked."

"Dead ?"

"As a nit."

"Ah, indeed ? So he won't want, then, his—his——"

"Half of the reward."

De Volence bit his lip.

"I did not mean to say that, my good friend, Tabby ; and, in fact, I am, of course, very sorry for the decease of Glass, whom I had a very high esteem for, upon my life."

"No doubt."

"But whom have you here ?"

"Gentlemen."

"Oh, of course, or they would not be in your good company."

"You do me but justice. I assure your honour that they are real gentlemen, and as a proof of it, I can tell you that from their being babies, though they never had a farthing of their own, they have never earned in the regular way a single groat."

"Indeed."

"No. But they have lived like gentlemen all the while, too."

"I don't doubt it."

"And drank of the best wine."

"Ah, it is fit that they should."

"Drank at the best tavern."

"Doubtless."

"And they are always ready to put a bit of cold steel into anybody upon certain terms, so I brought them here to introduce them to you ; for, to tell the truth, I didn't feel happy."

"Not happy ?"

"No—no !"

"What a pity !"

"It is a feeling. I mean, that I don't feel happy about the little job we have got on hand to-night."

"Ah !"

"Even so."

"And pray, my good friend, what should make you unhappy about this little job ?"

"I don't like it."

"Not like it ?"

"Oh, dear no. The fact is, I begin to have an idea that it is a deuced deal more dangerous than I thought it some time ago."

"Pho !—pho !"

"Well, it's all very well to say 'Pho—pho !' but that's my idea about it, for all that."

"Then I'll tell you what I will do."

"What ?"

"I will go, not only with you myself, but I will employ your two friends, and two more to the back of them, if you like, rather than not have the job done."

"You will ?"

"I will."

"Then you are a rich don, you are. Oh, what a thing it is to have to deal with a rich customer. None of your sneaking fellows who try to ape a gallant gentleman who has nothing but his rapier to depend on. None of your fellows, who, at the best, must feel as if they were only on sufferance in good society."

"Bah !"

"Well, I cannot say myself but I admire you. I say I admire you, noble sir."

De Volence made a mock bow, and then said, with a sneer—

"Of course I return the compliment in full, my good friend. And now for your comrades—pray introduce them."

"I will. Hem !"

At this sound the two rascals that

Tabby had brought with him, and who had waited at some little distance, came swaggering up.

"Noble sir," said Tabby, pointing to one of them, "allow me to introduce to your favourable notice Sir Hector O'Swagger."

De Volence nodded his head.

"At your service, sir, in anything," said Sir Hector O'Swagger; "from the cutting a throat, to the abduction of a heiress."

"Ah," whispered Tabby, to De Volence, "he is good at the abduction of a heiress, I assure you."

"Is he?"

"Yes, noble sir."

"Well, be it so. What is the name of your other friend?"

"This, noble sir, is Sir Blarney Ratcliffe, an Irish knight, as his first name implies, and of the most tremendous valour."

"He says nothing but the truth, sir," said Sir Blarney. "I make nothing of seven men."

"And kill them?"

"All, sir."

"And eat them?"

"Sir!"

"Oh, pardon me, I thought that you might possibly finish off the adventure by eating all you kill."

"Now, by the infernal gods and boisterous blazes, if any one but an honourable gentleman like yourself had said as much as that, I would have compelled him to test the blade of my rapier."

"Oh, it's only a joke."

"Cease all jokes, sir, say I! A joke, indeed! Fury and blue blazes, sir, say I!"

"As you please."

"You see," said Tabby, "that our Irish friend has a very great spirit."

"So I see," said De Volence, drily.

"I have, sir," said the Irish assassin.

"Well, gentlemen," added De Volence, who really scarcely took the trouble to conceal the contempt in which he held them all, "I daresay Tabby has informed you that I have a little business on hand?"

"He has."

"What is your price?"

They looked at each other rather oddly at this question, and at last O'Swagger said—

"Sir, we are gentlemen."

"Oh, I don't doubt it."

"Therefore we expect to be treated with delicacy, and we leave the price to you, with one stipulation."

"What is that?"

"That it shall not be under fifty crowns each."

"Agreed."

"Good. We are quite at your service, and without any further inquiry, we cannot help coming to the conclusion that your quarrel is a perfectly just one, and that, therefore, as men of honour, we are bound to aid and to assist you in it to the utmost of our ability and means."

HAPTER LXXIV.

DETAILS THE CONFLICT IN THE WOODY PASS.

HIS part being satisfactorily settled, Tabby slunk in by saying—

"And now that, as honourable men, we are all agreed so far, the noble De Volence has said that we may have two men, even yet, in strength if we like."

"Yes," said De Volence, "and if you know of a couple of vag—I mean gentlemen, who will aid you, you can fetch them."

"Hem!" said O'Swagger, "I do know of such, and I will engage, within one hour, that they shall be at any place you like to appoint."

"You can manage all that then, Tabby," said De Volence, "and any terms, in reason, mind you, that you may make I will satisfy."

"Your honour is a true gentleman, and we will be at the place appointed in due time, you may be quite certain of it."

"Mind you are. I, too, will be there."

With this the party left the church, and De Volence felt, in his own mind, very sure of his prey.

"Can he escape me now?" he said, with a tone of exultation. "No—no, and what a capital chance it will be if, now that I have such a force to contend against him, he should have that Lamont with him! Ah, that, indeed, would be to kill two birds with one stone!"

In the fact of Martin Lassamour having

the young Lamont with him, De Volence, as the reader is well aware, was likely to be gratified ; but that the two birds would be killed by one stone, in consequence, was quite another affair.

We will now leave De Volence and his rascally associates to form their own plans and to take what steps they can towards the completion of their designs, while we take a glance at the proceedings of Martin Lassamour for the purpose of foiling the purpose of the assassins.

His great object was to avoid, if possible, making any display of the force he had with him till a kind of conflict began ; for he well knew that if positively it was known that he was prepared, the cowardly assassins would fly.

With this object, then, he decided upon placing the guard he had got from the sheriff in such close ambush that they need not appear upon the scene of action, except upon a given signal to that effect and purpose.

At a convenient spot, then, he assembled his friends, and the sheriff's men, and then addressed the young officer who had the command, under him, of the party that the sheriff had given him.

"Sir," he said, "I do not wish these rascals that I am going to get your aid to foil to escape me. It is not to avoid their poinards so much as to bring them to justice that I wish."

"I comprehend you, sir."

"Therefore, what I want you to do, with your men, is to lie in ambush, if you will be so good, till I call upon you to act."

"As you please, sir."

Martin Lassamour was well pleased to find that the officer was so willing to act under his guidance, for it but too frequently happens that people who are very capable of accepting a subordinate position in any affair, are only too obstinate to do so.

As it was, though, in this instance, all was as it should be.

Martin was decidedly of opinion, and it was an opinion in which Sir Ralph Shard fully agreed, that the best plan of operation would be not to alarm the assassins.

The fact was, that the object in view was not so much to prevent the assassination, for that could have been easily done by not going to the place, but to take prisoners the assassins, or rather, the would be assassins.

Any display of force then, in or about the spot, would at once have the effect of defeating such an object.

In fact, any appearance of there being a suspicion, even, on the mind of Martin

Lassamour that all was not well, would have a precisely similar effect.

The very greatest caution was, therefore, necessary, in order that there should be nothing in the shape of suspicion excited with regard to the real state of affairs.

With this proviso, then, the proceedings of Martin Lassamour and his friends will be very easily comprehended, indeed.

Cyprian was well acquainted, as it turned out, with the precise spot mentioned in the anonymous letter, as that at which the assassination was to be attempted, and so at about one hour before the hour when it may be fairly supposed the rascally myrmidons of De Volence would be on or about the spot, Martin Lassamour called Cyprian to him to give him his instructions.

"Now, my good Cyprian," he said, " I will boldly tell you that what you have to do is of very great, and paramount importance to me."

"Yes," my good master," and to me."

"Well, Cyprian, I hope and trust it is to you, too."

"It is so."

"Have you any special reason to say that, my good friend ?"

"Ah, yes."

"Name it, then."

"It is this, my good master ; your success and your life, is my success and my life. Without your kind and good deed, how am I every to hope to call the fair and gentle Patience mine ?"

Martin smiled.

"Ah, yes," added Cyprian, quite raving with his subject, "it is so, indeed. Am I not indebted to your good and kind promise for all that is to make me the happiest of men.

"I will do all I can, Cyprian, for your happiness, as you well know."

"Yes, noble sir, that, indeed, I do well know."

"But now, Cyprian, attend to me in the interim, for I want you to do me good service."

"That I will, sir."

"Then, Cyprian, you will go with this officer, that the sheriff has put in possession of his guard, to the exact spot where it is expected that the rascals employed by the arch-traitor, De Volence, was to set upon me for my destruction."

"Yes, sir."

"And you will post them upon and about that spot, in such a position that they cannot be seen by any one."

"It shall be done, sir."

Martin Lassamour then again turned to the officer saying—

"The signal for you to appear with your men, shall be my crying out—'St. George to the rescue!' and the moment you hear that you will come to my aid, as quickly as you can."

"You will not find, noble sir," said the officer, "that either myself or my men will be at all backward in showing ourselves at that juncture."

"Be it so. And now off with you, and Heaven speed you."

"Amen, sir," said the officer.

"Shall I return, or stay with the sheriff's guard?" asked Cyprian.

"Return to me, good Cyprian, if you please, and you can then report to me if all be well."

"I will."

Cyprian, and the officer of the sheriff's guard, along with the sheriff's men, now made their way with rapidity to the spot intimated.

It was, in all respects, one that was well calculated for the sort of deed that was likely to be perpetrated there.

About an acre of hard, dry ground was covered with rather a thick little wood.

On one side of this wood there was a morass so treacherous, and so deep, that there were legends told about it of a fearful character.

One was that a man and horse had once, in the course of three minutes, completely disappeared.

Another was, that a deserter from one of the king's regiments, stationed in the Tower of London, had fled, with a party at his heels to apprehend him, and that they had all perished in the morass at the side of that little wood.

A third was, that a party of topers, from a tavern at Lambeth, finding themselves late in getting to their homes, and having a lively and married-man sort of fear of their spouses, had taken, what they hoped and expected would be found a short cut across the morass.

Instead, however, of finding it a short cut to their homes, they had found it a short cut to the other world.

In the morning nothing was found of this whole party but one pipe, the stem of which was sticking up from the morass, while the bowl of it lay buried in it.

This, then, was the character of the ground on the left side of the road that wound its way through the little wood.

On the right the ground was very unequal, and there were several deep clay-pits; but the most remarkable object there was rather a large barn-like structure, in a very dilapidated state, and which had once been a well known baiting place for horses.

A foul murder had been committed there.

" Murder most foul, as at the best it is,
" But this most foul, strange, and unnatural."

A son had murdered his father in that barn-like place.

From that time it had had so evil a repute that it had been suffered to go to ruins, and even the poorest wayfarer on Lambeth Marshes preferred the cold shelter of the trees to the lodging that the, at all events, standing walls of that barn might have afforded him.

This was the spot upon which De Volence hoped to be able to murder Lassamour.

CHAPTERL XXV.

THE EVENTFUL NIGHT PROCEEDS TOWARDS ITS CLOSE.

WE must now take the events of this most eventful night in regular order as they occurred, perceiving that we commence at the hour of eleven o'clock.

The moment Cyprian and the officer in command of the sheriff's guard came within sight of the place, the officer pointed to the dilapidated barn, saying—

"What building is that, my good friend?"

"Oh, that barn-like place?"

"Yes."

"With the old gable end to us?"

"The same."

"Well, that is called 'The Ghosts' Haunt.'"

"The Ghosts' Haunt?"

"Yes, even so."

"It is a strange name to give to a Christian building, is it not ?"

"Yes, granted if it was a christian building."

"What is it, then?"

"Nay, let me rather ask you, sir officer, what you are pleased to call a Christian building ?"

"A building built by Christians."

"Then it may be such ; but since the time it has been called the Ghosts' Haunt, it certainly has not been in Christian hands."

"You speak in riddles."

"Then I will explain them."

"You will much oblige by doing so."

"First and foremost, then, you see—"

"No I don't."

"You don't ?"

"Certainly not, good master page. I don't know exactly what you are going to assert that I saw, but it don't at all matter since it is too dark to see anything."

"Good."

"Bad, I think."

"Nay, I meant that your speech and its remark was very good."

"Oh !"

"But still I say you will see that this barn is in that state of dismemberment that it certainly is not inhabited by Christians."

"Or pagans either."

"Or pagans either, as you say."

"Go on."

"In the next place, then, I beg to say that it is likely to continue so ; for a foul, and cowardly, and awful murder has been committed in it, so that since that time it has been left to the undisputed sway of evil spirits, and so got its name, which causes all to shun it."

"Of the Ghosts' Haunt ?"

"Just so."

"Are you certain, master page, that it is quite deserted ?"

"Am I certain that I breathe ?"

"I suppose so."

"Then I am certain of that."

"I am glad to hear it."

"Glad ?"

"Even so."

"And why, pray, sir officer ?"

"Well, sir page, the reason why is soon stated, and it is, that if this be the spot upon which it is desirable, and in accordance with the views of good Master Lassamour that we should hide, inside that Ghosts' Haunt, I and my men will go."

"No."

"Yes, say I."

"Hem ! well, it's all a matter of taste. You are a brave man, sir officer."

"Sir page, I should not be fit for my duty if I were a coward."

"But, really now——"

"Well ?"

"You don't mean to say that you will take up your post in a place that may drive you and all your men out of your wits?"

"Why so ?"

"Oh, by the sights and the sounds that may come upon you in it."

The officer smiled.

"Indeed I do," he then said. "Now my men follow me, and as for you, master page, the sooner you get back to the noble Martin Lassamour, and let him know that we are here, and in good hiding, the better it will be, I take it, for all of us."

"Well, well, you really mean to go."

"I do, master."

The soldiers followed their officer, and in a few moments more he and they were ensconced in the Ghosts' Haunt, as it was in reality called.

Cyprian was not very superstitious, but he thought to himself that he would not have liked to take up his watch in such a place, so he at once turned, and went to where he had left his much respected master, Martin Lassamour, as quickly as he could.

Lassamour awaited the page's arrival with some degree of anxiety, and the moment he saw him, he cried out—

"Well, Cyprian, is all well ?"

"I hope so."

"You only hope so ?"

"That is all, noble master."

"But why is that all ?"

Cyprian shook his head.

"Upon my life," said Sir Ralph Shard, "they boy shakes his head as if he had brains in it.''

"Thank you, sir," said Cyprian. "I think and hope I have a few ; but the soldiers and their officer are well hidden. I can say that."

"Then that," said Lassamour, "is all that was required, was it not ?"

"Ah, but——"

"But what ?"

"What will you say, noble sir, if, when you want them, you find that they have been eaten up, or frightened into the morass?"

"Frightened ?"

"Ay, sir."

"By whom ? By what ?"

"Ghosts !"

Martin Lassamour laughed.

"Oh, no — no, Cyprian," he said. "Ghosts may be, or they may not.—Indeed, I have seen and heard enough at

Pleasaunce House to have very great doubts about the matter myself; but as regards them frightening any man deserving the name of a soldier, that is quite out of the question."

"To be sure," said Sir Ralph Shard. "Quite, as you say, out of the question."

"Well, noble sir, I am glad to hear that much, for in a word, they have taken up their post in that old crazy barn, that goes by the name of the Ghosts' Haunt."

"Ah, say you so ?"

"Yes, sir."

"How very strange."

"Yes, sir, it is ; but he would go."

"Pho—pho! I think he has done a good thing—and a clever thing, too, that officer, in going. What I meant when I said 'How very strange,' was, that it was very strange I had not thought of the existence of the place, and suggested it to him."

"After that, then, noble sir," said Cyprian, "I can really have nothing to say."

"No, Cyprian, but you have now something to do, and that is to follow me, if you please, in the way and in the manner that Sir Ralph Shard has agreed upon."

"That will I, sir, most willingly."

"Well, then, Cyprian, this will be the plan of our proceeding, as we have selected it out."

Cyprian listened intently.

"I am going forward, alone, towards the place where these rascally assassins are supposed to be, about the hour of midnight, in waiting for me, and you, with Sir Ralph Shard, and Lamont, and Robert Lee will follow me, but at such a distance as not to be at all observable to the foes."

"Yes, noble sir."

"Then, if they come out to attack me, I will retreat as fast as I can upon your aid, and at the same time I will give the signal to the sheriff's men to fly from their hiding place."

"I see it all, sir."

"Yes, Cyprian. You will perceive by all that that the rascals will be hemmed in on all sides, I hope, and killed or taken."

"Oh, kill them, sir, off-hand."

"You think so ?"

"Assuredly, noble sir. Why trouble the law, and the judges, and the hangman, and all that sort of thing with such gentry as that. The best way is to put them out of the way of doing further mischief as soon as possible."

"By the holy rood !" cried Sir Ralph Shard, "there is some truth in what the boy says."

Martin Lassamour shook his head.

"It would serve them right," he said. "I admit, freely enough, to shew them no mercy ; but if they cry for quarter, and are willing to surrender, it will, after that, be needless for us to kill them.

"Well, well, there is truth in that, too," added Sir Ralph Shard ; and when we come to consider that the men of the sheriff will be upon the spot, it is just as well to let them take them."

"Just so."

Cyprian nodded his head as much as to say :—

"Well, that is all very fine, but only let any of the rascals come in my way, and I will soon let them taste cold steel."

The time had now arrived when it was necessary that they should get their horses ready for the adventure.

"Come, gentlemen," said Martin Lassamour, "let us set off, or neither friends nor foes will think that we are coming tonight."

In the course, now, of five minutes more they were all well mounted and upon the road.

CHAPTER LXXVI.

DE VOLENCE TAKES HIS MEASURES FOR THE MURDER.

BUT while all this was going on with our friends, and with those who certainly had right and justice upon their side, the evil doers were far from idle.

That is to say, the rascally De Volence was very far, indeed, from faltering in the least in his blood-thirsty design.

The villains, Tabby, and the two gentlemen whom he had brought with him to Our Ladye Chapel, at Southwark, had gone in search of two other rascals whom they knew, for the purpose of bringing them to share in the danger, and in the reward of the little enterprise.

That is to say, they considered among themselves that it was to be all reward, and no danger.

They never for a moment imagined that Martin Lassamour would be attended by any one but, just possibly, the young Lamont.

That this young gallant would, in all likelihood, be with him, De Volence had told Tabby, along with an expressed hope that it should be so, and that he, too, should fall a victim to the daggers of the assassins.

So, with De Volence himself, the party that were to attack Martin Lassamour, and possibly, his young friend, Lamont, actually counted six.

They thought that by being such a force they made victory certain.

But even then it is a very doubtful thing if those six would have had the courage, in open and fair fight, to attack Martin Lassamour and Lamont.

On the contrary, they never intended any such thing as that.

What they meant to do, and what they looked forward to succeed in doing, was nothing of that sort.

They meant to hide themselves among the trees about the spot, and to pounce out upon Martin alone, or Martin and his friend, before they could draw their swords in their defence, and murder them in cold blood.

This was the design.

It was to be a murder—an assassination—by no means a fight.

Now Tabby, as well as all the four rascals that he was to have with him on the occasion, knew perfectly well all about the old ruined barn on the roadside.

But guilt is ever superstitious.

An innocent soul, or even one not stained with any very serious offences against God or man, may defy superstition; but the thoroughly guilty never can.

He who has imbrued his hand in the blood of his fellow man, is the slave of all such fancies.

Hence, then, was it that, tempting as one might suppose the ruined barn to have been to the rascally Tabby and his associates, they never one of them, for one moment, really considered the idea of making it their hiding-place.

It was just about a quarter past eleven o'clock when Tabby again presented himself in the cloister of the Ladye Chapel.

De Volence saw him, and was soon by his side.

"Well ?"

"All's right, noble sir."

"You are sure of that ?"

"Oh, yes. I have got two more gentlemen."

"Gentlemen ?"

"Hem ! Well, it is but civil to call them such, and I suppose they are, seeing that they do no work, but live by their wits."

"Well—well, we will not dispute about terms, my good Tabby. All I care for is, to have the work we now have in hand well and expeditiously done."

"It shall be so, sir."

"On my soul, I believe it ; and when that is done, we will still think of the girl."

"Hem !"

"You like not that ?"

"Oh, as far as liking it or not liking it goes, sir, it matters not. It is all in the way of business, and, after all, when I come to consider that, in all likelihood, that confounded Lassamour will be got rid of, I don't see that there will be much danger in the matter."

"None at all."

"Be it so, then ; I am yours in that affair again, on the understanding that it is not to be undertaken till mine, or some one else's dagger has been left to the hilt in the heart of Martin Lassamour."

"Agreed."

"Then that is settled ?"

"It is so."

"And now, noble sir, we are all quite ready to go and take our places in the wood, for in this little affair, you know, it is very much better to be too soon than too late."

"It is—it is."

"Then let us be off at once."

This intimation on the part of Tabby to be off to the place at which the murder was to be attempted to be committed was immediately attended to, and the consequence was that they were soon on the road to that very spot at which Martin Lassamour and his friends had taken such good pains to have for them a rather hot reception.

How they fared upon getting there we shall very soon see.

As for De Volence himself, and their general, Tabby, they kept rather in the rear of the others, for they both had the same thought, although they did not take the trouble to express it to each other.

That thought was, that should there be any immediate danger, it was just as well that they should keep out of it.

This conduct of theirs sufficiently showed how very incompatible true courage is with such crimes as these rascals had it in contemplation to commit.

Of course, as yet, there was nothing at all in the shape of danger expected, for

THE OFFICERS WAITING THE ATTACK IN THE GHOSTS' HAUNT.

the party of the bravos were but going, in their own idea, to take possession of the ground, in order that they might be ready to pounce out upon the unhappy passenger they expected.

This fact was very much exemplified in the conduct of De Volence in regard to Tabby at the present juncture.

There was De Volence, as proud and haughty as he could possibly be, rogue and assassin as he was at heart, and in all his actions—and there was Tabby, no doubt sprung from the very dregs of the population, and a bravo by profession, walking along very composedly.

And the haughty De Volence, now that it was possible there might be hard blows, did not disdain the companionship of the bravo.

In fact he talked to him in quite a friendly sort of way.

It is doubtful, though, whether Tabby fully appreciated the condescension.

"Tabby,' said De Volence.

"Ay, noble sir."

"When this Martin Lassamour is dead, we will go at once to Lambeth."

"To Lambeth Ferry?"

"Even so."

"Well, I see, noble sir, that that little disappointment with regard to the piece of lamb weighs heavily upon your heart."

"The what?"

"The piece of lamb!"

"Lamb?—lamb? what piece of lamb? I have no disappointment that I know, friend Tabby, connected with a piece of lamb!"

"Excuse me, noble sir, I mean the little female kid they call Amy Langdon."

"Oh!"

"Yes, that's her; but I call her a piece of lamb on account of her looking so soft and tender, you see, noble sir."

"Just so—I see now."

"Well, as I was a-saying—What was I a-saying?"

"That you thought the disappointment weighed rather heavily upon me."

"Ah, yes."

"Then I can corroborate that statement at once by admitting that it does so."

"Yes, noble sir, and as for your idea of going at once to Lambeth Ferry after we have settled this affair of Martin Lassamour, I think it a good idea, I can tell you."

"You do?"

"On my life I do!"

"And you will aid me in carrying it out?"

"I will. My hand on it."

Tabby stretched forth his ensanguined hand, and De Volence, with all the blood flowing in his veins, and all the pride of ancestry which he really had, did not refuse to take it."

"It is settled, then?"

"It is," said Tabby. "I tell you what we will do: as soon as this Lassamour bites the dust, and his friend, that young Lamont, I hope and trust, with him, I will say to our friends—'Now,' I will say, 'there is another hundred crowns to earn, and follow me, and I will tell you how to earn it.'"

"Good!"

"They will follow, and on the way to the Ferry Cottage we can tell them what we want them to do; and when we get there I recommend that Langdon be knocked on the head, and both the girls taken away at once from the cottage."

CHAPTER LXXVII.

MR. TABBY FURTHER DEVELOPES HIS PLANS.

DE VOLENCE looked a little surprised at this proposition.

"Both the girls?" he said.

"Yes, to be sure."

"Will that be prudent, think you?" said De Volence.

"To be sure it will. Don't you think it will, noble sir?"

"I have my doubts."

"Hem! Well, now, noble sir, look you here: the whole case lies in a nutshell, so to speak. If we take one of the girls, the other will not rest day nor night till she has found her out."

"It may be so."

"I am sure of it; but if we take both of them, where is the complaint?"

"Where, indeed?"

"To be sure, noble sir; you see how reasonable it is now."

De Volence smiled darkly to himself, and then he said—

"Have you no other good and special reason to urge, Tabby, why you prefer taking the fair Patience from the ferryman's house as well as the fair Amy?"

"Yes."

"I thought so. Out with it."

"Then it's just this: I begin to feel very lonely, and wish to retire from business into the bosom of my family."

"The what?"

"The bosom of my family, that's what folks call it, don't they?"

"They do; but upon my life I was not aware that you had any family to retire into the bosom of."

"No more I have, but I mean to have one, and so I think of proposing to the fair little Patience Langdon."

"You?"

"Yes, to be sure."

"You propose to her?"

"Ay."

"Oh, that is too absurd! Why the very sight of you will be enough to frighten the poor girl into fits."

"Oh, will it?"

"Yes, to be sure. You don't mean to say, Tabby that you have the slightest notion that any such girl as Patience Langdon will be so mad as to wed with you?"

"Yes, I have, though."

"Well, you can try your luck with her. So far as regards the taking her off at the same time with her sister, I don't care about it, and you can please yourself; but, mind you, you do it on your own account!"

"Of course—of course!"

"And you don't look to me for anything in the shape of payment for the extra job you take upon yourself to please yourself?"

"Certainly not."

"Then do it."

"I intend. Ah—dear me, from the first moment that I saw that nice-looking little kid, I said to myself, 'Tabby, my boy,' says I, 'your time has come.'"

"To be hanged?"

"No, to fall in love."

"Oh!"

"'Yes, Tabby, my boy,' says I, 'that's the sort of article for you;' and so, from that time, I have called her to myself Mrs. Tabby, and that's just what I mean to make her."

"If she consents."

"Oh—ah—yes. But how can she help it when she looks at me?"

"How, indeed!"

"Oh—oh! Ah, me! Eugh! Oh!"

"Good God, what is the matter?"

"Nothing."

"Then don't make those hideous sounds. See, you have brought your four friends back in consternation about it."

"What is amiss?" said one of the bravos.

"Ask Tabby," said De Volence.

"Oh, nothing—nothing, only I am in love, and it seemed to come over me, and to be rather too much for me just then, that's all."

"In love!"

"Yes, comrade; and why not?"

"Ha! ha!"

"What the duece do you mean by 'Ha! ha?'"

"Oh, it's so droll."

"Be off with you."

"Well, Master Tabby, don't make that horrid sort of noise again, that's all, old fellow. I thought you had all of a sudden come across some stray pig, and had him by the tail."

"Oh, did you!"

"I did."

"Then you thought wrong, stupid, that's all; so you needn't trouble your thick head any further about it."

"Ha! ha!"

The four bravos went on again, caring just as little for the anger of Tabby as they would have cared for his praises.

By this time, though, De Volence began to see that they were approaching so near to the spot of the intended assassination, that it was highly necessary that they should begin to be very cautious in their proceedings.

"Halt!" he said.

The whole party came to a pause.

"Now, gentlemen," he said, "yonder is the part of the path running through the trees at which, it appears to me, it will be desirable to stop our man."

"Ay, sir," said one, "it is a good place."

"Well, then, you understand my course of action?"

"Yes. He is to be put out of the way, and then thrown into the morass."

"Good."

"In a quarter of an hour, in the spot that we know of, and where we will take good care to throw him, he will disappear."

"Ah, that will be well."

"It shall be done."

"But are you quite sure that the morass will so swallow up the body."

"Oh, yes. We have had a little experience in that matter, I can tell you."

"I am content."

"Yes," said Tabby, you may look upon the job as good as done."

These words were a great consolation to De Volence, and as they now reached the precise spot where they proposed to lie in wait for Martin Lassamour as he should go home, they all looked about them a little.

"Well," said Tabby, "for my part, I think that we can't do better, all of us, than get behind, each of us, a tree."

"Be it so."

"And then as he comes up, you know, let a whistle which I will sound be the signal of attack upon him, and out we will all rush."

"Capital."

"It will go hard, then, but some one or other of us will be able to make his dagger drink his heart's blood."

"You enchant me," said De Volence, and then he added to himself, "and I will take good care to get out of the way."

"But," said one of the bravos, "it appears to me that as we may have a long watch of it, the very best plan we can adopt is to hide in the old barn."

Now in the barn was the sheriff's troop of armed men, with their officer at their head.

That officer had been prowling about the spot to reconnoitre, and he was now actually listening to every word that was spoken by the rascally assassins upon this occasion.

If, then, the idea of one of them, of taking the advantage of the sort of shelter that the old barn afforded, should happen to meet with general approval, a collision between his men and the assassins must take place at once.

Under these circumstances, the officer listened with some interest to the reply of the others.

It was Tabby who spoke.

"Do you mean the Ghosts' Haunt?" he said.

"The Ghosts' Haunt? Is that it?"

"Yes."

"Then I don't mean it. I didn't know it; though, to tell the truth, I have heard of such a place."

"Then you don't wish to go there?"

"Oh dear, no."

"Well, it's just as well you don't, for it strikes me, do you know, that if you did you would have to go alone to it."

"Drop it, Tabby."

"Drop it, indeed. I tell you, if you want to go in there, I will not desist."

"Well, well."

"Well, well, indeed. Hold your row, will you."

There was nothing for it but just to let the wrath of Tabby evaporate in words, as it was doing, so they let him go on.

"The Ghosts' Haunt! Ah, a pretty idea, indeed, to have us all eat up by ghosts, let alone having a fellow's hair made to stand on end so that it won't come flat again. Ah, indeed."

Tabby's indignation died away in indistinct mutterings.

"Come, come," said De Volence, "enough of that. Take your place behind these trees, and be on the alert. Tabby will give the signal of attack after me. I will look out here at the very commencement of this narrow part of the wood, as I know the man well, and when I whistle you will know that he is coming."

"That will do," said Tabby. "That will do."

CHAPTER LXXVIII.

THE LITTLE BATTLE IN THE WOOD TAKES PLACE.

RULY these were the rascally arrangements made for the destruction of Martin Lassamour and those brave friends who might be with him on this occasion.

But it will in good truth soon be seen that the villanous De Volence reckoned quite without his host when he thought that it would be an easy thing to take the life of such a man as Lassamour.

Every preparation that the villain had made so to do appeared to recoil upon his own head, and as often happens with a great and glorious principle of retribution, he, in seeking the destruction of one whom he hated, only prepared to the full his own.

But the time is drawing nigh.

Martin Lassamour and his little party are now quite close at hand to that appointed spot, on which, had he not been properly warned, and well prepared for what was intended, there can be no doubt but that he would have met his death.

But that was not to be.

As Lassamour came still nearer and nearer to the place, and as he waited upon going on a little in advance, so as not to go there alone to his foes too soon, strange thoughts came over him.

"Is this," he said to himself, "really and truly a crisis in my life. Ought I, even if I escape this one great peril, ought I to take the officers of justice to the chamber of Margaret, and deliver her up to them upon the idea of her guilt?"

It was out of the abundant and full generosity of his soul that Martin Lassamour then reflected, for of the guilt of his wife—the wife of seven husbands—it was quite out of all question that he could entertain any sort of doubt.

But his was a devotive kind of soul.

No wonder then that now he had, so to speak, the affair all his own way—now that he had arranged everything for the detection of the guilty woman, he should shrink from the consequences of so doing.

It was weakness.

But it was weakness of the right sort, after all, and so not to be blamed.

"Poor Martin Lassamour!

His heart felt very heavy.

But as he neared the little wood he felt the full necessity for other thoughts, and he began to drive away the phantoms of a vain and too sensitive regret, and to look about him with anxiety and caution lest he should be attacked unawares.

It was a very great object with him, if possible, to carry out this little adventure with the villanous De Volence without loss to his own party.

The idea of sacrificing any life of those whom he brought with him, even in the capture, or in the death of such a man as De Volence, was to Martin Lassamour a most uncomfortable thought.

He felt such an appreciation of the detestable character of De Volence, that his death at the hands of the common executioner was, he felt certain, the only real fate he merited.

To die in honourable fight was not the sort of end for the assassin.

Lassamour was right.

De Volence was an assassin.

Nay, of the two, De Volence was a degree or two worse than the hired assassin.

He sunk, we think, even below the level of such men as Tabby and Glass.

They were the mere tools of his bad passion—they were the bold, but unscrupulous instruments by which he strove to carry out the hatreds that he engendered in his own breast.

The friends of Martin Lassamour took good care to keep his figure, as he advanced, dimly in sight.

And yet with that they took as good care that they themselves should not be seen by the ambuscade.

We shall now see how all this fared with them.

But for a certain precipitancy now on the part of De Volence, Martin Lassamour might yet have had a hard fight for his life.

But the villain who was waiting for him was so full of exultation at the seeming fact of having his foe in his power, that he had not the patience to wait, to be quite sure of it

He could have shouted with delight.

He saw, as he felt certain, Martin Lassamour advancing, and alone, too.

Then he was, in all likelihood, so thought De Volence, full of wine.

Then he was unsuspicious of danger, wending his way home to his splendid house at Richmond—that house which he, De Volence, chucklingly told himself he meant that Martin Lassamour should never see again.

How greviously for himself was this rascal mistaken in his calculations.

But we shall soon see.

Now, according to the nature of the ground, and the disposition of the trees, if De Volence had only let Martin Lassamour get about fifty paces further on before he gave the signal of attack upon him, he, Martin, might have had a good deal of difficulty in getting back.

But De Volence did not so wait.

On the contrary, as soon as he saw that Lassamour had fairly passed the spot on which he held watch, although it was but a pace or two, he placed the whistle to his lips.

La samour heard the sound.

So did Tabby and the other rascal who was on the alert to commit the terrible crime of murder.

Martin Lassamour paused on the moment.

He drew his sword.

De Volence turned and plunged into the wood to join his force further on.

"All's right," cried Tabby.

"On! on!" shouted one of the other bravoes.

There could be now no doubt of what was fully meant by all this.

If Martin Lassamour had not been upon his guard, a little hesitation might yet have given his foes great advantage over him; but as it was, they had none.

Wrapping hastily his cloak around his left arm, he began, according to the arrangement he had made with his friends, slowly to retreat backwards.

But he kept his face to the foe.

The long rapier that he held firmly in his right hand glared in the night air.

"On—on!" cried Tabby.

"It's but one man," said another of the rascals.

This was said as an encouragment to the others and to himself.

They all rushed forward with their swords in their hands to the slaughter of this one man, whose death they now made so very sure of that it did not seem to them as if it for one moment admitted of a doubt.

We shall see.

Little did they suspect that Martin Lassamour was relying upon the support of a body of his friends.

Little did they suspect that the slowness of that retreat was for the express pur-pose of wiling them on to their own defeat.

But least of all, as they passed the old ruined barn, did they suspect that from its dark and gloomy shelter would issue another force to hem them in, and take them in the rear.

And yet that was precisely the condition to which De Volence and his party of cut-throats were brought.

"On—on!" cried Tabby again.

"Ay—ay, we have him!"

"Rascals, what do you want?" shouted Martin Lasssamour, in a loud voice.

He spoke thus loud for two objects.

In the first place, he wanted to let his own friends, who were behind him, know by his voice that he was uninjured, and that he was near them; and in the next he wished to urge the others to make an advance.

CHAPTER LXXIX.

THE FIGHT CONTINUES IN THE OLD WOOD.

 ARTIN LASSA-MOUR, by calling out the words that he did, succeeded in both the objects he proposed to himself by so doing.

His friends, who were some distance behind him, became well aware that the time for action had fairly begun.

The assassins were assured that they had made no mistake, and that it was their man upon whom they pounced.

Indeed, a very unexpected result ensued from Martin Lassamour speaking in this way.

De Volence heard him.

Now, every awful and bad passion that could deprave the nature of such a man as De Volence came up in arms by this time.

He had hurried his way through some thickets, and so got to the rear of his own party; but he so thirsted for the blood of Martin Lassamour, that upon hearing what to him was his hated voice, passion got the better of prudence.

He pushed forward, sword in hand, crying out as he did so—

"Fifty gold pieces more to the man who first strikes Martin Lassamour dead!"

"Ah!" cried Lassamour. "De Volence?"

"Yes, and your foe."

"Come on, then."

"I will—I do!"

"To your own peril, villain!"

De Volence did make a sort of show of pushing on in the foremost of the rank of the assassins; but it was only a show, for he took good care not to come within reach of the long blade of Martin Lassamour's rapier.

"Down with him! down with him!" he cried.

"On! on!" shouted Tabby.

Now, one of the rascals that Tabby had employed had a little more animal courage than the others, and as the fifty gold pieces De Volence spoke of was, to him, a very sore temptation, indeed, he thought he would try and earn them.

But the only way to do so was to be the first to strike down Martin Lassamour.

And that was not an easy thing to do.

But he attempted it.

Treasuring up his courage, as we may suppose, to its utmost tension, he made a dash forward, crying out as he did so—

"Hurrah! hurrah for fifty gold pieces!"

There was one clash as the sword of the assassin and that of Martin Lassamour came together.

Then with a yell of rage and pain the foolhardy villain, who had little reckoned upon the skill of the adversary he thus chose to encounter, felt the cold steel plunge through his heart.

He fell a corpse!

Martin Lassamour coolly and slowly retreated as though nothing particular had happened.

"Come on, cowardly De Volence!" he cried. "You can talk, but you cannot fight."

This sudden death of one of their

comrades all at once appeared to damp the energies of the assassins.

They paused a little.

The idea just struck them that they might be trying to earn even the gold pieces of their bad employer at too dear a rate

This pause appeared to drive De Volence very nearly to distraction.

Rage, for the moment, gave him some kind of spurious courage.

Riding forward, he cried out—

"What, are you all afraid of one man? On—on! Follow me, or leave me, as you will!"

Now the idea of leaving him rung disagreeably in their minds, without the idea of leaving all prospect of the reward too, so, as that was not at all pleasant, and as he chose to take the lead, they did follow him.

This suited Lassamour very well.

He longed to cross swords with the villain, De Volence.

But Martin had, by this time, got far enough back to be quite close to his friends.

Then, with a shout of congratulation at the success of their plans for driving the assassin into a hand-to-hand contest, out flew, from the shadow of the hedge, Lamont, the pedler, Cyprian and the others.

If an apparition had suddenly started up in the paths of these men, and with awful gesture, and blood-stained hands warned them back from the perpetration of the deed they meditated, it is very much to be doubted if they would have been one half so much affected by it as they now were by finding that Martin Lassamour had friends at hand.

They staggered back.

They felt all their courage ooze away.

That is to say, if the spurious feeling that they, no doubt, would have called by that name, deserved it.

"Forward!" shouted Lamont.

"Down with the rascals!" cried the pedler.

There was one rush, and just a few strokes with the sword, and then the assassins turned to fly.

No doubt they thought that that resource was, at all events, open to them.

What coward is there who does not suppose that, at the worst he can run away?

But even this solace was now denied to them.

Of course the tumult that had taken place had not escaped the ears of the sheriff's guard in the ruined barn. They felt that the time of action had arrived.

No sooner, then, had the assassins fairly passed by that spot in the pursuit of Martin Lassamour, than the door of the old ruined building was at once flung open, and out bolted the sheriff's guard.

The noise that Mr. Tabby and his friends made as they rushed after Martin Lassamour, of whom they, no doubt, thought to make so easy a prey, had the effect of drowning the sound of the footsteps of the sheriff's guard.

It was not until they turned to run away that they became at all aware that they had foes in that direction as well as in the other.

"Lost!" cried Tabby.

"Mercy!" shouted two of the others.

With a yell of fury, now, De Volence sought to escape from the spot.

But whichever way he turned he found a foe.

With great speed a couple of the sheriff's men lighted flambeaux, and then there was a brief clash of swords, and Tabby and his friends were prisoners.

All with the exception of De Volence!

A couple of the sheriff's men were about to throw themselves upon him and make him a prisoner, when Martin Lassamour called out—

"Hold!"

They drew back.

"I will settle with this villain! Bring the flambeau hither."

The blazing torch cast a strange and a lurid light upon the scene.

De Volence was as pale as death.

With his rapier still in his grasp, and a dagger tightly clutched in his left hand, he stood in the narrow roadway.

The lights flashed upon him, and as Martin Lassamour advanced, the villain, for one moment, shook from head to foot.

"Villain!" said Martin Lassamour, "worse than ordinary villain—assassin!"

"No! no!"

"No, say you?"

"I do."

"'Tis false as thyself, that negative. De Volence, I scorn, and I defy you."

De Volence glanced at him like a fiend.

In a guttural voice, he said,—

"Martin Lassamour, what want you with me?"

"What want I with you?"

"Ay."

"Can you ask?"

"I do ask. For I know not what great offence I have given to you."

"You know not?"

"In sooth not."

Even Martin Lassamour wa staggered

at the effrontery that could put such words into the mouth of even such a man.

Here was one caught in the very fact of trying to perpetrate a cold blooded and most diabolical assassination, pretending to wonder that his victim should be angry with him.

There was a silence of the duration of a few moments now, for all were amazed at the effrontery of De Volence.

CHAPTER LXXX.

DE VOLENCE GOES TO HIS LONG ACCOUNT IN ANOTHER WORLD.

IT was a last desperate game that De Volence was now trying to play. It was such a game as none but one in such an extremity of fortune, and in such an agony of pain as he was in could ever have thought of playing.

Turning to the prisoners, he cast upon them what he thought would prove a meaning look, and then he said,—

"I was travelling this way, and heard a whistle, and so approached the spot, sword in hand. I know nothing further of this matter."

"Oh, outrageous villain!"

"On my soul——"

"Hold!" cried Martin Lassamour. "Do not further pollute that soul with crime, which may soon be in the face of its maker. You are the employer of these assassins."

"I?"

"Even you."

"Good sir, you wrong me."

"Wrong you?"

"Yes. In truth you do."

"As how?"

"I never saw them in my life before!"

"Oh, monstrous."

"Oh! oh!" said Tabby. "Oh!"

"Who are you, fellow?" said De Volence, looking at him with a not badly dissembled surprise.

"Oh! oh!"

"Your own base tools will contradict you," said Martin Lassamour. "I can see it in their eyes."

"They cannot."

"They will."

"My good Martin Lassamour, they may lie, as no doubt such base knaves are accustomed to do, but if they accuse me of any complicity with them, surely you will not believe them."

"I will."

"What, against my honour?"

"Against your honour? No."

De Volence breathed again, but his respite from fear was but of short duration.

"You have no honour!" added Martin Lassamour, in a calm, determined tone of voice. "There is no possible mode to bring it down to a feeling which you do not possess."

De Volence's heart sunk within him again.

"Oh, noble sir," began Tabby, now in a low and whining tone of voice, "if you will let a poor fellow go, who, in a moment when the wine was in him, and the wit was out, consented to do a bad thing, I will tell you all?"

"'Tis false!" cried De Volence.

"False!" shouted Tabby. "Go to the devil, you know it is all true enough."

"It's false."

"False be hanged. You know very well that you employed us all to assassinate good Master Martin Lassamour here, because you were by far too cowardly to do it yourself."

"No—no."

"But I say yes. And now let me go, as I have told the exact truth to you all."

"You have confessed your rascality," said the officer commanding the little party of five sheriff's men; "but I don't see any reason why you should be let loose on that account."

"But I do."

"Then we differ."

"Oh, but my good sir, that was the bargain that I made with the noble Martin Lassamour, and he is not of the sort to break his word."

"You say truly," returned Martin Lassamour; "that I am not one of the sort to break my word."

"Then—then you believe him?"

"I do."

"But," added Martin Lassamour, "I

THE DEATH OF DE VOLENCN.

am not aware that I even was pledged in this case. The fact is, you and your rascally employer were so intent upon abusing and criminating each other, that there was no occasion for me to speak at all."

Tabby looked confounded.

Martin Lassamour had certainly promised him nothing, and he had, in his anger, told the truth, for once in a way, and got nothing by it.

This was desperately provoking.

De Volence knashed his teeth with rage, and looked round him like some caged wild beast.

Watching, then, a moment when he thought Martin Lassamour was off his guard, he made a sudden rush upon him, exclaiming, as he did so—

"I will fight thee!"

His object was about as far from fighting as it very well could be.

What he wanted to do was to put an

end to the prospect of a fight at all with Martin Lassamour, by plunging his dagger into his heart.

But he was foiled.

From the first moment that they had come face to face, Martin Lassamour had never taken his own eyes off those of De Volence.

He well knew the treacherous foe he had to deal with.

By this means he was able easily to foil him in the base attempt to take him at unawares, and De Volence reaped nothing from it but a wound in his own shoulder, which made him howl with rage and pain.

Martin Lassamour followed him up.

And now, for once in his life, De Volence did fight, and fight well.

It seemed as if a sort of wild insanity had now seized him. No doubt he felt that it was a matter of life and death with him, and that it was far better he should try his chance than quietly submit to the sword of Martin Lassamour.

And so, after all, the combat was fierce, though brief.

The clash of the rapiers together did not last more than half a minute, and then, with a deep groan, De Volence dropped his sword, and fell beneath the point of that of his adversary.

Martin Lassamour had run him right through the heart.

We may presume that even that villain had such a thing as a heart, bad, though, it no doubt was.

He first sank on his knees, and then fell on to his face.

From that position he rolled on to his back, and there he lay, with death visible upon his pallid features.

The men with the links approached, and cast a good light upon him.

Martin Lassamour calmly wiped his sword; and then, as the dying De Volence cast his eyes upon him, the awful expression of them induced Martin Lassamour to turn aside.

"Curses!" muttered De Volence. "My dying curses be upon you all—all! May the curse of a dying man cling to you for ever!—for—for—ever——"

His eyes became fixed and glassy, and he was but a clod of earth.

"Gone," said one of the sheriff's men.

"Dead?" said Lassamour.

"Yes, sir, after cursing us all."

"Heed not that. Heaven does not delegate the power to curse to such as he."

"I should think not, sir."

Lamont gazed at the dead body.

"Well," he said, "there is an end, at last, of one of the greatest rascals that ever disgraced human nature."

"There is," said the pedler. "And what are we to do next?"

Martin Lassamour, upon this, spoke—

"Sir Officer," he said, addressing the officer in command of the sheriff's men, "it is to you I now address myself."

"I am to obey your commands, noble sir, be they what they may.'"

"Sir, I thank you."

"No thanks, sir. Such are my orders."

"Then, sir, will you despatch so many of your men to London with these prisoners as may suffice to lodge them safely in jail in the first instance?"

"It shall be done."

"And then will you, with the remainder of your force, and such men of my own party as are willing to come with me, repair to Pleasaunce House?"

"Yes, sir."

Sir Ralph Shard touched the arm of Martin Lassamour.

"This night will end all," he said.

"It will."

"With Lady Margaret."

"Even so. Now come with me, friends, and what I mean to do I will tell to you all as we go along. I have a great duty to perform, although it is one that is most fearful to my heart and soul."

"We attend you, sir."

The officer commanding the sheriff's men sent the prisoners to London with a sufficient escort, and then he, with the remainder of his men, accompanied Martin Lassamour to Richmond.

CHAPTER LXXXI.

LADY MARGARET MAKES HER PREPARATIONS AT HOME.

HILE all this was going on, where was the Lady Margaret Lassamour? What was she about? Had she no sort of presentiment that her last act was about to be prevented? Had she no idea that it could not be, as it had been, for ever with her; that she had but to will the death of aught human, and that human thing in due time became a corpse?

She did not.

Guilt, long concealed, and long triumphant, will, in time, beget a feeling of false security.

The soldier who has gone through very many battles with impunity, begins at last to think that he must surely be invulnerable.

So was it with the Lady Margaret.

That she was the murderess of the six husbands who had gone before Martin Lassamour the reader can now entertain not the shadow of a doubt upon.

And so as she had sent them all to

"That bourne from whence no traveller returns."

she thought she had only to make up her mind so to do in order to send him after them.

There was she mistaken.

But had she quite made up her mind to this course, or did she really, for the first time in her life, love, and was that love waked by Martin Lassamour?

That is the question.

From all concurrent testimonies we are led to the belief that she did love Martin Lassamour—that for once her fancy was attracted, and that she would have put up with much to retain him in life, but it is at the same time a pretty candid proposition that with that love there was associated such a world of mad jealousy that it lost its proper influence.

Jealousy!

That monster passion which truly

"Doth make the meal it feeds on."

it had possession of her whole soul, and as such a wild mad passion will always be much more than a match for anything in the shape of sentiment, there can be no wonder that it became the guiding principle of the mind of the Lady Margaret, instead of love.

And so she told herself that she and Martin Lassamour would part for ever on that night.

She was right there, but not after the manner which she anticipated.

She meant to kill him!

Yes, she had made her resolve. You may call it insanity, if you will, on the principle that all conscience must be insanity. But still, be it what it may, it was a resolution that she had taken.

And while Martin Lassamour was engaged in his conflict with the villain De Volence, and his assassins, the Lady Margaret made her preparations.

She had no one to watch her now.

The only person whose knowledge of her past acts she might well dread was in the grave. The waiting-maid was no more, and so the Lady Margaret felt that she could look upon the mighty secret of her great crimes in her own heart alone.

The evening wore on listlessly with her—it deepened into night, and her fell purpose gathered strength with it.

She sat alone in her chamber—that chamber that by the secret panel in the wall, and the narrow passage beyond it communica'ed with the state bedchamber in which Martin Lassamour was wont to repose when he returned late in the night to Pleasaunce House.

Yes, there she sat!

Like some evil genius, brooding over the destruction of a soul, she sat there; but it was her own soul that was the victim!

Strange infatuation!

Upon the hearth there was a brasier that contained charcoal in a state of red heat, and ever and anon she heaped up upon it small pieces of charcoal, so as to keep it to a certain point.

At eleven o'clock she rung her bell; but she did not mean that any one should enter that little chamber; so she walked out into the corridor to meet whoever might reply to the summons.

The servants in their own great kitchen heard the summons; for somehow they had all, upon that night, been fearful of retiring to rest.

A clap of thunder about ten o'clock had had the effect of alarming them all, and they had sat up telling old tales of ghosts and murders, until no one liked to make the move to retire to rest.

The tinkling of the bell of the Lady Margaret at once startled them all, and they jumped from their seats.

"The Lord be good to us!" said one, "the Lady Margaret is not to rest yet."

"Of course not," said another.

"Why of course?"

"Why, Martin Lassamour is not at home, and though she seems to go to rest, you may take my word for it she don't do so."

"Likely enough."

"Ay, and what is more, I can tell you that in the very middle of the night— Good Lord, there is the bell again."

"Who will go?"

That seemed to be as great a question with the servants of the Lady Margaret as the one that in the fable agitated the mouse community with regard to who should tie a bell round the cat's neck.

They looked at each other in blank dismay.

The fact was, that the route to the chamber of the Lady Margaret lay through a very great portion of the house, and no one, particularly after the terrible tales they had been telling each other, exactly liked the job of going.

"Where on earth," said one, "can be that Cyprian? He is the proper person to go."

"To be sure," said every one.

"Or her own maid," said another.

"To be sure," was the chorus repeated of assent.

But Cyprian was with Martin Lassamour, and the own maid was in the tomb—at least, such a tomb as the Lady Margaret had chosen to provide for her.

There was, however, a young lad who had but recently joined the establishment, and who had gone fast asleep, while the rest of the servants had been telling to each other tales of terror.

Now, as if by one impulse, all eyes were turned upon this boy.

"He'll go," said one.

"To be sure," said another.

"Of course," said a third.

"Send him," said a fourth.

"Ay, send him. Wake him up, and send him," cried the whole together.

The boy was awakened, and looked about him with a stare of only half consciousness.

"Hilloa! hilloa! Hugh! Hugh!"

"Anon!"

"Hugh?"

"Eh?"

"You are wanted."

"You don't mean I?"

"Oh, yes, we do. The Lady Margaret has sent for you; so be off."

"Anon!"

"Confound the fool, he is not half awake yet, give him a good shake."

The good shake was duly given, along with several boxes on the ear, and then Hugh was supposed to be thoroughly aroused, although it is very doubtful if the last part of the process had any sort of effect upon him.

"Now, Hugh, attend."

"Oh lord, yes. What is it?"

"Do you know the way to my lady's room in the grey turret?"

"Yes."

"Then go, for she wants you."

"Wants me?"

"Yes, stupid."

"Well, I'm a going."

"Be quick, good Hugh."

Hugh, stretching himself, and yawning as he went, did not feel that there was anything out of the way in the matter. His imagination had not been sufficiently cultivated to make him a slave to any of the terrors of the supernatural world.

Indeed, if Hugh had met the ghosts of the whole six husbands of the Lady Margaret on his route to the chamber, it is doubtful if he would have done anything but say—

"My service to you all, gentlemen!"

CHAPTER LXXXII.

MARTIN LASSAMOUR PREPARES TO PLAY HIS PART.

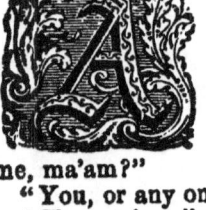GAIN the Lady Margaret rung the bell. In the course of a few moments she heard a footstep coming, and then Hugh appeared.

Did you please to want me, ma'am?"

"You, or any one.'

"Yes, ma'am."

"Is Cyprian returned?"

"No, ma'am."

"Are the domestics retiring for the night."

"No, ma'am."

"Go and say that it is my order that they one and all retire to rest. Mark me, it is my distinct orders."

"Yes, ma'am."

"You can go now."

Hugh made no remark at all upon the subject, but slowly turning round, he retraced his way to the kitchen again, and delivered his message.

"Well, then, we must all go, that's quite clear."

"Ah, yes, and time enough, too, if we are to get up at all in the morning."

"But Hugh, my lad," said a third. "Did you see anything as you went along the gallery?"

"Yes."

"Oh, what?—what?"

"The floor."

"The floor only?"

"Yes, that's all. Why, what else was there to see I should like to know, eh?"

"Ghosts."

"What?"

"Ghosts."

"No," said Hugh, after looking very dubious for a few moments, as though the subject required a little consideration. "I didn't never see none of them as I know on."

After this, there was no resource but for the domestics of Pleasaunce House to retire to rest, as they had been ordered to do by their somewhat imperious mistress.

In another quarter of an hour a death-like stillness reigned in the mansion.

We may now return to Martin Lassamour, and the party with him, who had just, with them, reached the small postern in the park door of Pleasaunce, and then came to a halt, to arrange every minute and important particular of their next proceedings.

It was past the hour of midnight when they all came to a halt at that little door in the wall that bounded the domain of Pleasaunce House.

Martin Lassamour spoke in a voice in which could be discovered tones of very deep emotion.

"Now, my friends," he said, "I am afraid that what we are about to try to-night is, after all, not much of an experiment, for we are pretty well sure of how it will turn out. But yet it is a something by which we seek to be assured of the guilt of the Lady Margaret, not yet being quite assured of it."

"To be sure," said Lamont. "That is it, I take it. That is just my feeling, and I pray to Heaven that it may yet turn out we are all very much mistaken."

"Amen!" said Martin Lassamour, in a tone of deep and heart-felt feeling.

"Amen!"

"Well," said Sir Ralph Shard, "it is very natural for you, my good friend, Lassamour, no doubt, to have those feelings, and they don't do you discredit—but—"

"You think differently?"

"I do."

"I fear that you are right, sir."

"My good friend, I am quite sure of it; so let us get on, for the sooner all this affair is settled the easier you will be in heart and in brain."

"True—most true."

"That is true, indeed," said Lamont.

"Cyprian," said Lassamour.

"I am here, noble sir."

"Open the small door for us."

"I have done so already. There is nothing to hinder you and all these good gentlemen from entering the garden."

"Come on, then."

They all passed through the little door in the old red brick wall, and then they were, so to speak, fairly within the precincts of Pleasaunce.

They came to a halt.

"Let me, now," said Martin Lassamour, "clearly explain to all the line of conduct that I propose to lay down for myself to-night."

They all gathered around him, and listened with marked and serious attention.

"It is believed that the Lady Margaret has made away, in some mysterious manner, with her six husbands preceding me, for two reasons."

"Ay, ay," said Sir Ralph Shard ; "go on."

"These two reasons are, jealousy and intoxication."

"Good."

"Well, then, what I propose is, to-night to simulate intoxication, and in that seeming state, to say things that will tend to awaken the other feeling, namely, jealousy."

"Good, again."

"If, then, she thinks proper to attempt my life on that provocation, I, keeping all my faculties, as I shall, on the alert, shall be able to find out the obscure and the mysterious means she employs."

"Good, again."

"While this experiment is in progress, then, I would have you all in hiding in the long picture gallery, close to the state bed-chamber, in the which I will make a pretence of lying down to sleep."

"That will do."

"Upon my calling out for help, you will then be pleased to consider that it is time to rush in and seize her."

"All's right."

"And yet," said Robert Lee, the pedler, "will you, good sir, allow me to make one remark?"

"Assuredly."

"To my simple judgment, then, it seems that this plan is not without a serious objection."

"Think you so?"

"I do, noble sir."

"Pray state it, then."

"It is just this : If the Lady Margaret be a guilty woman, and if it be true that she has made away wih her former six husbands by some very mysterious means, we may well come to a conclusion that those means, be they what they may, are at all events, efficient and prompt."

"Just so."

"Then, my good lord, as you have to lie down, and simulate sleep, is it not possible that her means of accomplishing your death may be so sudden, and so good,

that you may perish, perchance, before you have time to utter any cry for aid to us."

"Body o' me !" cried Sir Ralph Shard, "but there is much reason in that."

"There is," said Lamont.

"You have staggered me," said Martin Lassamour.

"I merely threw this idea out as a suggestion."

"It is a good one."

"Ay," added Sir Ralph Shard, " and one well worth the considering, in more ways than one."

"It is—it is."

"But, my good friend, Lee," added Martin Lassamour, after a pause of thought, "I don't take you quite to be the man to start an objection without some way of getting over it. Tell me if it be so."

"I have a thought."

"Ah, yes, I could have sworn you had."

"Speak out, man," said Sir Ralph Shard; "for I do begin to think your head-piece is worth all ours put together. Speak out, my good fellow."

The pedler, thus encouraged, spoke clearly and calmly to the purpose.

"My idea is simply this, that Master Martin Lassamour will at the first take me into the state chamber with him, and rapidly let me hide where I can, so that while he is feigning to be asleep, and lying down somewhat helplessly, I may be on my feet, and ready for immediate action."

"That's it!" cried Sir Ralph Shard. "That will do it."

"I think so too," said Lamont.

"Be it so, then," said Lassamour. "Be it so."

Martin could not but feel that this was an arrangement that made his safety much more assured than it would otherwise have been. He turned to the pedler, saying—

"It is likely enough, my good friend, that you will, in truth, save my life to-night."

"It will give me great joy to do so."

"I know it will."

"I speak from my heart, sir."

"Of that I am well assured. So now come on, as I think that we all well comprehend what we have to do."

We do—we do."

Walking slowly and lightly as foot could fall, and looking like so many spectres, they took their way towards the house.

CHAPTER LXXXIII.

GAMIEL GANDER IS OF SOME USE AFTER ALL.

E must now leave Martin Lassamour and his friends for a brief period, in order to recount a something of importance to our story, which took place at the ferry house of Langdon.

Far from in any way abandoning his idea of quitting possession of the ferryman's daughter, the villanous De Volence had, as often as he had had anything in the shape of conversation with the assassins in his employment, reverted to it.

This then had had the effect of inducing them to think of some little piece of business on their own account.

They began to think that this over anxiety upon the subject of the abduction of Amy Langdon must have more in it than the mere admiration the beauty of the young girl inspired.

In fact, these coarse-minded and most thoroughly mercenary rascals could not possibly make up their minds to anything being true that had not money or money's worth in some sort of way as its basis and beginning.

Hence, while a considerable portion of time had been spent by De Volence in waiting until he thought it would be prudent to go. to the little wood and wait for the coming of his foe, Martin Lassamour, Tabby had made some arrangements of his own.

These arrangements were very inimical indeed to the peace of Amy Langdon.

But they had reference solely to the money part of the matter.

So far, poor Amy had rather less to fear from Tabby than from even his rascally employer, De Volence.

And what made it so much more easy for Tabby to continue a something against the peace and the liberty of Amy Langdon was, that Martin Lassamour and the pedler both thought that all danger to her would be sure to come through De Volence.

Hence in watching him, and in knowing well of his whereabouts, they considered that they were doing all that was necessary to do in that particular.

And so it seemed reasonable to thk. in

But the case was in reality very different, indeed, as we shall see.

Tabby then seized the opportunity, after the discomfiture of the plan to carry off Amy Langdon in the sedan chair, to try a little plot of his own.

We shall briefly detail how he set about it.

Feeling that he was not wanted by De Volence for some hours, he started alone to that not very salubrious locality, Whitefriars.

Whitefriars now has nothing to boast of but a great quantity of dirt, and a great quantity of vulgarity, but at that time it was the known, and the chosen resort of a class of desperadoes, the very existence of whom was a shame and a disgrace to any country calling itself civilised.

Assassins, cut-throats, robbers of all sorts and description found a home of safety in that region.

It was perfectly well known that if a man wanted a rascal to do anything which he either had not courage to do himself, or had not power, in Whitefriars he would find such a man.

We will, then, follow Tabby to that favoured spot.

He was well known there.

More than once had he been in hiding in that place from the officers of the law that were in search of him; and, in fact, from his roguery and his boasting, and his capacity for holding an enormous quantity of drink, he was considered quite an ornament to the community.

Fame takes different complexions, according to place, time, and people.

Perhaps Tabby was as proud of the sort of distinction he enjoyed in Whitefriars as any bowing, smirking courtier at St. James' might be of his ridiculously contemptible position.

No doubt of it.

In Whitefriars there was one very ancient house, of large size, kept by a man who called himself Captain Augustus Cæsar.

Of course that was an alias that, no doubt, he thought peculiarly fitted his capabilities.

The house had been at one time a large mansion belonging to a noble family, bu that was before Whitefriars became so degraded as it then was.

With the decaying portion of the neighbourhood, and the bad repute of it, all persons who resided within its precincts, had got rid of their houses there, and given up all idea of even ever visiting them again.

This large, and once handsome house, then, had fallen into the hands of Captain Augustus Cæsar.

The gallant captain had connected it with a sort of hostelry, so that when a gentleman had got into any little difficulty with the police, or with any one to whom he had given a quieter, in the shape of a blow with a dagger, he might fly to the sanctuary of Whitefriars, and at once take his ease, as at his inn, at the abode of Captain Cæsar.

That is to say, he might do that upon one little preliminary condition.

He must come to with a full purse.

If he did not come with that essential, Captain Cæsar would, of the two, rather not have his company.

But this is all by the way.

Let us follow Tabby, now, to Whitefriars.

He made good speed, and soon reached the door of Captain Cæsar's house.

That door stood always very invitingly open to all comers; and there was a very strong odour of stale tobacco and strong drinks for ever, apparently, rolling out in clouds from the hostel.

The Babel-like sound of many voices came upon the ears of Tabby as he crossed the threshhold, and he caught the following stanza:—

CAPTAIN CÆSAR'S SONG.

Drink, drink, drink, boys,
And care you will forget it;
Never leave off drinking, boys,
Except—when you can't get it!
   Hurrah! Hurrah!

Love, love, love, boys,
When a pretty girl is nigh;
Never leave off loving, boys,
Except—her friends are by!
   Hurrah! Hurrah!

Tabby pushed open a door upon the ground floor, and entered a large room that had been once the dining-room of the house.

A very motley sort of assemblage then met his gaze.

Some twenty-five men were in the room, all drinking, smoking, laughing, talking, singing, and quarrelling, as it seemed, together.

Upon a chair, placed on the table, sat the redoubtable Captain Cæsar himself, evidently very far gone already in intoxication.

"Hilloa!" he cried; "who comes?"

"A friend!".

"Ha! ha! A bon comorado, is it?"

"It is."

"His name? What do the profane and wicked call him, eh?"

"Tabby!"

"Ha! ha! He is right welcome! Come to my arms, my Tabby!"

"Go to the devil," said Tabby, as he coolly sat down at as good a distance from Captain Cæsar as he could.

"What was that?"

"What?"

"What did you say?"

"I said go to the devil!"

"Take that, then."

Captain Cæsar caught up a flagon full of hot mulled wine, and flung it at the head of Tabby, but that worthy saw the missile coming, and just ducked in time to avoid it. It flew over his head, and hit a surly-looking man behind him full in the face with considerable violence.

With a roar like that of some wild bull in an arena, the surly-looking man sprang to his feet, and drew his sword.

"What fiend did that!"

Everybody was on his feet in a moment, and with the prospect of a severe row, Tabby moved to the door.

As he did so, he placed his mouth to the ear of a man with a huge red moustache, and whispered—

"Come with me, I want you on business."

HAPTER LXXXIV.

SHEWS THAT AMY LANGDON WAS IN MUCH DANGER.

 HE man with the red moustache gave Tabby a nod, and then rose, and followed him from the room.

As they both left it, bottles, and decanters, and glasses, and drinking cups, were beginning to fly about in very great profusion.

Oaths and imprecations were abundant, and in fact, a complete row, such as not unfrequently brought to an end some of the orgies of Captain Cæsar, appeared to be getting up.

TABBY AND HIS COMPANION IN WHITEFRIARS.

"Follow me," said Tabby.

"Ay, ay."

Tabby walked on till he and the man with the red moustache got under the archway of an old, and apparently deserted house, and then they paused.

"Well, Tabby," said the man, "what is it now?"

"Why, Houseman," said Tabby, for the first time addressing the man by his name, "it is a something that I think will pay."

"That's the thing."

"Of course it is."

"To be sure."

"But it is likewise a something that will require skill, prudence, and courage."

"Indeed!"

"Yes."

"Is it a fencing match, then?"

"Oh, dear, no."

"What then?"

"Listen, and I will tell you."

"I am all ears."

"There is a nobleman with plenty of

money, and there is a young girl with none. The young girl is pretty, and the nobleman has taken a fancy to her."

"Oh, the old story."

"Just so."

"Well?"

"Well, then, the girl is coy."

"Ah."

"She is what she calls virtuous, and all that sort of stuff, you see."

"Go on."

"So the nobleman has said to me that he will give a certain sum if I get her out of her own house, and place her somewhere where he can pay her a visit, and where a little squalling won't be attended to."

"Good."

"Yes, so far as it goes. But——"

"But what?"

"I think that he will pay double—ay, treble, for the girl, and so what do you say to the speculation of taking her away on our own account, and then making our own price with him?"

"Capital."

"You think so?"

"I do."

"Then give me your hand, Huseman, and we will do it."

"We will. And all I can say is, Tabby, that you are a genius."

"Oh, don't. You know how modest I am, so don't praise me."

"But you are a genius for all that, my ad'mirable Tabby."

"Don't—don't."

"Well, well, I won't distress you by my praises, though you deserve 'em, but all I will say is, that I am quite at your service."

"Many thanks."

"When shall we set about it?"

"To-night."

"To-night?"

"Yes. This very night, or it will be too late, and it is a matter of great regret to me that I shall not be able to be with you."

"Ah?"

"I cannot."

"Humph!"

"You don't like that."

"I don't."

"Well, Huseman, if you don't like it, you know I can find some one else to take the conduct of the affair, for there is no difficulty in it, and when I tell you why I can't come with you, you will feel differently to what you do now."

"Why can't you?"

"First, because I shall be engaged in keeping everybody employed who otherwise would be likely to interrupt you in the little affair."

"Oh, that's it."

"It is. And what do you say now?"

"I will do it."

"Right. Now we understand each other, and let me hope that there will be honour among——"

"Thieves!"

"Well, well, I was not a going to say that, exactly, but it will require only three of you, so if you can get a couple of friends to aid you, it will do."

"Oh, yes. But where is the girl? Who is she, and where shall we take her to?"

"Take her to old Mother Hill's, in the Mint, she will take care of her."

"I believe you."

"And as for her name, it is Amy Langdon, and she is the daughter of the ferryman of Lambeth."

"The devil!"

"Well, what of that?"

"Well, I don't know that it matters much, but that Langdon is rather an ill-conditioned, and big sort of fellow."

"Give him six inches of cold steel, and were he as big as Goliah, it will settle him."

"That's true."

"Of course it is, and you can do it, too."

"Well, well, let it be so."

"Good. Now Huseman, I leave this little affair entirely in your hands to arrange, and to settle, and I promise you truly that it shall be a case of share and share alike."

"Agreed."

"Good again. And now set about it as soon as you can, for I have to go to our Lady Cheerful to meet some one, and be careful, whatever you do, of who you engage in the matter."

"Oh yes—yes."

"Have you a thought of any one?"

"Well, if Glass could be found——"

"Glass?"

"Yes, your old friend."

"Hem! I—a—that is—I'm afraid you can't find him again in a hurry."

"Indeed."

"No. He has met with a little bit of an accident, and by this time he is out of his troubles."

"Dead?"

"Yes."

"You don't say so?"

"I do though, Huseman, and it will satisfy you to know that one of the reasons why I can't go with you on this little affair, is that I am on an expedition, to-night, that will send the man who did for poor Glass after him."

"Then I excuse you, indeed."

"I knew you would."

"Alas! poor Glass."

"Ah, alas! indeed."

"What a lot he could drink."

"He could."

"And how handy with his poinard."

"He was."

"And what a humour he had too, what a fine wit!"

"True—true! He had all that."

"And so he has gone at last."

"Quite gone."

"Well, it's no use grieving, Tabby; so, now, good evening to you, and I will set about the job, and in the course of an hour shall have two brave comrades."

"Do so; but mind you don't bring the wrong girl from the ferryman's."

"What, is there a lot of them."

"No, only two; but the younger one is not just now wanted; you will know the one they call Amy, by her being the tallest, and rather the darker of the two."

"All's right."

"Good luck to you."

"Thank you. Perhaps I shall take a fancy to the little one myself, and if so I will bring them both off, and then, you know, there can be no mistake."

"Ha! ha!"

"Good evening. I will set about it at once.'

They parted, and Tabby hurried from Whitefriars as fast as he could.

CHAPTER LXXXV.

HOUSEMAN AND HIS FRIENDS MEET WITH A DISAPPOINTMENT.

HOUSEMAN had far better, so far as his own person was concerned, have been not at home when Tabby called. This little treacherous proceeding on the part of Tabby was doomed to disappoinment, as we shall presently see.

Houseman was very sorely in want of cash, and he was just like the rest of the world in that particular, that is to say, he did not care one straw where, or how he got money, so that he did get it.

So soon, then, as Tabby had left him, he set about making the necessary preparations for carrying out the precious plan with which he had been entrusted.

It became necessary that he should find his associates.

This was not difficult. You might find some difficulty in getting three dogs, cats, or horses together to commit some iniquity in concord, but there is none at all in procuring three human beings to do so.

Therefore, Houseman was soon in the company of a couple of as great rogues as himself, and they were discussing the minor arrangements of their plans.

"How is it to be done?" said one, "that Langdon, the Ferryman, is not a very agreeable customer to come across, I rather think."

"He is not," said the other.

"Well," replied Houseman, "of course, in a littly piece of business like this, you cannot expect it to be all plain dealing."

"No, no."

"Then we must just take the rough with the smooth, I rather think."

"But if we rouse him up—"

"Then knock him down."

"Well," said the one who had just spoken, "my idea about all these sort of affairs is just this, that it is best to find out where the greatest difficulty lies, and the greatest chance of failure, and set about putting a stop to them."

"As how?"

"Why, now, look you here. It is this Langdon, the Ferryman, who is likely to be the principal difficulty. Suppose, now, we go to the cottage—suppose we get into it, and get hold of the girl we want, and then suppose she begins squeaking, as they will do you know—where are we then?"

"Rather in for some danger."

"Yes, and so I say tackle the danger first. Go to the cottage, and let the first visit be to the room of old Langdon."

"Ah!"

"Yes, you see what I mean. Silence him first, and then we have the rest of the business all our own way."

"There is something in that," said Houseman.

"A good deal," said the other.

"Let it be so, then. After he is settled,

it will, indeed, be all plain sailing, I should say."

"It will—it will."

"Come on, then. Let us be off about it, for the sooner we bring the affair to an end the better I shall be pleased."

"And so shall I."

With this, Huseman and his two rascally associates started at once from Whitefriars to Lambeth, to carry out the exceedingly amusing plan of Tabby.

Little did Tabby think that on that very night the death of his rascally employer, De Volence, would at once put an end to the abduction of Amy Langdon being a good speculation at all, even should his associates succeed in it.

But they did not succeed, as we shall see.

Huseman and his two friends went at a very good rate of speed, and being tolerably intimate with both the highways and the byeways of London, they very soon reached the appointed spot.

They stood, in fact, on the outside of the palings of the garden of Langdon's house within one hour of the time that Tabby had left Huseman.

"Is this the place?" said one.

"It is."

"Yes," added Huseman, "there can be no sort of mistake about it. There is no other cottage and garden, at all like it, hereabouts."

"Good."

"Now we had better get as quickly as we can over the garden wall."

"Agreed."

They assisted each other over the paling, which, to tell the truth, was not a very difficult enterprise, and they soon stood within the precincts of that pretty little garden which had been for so long the quiet pride and care of the fair sisters, and in which both Cyprian and Gamiel Gander had wandered full of love and admiration of the rough ferryman's daughters.

But although these three ruffians thought that they had carried on their proceedings with great secrecy, they were observed.

The person who observed them was just about the last from whom they would have expected any danger, or who they thought might be at all likely to be stirring at that time of the evening.

It was no other than our old friend, Gamiel Gander.

Now it so happened that Gamiel Gander's poor old grandmother was in a very queer state of health all that day, and after Gamiel had come home and duly related to the old lady the trials and remarkable adventures he had met with at the ford, she got rather worse.

"Oh, my Gamiel, she said, "I'm afraid that little wretch of a page, Cyprian, must have sold himself to the devil."

"You don't mean that!"

"I do—I do."

"But why—how?"

"Well, my dear, how could he get the better of you, with all your beauty, if he had not?"

"There is something in that, granny."

"There is, indeed, my love. You so nice and fat, too—why, good gracious me, where can the eyes of that little wretch, Patience Langdon be, I should wonder, that she can't see how beautifully plump and fine you are."

"Well, I am that."

"You are, my love—you are. Oh! oh! oh!"

"What's the row?"

"Oh! oh! oh!"

"Good gracious, what's the row now?"

"The spasm !"

"Stuff !"

"Oh! oh! I'm going—going——"

"Where?"

"To the grave, if you don't get some *eau de vie*. Oh! oh! Go to the 'Lamb and Wolf,' my dear Gamiel, and say it is for me. Oh! oh! The spasms! Oh! oh!"

Gamiel, when he saw the old lady now fall flat to the floor, began to get rather seriously alarmed, and he made a rush out of the cottage to go for the *eau de vie*, to the "Wolf and Lamb," which was a hostel not above a couple of hundred yards from his grandmother's house.

But to get to the "Wolf and Lamb" Gamiel Gander had to pass a portion of the garden wall of Langdon the ferryman.

What was his surprise, then, and consternation to see a man's legs just disappearing over the palings as he reached that spot.

Gamiel forgot all about his poor old grandmother and the spasms, and came to a dead halt.

"Oh, lor! he said, "what is the meaning of this 'ere, I wonder?"

It was not at all likely that by waiting there wondering, he would be able to come to anything like a good opinion as to the meaning of it, so he adopted another plan.

Now to Gamiel Gander, who had roamed around the garden palings of that little abode by the hour together, like a cat round a dairy, the paling was so familiar that he knew all the crevices through which a peep could be got inside.

Applying his eye, then, to one of them, he tolerably distinctly saw three men tanding in one of the flower beds of the garden, apparently in deep and earnest conversation

Gamiel, too, heard what they said.

"All's right so far," said one.

"Yes, yes."

"And not a soul saw us."

"To be sure not."

"That's a comfort."

"Come on, then, slowly and quietly," said another. "There is no hurry, and all we have to do is to put a poniard up to the hilt in the heart of Langdon, and then carry off the girl."

Upon hearing these words, poor Gamiel Gander tumbled backwards right into a wild blackberry bush, and was fixed in it for some few moments.

CHAPTER LXXXVI.

GAMIEL GANDER GIVES THE ALARM.

POOR Gamiel Gander's situation in the black-berry bush was far from pleasant.

No wonder, then, that he rescued himself from it as quickly as he possibly could; and the fact that he had some physical pain to complain of, no doubt aided very materially in the awaking of his faculties to the consciousness that things were anything but right in the garden of Langdon the ferryman.

That Langdon was to be murdered, and that one or both of his daughters were to be abducted from their old house was a proposition that had struck his ears with dismay.

"Oh, what shall I do!"

That was the first sentence into which the fears and the horror of poor Gamiel Gander shaped themselves.

"Oh, what shall I do?"

This, at that period, was a question very much easier to ask than to answer, for at that time there was no police station to run to, and the watch was so totally inefficient that, if it depended on them to stop it, one half the parish might easily be murdered without let or hindrance of any kind whatever.

Poor Gamiel Gander was for a little time at his wit's end.

Then a thought struck him.

"I will run down to the river," he said, "and see if I can get any of the young fellows of watermen to come and do a good act for once in their lives."

No sooner was this thought of than he started at great speed to carry it out. Several times he fell down in his flight and hurry, and rolled on and on, but he contrived to scramble to his feet again, and

on he went till he got down to a stairs by the side of the river, and close to Bishop's Walk, Lambeth.

As soon as he got there, he placed his hand to his mouth in the shape of a trumpet, and shouted out—

"Murder! murder! murder!"

Such a cry, of course, was not likely to be raised without some efforts, and in a few moments Gamiel Gander was surrounded by some half dozen stout watermen, all eagerly inquiring who was murdered.

"Oh, I'll tell you. Oh! oh!"

"Do so at once, then, stupid."

"Yes, I am."

"We know that."

"Oh, you know me, then."

"To be sure. You are the little fat Gander."

"I is—I is!" cried Gamiel, quite heedless of everything in the excitement of the moment.

"Well, what's the row?"

"Oh, I'll tell you. Do you know old Langdon the ferryman?"

"To be sure."

"An old curmudgeon!" cried another.

"And as stingy as the devil," said a third.

"Ah, but," said a fourth, "only think of the two pretty loves, his daughters."

"Yes, yes," cried Gamiel Gander, "its about them."

"About them?"

"Yes, yes."

"Why—why you don't mean to say that they are murdered, do you?"

"Worse! worse!"

"Worse?"

"Oh lord, yes!—oh lord, ye!"

"How so?"

"They will be ruinated if you don't all

of you interfere. There's three ruffians got into the garden, and they are going to cut old Langdon's throat, and run off with the gals."

"The devil they are !"

"Yes, yes, yes."

" Well, but you don't mean to say that it's really true?"

"I do—I do !"

The questioner turned to his fellows, and cried out—

"I say, comrades, this won't do."

"Certainly not."

"We may not like old Langdon, for a crusty old wretch, as he is; but it won't do to let his throat be cut, and the two young girls be run off with before our faces."

"No, no."

"Oh, come along—come along," said Gamiel Gander ; " don't stand talking about it, but come along at once, do, and do something to save 'em."

"All's right. We will come."

The party of watermen, to the number of seven, now, without more ado, set off towards the cottage of the ferryman, fully determined to rescue the two young girls from the ruffians that had got into the garden, according to the account given by Gamiel Gander.

As for poor Gamiel, he was very soon distanced by the watermen, for he was never very good at running, and he had so completely exhausted all his power in that way to get to the little landing-place by the bank of the river, that the idea of running at full speed back again to the ferryman's cottage was quite out of the question, as far as he was concerned.

But Gamiel Gander did arrive in time to do some good for all that.

We will, now that we have fully possessed the reader with all that is being done for the safety of the young and beautiful sisters, once more beg to join the company of Mr. Houseman and his rascally friends in the garden of the little cottage home.

The rascals certainly had not an idea that they were in any danger.

On the contrary, they really considered that they had managed the affair so well that the success of their villanous enterprise was quite beyond a doubt.

"Ha !" said Houseman, in a low tone, "this will do, I rather think."

"It will," growled one of the others.

"Yes," said the third, "and if the girl is pretty one may make a little love to her oneself."

"That would be rather dangerous."

"Dangerous?"

"Yes."

"Why so?"

"Because she is meant for Sir Warenne de Volence, as you well know, and you don't suppose he wants any second-hand goods, do you?"

"Oh, that's nothing."

"Is it nothing?"

"Nothing at all. How is he to know? She wouldn't tell him, I'm quite sure, and besides, I am so good-looking that the girls can't help falling in love with me whether they like it or not."

"Curse your vanity."

"Vanity do you call it?"

"Silence and be hanged to you both," said Houseman. "You talk too loud. Do you think that the way to carry out such an adventure as this is to be gossiping in this fashion about it?"

"Well, well, mum is the word."

"Yes it is, if you have the sense to keep to it. Come on, we must find our way into the cottage by some window or another."

"Yes, that's the way."

"Follow me."

They crept on after Houseman right through the garden to the cottage, and then they paused, while he who was considered to be quite an experienced hand in such matters, made a sort of reconnoitering expedition all round the premises.

When he returned to them he spoke in a low tone.

"This way—there is a little window at the back that can be easily opened."

"All's right."

"Follow me."

They trod now very gently as they followed Houseman towards the little window at the back of the cottage, to which he had alluded.

When they got there they looked rather doubtingly, for it was a very small square window, and rather high up from the ground.

"Do you think one of us can get through that?" said one of the fellows to Houseman.

"Yes."

"Well, if you think so——"

"I know it."

"Well, you ought to know, for you have seen a little of this sort of fun in your time."

"I have, indeed. Come, now, you are the thinnest of us all three, so you will go."

The thin ruffian looked rather downcast at this idea, and, no doubt, at that moment he very devoutly wished himself the stoutest of the party instead of the thinnest; but there was no help for it. He had come upon the enterprise, and it would be very ridiculous to hold back.

"Well, well," he said, "I'll go."

"That's right. We will both hoist you up, and you can go through head first, or feet front, as you like; but I should advise you to go feet front."

"Be it so, then."

CHAPTER LXXXVII.

LANGDON CARRIES HIS SELFISHNESS TO THE OTHER WORLD.

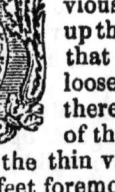OUSEMAN had previously, by clambering up the wall, ascertained that the window was loosely fastened, so that there was no difficulty of that sort to entertain.

But yet to the thin villain, who was to be projected feet foremost into a house of which he knew nothing, it was rather a curious sort of affair.

No wonder that this fellow, who was by no means the most courageous of the party, looked a little blue over the part he had to play in the matter.

"But—but," he said, "don't you know at all what's inside?"

"Oh, yes."

"What, then?"

"A room."

"Oh, any fool knows that."

"It seems that you didn't, so any fool did not, for once in a way," said Houseman. "But what is the use, now, of making a fuss about it, you have to do it."

"Well, I suppose I have, but I ought to get something extra for going in first in this sort of way, that I ought."

"So you will, perhaps."

"As how?"

"Why, a knock on the head when you get in if the ferryman is on the alert, as he ought to be."

"Ought to be?"

"Yes, ought to be."

"Well, but——"

"Bah! Oughtn't every man to be on the alert who has such ticklish property on his premises as a couple of girls?"

"Oh, ah!—to be sure."

"Come, come, be quick."

Houseman and the other one now managed between them to lift up their companion in such a way that his feet projected against the window, which gave way before them, and in they shot him.

It was rather an awkward kind of fall that he had inside, for it so happened that just below that little window there was a leaden sink and chair, and several pieces of crockery lying about.

With something of a smash, then, the ruffian alighted in the dark among all these things, and then he rolled on to the floor.

"Curse everybody and everything!" was the discursive sort of exclamation that came from his lips.

He sprung to his feet, though, and drew a long dagger from it's sheath, and put himself in an attitude of defence, for he did not know how soon he might be attacked.

That the noise he made was more than likely to give some alarm in the cottage, he could not conceal from himself, and his fright was rather great.

"Hist! hist!" cried Houseman, from the garden.

"Yes."

"Is all right?"

"No."

"What's amiss, then?"

"I don't know."

"Well, but——"

"Silence! Silence!"

"Hilloa!" cried a gruff voice, from the upper story of the little cottage. "Hilloa! what the devil is all that, I should like to know!"

This was no other than Langdon, the ferryman, himself, who had been awakened by the clatter in the little scullery, and who, upon the impulse of that alarm had sprung out of bed.

The intruder slunk behind the door of the room in which he was, and waited the event.

"Hilloa!" he heard Langdon call out again. "Hilloa!"

He then heard him knocking with his knuckles at some door on the upper landing.

It was the door of his daughters' chamber.

"Hilloa, Amy! Amy, I say!"

"Yes, father," replied Amy, from within.

"Did you hear any noise, girls?"

"Yes, yes."

"Then I didn't dream it."

"Oh, there was a noise, father, but Patience thinks it was the cat."

"The what?"

"The cat."

"Bah!"

"Yes, father."

"Bah! I say, bah! It was no cat. A two legged cat, in all likelihood. My life is a torment, and all on account of you two. I dream all night, and think all day of some vagabonds coming after you."

"Oh, father, how can you?"

"How can I do otherwise?"

"Well, it's the cat."

"I'll go and see. I'll soon find out; if I don't I shall get no sleep all night with watching and listening to every mouse that stirs in the place. It may be the cat, but I don't think it is—I don't think it."

Langdon, with a rushlight in his hand, began to descend the stairs; but that it might be the cat, who was a great pet of his daughters, he evidently had an idea, for he muttered to himself—

' If I catch that cat I'll smash her, and there will be an end of that trouble."

He paused when he got nearly to the foot of the stairs, and called—

"Puss—puss—puss!"

The cat was in the cottage, but she had by far too bad an opinion of Langdon to come to him. If Amy or Patience had called her it would have been a different thing.

He waited the appearance of the cat in vain.

"It is not the cat," he muttered. "It is not the cat at all—I'm quite sure of that. It is a two-legged cat."

It now struck Langdon that he was quite unarmed, so he went back again to his room, and got hold of an old sword that was about as rusty as it could be, and with that in his hand, he again began to descend the stairs.

As he passed his daughters' room Amy looked out.

"What is it father?"

"I don't know."

"The cat?"

"No, I tell you it isn't the cat. Go to bed again, do. I'll soon see what it is. Go to bed."

Langdon went down the stairs slowly and cautiously, holding the sword well poised in his right hand, and the candle in his left, and as far above his head as he could reach, so as to throw as wide a light about him as possible.

There was a very small passage just outside the door of the room in which the villanous comrade of Houseman was in hiding.

Langdon paused in that passage a moment to listen.

All was still.

"What could it have been?" he said to himself.

A strange feeling of nervous apprehension crept over him, and more than once he thought ne would abandon the affair, and go up to his room again; but the natural ferocity and anger of his nature fought hard against any such notion, and he pushed open the door of the scullery, calling out as he did so —

"Hilloa! Any one here?"

No reply.

Houseman's associate was behind the door, and as Langdon opened it he was jammed close to the wall by it. If Langdon had only pushed it another inch or two, he must have been aware that some one was behind it.

But he did not do so.

On the contrary, he made his way into the scullery in a very incautious manner.

"The window open!" he exclaimed.

These were the last words he ever uttered in this world.

With one step forward, the ruffian who was hidden in the room rushed upon Langdon, and the long blade of the dagger he held in his hand was, with one blow, plunged up to the hilt in the back of the unhappy man.

The dagger, thus directed, found its way to the heart of Langdon the ferryman, and he fell to the ground with but one deep and awful groan.

One sharp convulsion then ensued, and he was a corpse.

"That's done," said the fellow. "Ha! ha!"

He was quite elated at the idea of having committed a most dastardly murder.

The ferryman was no more, and although our readers have seen quite enough of him to be quite well aware that he was no great loss to society, yet the criminality of the man who had murdered him was none the less on that account.

Little did Amy and Patience think that the moment had at length arrived when they were both orphans, in the true acceptation of the word.

But they were so.

The assassin now stepped over the dead body of Langdon, and reached the window.

THE ASSASSIN HOUSEMAN ATTACKED BY THE NEIGHBOURS.

"Houseman!—Housemam!" he whispered.

"Yes."

"It's done."

"What?—what?"

"The worst part of the job. The ferryman is a dead man.

"You don't say so?"

"Yes, I have done it, and I ought to have a clear half of the reward, for neither yourself or our brave companions had any hand in the matter, as I had all the honour I ought to have a large portion of the reward."

CHAPTER LXXXVIII.

GAMIEL GANDER PERFORMS PRODIGIES OF VALOUR.

BOTH Houseman and the other rascal, waiting in the garden of Langdon's cottage, were quite elated at the intelligence that the deed, which they had thought the only difficulty of the whole affair, had actually been done.

The death of the ferryman appeared to them to place the cottage and its other inmates quite at their mercy.

And, in truth, so it would under ordinary circumstances.

But it is strange how the most trifling incidents will alter the whole aspect of a case.

Now, if Gamiel Gander's old grandmother had not had the spasms on that particular night, it might have fared very badly with poor Amy and Patience Langdon.

But the old lady had the spasms, as good luck would have it, and so she sent Gamiel for the *eau de vie*, and so he saw the ill-looking fellows in the garden of Langdon, and so he got the watermen at Lambeth Quay to go to the rescue.

We see by this that there is nothing in this world, however bad an aspect it may wear at first, that may not in the end be productive of good; for even the spasms of an old lady became the means of saving a world of misery to those fond young girls, who else would have been in such jeopardy.

Houseman and the other rascal, though, could very well guess that it was to some lucky accident, and by no sort of means to the courage of their associate in the cottage, that the death of the ferryman was owing.

But they soon had an opportunity of finding out all that, for the fellow coolly enough, now that he expected no sort of opposition, opened the back door of the cottage, and called to his comrades to walk in.

"It's all right. This way—this way."

"Hush!—hush!"

"Oh, it's all right."

"What do you mean by all right?" said Houseman. "You don't mean to say that you have killed everybody in the place?"

"No, no; but I have settled the ferryman."

"Well, well, but the girls?"

"Oh, they can't fight."

"But they can scream."

"Well, to be sure they can do that; so after all, it's as well to keep quiet."

"Ah," said the other, "you are so elated at the death of the ferryman, that you lost your head for the time. I suppose he committed suicide."

"Suicide?"

"Yes."

"Whatever puts that into your stupid head?"

"Why, his death to be sure."

"I killed him."

"You?"

"Yes, I did it. I got behind him when he didn't see me, and did it."

"Oh, that was it. Now I can comprehend it."

"Do you doubt my courage?"

"Oh dear, no."

"You had better not."

"I don't mean."

"Silence," said Houseman, "you know as well as I do that you are a couple of as arrant rogues and cowards as ever stepped, so what is the use of pretending otherwise to each other."

"Ah," said the rascal who had assassinated the ferryman, "if any one else had said that——"

"Well, what then?"

"Never mind."

Houseman laughed.

"Come, come," he said, "let us get this little job over, and if the worst of it is done, it is all the better. Come on."

They were all three, now, in the little narrow passage of the cottage, and then they paused to light a match, and from that to light a bit of wax candle that they had brought with them for the express purpose.

But what were Amy and Patience about all this time.

We shall see.

The question that Langdon had asked of them, had, although it had not alarmed them, the effect of keeping them awake. The murder of their father had been perpetrated with so much silence that, although they thought they heard a something like a heavy fall, they did not, in their own minds, associate it with any thought of such a fearful deed.

They remained awake and listening.

"Amy," said Patience, "do you really think that there is any one in the house?"

"Oh no, no."

"You think not?"

"How should there be?"

"That I don't know; but I feel very nervous, and a strange feeling of agitation has come over me within the last few minutes, that I cannot at all account for."

"You foolish Patience go to sleep."

"Oh, no, no."

"No?"

"How can I, till I am quite sure that all is well?"

"But all is well."

"Oh, I don't know. Hark!—hark! I hear voices. Oh, Amy, there is, indeed, something amiss."

Amy heard voices likewise, and from the

moment that she did so, she could no longer persuade herself, or attempt to persuade Patience that there was nothing to be alarmed at.

Of course, voices proved that there was some one or more persons in the cottage than Langdon.

Without a word Amy rose, and began hastily dressing herself to prepare for the worst.

"Oh, Amy, Amy," said Patience, "you are now alarmed."

"Not alarmed, dear Patience ; but I think it is as well to get up and to dress quickly."

"Yes—yes. Oh yes, I will, too."

The two young girls set to work dressing themselves with all the expedition in their power, and as they were not fine ladies, they got through that operation in a very few minutes, indeed.

By the time it was completed, they distinctly heard footsteps on the stairs of the cottage.

Amy listened for a moment, and then turning to Patience, she said.

"Patience, help me!"

What Patience was to help her in, Amy by her movements at once showed, for she laid hold of one corner of a long, old fashioned wardrobe that was in the room, and by a glance at the door, let Patience see that her object was to use it as a means of barricading it against any sudden intrusion.

How these two young girls contrived, at the moment, to muster up strength sufficient to move the heavy piece of furniture it is difficult to say, but on the impulse of the moment, without the exchange of a single word till it was effected, and the wardrobe was jammed against the door, they did it.

Then they looked at each other, and Amy said—

"Thank God !"

"It will protect us," said Patience.

"It will—it will."

"Oh, Amy, Amy, what has happened? What can it all mean?"

"I know not."

"Our father?"

"Oh, hark ! Oh, hark ! I hear voices again."

The two girls were as still as death.

And now Houseman and his two associates having looked into all the other rooms of the cottage but that one, of course came to the conclusion that it was the chamber of the two young girls, and they all halted at the door of it.

"What shall we do?" whispered one.

"Hush. Be cautious."

Houseman considered for a few moments, and then he said,—

"It's their squalling that I dread."

"Yes—yes."

"But how to prevent it I don't know."

"Suppose," said one of the others, "I call to them."

"You?"

"Yes. I have a soft enough voice when I like, and I will call to them, by name, that Langdon wants them below, and so try to get them to come out, when we can lay hold of them and stop their mouths if they try to cry out."

"Well, try it."

Upon this permission the assassin, who fancied he had a soft and persuasive voice when he liked, advanced close to the door, and spoke.

"Hem !—hem ! My dears? My dears?"

There was no reply.

"My good girls, your father desires me to say that if you will step down stairs he wants to see you."

"Amy," whispered Patience, "what shall we do?"

"Nothing."

"Nothing ! But——"

"Hush ! Not a word."

"Hem !" said the assassin, again. "My good girls, your father, the good, and amiable Langdon, is below, and wants you. Pray come down at once, if you please, there is no danger."

All was still.

"That won't do," said Houseman.

"It don't seem like it," said the other.

Houseman lost patience. Advancing to the door, he in the first instance gave it a hasty kick, and then he said,—

"Hark you, girls. We know you are in this room, and all I have to say to you is that if you force us to break the door down it will be the worse for you; but if you open it at once, and be civil, no harm will come to you."

This speech produced no more effect than the other; but it sufficiently proved to the young girls that there was danger, and that they had acted prudently in barricading their door.

CHAPTER LXXXIX.

AMY AND PATIENCE LANGDON ARE RESCUED FROM DANGER.

INDING that neither threats nor dissimulations had any effect upon the two girls, Houseman lost the little grain of patience he had up to that moment kept, and he cried out,—

"Now break the door open at once. It is but a squall or two, and then we have them prisoners."

He made such a dashing kick at the door with the heavy riding boots he wore, that there is very little doubt but that it would have been burst open but for the wardrobe that was close to it on the other side.

As it was, there it stood as firm as if it was a block of stone.

Houseman was surprised.

"Curse the door!" he cried.

"Try it again," said the others. "Let's all try it together."

They all three now made a simultaneous dash at the door, but with no better effect than before, and then rather bruised by the effect, they looked at each other in confusion.

"This won't do," said one.

"Not at all."

"But what will do?"

"Ah, that's the question."

"They don't squall, either."

"No—it's very odd."

"It is, indeed."

"But suppose they are not there, after all."

"I don't think that," said Houseman; "but step this way. They may, for all we know, be listening to every word we say. Now it isn't a very likely thing that the room in which these girls sleep has no window, and so what do you say to one of you two going into the garden and looking for it, while the others make a racket at the door to attract the girls' attention."

"Good."

"Well, then, you go."

"I will. I'm not afraid—not I. Didn't I settle old Langdon, the ferryman, that all the parish was afraid of? To be sure I did. I'll go."

The rascal set off upon his mission, and the moment he was gone Houseman com-menced a furious kicking at the door of the room, and then called out—

"Hilloa! hilloa, there! I tell you what it is, my girls, we don't mean any harm just as yet, but if you provoke us we may mean it when we do catch you."

Still no reply.

"I don't mind telling you both," continued Houseman, for he thought it as well to go on talking, in order to engage their attention, "I don't at all mind telling you what we came for—it is for money, that's all; and if you will come out and give us what you have, why, of course, we will go at once."

"Oh, Amy," whispered Patience, "give them all."

"Peace—peace, Patience; that is all pretence. Do not say one word to them. We are safe as yet, and it is our silence that is the puzzle to them."

But the young girls little thought that they were about to be attracted by the window.

The rascal who had been sent upon that errand, soon found that the window of the girls' room overlooked the little greenhouse in the garden, and by climbing on to the roof of that he was quite on a level with the window.

Now, by continuing to talk, Houseman really did succeed in attracting the attention of the two girls, so that the fellow who had got to the window was able to burst it suddenly open, and make a rush into the room before they were at all aware of his presence in the place.

Amy did not utter any cry; but Patience uttered a shrill scream, and the rascal sprung at her and tried to place his hand over her mouth.

In this he was foiled, for Amy, with instinctive courage, seized rather a heavy poker that was in the fireplace, and dealt him such a blow with it, on the head, that he staggered back half stunned.

"You little she-devil!" he muttered, "I will have you life for that—I will."

"No—no!" cried Patience. "Help! Oh, help!"

"I'm a-coming!" said a voice from the garden.

It was the voice of Gamiel Gander. For once, oh, how welcome was its tone.

"I'm a-coming!"

"Help! help!" cried Patience again. "Oh, help!"

"Yes, yes."

The ruffian in the room was staggered as much by the voice of Gamiel Gander from the garden as he had been by the blow with the poker. A glance showed him what it was that hindered the door of the room from opening, and he made such an effort that he displaced the wardrobe, and called out—

"Push the door!—push the door!"

"Yes," cried Houseman.

The door was dashed open!

Houseman and the other rascal rushed into the room; but at the moment that he did so there arose from the ground floor of the house a loud cheer.

The watermen had got the front door open, and were rapidly ascending the stairs.

"We are lost," said Houseman.

"Lost!" howled the other.

"Yes, the lower part of the cottage is full of men."

"Let us kill the girls, then!"

"No—no. And yet——"

"The window!—the window! We may escape yet by that!—The window!"

"No."

"Why not?"

"There is some one in the garden, I heard him say he was coming."

"Never mind that. One is better than a dozen. Here goes for one at all events."

The villanous Houseman made a rush to the window.

He darted out at it, for it was open, as it had been left by the bravo who had effected an entrance to the chamber by that mode.

He fell right on to the roof of the green-house, and a crash of broken glass proclaimed the fact.

At the same moment there was the loud report of a blunderbuss that Gamiel Gander had possessed himself of, and then all was still for about the space of time in which you might have counted six rapidly.

It was the voice of Gamiel Gander that broke the silence, as he called out—

"Pepper for one! In for a penny in for a pound. I rather think he's settled."

The two rascals still in the chamber, now with all the cowardly vindictive character of their race, drew their daggers, and turned upon the sisters.

But Amy had taken good care to have some sort of defence ready.

She had dragged the bewildered Patience into a corner of the room, and with a rapid hand she had overthrown a table and several chairs before them, so as to make a kind of barricade for the moment.

It saved them.

It was only for the moment that the simple defence was wanted. The rush of the assassins was baulked, and then the party of watermen was in the room, and both the assassins were secured.

"All's right!" cried a young waterman, who had put himself foremost in the adventure—"all's right! Miss Langdon, you are quite free now."

"Oh, yes—yes. Oh, God! How can we thank you?"

"Don't mention it."

Patience burst into tears, and sobbed like a child.

"Father," she said; "oh, where is he?"

"Well, miss, the truth had better be told at once. He is no more."

At this intelligence Amy turned pale and she felt as though the strong courage, and the indomitable will that had hitherto supported her had given way.

Langdon had been ever a harsh and selfish parent to her; but still the sacred tie of consanguinity that united her to him could not be altogether of no account. She felt his death keenly.

As for Patience, her tears flowed afresh, and she exhibited all that violent grief which is the characteristic of a young and ardent spirit.

Such grief, though, is but evanescent.

"Don't fret," said the young waterman. "We must all die, you know, some day, and, for my part, I would rather go off at once, as Langdon, no doubt, has done, than lie on a bed of sickness till everybody wished me at the devil, and till the doctors made an end of me."

"Oh, don't—don't speak so," said Patience.

"Well, I won't, miss, if so be as you don't like it. But who are these rascals?"

"We don't know," replied Amy. "We only know that we were assailed by the house being attacked, and then we heard the voice of Gamiel Gander."

"Yes, Miss Amy. It was he who brought us all here."

"Then we have very much to thank him for. Where is he?"

No one knew what had become of Gamiel Gander till he was found lying on his back in the garden, with a blunderbuss in his hands, which, in its discharge, had knocked him over; but he had killed Houseman, whose body was found in the greenhouse, with its head nearly blown off.

The sisters went to a neighbour, and the two assassins were conveyed to the round-house.

CHAPTER XC.

RETURNS TO MARTIN LASSAMOUR AND THE LADY MARGARET.

E now return to Martin Lassamour.

It will be remembered that we left Lassamour, accompanied by his friends, just within the little door in the wall of what might be called the park around Pleasaunce.

Those friends were—

The gallant young Lamont.

Robert Lee, the pedler.

Old Sir Ralph Shard, who had ever had so great a cause to feel a hatred to Margaret Lassamour, and the sheriff's men-at-arms, together with Cyprian.

By-the-by, poor Cyprian was quite in a state of agitation upon the occasion, and the expression of his face was that of grief and distress.

This was so much so, that Martin Lassamour laid his hand upon his arm, and took him aside to say to him—

"Cyprian, what ails you?"

"What ails me, noble master? Ah, I am sick at heart."

"Indeed, boy?"

"I am, indeed, sir."

"On what account?"

"On account of the Lady Margaret."

"Ah?"

"Yes, noble master. I cannot conceal from you, and I do not wish to do so if I could, that such is the case; I do not for one moment try to defend her. Indeed, in my heart, I think her thoroughly guilty, but I have lived long with her, and I have a foolish knack of loving those that I have had frequent associations with."

"Alas, poor Cyprian!"

That was a knack that was not likely, in this cold and wretched world, to do him much good.

Martin Lassamour was silent for a moment or two, and then he said—

"Cyprian, I am far, indeed, from blaming you."

"I thank you, sir."

"No thanks to me. The feelings that you have given utterance to, just now, do you honour, my young friend. I, too, cannot but believe the Lady Margaret guilty, but that is no reason on earth why both of us should not pity her."

"It is not, sir."

"So, my good Cyprian, we will pity her, let the cold world say what it may of us for so doing."

"Ah, yes, sir. I knew you would."

"From my heart, I do. But say nothing of this to others, Cyprian. Let it suffice that on this matter you and I understand each other thoroughly and completely."

"I am happier now," said Cyprian.

"Come, gentleman," said Martin Lassamour, now turning to the others, "you will now be so good as to place yourselves under the guidance of Cyprian, with the exception of you, my good friend, Lamont, and you shall go with me to the state chamber."

"Yes. And the moment I get there I will hide myself."

"Do so."

Thus, then, as it had been all pre-arranged, did they proceed towards Pleasaunce House.

Cyprian led the strong party, the charge of which had been devolved upon him, by a circuitous route through the garden, intending still to bring it to the gallery immediately beside the state bed-chamber of the house.

It was in that state bed-chamber that every one fully expected such an explanation of the mysteries of the conduct of the wife of seven husbands would take place.

And it did so.

As for Martin Lassamour, he alone, with young Lamont, went by the most direct route to the house.

As they went they spoke but little.

The heart of Martin Lassamour was full. He had a part to act which he did not like, and yet he could not see that there was aught of dishonour in it, or that he could in any way now avoid it.

It might be none the less repugnant though, to him, on that account, nor was it.

He had to betray, so to speak, his own wife.

But that was quite another thing, when it was his life that she aimed at, and that, too, by some diabolical means which had had the effect of already sending to the grave no less than six before him.

That, indeed, altered the case.

As they neared the private entrance to the house, of which Lassamour had a key, he spoke to Lamont.

"My friend?"

"Yes, Martin."

"You will require all your caution, and all your circumspection, now."

"I know it."

"You had better keep close behind me, treading in my footsteps as much as possible."

"I will."

"For if she should but for one moment suspect that I am not alone, all this preparation to catch her in the snare laid by her own guilt, in reality, will fail."

"It will, indeed."

"And the moment we both get into the state chamber, you must dart behind the heavy hangings of the bedstead, where you will be secure from observation."

"It is the only way."

"Let it be so, then, and I will leave the rest, along with my life, to your discretion."

"You may do so, my good friend, and with my own life, I will answer for yours."

"I know that it is so. On—on."

Martin Lassamour, with the key he had with him, opened a door that led them into the great hall of Pleasaunce House, and then, without exchanging another word, they ascended the splendid staircase together.

They reached the long picture gallery

Then for one brief moment Martin Lassamour looked about him, at the portraits of the husbands of the Lady Margaret, on the wall.

He shuddered.

Lamont suddenly, then, touched him on the arm, and whispered to him—

"Look!"

"At what? Where?"

"Here."

By the rays of the dim night-light that was in the picture gallery, and which it was the custom to have there burning from sunset till sunrise all the year round, Martin Lassamour saw a fresh portrait on the wall."

One glance sufficed to let him know whose it was.

It was his own!

Yes, the Lady Margaret had, at length, finished the portrait of her seventh husband, and hung it up only two hours before that time when her own fate was all but determined.

"It is myself," said Martin.

"It is, indeed."

"And wondrously like."

"The very image."

"Come on—come on. Not another word—not another word."

Martin Lassamour had made up his mind to the part he had to play.

It was that of drunken hilarity. He fully intended to try whether, for such an offence as coming home at a later hour than she approved of, and that, too, with a cup of wine too much, it was possible that a woman who affected to love him could deliberately and savagely murder him?

That was the question.

And now Martin Lassamour paused at the door of the state bed chamber.

He placed his plumed cap rakishly on the side of his head. He disarranged his doublet, and he twisted his sword belt round to the wrong side, so as altogether to give him the appearance of coming home in tipsy tumult, and then he whispered to Lamont—

"Ready?"

"Quite."

Martin Lassamour dashed open the door, and staggered into the room. Lamont followed him closely, and then, with great rapidity, darted behind the hangings of the huge state bed that was in that room.

This was done with sufficient adroitness to render detection quite out of the question.

Martin Lassamour, now, at once began to play his part, and well he played it too.

"Bravo!" he cried. "Long life to old wine—and long life to good fellowship—and long life to pretty girls! Ha—ha! This is capital! This is—Damn everybody!—Now some fellows would call me drunk, but I am as sober as a judge—as sober as a judge, who is a good fellow!"

He pretended to stagger across the room, and half to fall on to the couch that was near to the rich old fire-place.

"Capital, this—upon my soul! Bravo! say I. Bravo! and long life to wine and pretty girls! What the devil would be the use of life if it wasn't for both of them? That confounded old curmudgeon, the ferryman of Lambeth, how the deuce did he come by such pretty daughters—eh?"

Martin Lassamour, then, in a tipsy tone of voice, broke out into a song:—

Wine! wine! wine!
There's nothing like wine.
Give me rosy lips, and the grapes
Ever next to mine!

"Ha! ha! Bravo again! That isn't a bad song by any manner of means, upon my honour."

CHAPTER XCI.

LADY MARGARET QUESTIONS MARTIN LASSAMOUR.

THE rich silver lamp that hung from the centre of the ceiling in the state bedchamber of Pleasaunce House shed quite a sufficient light around the room to render every object plainly visible.

There was ho Lady Margaret there.

But Martin Lassamour had an idea that every word he said was heard by her, and he did not know but what every action came under the cognisance of her observation.

So he did not relax in the perfomancee of the part that he had set himself.

"Well," he said, with apparent tipsy gravity, "there's nothing in all the world like bright eyes, except bright wine ; only the older the wine is the better it is; but it isn't so with the eyes. Oh dear, no !—oh dear, no !"

He unbuckled his sword belt, and flung his rapier on to a chair, saying as he did so—

"Confound you, lie there. I don't know how or why it is that, at times, one's sword has such a propensity to tangle itself about one's legs, and tip one up. It isn't as if I was drunk. Oh dear, no."

He glanced around him, and he saw a small door in the wall open, and the Lady Margaret enter the chamber.

The heart of Martin Lassamour beat quick.

"She comes ! She comes !"

But there was nothing at all indicative of a deadly purpose in the habit, or the manner of the Lady Margaret. On the contrary, she looked quite calm and composed.

Lassamour was rather perplexed.

Margaret advanced.

"Martin?"

"Hilloa! Is that you? Bravo! bravo! The more the merrier, say I."

"Martin?"

"Well, what's the row? The room goes about in a very odd way."

"Martin, I say."

"What is it? Wine!—wine! Rosy wine !"

"It is late."

"Late, is it ?"

"It is more than an hour and a half beyond the time at which I told you I expected you home."

"Oh."

"And what is more, and worse, when you do come home, you are in a shameful state of intoxication."

"In—tox—ti—what?"

"Intoxication !"

"You don't say so."

"It is but too evident."

"Is it?"

"Yes, Martin, it is so."

"Well, what then? I suppose—tol, de rol, de rido—that a man may take a cup of wine too much once in a way, and not be hung for it."

She was silent.

"What if I do go over the—a—traces in a little way, all I have to say is—

" Fill the goblet to the brim,
Then shut both your eyes, boy,
Quaff the dainty draught——

"Silence!" cried Lady Margaret, with the voice and gesture of a fiend. "Silence!"

"Oh, well."

"Hear me!"

"Hear you? Well, it isn't your fault, my lady, if I don't hear you."

"What do you mean?"

"Just that you speak loud enough."

"Indeed."

"Well, don't you?"

"It matters not. Listen to me, Martin Lassamour. You have other attractions than the wine cup."

"Have I?"

"Yes. The daughters of Langdon, the ferryman of Lambeth, are fair."

"Fair ?"

"Yes. I said fair."

"Then, my good Margaret, you don't say one half that they deserve, for they are the fairest of the fair, by all that's sacred. Why, they are perfect in form, and in feature. Fair, indeed ! By St. George, they are fair."

The Lady Margaret's eyes flashed with a strange fire as Martin Lassamour spoke.

"So," she said, "you have thought much of them?"

"Of course I have."

"Is it of course?"

"Yes, it is of course with me, and

MARTIN LASSAMOUR AND LADY MARGARET.

always was, and always will be, to love all that is beautiful."

"Do you forget?"

"What?"

"That you are a married man."

"Oh dear, no. I can't help remembering it, but my heart is quite large enough for my wife, and for plenty of others besides. You will not, Margaret, tell me that you are jealous."

"Jealous?"

"Yes. It is an worthy passion, but I feel very sleepy, and the fumes of the good wine are darting about my head like so many will-o'-the-wisps. Ha! ha! this is life, is it. A jealous wife, and pretty girls, and the wine cup."

"Is it life?"

"I suppose so."

"It may be something else, Martin Lassamour."

"What else?"

"That you will find out."

"Shall I?"

"You will, indeed."

"Well, then, the sooner the better."

"Ah, say you so, sot—fool—drunkard—wretch?"

"Hold! hold! Upon my life these are not at all pretty names for a lady to call her husband."

"Husband?"

"Yes; seventh husband!"

The Lady Margaret recoiled as if an adder had stung her.

"So," she said, in a deep, low voice, "so you cannot forget that?"

"Forget it? Upon my life it isn't at all likely I should; but where's the odds? Let's sing and be gay. Ha! ha! ha!

> Care is a haunt shunned by all:
> He lives where there's no sunshine;
> So let him rot in a mouldy cell,
> And give us bright eyed wine.

There's a delicate sort of ditty, now, for you, to be knocked off at once without any premeditation. It's my own, I assure you, and though full of faults, yet there is an idea in it. Bravo! bravo! Ha! ha!"

Martin Lassamour flung himself back on the couch, and raved in apparently tipsy delight.

The Lady Margaret approached him.

"Martin?"

"Well, what now?"

"You think it unkind of me to grudge you the wine cup now and then?"

"I do."

"And you think that my jealousy is too easily aroused about the fair daughters of Langdon, the ferryman?"

"Well, Margaret, upon my life I think so too."

"This is the last time."

"What last time?"

"That you will hear aught from me upon the latter subject; and as to the former, I will convince you I am no foe to your enjoyments, by filling you a tankard of Burgundy myself."

"You will?"

"I will."

"What am I to think of this?"

"What you please, so that you think kindly of it. Tarry here a few moments, and I will soon return to you."

"I will."

She left the room.

The moment that she did so Martin Lassamour could not help darting a glance in the direction of the hangings of the bedstead, behind which Lamont was so well and so securely hidden.

Lamont, who had been cognisant of everything that passed, was on the look-out, and saw him.

"Martin! Martin!" he whispered.

"Silence, on your life!"

"Don't drink—don't drink her Burgundy."

"I don't intend. Hush!"

Lamont said not another word. He had only been anxious to guard against the possibility of Martin Lassamour drinking anything from the hands of the Lady Margaret, for he judged rightly enough that it would be drugged.

But he was, in a manner of speaking, both right and wrong.

It was true that the wine that the Lady Margaret went for was drugged; but it was only with a harmless opiate that would, for a time, steep the senses in oblivion; but leave no trace of poison in the system.

It was not by poison that the Lady Margaret disposed of her victims. She had what she considered a better and surer mode of operations than with drugs.

CHAPTER XCII.

THE DENOUEMENT RAPIDLY APPROACHES.

AND now the end of our story is close at hand, and it will be seen how the wretched woman, actuated by the passion of a fiend, contrived to be so many times a widow.

She was absent from the state bed-chamber about five minutes, and when she returned she brought with her a silver goblet, and a flask of Burgundy.

"Come, Martin Lassamour," she said, "we will not part to-night in positive, unkindness; so you shall pledge me in this rich Burgundy."

"And you?"

"Oh no—I—that is, wine just before going to rest ever gives me a sick headache for the following day."

"Well," cried Lassamour, still keeping up his tipsy character, "that is because you don't take enough of it. If you did you would be all right."

"Oh no."

"Yes, you would; but never mind. Give me the goblet, and I will drink to all the bright eyes that ever were, and that are, and that ever will be; and if that is not a comprehensive toast in that line, why, I'm a Frenchman, that's all, and have lived upon frogs all my life, and cheese pairings."

"You are full of high spirits, Martin, to-night."

"I am full of good wine, too."

"No doubt of that. But come, now, drink off the old Burgundy, it will do you a world of good. It is a rare old wine, and I will take upon myself to say that there is none such at any of the taverns you are in the habit of frequenting."

"It may be so, wife. It may be so; but don't you say anything against the taverns."

Martin Lassamour took the goblet in his hand, and Lamont was full of wonder to know how he was going to contrive not to drink it.

Suddenly, though, Martin Lassamour fixed his eyes upon the large bay window of the room, and in a low voice he said—

"What—what can it be—crossing the window? There—there—there!"

It was not in human nature to resist glancing in the direction so indicated, and Lady Margaret turned her eyes and head full to the window, while she uttered a cry of alarm.

The moment was seized by Martin to cast the wine from the goblet over the back of the couch, and when she turned again the empty vessel was at his lips, and he drew it away with a long breath.

"What was it?" she said.

"A something passed the window, I thought."

"Nothing—I saw nothing."

"Ah, it was one of the boughs of that old cyprus tree. See it again."

"Yes, yes. The Burgundy!"

"Curse the Burgundy."

"Why so?"

"It has a queer taste."

"No?"

"By Jove it has, though."

"What sort of taste?"

"Well, I hardly know what to compare it to. It is a kind of I don't know what."

Martin had taken good care that not one drain of it should pass his lips.

Lady Margaret fixed upon him a peculiar look, and then she said, slowly—

"Do you feel drowsy? If you wish to sleep I will no longer interrupt you."

This gave Martin Lassamour a hint of what she expected the effect of the Burgundy would be.

He acted upon that hint at once.

Stretching out his arms, and gaping furiously, he pretended to be scarcely able to keep his eyes open.

"You are drowsy."

"Most cursedly."

"Then I will leave you to repose. It will do you good."

"Well, I—a—oh, dear—I—eh—suppose it will."

"It will."

"Ah!"

"You will have a long sleep."

"Oh, shall I?"

"A very long sleep."

"Ah!"

"Good night."

Martin Lassamour did not reply. He pretended to fall back upon the couch in a state of complete lethargy. The Lady Margaret glanced at him for some few moments, and then she spoke.

"Yes, a very long sleep," she said. "The long sleep of death."

She went from the room with a very quiet step.

"Martin?" whispered Lamont.

"Yes."

"You are on your guard?"

"Fully. Hush!"

The Lady Margaret came slowly into the room again. In her right hand she held a small iron ladle, in which was about a couple of ounces of *melted lead!*

She approached the couch.

For one moment she paused, and Lamont could see that the little iron ladle was of a red heat.

"The seventh!" she said. "Yes, this will make the seventh! What is hereafter to me? There is no hereafter! This lead once poured into his ear will seek the brain at once. There may be one shriek; but that will be all, and then he is no more than a lump of clay, as we shall all be."

The horrible purpose of the wife of seven husbands was now but too apparent.

She intended to pour the liquid lead into, as she supposed, the slumbering brain of her husband, through his ear.

This, then, was the truly horrible method by which she had managed to put to death all her six husbands, and as the lead offered no external hurt or injury, no one had thought proper to look into the heads of the dead men for the little thread of lead that had killed them.

Modern sciences would very soon have detected the Lady Margaret ; but in those days human life was not so carefully looked after as it is in our own, nor was, indeed, science in its present state.

Martin Lassamour did not stir.

He depended solely upon Lamont.

Slowly but steadily, and without the appearance of the smallest terror, the murderess approached the couch on which she fully believed that the unconscious victim lay.

"He sleeps," she muttered—"he sleeps. "I have been more merciful to him than to the others."

She meant in giving, as she thought she had given him, a sleeping draught.

Another step and she was by the side of the couch. The ladle, with the molten lead in it, was still red-hot, and there lay Martin, as still as though already she had found a means of sending him from the world.

"Now—now !" she cried.

With a bound that cleared at once the space between him and her, Lamont was at her back. He flung his left arm around her waist, and with his right hand he grasped her right arm, in the hand of which she held the ladle.

"Hold, murderess !" he cried. "Your time has come, and you will make no more victims !"

The Lady Margaret uttered one shriek, and the ladle, with the hot lead in it, dropped from her hand to the floor of the room.

Martin Lassamour sprang from the couch !

"You are saved !" said Lamont.

"Yes, and by you. Oh, Margaret—Margaret, and has it, indeed, come to this ? Are you the murderess people deservedly accused you of being ?"

"Help ! help !" cried Lamont.

The door leading from the picture gallery to the state bedchamber was dashed open, and Robert Lee, with Cyprian, and the men-at-arms of the sheriff, rushed into the room.

"Seize her !" cried Lamont. "The Lady Margaret is a murderess !"

A couple of the sheriff's men sprung forward to lay hands upon her, but she cried out—

"Hold ! I cannot escape ! Martin, you see I cannot escape ! Save me from them !"

"Guard every avenue," said Lassamour, "but touch her not. Oh, Margaret, Margaret, this is a sad hour !"

She had sunk to the floor, but now she rose to her feet and looked at him. Her eyes looked preternaturally bright ; but her face was as white as a fair sheet of paper.

"Martin, you—you—are sober ?"

"Quite."

"Then this was——"

"A plan to test you."

"Ah, I see it all, now. Lost—oh, God, lost !"

"Wretched woman !" said the officer of the sheriff's men, "your guilt is but too apparent."

"Guilt ?"

"Yes," added Lamont, "I have been in this chamber from the moment of the arrival of Martin Lassamour, and have seen all."

"All ?"

"Yes, all ; from your attempting to give him the drugged wine, to your attempt to pour molten lead into his ear while you thought he slept."

CHAPTER XCIII.

THE CONCLUSION APPROACHES.

 H E Lady Margaret pressed her hands upon her face for a moment, and then she looked at Martin again, and said—

"Why did you do this?"

No one replied to her.

She repeated the question, looking intently at Martin.

"Why did you do this?"

"Can you ask?"

"I do ask."

"Wretched woman, can you deem it necessary that there should be aught more special as a reason for such a plan as I laid for you detection than a full and a complete consciousness of your guilt."

"My guilt?"

"Yes, your guilt."

"Surely you will not to attempt to deny," exclaimed Lamont, "that your guilt is but too apparent. This is the very effrontery of iniquity."

Lady Margaret turned towards him, and looked him in the face with such a petrifying gaze that it would have required more, by ten times the command of countenance than so young a man possessed, to withstand it.

Lamont made the effort, but he was, in a very few moments, compelled to withdraw his eyes from a contemplation of those wild orbs that Lady Margaret fixed upon him.

"I have no more to say," he added. "It is not for me to reproach you."

"Wretch!" exclaimed the Lady Margaret, "how dare you speak? Who, and what are you, that you should be even here at all, or utter one word in this house?"

"I am the friend of Martin Lassamour."

"Friend?"

"Yes, lady, the friend of your husband."

"His friend?"

"Even so."

"Now, marry, but this is some jest! You do him a rare act of friendship, sir, when you sow in his mind the seeds of suspicion—when your whole effort is to despoil him of that peace of mind which I will take upon myself to say, after this night, he shall never know again in this world."

Martin Lassamour uttered a deep sigh.

"You hear him," said Lady Margaret; "he acknowledges the truth of what I say."

"No—no," said Martin.

"Not so?"

"Not so, Margaret. It may be that the shadow of the events of this night may yet rest upon my soul in such a fashion that they may disturb my peace. It may be that I may never possess the same hilarity of spirit that once I had, but that is no fault of my young friend, Lamont."

"Indeed!"

"No, it is your guilt!"

"Truly so," said Lamont.

Lady Margaret uttered a short, bitter laugh, as she then added—

"Well, gentlemen, this is brave of you all. You all are leagued against one poor, defenceless woman."

"Come, come, madam," said the officer,

we must take you with us; and there is one thing which, out of charity to you, I would say."

"Charity, sir?"

"Yes, lady, I don't mean alms-giving when I say charity, but I mean good feeling to you."

"Say that again, sir."

"What again?"

"Good feeling. Is it possible that there is such a thing as good feeling to me in this place?"

"It is true, as well as possible."

"Well, sir, what does your good feeling and charity suggest to you in my favour?"

"Simply, madam, that any word you now say is being listened to by my men here, at the door, and that they will deem it to be their duty to report all such words."

"You do not tell me so much?"

"I do, lady."

"Then, sir, let them report that the Lady Margaret Lassamour requests to know of what she is accused."

At this audacious speech the persons in that state bedchamber looked at each other in surprise.

"I repeat my question," she said; "of what am I accused?"

"Murder!" said the officer.

"Murder?"

"Yes, lady."

The officer was getting a sort of respect for this cool, and this determined woman, who, now that she had recovered from her first surprise, did not seem at all inclined to give way, even to the force of the circumstances then around her.

"Yes, murder!" repeated Lamont.

"Silence, sir!" said Lady Margaret "The murder of whom?"

"Your husband."

"My husband lives. There he stands, coward-like, to hear me so accused, when his sword should leap from its scabbard at the thought of such a charge."

Martin Lassamour shook his head.

"This bravado will not do, Margaret," he said.

"Bravado call you it?"

"I do, indeed."

"And you accuse me?"

"What other can I do? Oh, Margaret, if I saw but the smallest loophole for a doubt as to your guilt—if I saw but the most faint and glimmering probability, or I may say possibility, that we may all be mistaken, I would cling to you to the last."

A visible emotion shook Margaret.

"Yes," he added, "I would stand by you, sword in hand, were the whole world. leagued against you."

"But you will not?"

"I cannot."

Lady Margaret uttered a low groan.

"Be it so," she said. "Let me then be deserted by all ; let me die so deserted."

The officer advanced, and laid his hand upon her shoulder.

"Madam !"

"Well, sir ?"

"You are my prisoner.'

"Well, sir ?"

"He turned and motioned to a couple of his men to advance. There was a jingling noise of a pair of fetters which they were about to place upon her wrists, and she started.

"What is that ?"

"Oh, only a pair of our bracelets, my lady," said one of the men.

"Silence !" said the officer, "it is not your place to reply."

The man shrunk back.

"Monster ! Monster !" cried Lady Margaret.

"What would you ?"

"Spare me this !"

She pointed to the fetters in the man's hand, and Lassamour, looking as pale as death, turned to the officer, saying to him,

"Must it be so ?"

"It is right that it should be so."

"You will spare this ceremony for my sake."

"As you please, sir, but—"

The officer drew Martin Lassamour aside and added, "I can assure you, sir, that, in my opinion, that unless she be secured in some way, she is just the sort of person, in some sudden access of fury, which, I think, is even now kindling in her eye, to do herself, or some one else an injury."

Lassamour looked distressed.

"Alas ! What can I say ?"

"Let me place the fetters on her hands, sir."

"No, no. Take this scarf, and find from it strength sufficient to bind her, if it must be so."

The officer took the scarf, and gliding behind Lady Margaret, he bound her arms with it in a moment.

She did not resist.

At this poor Martin Lassamour, who, to tell the truth, was throughout the whole scene suffering far more than he would have suffered if the Lady Margaret had succeeded in pouring into his ear the molten lead, turned aside with deep emotion.

Lamont observed him, and stepped up to him.

"Courage, courage, my dear friend," he said.

"Ay, Lamont, I will strive for courage."

"Do so, and it will come, as it ever does for the striving."

"Think you so?"

"I know it."

"But still, all this is very terrible."

"It is so."

"Oh, my friend, there is no doubt? There can be no doubt——"

"Of what?' "Of her guilt ?"

"Do I hear aright, Martin Lassamour? Is it possible that, now, you can want an assurance upon such a head? What doubt can there be? But for my interposition, at the last moment, I can tell you that you would have been now a corpse, having passed from life to death in the midst of a most cruel torment. Oh, there is no room for doubt."

CHAPTER XCIV.

LADY MARGARET GIVES HERSELF UP TO DESPAIR.

URELY there was no room for doubt, and that truth was one that Martin Lassamour felt to its full extent. But yet his mind was in so much confusion, and in so much agony in consequence of the whole affair that he could not avoid saying what he had said to Lamont.

Truly the situation of Martin Lassamour was very pitiable.

And yet it was a situation that he could not avoid. It was quite out of the question that he could go on suspecting his wife of such terrible crimes, and not make some sort of effort to convince his mind of her guilt or her innocence.

And so we must look upon Martin Lassamour as the victim of circumstances, far beyond his own control.

Lamont looked at him with eyes of pity and commiseration.

"Come, come, my dear friend," he said,

"this state of depression will soon pass away, and you will forget it all."

"Ah, no—no; you do not think what you say, Lamont."

Lamont was silent. He did not, indeed, think what he had said; and yet it was a friendly deceit that he had practised. He wished, if possible, to assuage the grief of Martin Lassamour.

This little conversation between the friends took but a very short time, indeed, and then they both turned to Margaret Lassamour, and to the officers of justice, who had her in their possession.

Sir Ralph Shard, who had hitherto kept rather in the background, had now advanced, and was looking at her fixedly.

"Well," he said, "on my soul I am sorry for you, and now that I have had a good look at you, and feel that you have a mind above the common, I don't at all wonder at my unfortunate nephew becoming so enamoured of you as he did."

"It is false," said Lady Margaret.

"False!"

"Yes, as a dicer's oath."

"As how? How mean you, lady? Body o' me! was he not one of your seven husbands, of whom this poor benighted Martin Lassamour is the seventh?"

"Yes, but he loved me not."

"Loved you not?"

"No. He was a sot, like his old uncle. He loved the wine cup, and so he loved the large resources of the woman who could furnish him with the means of such indulgence."

"Hem!"

"Yes, Sir Ralph Shard, such was your nephew, and you know it well."

"Hem! I—a—well certainly, he did drink his wine like an honest gentleman— I will admit that; and I must say that he scorned to leave his glass when it was full."

"Enough of this," she exclaimed. "I am ready to meet whatever conviction my husband and all his friends have to prefer against me."

"By the mass, you are a bold, brave woman!"

"I desire not your compliments, Sir Ralph Shard."

The officer was about to lead her forth, but Martin Lassamour called out to them—

"Hold! Lady Margaret Lassamour is as yet only accused. It is my duty to see that justice is done to her, and to see that all possible comfort shall surround her present unhappy position. Pause a moment, Sir Officer, till her coach is ready."

"As you will, sir."

"It is to London you would take her?"

"Even so, sir. To the prison by Blackfriars she will go until to-morrow, when the justices will, no doubt, take cognisance of her case."

"Be it so."

"Yes," said Lady Margaret, "Be it so."

There was a very strange tone about her pronunciation of these words.

Martin Lassamour now called out to some of the terrified attendants who were in the state bedchamber to get the coach in readiness to proceed to town.

Turning, then, to the Lady Margaret, he said—

"Be assured that, in no regard, will I neglect my duty to you. On the morrow I will take care that you have skilful and learned men of law to aid you, and you shall not be declared guilty of the heinous crimes laid to your charge without the most full inquiry into the grounds of the accusation."

"How very kind of you, after being so unkind."

"Nay, call me not unkind. This fatal and terrible career of yours was sure to come to some such a close as this."

"It should not have been your hand that struck the blow, Martin Lassamour."

"Spare me reproaches."

"I loved you."

"No more! No more!"

"Yes, I loved you much."

"And so," said Sir Ralph Shard, "you would, to show your love, have poured a ladle of melted lead into his ear. The Lord preserve us from such affection!"

Lady Margaret darted such a look at Sir Ralph Shard, that if looks had had any power to kill, would certainly have done so on the spot; but luckily they have not, so the good old knight escaped.

An attendant now appeared, looking quite pale, and trembling.

"Well?" said Lassamour."

"My lady's coach, noble sir, is quite ready, if you please."

"'Tis well. We will proceed."

Lamont laid his hand upon the arm of his friend.

"Go not to town to-night."

"Why not?"

"You will but vex yourself in vain. By the morning, which is so near at hand now, you can do all that you wish to do for your lady, and there may be something to do here ere you see her judges."

"What can there be to do here, Lamont?"

"I know not what may come of it; but

I should advise, as I feel quite sure that you will take no rest to-night, that you spend the remainder of it in an active search about the chamber and the private cabinet of your lady. It may be that you will find further evidences of her guilt."

"It may be so, or some evidences of her innocence."

"Innocence! Impossible!"

"Well—well, I will stay."

"Be it so. You have well and wisely determined. I will say as much to the officer."

Lamont intimated to the officer that he was now at liberty to depart with his prisoner.

He bowed in acquiescence, and then took the arm of Lady Margaret, saying—

"Now, madam, your coach awaits you, if you please to come with us."

"Do not mock me with such hollow words of courtesy. I do not please to go with you; but I must go perforce, it seems."

They led her from the apartment; but as she left it she cast one lingering look at Martin Lassamour, as though it were the last she was likely to have of him in this world.

Martin averted his eyes, and when she was gone he sank upon a seat in a great agony of woe.

The old knight, Sir Ralph Shard, approached him.

"What!" he cried, "a soldier, and cast down at the loss of a woman? Shame upon you!"

"Nay, bear with me," said Lassamour. "She had, in some strange way, wound herself around my heart, and I assure you, noble sir, that my grief at this unhappy circumstance is great."

"Well, there is no accounting for tastes."

"How mean you?"

"Why, to my mind the lady, by the number of husbands she had had before you saw her, had placed herself far beyond anything in the shape of sentimental sympathy or feeling."

"It may be so."

"Well, well," said Lamont, who, with a finer feeling than the rough old knight, saw how distasteful this style of conversation was to Lassamour, "Well, well, say no more on this head."

Lassamour thanked him by a look.

"As you please," said Sir Ralph Shard, "I don't at all want to say anything about her; but I have a request to make on my own account."

"You have but to name it, sir."

"It is, then, that you will oblige me with bed and board till morning?"

"With pleasure, Sir Ralph. My home is much honoured by your presence."

Lassamour now gave orders for all the attention possible to be paid to the comfort and accommodation of the old knight, and when he had retired Lamont and himself set about the examination of the Lady Margaret's room.

They found nothing that in any way related to recent events, with the exception of several male disguises, among which was one of a monk.

Wearied and exhausted, at length, by the events of the last twenty-four hours, Lassamour dropped into a deep sleep on a chair.

CHAPTER XCV.

THE EXHUMATION OF THE DEAD TAKES PLACE.

WHEN Martin Lassamour started from his sleep, the sun was shining in at the windows of Pleasaunce House.

At first he was too confused to know exactly where he was, and even when the events of the night before came crowding to his recollection, he was half inclined to dismiss them as the records of some wild disordered dream.

The sight of his young and gallant friend, Lamont, asleep, wrapped in a cloak, upon a couch, however, awakened him to the truth.

"Lamont! Lamont!"

"Here, Lassamour! Here!"

Lamont sprung to his feet, and laid his hand upon his sword.

"There is no danger."

"Ah, no! Now I recollect—you have had, I hope, a refreshing sleep, Lassamour?"

"I hope so, too. I have slept, but feel not much refreshed."

"Nay, you will be better soon."

"Yes, yes," sighed Lassamour. "And now we will but snatch a hasty breakfast, and then to town."

This was soon done, and in the course of another half hour the friends were mounted, and going at a good pace to London.

Sir Ralph Shard accompanied them; and, in fact, he had breakfasted before either of them awakened, since he had enjoyed a sound repose of some hours' duration in one of the soft beds of the mansion, before they had finished their search in Lady Margaret's room.

They all three, now, made their way, in the first instance, to the sheriff, who had given them such efficient assistance, as well against De Volence as in the affair of the Lady Margaret.

The sheriff received them kindly.

Lassamour looked at him fixedly, and then said—

"She lives?"

"Lives! Who?"

"My wife."

"Oh, yes. Did you expect otherwise, my good sir?"

"I did, indeed."

"And I, too," said Lamont.

"Well," said the sheriff, "I will not say but that some such idea possessed us all, but I had her well watched by women during the night."

"Body o' me!" cried Sir Ralph Shard, "but, with all due deference to you, Master Sheriff, if she had put herself out of the world, I don't think the world would have taken it to heart much."

The sheriff shook his head.

Lamont, in his own heart, echoed the sentiment of Sir Ralph.

It is possible enough, too, that even poor Lassamour would have found it some sort of relief had he been told she was no more.

Such an event would at once have put an end to an inquiry, and to an amount of publicity that could not but be painful in the highest degree to him, but he made no further remark upon that head.

"I may now tell you, gentleman," said the sheriff, "what is the course to be pursued in this matter. It is necessary that something in the shape of a preliminary inquiry should be made in the case, in order that the law may have a fair excuse for the further detention of the Lady Margaret."

Lassamour assented by a bow.

"That inquiry will take place this morning before two justices; but it will be made as short as possible, for to-night we purpose exhuming the bodies of her deceased six husbands."

Lassamour started.

"Indeed!"

"Yes; it is to be done by order of the king."

"The king?"

"Even so. The matter was of such strange and singular importance that it was deemed, at once, advisable to communicate it to the court, so that proper order should be taken in respect to it; and such is the order."

"Be it so, then."

"We expect, my good sir, doubtless, to find, from such an examination, abundant evidence of the guilt of the Lady Margaret."

"Alas, there is no doubt!"

"Alas, say you?"

"I do, indeed, Mr. Sheriff."

"Can it be possible that you regret her, then?"

"It is not only possible, but it is true that I do regret her with all my heart and with all my soul."

"Then I pity you."

"You may do so, sir, for in me you see a man who, acting under a stern sense of duty, has done that which will embitter the remainder of his existence."

"It is sorrowful, but yet—"

"What would you say?"

"Excuse me, sir."

"Nay, I know that you have a kind heart and a friendly feeling towards me, and so I would fain hear your thoughts. You were about to say a something which it might be wholesome for me to hear, but which you feared might jar with my feelings."

"It is so."

"Then be assured that I shall construe you rightly, and that I would rather hear that which you had to say than be left to conjecture it."

"You shall hear it, then."

"I shall be, Sir Sheriff, the more beholden to you."

"I was going to say, then, that out of evil we generally find come some good; and so, in her guilty career, the Lady Margaret has accumulated a fortune which I am glad to see come into your possession."

The colour for a moment mounted to the cheeks of Martin Lassamour, and then it left them paler than before.

"I have thought of that," he said.

"No doubt."

"Yes, it has forced itself upon my consideration."

"Surely yes."

"But not as you take it."

"How so?"

"I do not, sir, congratulate myself upon any such event."

"Nay, but——"

"Pardon me, sir, and hear me out. At this juncture I should not have mooted such a subject, but since it is mentioned, it is as well that I should tell you what my own ideas are regarding it."

"I listen to you, sir, with attention."

"Then if it should please Heaven that the guilt of this wife of mine should be so apparent that she can no longer continue in life, and her fortune revolves to me, I will make such an immediate use of it for pious and benevolent purposes as shall leave me as I was when I first saw her."

"Indeed!"

"Even so, sir."

"And—and what were you then?"

"A soldier of fortune. I never drew my sword, to my own knowledge, in a bad cause, but I lived by my sword, nevertheless, and I can do so once again."

"You surprise me."

Lassamour smiled faintly.

"Nay, Sir Sheriff," he said, "from what I have seen of you, I take you to be a man of fine honour, and were you situated as I am, I cannot help thinking you would do very much the same as I do."

"It might be so."

"I think, sir, it would be so."

At this moment there came a messenger to inform the sheriff that the justices were met to conduct the preliminary inquiry that he had spoken of.

He turned to Lassamour.

"You will come?"

"It is a duty."

"Then follow me, sir, and believe me that in all I have to do in this case, I consult an imperative duty, and not an inclination."

"I know it, sir."

"Knowing it, then, you will view with an indulgent spirit all that I may say or have to do in it."

"I will, indeed."

"For that I owe you many thanks. The office ofttimes that a man has to fill makes the man, himself, seem to be ungracious."

"That I can readily imagine. But you will find no such feeling towards you, Sir Sheriff, in my mind."

"Come on, then, Martin Lassamour," and as we proceed, let me beg of you to keep your feelings as much under control as may be."

"I will strive so to do."

CHAPTER XCVI.

THE GUILT OF THE MURDERESS IS FULLY ESTABLISHED.

IT was quite a wonder, to tell the truth, to Martin Lassamour that the Lady Margaret had not committed suicide.

To his apprehension, she was just the sort of person likely to do so.

That she was still there, in the land of the living, on that eventful morning, was, to him, quite an unexpected event.

But did he wish her to commit that dreadful act which there is no recalling?"

Perhaps he did.

He looked upon her guilt as so completely established, that no possible sophistry could in any degree explain it away.

Nay, it appeared that nothing in the ordinary course of things could, in any way or shape, even palliate it, and so it was well to wish her at once with the dead, than to look forward to the trouble and painful scenes that otherwise were sure to await her.

No wonder, then, that it was with a sigh that Martin Lassamour heard that she had survived that night.

He followed the sheriff, however, from the room in which they then were to a room where the magistrates charged with the preliminary examination of Lady Margaret sat.

Although, so far as the public was concerned, in those days there was nothing at all like the sort of open publicity to legal proceedings that we now consider essential, yet the room was crowded with persons of rank and station.

From one to the other the rumour had got abroad that, at length, the long suspected Lady Margaret, of Pleasaunce House, Richmond, had been arrested on the charge of murder.

No wonder, then, that curiosity to see her, and to hear the particulars of the special charge laid against her should congregate a number of persons to the examination.

And when we come to consider the very special circumstances of the whole case, we shall see at once how more than likely it was, that anything at all connected with the lady of Pleasaunce House should excite an extraordinary interest.

She was the wife of seven husbands.

Of course the whole of those husbands had friends, relations, and connections of all sorts, and of all descriptions.

The six who were dead, probably, had more of such than the one who was living.

As for Martin Lassamour, the fact is, that in connections of a family character, he was less to be considered than any of his predecessors.

But he had friends, too, about him. Friends who knew him well, and who valued him for the very many sterling qualities of heart and head that he possessed.

But for all this, it was with the relatives of the six deceased husbands of Lady Margaret that the room in which the judicial examination was to take place was chiefly filled upon this deeply interesting occasion, and many were the singular remarks made respecting the probabilities of the case before it was heard.

At the sight of the sheriff, and of Martin Lassamour, and Sir Ralph Shard, a sort of whisper ran through the assemblage.

This was hushed by the officials of the court, as quickly as possible.

A couple of magistrates, by order from the crown, had come to listen to the preliminary statements of the case, and when Martin Lassamour came, they at once proceeded to their duty.

We have stated there was no sort of intention, on this occasion, of trying the case. On the contrary, the object of the magistrates was to go as little into it as possible.

But consistently with that strong sense of justice, and of individual liberty in this country, which even at that period was beginning to be well comprehended, and to pervade all classes of society, it was sought to hear just so much of the charge against Lady Margaret as should thoroughly justify the law in withholding from her her liberty.

Then a thorough and searching examination, with all the circumstances of her guilt, could be made at sufficient leisure.

Martin Lassamour, from what the sheriff had, in a friendly way, told him, fully comprehended all this.

The silence in the court was intense for a few moments, and then one of the magistrates said—

"Mr. Sheriff, what have you to say to us?"

"Your honours," said the sheriff, "I have to state that the Lady Margaret Lassamour has been given into my charge upon suspicion of murder.

"Have you the prisoner in your custody?"

"I have."

"Who charges her with murder?"

"Her husband, Martin Lassamour."

"Is he here?"

"He is."

Lassamour bowed, but he looked very pale, and sad."

The justice then, who had asked those questions as a matter of form, now whispered to his colleague for a moment, after which he said,—

"Produce the prisoner, Mr. Sheriff, if you please, at once."

The sheriff gave an order to the officer who had apprehended the Lady Margaret at Pleasaunce, and he at once left the apartment.

This officer was not gone above three minutes, but to those who were anxiously awaiting his return, it seemed three hours.

As for poor Martin Lassamour, he would far rather have gone through a battle than have had to pass such moments of intense anxiety as he now suffered.

At length, however, the door was flung open.

All eyes were turned towards it.

Lady Margaret appeared, and was conducted to the table at which the magistrates sat.

Oh, how pale she was! She looked more like some exhumed dead body than a living, breathing creature of this world.

She slowly cast her eyes around the court, and for one moment they rested upon those of Martin Lassamour. She seemed, then, as though she was about to speak to him, but she did not do so, only her lips slightly moved.

Lassamour was much affected.

"Lady," said the magistrate who assumed the office of spokesman in the matter, no doubt by arrangement with his colleague, "Lady, will you disclose to us your name."

"My name?"

"Yes, if you please."

They treated her with an involuntary respect—that kind of respect that one whose fate is sealed in this world is treated with.

"Yes," she added. "My name is Margaret, and I am called the Lady Margaret Lassamour."

"Your residence?"

"My own house at Richmond, usually; but last night a prison."

"Margaret Lassamour," said the magistrate, "commonly called Lady Margaret Lassamour, you are brought before us accused of a capital offence."

"Indeed, sir."

"Yes. The offence of contriving and attempting the murder of Martin Lassamour, your husband. It is our duty to turn what is said against you on that charge, and to hear all you may please to say in answer to it, if you please to say anything."

"And my accuser?" said Lady Margaret, turning and looking at Lassamour.

He uttered a deep sigh.

"Is my accuser here?"

"He is here."

"Which is he?"

"I am he, Margaret," said Martin Lassamour. "I am he by the force of circumstances which man may not control; and I would go to death with joy this moment, if I could carry a conviction that this was all some hideous mistake, and you were innocent."

"Indeed!"

"You doubt me?"

"I do doubt you."

"Heaven have mercy upon you."

"Which means, if you would finish the sentence, Martin Lassamour, that you intend to have none."

"No, no, you do me wrong, Margaret, you do me wrong."

"Well, I hope I do."

"On my soul you do!"

"Be it so. From a man's actions let him be judged."

CHAPTER XCVII.

THE EXAMINATION OF LADY MARGARET IS CONTINUED.

THIS little episode between Martin Lassamour and the Lady Margaret did not take so long in the passing as it has necessarily taken in the telling.

It was only the rapidity of it, and the very exceptional character of the whole proceedings that induced the two magistrates to permit anything so very irregular as a conversation between the accuser and the accused in court.

To Martin Lassamour it was quite evidently a matter for deep affliction that he should have to say what he did say to the Lady Margaret, and that he should be so situated as he was.

These few words, then, between them being over, he turned aside, and did not seem disposed to look at her again.

The magistrates then turned to the sheriff, saying—

"What have you to urge against Margaret Lassamour?"

"That I will at once depose to," he replied.

The oath was then adminstered to the sheriff, after which he said—

"Martin Lassamour came to me in the good company of Sir Ralph Shard, and they made such statements to me that I was induced, at once, to place under their orders one of my most active officers, together with such a force as should be able to act with ease and decision."

"What was the statement made to you by Lassamour?"

"It was to the effect that he suspected his wife of a design on his life."

"Is the officer here whom you entrusted with the conduction of the affair?"

"He is so, and will now, if you please, give his evidence."

"Call him."

The officer who had been in command of the sheriff's guard, throughout the proceedings which had ended in the discomfiture and death of Sir Warenne de Volence, and the arrest of the Lady Margaret, was duly called, and made his appearance.

He was sworn.

"Depose to what you know of all this," said one of the magistrates to him.

"I will, sir."

"Be brief."

The officer detailed the events of what is already known to the reader, and plainly stated how he had kept watch in the gallery, or corridor, outside the state bedchamber of Pleasaunce House on the night before."

"What saw you there?"

"Nothing."

"Nothing, say you?"

"Nothing, sir; I could not see through a three inch plank. But after a time I was called to by the youg gallant, Lamont, and then the prisoner, now present, was given into my custody, and I brought her to London."

"Were is this Lamont?"

"Here," cried the young friend of Martin Lassamour, and he stepped forward.

"You have evidence to give?"

"I have, indeed."

It was quite evident from the manner of Lamont, that he not only had evidence to give, but evidence of very great importance, too, as regarded the affair at issue.

He was duly sworn.

"Now, sir," said the magistrate, "pray relate to us, at once, and without fear or favour, all that you know of this affair."

"I will."

"Proceed, my friend," said Lassamour.

"I think, then," said Lamont, "and it is a thought that gives me much pleasure, that, under Heaven, I was, last night, the means of saving the life of this gallant gentleman, Martin Lassamour."

"Tell us how, sir."

"I will do so."

"Take your own time, and tell the tale in your own words; we do not hurry you."

"Thanks—thanks."

Lamont paused a moment or two, as though to collect his thoughts, and then he said—

"Sirs, I may commence by saying that I am a friend of Martin Lassamour, and a sincere one, too."

"I know that," cried Lassamour.

"Silence, good sir ! Let him proceed."

"Last evening, then, from circumstances which I need not detail, inasmuch as they do not come within my own knowledge, there seemed to be good reason why Martin Lassamour should suspect a design upon his life by the Lady Margaret."

"Had you suspicions before that communication?"

"I had."

"But no facts to go upon?"

"None."

"Proceed, then."

"Martin Lassamour agreed, then, with me, that he would go home affecting to be intoxicated, and that he would lie on a couch in the state bed-chamber, and affect to go to sleep, and that the while I should conceal myself behind the thick and ample hangings of the state bedstead in the room, and keep a wary eye on all that passed."

"You did this?"

"I did."

"Proceed."

"It was an easy part to play, and Martin Lassamour played it well, and at last affected to go to sleep on the couch, as it had been arranged."

"And then?"

"Then, gentlemen, when all was still, and when, no doubt, she fancied no human eye was upon her, or could possibly be upon her, the Lady Margaret glided noiselessly into the room."

"Alone?"

"Yes, quite alone."

"Go on, sir."

"In one hand she bore a small iron ladle, in the which, as it afterwards turned out, though I could not at the time well see it, there was some molten lead."

There was quite a movement among the auditory as young Lamont made this statement.

"Pray proceed, sir," said the magistrate, "we are all attention to your remarkable evidence."

"From what she muttered to herself then," added Lamont, "and from her actions, I could entertain no sort of doubt as to what her object was."

"And what was it ?"

"To pour the molten lead into the slumbering brain of Martin Lassamour, through his ear."

A shudder pervaded the assemblage.

"Into his ear, said you?"

"Ay, sir."

"Are you sure?"

"As sure as that I am now a living man."

"It is horrible !"

"It is so."

"From the actions, then, of the prisoner, you came to the conclusion that such was her object ?"

"I did."

"And what did you then ?"

"I let her proceed as far as I dared do, without in any serious way compromising the life of my friend, Martin Lassamour, for I was anxious that there should be no possible mistake as to her intentions, and then I sprang from my hiding-place and secured her."

"Did she resist ?"

"No."

"And what happened then ?"

"Martin Lassamour, on the instant, sprang up from his feigned sleep, and then confronted her, and reproached her with her baseness and her criminality."

"Is that all you know?"

"It is."

"And enough, too, I think. It is very fearfully conclusive."

"Yes, your worship," cried Sir Ralph Shard ; "but there is yet another proof to be found."

"What is that, sir?"

"If there be not found in each of the brains of her dead husbands a pullet of lead that has been poured into their ears, even as she would have poured it into the ears of this Martin Lassamour, the Frenchman."

Lady Margaret gasped as if her breath had left her.

All eyes were fixed upon her.

The magistrate then said—

"Prisoner, have you any questions to put to the witness, Lamont."

"None. But—but——"

"What?"

"You cannot mean to disturb the sacred repose of the dead upon such a pretext as this wild supposition of Sir Ralph Shard's?"

"The law will take its course."

"But that is not the law."

"It is a matter which we will not discuss here. It is sufficient for you to meet the charge against you."

"Be it so."

"What say you to it, then?"

"It is false!"

"Can you prove so much?"

"I can assert that the molten lead I had was for the purpose of casting a nativity?"

"A what?"

"A nativity, or horoscope."

The magistrate shook his head, and the spectators in the court looked incredulous.

"Explain yourself."

"I will do so. I had reason to suspect the fidelity of Martin Lassamour, my husband. I think I was wrong, now, but I thought myself right then. Well, it is a fact, that if you do suspect a husband, and pour some molten lead into water, it will, if he be really unfaithful, assume the shape of the person who is the rival of his true wife. That was my object."

"But where was the water in which to pour the lead. You had nothing of the sort, as it appears."

CHAPTER XCVIII.

THE EXHUMATION OF THE DEAD BODIES TAKES PLACE.

LADY MARGARET had well concocted this tale that she meant to tell. She answered at once, and without the least degree of hesitation or confusion.

"It is true that I had not with me water wherewith to carry out the experiment, but I had it in my own chamber."

"Why not, then, carry it out there?" said the magistrate. "Why bring the molten lead into the other apartment."

"Simply because the charm would not be complete if the breath of the person concerned were not to touch the molten lead, and that was why I brought it so near to the face of Martin Lassamour."

The judge shook his head.

"I would that this were true," he said.

"And I, too," said Martin Lassamour, in a mournful tone of voice, "I wish it with all my heart and soul."

"It is true," said Lady Margaret.

"Never mind," cried Sir Ralph Shard, "we shall soon find out something by digging up the bodies of her other six husbands, I take it."

"Yes," said the magistrate.

"I forbid that act," said Lady Margaret, with a look of stern composure.

"You forbid it?"

"I do!"

"And upon what ground?"

"Simply that they are all interred in my family vault, which is my own freehold property, and which no one dare, without my consent, disturb."

The cool effrontery of this speech was such that, as may be supposed, it made the profoundest impression upon every one present.

Poor Martin Lassamour, who really did feel so much earnest sympathy with the prisoner on many accounts, shrunk back, and those who had an unfriendly feeling to the Lady Margaret looked at each other, as much as to say—

"This is in keeping with the bold and the reckless character of the woman."

It was some few moments before any one replied to her.

Then it was the justice who did so, and whose duty it was to do so.

"Prisoner at the bar," he said, "did I hear you aright on this point?"

"I know not, sir."

"You know not?"

"Just so—nor care I."

"I am afraid, madam, that you are hardened in the career of deep iniquity which you have thought proper to carry on."

"That, sir," she said, "is an imprope

remark for you to make, in your position."

The magistrates looked at each other, and then they whispered a few words together, after which one said—

"We have, we consider, heard enough to fully warrant us in remanding the prisoner for one week from this date."

"This is gross injustice!" cried the Lady Margaret. "It is vile injustice!"

"How so, madam?"

"Can you ask?"

"I do ask."

"Then your own conscience should tell you that you have no evidence, as yet, against me."

"We have."

"What is it, then?"

"This much, that you were, by the young gallant, Lamont, prevented from pouring molten lead into your husband's ear."

"Which I deny."

"That he prevented you?"

"No, but that such was my intent."

"We scarcely expected you to admit it, madam."

Lady Margaret inclined her head for a moment, and then said—

"Is Martin Lassamour here?"

"He is."

"Then before I am what you call remanded, I claim the right to ask him a few questions."

"You may claim the right, but he may not choose to answer you."

"We shall see."

"I will answer," said Lassamour.

He at once stepped forward, and confronted the Lady Margaret. He was very pale, but it was easy enough to see, too, that he was very determined.

For a few moments they looked at each other in silence, and then she said—

"Martin Lassamour, am I your wife?"

"You know you are."

"For how long have I so borne your name?"

"For over twelve months."

"Have I by word, or look, or deed shown myself to be other than kind and loving, and gentle to you?"

"Until this dreadful act—no."

"What dreadful act?"

"That of which you stand accused."

"Ah, Martin, if, now, I should be innocent?"

"If you should be innocent?"

"Ay!"

"Oh, Margaret, if you could prove yourself so, no power on earth should part us."

"Indeed!"

"I swear it!"

"Why, then, Martin, that is all I wish to ask of you, just now, so you may go your way in peace, if you will."

"Oh, Margaret! Margaret!"

"What would you?"

"Nothing—nothing."

Poor Martin Lassamour, who had really been deeply affected by the little conversation he had had with her, turned aside to hide his grief.

"Have you anything else to say, prisoner," said the magistrate, "against this remand?"

"No, sir. For I can see it in your eyes, that you would remand me, evidence or no evidence, so take your course, sir."

"You wrong me."

"Nay, sir, I do not. But it matters not."

"Then you are remanded until this day week. Officers, remove your prisoner."

"One moment, sir."

She turned to the sheriff, and to Sir Ralph Shard, saying as she did so—

"Beware, now, how you attempt to carry out your foul and dastardly threat of disinterring my dead husbands. The vengeance of both the dead and the living will be upon you, if you do."

"Pho!" cried Sir Ralph Shard, as he snapped his finger. "That for the vengeance of both dead and living."

Lady Margaret smiled contemptuously.

"I shall do my duty," said the sheriff.

"But no wrong," she said.

"Be it so."

"You wrong me, then, if you attempt to invade the sacred precincts of my burying place. Do you hear that, sir?"

"I do."

"Act as if you heard it, then."

The justices made a sign to the officer to withdraw her, but when one laid a hand upon her, and said,—

"Now, madam."

She started back, and struck him from her, saying—

"Hands off, sir."

"It is my duty, madam. Will you please to follow me?"

"To where?"

"To prison."

"Well, fellow, I suppose it is your duty, so be it so; but yet another word ere I go."

They all paused, and waited what she should say.

"May my curses," she said, "light upon the head of all who shall have any hand by actual work, or by command, or implication in the desecration of the grave you threaten!"

It was not so much these words them-selves that made an impression upon all who heard them, but it was the tone of awful denunciation in which they were uttered that struck a chill to their hearts.

"I am now ready."

"Remove her," said the justice.

Another moment, and the Lady Mar-garet was taken from the court by the officers.

Then everybody drew a long breath, and even Sir Ralph Shard spoke in a voice that savoured a little of emotion, as he said—

"By Heavens her dead husband, who was my near kinsman, shall be exhumed, were she to go on cursing to all eternity against all who aided in it!"

"It shall be done," said the magistrate. "Mr. Sheriff, you will see to the ordering of all this."

"Yes, sir. I have already made some of the necessary arrangements for that object."

CHAPTER XCIX.

THE VAULTS OF OUR LADYE CHAPEL AT SOUTHWARK.

HEN the Lady Margaret stated that her six husbands were interred in a vault that was her own property, she did not in any way or shape enlarge upon the truth of what she had stated.

Such was the fact.

It appeared, from authentic inquiries that had been made long after the events connected with this story, that upon the sudden, and the very unaccountable death of the first of her six husbands, she bought a freehold vault beneath the church of Our Ladye at Southwarke.

It was in that vault, then, that she had had laid the whole of the deceased husbands, and circumstances afterwards proved that she flattered herself she had taken good care that nothing should appear against her with relation to their dead bodies, even if they should be exhumed at any time.

But of this we will speak soon more in full.

It is our duty, now, to follow the sheriff and his men to the loathsome duty they had set themselves, of an examintion of the corpses of the six deceased husbands of the criminal Lady Margaret.

This course was recommended by the crown lawyers at the time, because it was thought better to examine her, and commit her for the actual murder of her husbands, than for the attempted one of Martin Lassamour.

The hour is close to midnight, then, when in the sacristry of the church of Our Ladye at Southwarke, a little party was rapidly assembling.

The bishop of the diocese was there, and several priests, too, from a neighbouring abbey, and the sheriff with some of his assistants arrived very soon.

They looked at each other, all these people, with rather agitated expressions, and the sheriff, addressing the bishop, said—

"Holy sir, I cannot but feel that this is, in some sort, a desecration of this place that we are about to engage in."

"Heed not that, my son," said the bishop. "In the holy name of justice, the vault should give up its dead."

"You are kind and good, holy sir."

"It is among the commandments of Heaven," added the bishop, "that 'Thou shalt do no murder;' and so, if it be even suspected that murder is done, it cannot be the will of Heaven that even the dim receptacle of the dead should hide the evidences of the crime."

The sheriff bowed low.

At this moment some footsteps approached the sacristy.

"Who comes," said the bishop.

The door was opened by a monk, who in a low tone, said—

"Master Lassamour, with his friends, the young Lamont, and Sir Ralph Shard, are here."

"Let them enter."

The three gentlemen entered the sacristy together, and bowed low to the bishop.

"My son," said that dignitary, addressing himself to Martin Lassamour, "I am told that you have certain intentions as regards the wealth which this unhappy woman, who is your wife, has brought to you."

"I have, holy sir."

"What are they?"

"I feel as if gold so obtained, and appropriated solely to my own uses, would be accursed, so the bulk of it I look upon as in trust in my hands, to dispense for good uses."

"You are right, my son; and what portion did you purpose to give to the church?"

"If you, my Lord Bishop, will accept of one half the total fortune, and found with it some charitable institution which will be for the good of poor souls, and the glory of the church, it will please me much."

It was quite evident, now, from the expression of the face of the bishop, that such a proposition pleased him quite as much as it could, by any possibility, please Martin Lassamour.

"Kneel, my son—kneel," he cried—

Those were superstitious days, and Martin at once knelt at the feet of the bishop.

"The blessing of the Holy Catholic Church be with you and about you for evermore!"

"Amen!" chaunted the priests who were present.

Lassamour rose.

"Thanks, holy father," he said; "thanks, for this great boon to me."

In those days it was considered that such words from a dignitary of the church to any one, were a passport to Heaven that no one would think for a moment of disputing.

Martin Lassamour was not a weak nor a vain superstitious man, but he was a catholic, and had been brought up to think what we have stated; therefore, he was well enough pleased at the benediction of the bishop of his church.

"And now, are we all here?" said the bishop.

"All, holy sir," said an abbot of the monastery attached to the church.

"Then let us proceed."

An aged man—the sacristan of the church, with a huge bunch of keys at his girdle, and followed by his two assistants, stood without the door of the little gothic room.

The two assistants carried torches; but when the party reached the door, Martin Lassamour said, suddenly—

"Nay, we are not all here yet."

"Who is wanting, my son?"

"Master Arrowdale, the cunning leech, who was to examine the dead."

"Ah! that is true."

"I am here," said a voice, and a small, thin old man, dressed in black, and with a Geneva skull-cap on his head, slowly advanced.

"You are welcome."

"Is all ready?" said the surgeon.

"Quite—quite."

"Then let us proceed; for by my faith, gentlemen, in thus attending to the dead, I am rather neglecting some urgent wants of the living."

"I hope that we shall not detain you long," said Martin Lassamour.

The bishop and Martin went first, and the little party entered the old church.

The torches from which there came, while in the narrow passage leading from the sacristy, a good light enough, now seemed in the large space of the church to burn dimly, and large shadows flitted on the walls.

"Where is the vault?" said the bishop.

The old sacristan stepped forward.

"Here, holy father, here," he said, as he pointed to a flag-stone in the flooring of the church. "It is here, an' it so please you."

"Remove it, then."

The sacristan made a sign to his two men, and then, while some others of the party took the torches, they set to work to raise the slab of stone that covered the entrance to the vault which the Lady Margaret had purchased, and, no doubt, given a liberal price for, to the monks of the church of Our Ladye at Southwarke.

The stone soon yielded to the practised efforts of the two assistants of the sacristan, and they turned it over from the entrance to the vault.

Every one drew back instinctively.

"There may be foul air in the vault," said the bishop. "Stand back!"

"It is probable enough," said Martin.

"Nay," said the sacristan, "scarcely so, for there are many gratings to the open air from the vaults that let vapours escape, and the free air into them again."

"It is well that it should be so," said the bishop; "for, at least, it is not often that such as we are born to, descend to such places; yet it is not meant that the congregation of the churches should worship over a mass of contagion and foul odours."

"It is anything but well, my good lord bishop," said Sir Ralph Shard, "and the church, as well as the laity is much beholden to you for your good regard to such matters."

"Let us descend," said the bishop.

He drew back himself so, and there was a little sort of hesitation, and then the sacristan took one of the torches, and said, in a low voice—

"Follow me, gentlemen. I will go first."

CHAPTER C.

THE VAULT OF THE MURDERED DEAD.

IM and dark, indeed, was the entrance of the vault; and for any one not accustomed to such places, and not well knowing whither such a dreary-looking flight of narrow stone steps were likely to leae to, it would have been rather a fearful thing to attempt the descent of them.

But the vaults of Our Ladye church were all familiar to the old sacristan.

He felt no fear at all upon the subject. The only thing that he dreaded in the whole affair was a fresh attack of the rheumatics, in consequence of being up at such an hour of the night in the damp air.

His two men followed him with their tools for opening the coffins, and then the surgeon descended.

The bishop signed to Martin Lassamour to precede him, and then he followed, and the rest of the party brought up the rear.

It was a steep and narrow staircase that led to that last home of poor humanity.

Damp exhalations were upon the walls, notwithstanding all that the old sacristan had said about the good ventilation of the vaults, and the torches evidently gave evidence of the air being rather foul, by not burning so brightly as in the upper air.

But still there was nothing sufficiently ominous to prevent the party from descending.

The stairs were twenty in number, and at the foot of them there was a thick layer of sawdust with which, in fact, the whole of the vaults, and the passages leading to them, were covered.

They did not find themselves at once in the vault upon reaching the foot of this flight of stairs from the church, but in a narrow passage that seemed, in a tortuous manner, to wind like a snake, far away under the foundations of the church.

"Where is the vault?" said the bishop.

"Here, my good lord,—here," said the sacristan, and producing one from the many keys he had at his girdle, he fitted it to the key hole of a small gothic door to the left of where they stood.

The lock was stiff and rusted, but at length it yielded to the key, and with a harsh, grating sound upon its hinges, the door opened.

"And this, then," said the bishop, "is the vault that belongs to the Lady Margaret?"

"It is so."

"You are certain?"

"Quite, holy sir. Oh, quite."

They crossed the threshhold of the vault, now, and not without some apprehension of finding the air there even worse than on the outside of it, but such was not the fact.

There was a grating in the wall just above the door, which at all events had the effect of equalising the quality of the air.

The vault was about twenty feet square, and there were deep narrow recesses in the walls, into which coffins could be placed.

On the floor of it, too, there were iron and stone biers, on which coffins could be rested. The floor was thickly strewn with sawdust, and when the torches were placed on brackets that were evidently constructed and fastened to the wall for that purpose, they sent up a clearer flame, and the whole interior of the vault was very plainly to be seen by the little party.

There was a complete silence, now, for a few moments, which no one seemed inclined to break, till the bishop said—

"Master Sacristan, let us proceed, at once, with this business, for the sooner it is over the better it will be."

"Ay, holy sir, it will."

"Can you point out to us the last coffin that was placed in this vault?"

"Ay, can I, holy sir."

"Where is it?"

The sacristan, with one of his keys, tapped on the end of one of the coffins, in one of the recesses.

"It is this."

"Have it out then."

The sacristan motioned to his men, and with a harsh, and grating sound, the coffin was dragged out.

"Place it here," said the sacristan, pointing to one of the stone biers on the floor of the cell.

The coffin was thus placed.

A cloud of dust was upon the surface of it. The cloth had rotted away, and hung in shreds, and the nails were as black as ink. One of the handles came off with a touch, and the plate upon the lid was with some difficulty distinguished from the cloth and wood surrounding it.

"You are sure this is the last?" said the bishop.

"Oh yes, holy sir. I am quite certain."

"I will soon see that," cried Sir Ralph Shard. "Give me one of the lights."

One of the torches was handed to him, and he threw a broad glare upon the coffin lid, and the plate.

Then, in a voice that had in it considerable emotion, he said—

"'Sir Thomas Shard.'"

"Yes," he said. "This is the receptacle of the mortal remains of my poor nephew."

The surgeon stepped forward.

"How long has this body been here?"

"A twelvemonth and a week."

"Humph!"

"Think you, sir, it will be much decayed?"

"I can't say. It all depends upon circumstances, but be so good, Master Sacristan, as to let your men remove the lid of this coffin as soon as possible, and then we shall see."

"Yes, sir—yes, sir."

Sir Ralph Shard drew back as the sacristan's men advanced to the coffin.

One of them, with a broad flat chisel, and a hammer, set to work. There was a sharp crackling noise, and the lid was loose.

"It is open."

Curiosity now induced Martin Lassamour and Lamont to step forward. There was a pause of a few moments, and then the bishop made a sign.

The lid of the coffin was lifted off.

There lay the body of poor Sir Ralph Shard, and in such a good state of preservation that one would have fancied he had died but the day before.

"Ah! good," said the surgeon; "it is so!"

"What is so?"

"Why, I may mention to you all that my good friend, the learned leech, Anthony Brown, was called in to see this gentleman on his sudden death."

"Indeed!"

"Yes, holy sir."

"And what thought he?"

"He thought the death so singular that he would fain have opened the body."

"And why did he not?"

"The Lady Margaret would not let him. But still he had his suspicions of foul play, and he placed in the coffin, along with the corpse, some precious herbs, which he knew would have the effect of preserving it from all decay. And see, it is as fresh as if only just dead."

"It is so."

"And can you not smell the herbs?"

They did all smell something of a rich aromatic odour.

"Yes—yes."

"Well, then, my friend's plan of preserving the body in case there should arise any future questions about the cause of death has, so far, very greatly facilitated our progress."

"It has, indeed," said Martin.

"It was a piece of wise and learned forethought," said the bishop.

"It has, too, stopped the job," added the surgeon, "of much that would otherwise have been loathsome and unwholesome in it; and now I will proceed at once with my examination."

"Do so—do so."

Sir Ralph Shard was by the side of the coffin, and he fully had the intention of seeing the investigation made, but in such a thought he rather miscalculated the strength of his nerves.

When, with all the coolness and nonchalance in the world, the surgeon lifted up the head of the body, the poor knight was compelled to draw back.

"I can't—I can't—" he said.

"You cannot what, my dear sir?"

"I cannot look on. He was my own nephew. Perhaps, had he been a stranger to me, I might."

"Oh, that is it."

The surgeon motioned to one of the sacristan's assistants to help him.

The man stepped forward.

"Hold the head, sir."

"Yes, master."

"Steady!"

"Yes, master."

The surgeon took from his pocket a black case, and opened it. He took from it a saw and other neatly made implements.

"What are you about to do?" said the bishop.

"Open the skull!"

Even the bishop drew back a pace or two.

CHAPTER CI.

THE EVIDENCE AGAINST THE LADY MARGARET IS CONCLUSIVE.

THE surgeon glanced at the faces of those around him, and seemed rather amused at the looks of horror that they had on them.

"Gentlemen," he said, "I am sorry to shock you all in this way, but really a very little reflection ought to get you quite over such feelings, I think."

"It ought, indeed," said Lassamour.

"Yes," said Sir Ralph Shard; "but I tell you that, so far as I am concerned, he was my sister's son, and so you see my case is rather special as regards him."

"It is so."

"And I, too," said Martin Lassamour, "may well be supposed to feel a more than common interest in the fate of this poor corpse, for what its fate was might have been mine."

"That is true, my good Martin Lassamour," added Sir Ralph Shard; "and you may depend it is next thing to a positive miracle that it was not so."

"I am of that opinion, too."

"My son," said the bishop, "it is quite clear that you were, by the special favour of Heaven, preserved for the express purpose of bringing to light the terrible guilt of that woman who has committed such awful crimes.

"You assume her guilty, holy sir ?"

"Can I help it?"

Lassamour was silent.

It was next thing to impossible, indeed, to suppose in any human probability that the Lady Margaret could be innocent.

And yet he shrunk from the supposition of her guilt, even then.

"Now gentlemen," said the surgeon, "I think you told me that the supposition was that the six husbands of the Lady Margaret had come by their deaths owing to molten lead being poured into their ears ?"

"Even so, sir," said the sheriff.

"Then if we find evidence of such a fact in this one case, it will, I think, carry the others ?"

"It will, indeed."

"And the investigation need be pursued no further?"

"No further, sir."

"Then, gentlemen, I may as well tell you that such an act as pouring molten lead into the ear of any one asleep would be certain and immediate death."

"And most agonising."

"Yes, while it lasted."

"It would be but for a moment," said Lassamour.

"As you say, but for a moment; and yet——"

"What, sir?"

"There is no knowing what length of time a moment might appear to the struggling soul at such a time."

Lassamour shuddered.

"The Lord have mercy upon us!" whispered Sir Ralph Shard, "I fear my poor nephew suffered much."

"He is at peace, now," said the bishop, "and if he should not be, I will order some masses for his soul."

"Thanks, holy sir."

"They will avail him much."

"Oh yes, poor fellow, they will ; and yet the pangs that he must have suffered ought to be sufficient to free him of purgatory."

"Hush! hush! That is impiety."

Sir Ralph Shard bowed his head to the reproof of the bishop, for in those days the church had a great power over all men.

"Proceed, sir, I pray you," whispered Martin Lassamour to the surgeon.

"Yes—yes."

There was a silence now again, and the surgeon, after a few moments, said—

"Gentlemen, I think that all of you, or at all events, as many of you as may feel inclined so to be, ought to witness what I am about to do."

"Yes," said Martin.

"Exactly so," said Lamont.

"If, in the dissection which I am about to make of the skull of this corpse, I find anything which ought not to be there, it is better that there should be plenty of evidence that it was found there."

"You are right, sir."

"Come round me and the coffin, then, and see what I do."

This was so reasonable, and to the purpose, that they could none of them object to it, and even Sir Ralph Shard, after a severe mental struggle, whispered to Lassamour—

"My good friend!"

"Yes."

"Advise me!"

"To what?"

"Ought I to see this?"

"Yes."

"You think so?"

"On my soul, I do."

"Then I will."

This seemed to decide the good old knight, for although his face was very pale, he finally took his stand at the side of the coffin."

"Are you all ready, gentlemen?" said the surgeon.

"We are."

"Then I will proceed, if you please."

"Proceed, in God's name!" said the bishop.

"Hold the light lower."

The sacristan himself took the light from the man who was holding it, and held it in the position required by the surgeon, and so that its beams fell full upon the skull of the corpse in the mouldering coffin.

The surgeon then laid his saw across the skull, and, with all the coolness possible, began to work away to divide the bone into two portions right through.

It would be quite out of the question to attempt, in any way, to do justice to the feeling of those assembled in the vault of the dead at this time. Every one of them had his feelings and his imagination wound up to the highest pitch of intense excitement by the scene that was going on.

And who will wonder at it?

The grating sound of the saw, as it bit through the bone of the skull of the corpse, was terrible to hear, and jarred awfully upon the nerves of the whole party.

The saw was a good one, and it soon did its work. The harsh grating sound ceased all at once.

The bone was divided.

"So far, so good," said the surgeon.

"Is it done?" said Martin.

"Nearly."

The saw was laid aside and from the case of implements the surgeon took a powerful pair of pincers. He laid hold of a portion of the skull, and with one skilful, and well directed wrench he separated the entire head into two portions.

"Behold!" he cried.

They all shrunk back with horror.

Lying, like a thread of silver, so bright and fine did it seem, and in a direct line from the ear to the brain, where it ended, was a long thin thread of lead.

"Do you see it?" said the surgeon.

"We do," gasped all.

He took another instrument from the case, and in another moment he picked out the piece of lead. He held it up.

"Behold!" he said, "the cause of the death of this man. This lead has been poured into his ear while molten, and it has just reached the brain, and so produced death."

"Horrible!—most horrible!" cried Martin Lassamour.

Sir Ralph Shard sat down on one of the stone biers and covered his face with his hands.

"May the Lord punish the wicked," said the bishop. "Blessed is the name of the Lord."

Then there was, so far, the evidence as against the Lady Margaret quite conclusive.

No one, after the awful discovery that had been made in the brain of Sir Thomas Shard, could doubt for a moment how he, a strong young man, in perfect health, had come by death.

And a truly horrible death it was, too.

Oh, what must have been the agony of that moment when the molten lead ran hissing into the very brain? It is too awful to contemplate!

The more rapid, then, that death came to release the poor victim of such a diabolical deed from the agonies he must have endured, the more merciful it was.

By what terrible thought it was that the wicked woman came first to dream of such a mode of putting her husbands out of the world, it is quite impossible to say.

Certainly, if any human crime could be supposed, more than another, to be specially suggested by the spirit of all evil, this was just that one.

No wonder was it that the bishop and the sacristan, and Martin Lassamour, and Sir Ralph Shard, and their other friends made what haste they could out of the vaults.

It was an immense relief to them all to get up the narrow staircase into the church.

Just as they reached it, the old clock struck the hour of one, so that they had been only about half an hour in the vaults.

But what an half-hour it had been!

How fearful had been the state of feeling of those who had to endure even that comparatively short space of time in the dreary home of the dead.

Well—the investigation was over.

With all the force of a fearful truth, the fact was now established that Sir Thomas Shard, at all events, had come by his death by having molten lead poured into his ear.

That was all that was required.

One case on which to proceed safely and surely against the murderess was, for the purposes of justice, as good as a thousand could be. It would fully and amply meet the requirements of the case.

CHAPTER CII.

THE FATE OF THE MURDERESS IS DECIDED.

IT would be difficult to analyse the feelings of Martin Lassamour upon this occasion.

Perhaps, after all, notwithstanding the terrible evidence which the dissection of the skull of Sir Thomas Shard had produced, he felt a sensation of relief.

First of all, he could not from the first have had any real doubt of the guilt of the Lady Margaret.

Then again, it was a very great relief to him that it would be upon some other charge than the one which he alone could support that she would now be tried.

Of course the law would prefer to attack her for an actual murder accomplished, than for one that, at the fullest, had been only attempted.

He felt that now she would be arraigned for the murder of Sir Thomas Shard.

That, then, was in itself, in so far as it made him a mere spectator of her trial, instead of a prominent witness at it, so much a relief.

But still Martin Lassamour felt anything but happy under all the circumstances of the case.

The course of our story proceeds, though, hastily now, and irrespective of the special personal feelings of any individual.

The week soon passed away during which the Lady Margaret had been remanded by the justices, in order that the fact of whether the deaths of her other husbands should be attributed to her or not might be clearly ascertained.

Now upon the occasion of the inquiry into the fate of Sir Thomas Shard, and the dissection of his skull, no one had thought it at all necessary to pursue the inquiry further.

In fact, they had all left the vault as soon as they could after the finding the lead in his brain, for they considered they had gone far enough.

But no sooner did the friends and the relatives of all the other dead husbands of the Lady Margaret hear what had been done, and what had been the result, than they were all seized with a desire to have their own individual relatives similarly examined.

This was a desire which the authorities found it difficult to resist.

It was so natural that it should arise, that after some consultation, and some correspondence upon the subject, it was determined that free leave should be given.

Upon that being settled, then, the vault of the Lady Margaret, in which lay the dead bodies of her husbands, was thrown freely open to all, and in the course of another twelve hours it was ascertained that all had perished in the same way as Sir Thomas Shard.

The fate of the Lady Margaret, after this, was quite a certain thing.

At least, so said every one.

But the week, as we have said, passed away, and for the second time she was brought before such a crowded court as never was seen before, in order to be committed in due form for trial.

The friends and the connexions of her six dead husbands alone formed a large throng of persons, and when we add to them the crowd that was collected from curiosity, it may be fairly imagined what a state the limits of the court was in.

It was with difficulty that the officers could get to their places, and even when they did so, it took half an hour to get the throng into anything like order.

At ten o'clock in the morning, the prisoner was put to the bar.

She was attired in a complete dress of black velvet, and that tended to make her look more ghastly pale than she otherwise would.

She cast a hasty glance around her.

There was a look of curiosity upon her face, for it had been carefully concealed from her that the inquiry and investigation she had so firmly denounced, had taken place at all.

But this state of incertitude was not likely to last.

The clerk of the court rose, and said—

"Margaret Lassamour, you are charged with the wilful murder of Sir Thomas Shard, your late husband, and it will be to that charge, at present, that you are required to attend."

She started.

"Sir Thomas Shard?"

"Yes. Sir Thomas Shard."

"He is not my husband."

"But he was," said one of the justices.

"Ay, before God took him."

"Before you sent him to that place wherein it is to be hoped he lives in glory."

"Amen. But send him I did not."

"We shall see."

"No. We shall not see. Allow me, sir, to ask, do you believe in God?"

"As I live, I do."

"Then do you think man more powerful than he?"

"Assuredly not."

"Then you think God can do as he pleases with the great world?"

"I do."

"And that he can permit or not permit things to happen, as he chooses, and that none of his creatures can cease even to live without he so wills it?"

"Be it so."

"Then it is clear that, let Sir Thomas Shard have apparently come by his death how he may, it was in truth by the will of God, and the will of God, you see, is the act of God."

"This sophistry will not save you."

"It is truth."

"Call the witnesses."

The surgeon who had cut open the skull of the deceased Sir Thomas Shard was produced.

He was duly sworn.

"Did you examine a dead body?" asked the magistrate, "in a vault at the church of Our Ladye at Southwarke?"

"I did."

"Whose body?"

"The plate on the coffin lid had the name of Sir Thomas Shard."

"What did you do?"

"I opened the head."

"And what appearance did you find?"

"I found a piece of lead that had passed into the brain through the right ear."

"Have you the lead?"

"This is it."

Lady Margaret shuddered, and they thought that she was about to faint away, but she did not.

One of the turnkeys, indeed, placed a hand upon her shoulder to support her, but she turned and said, in a cold, stony sort of way—

"Well?"

"You are faint."

"Who told you so?"

"No one. But I thought——"

"Keep your hand from me, sir. When I need your aid I will ask it."

"Proceed with your evidence," said the magistrate to the surgeon.

"I have nothing further to say but that this has been, to the best of my judgment, the cause of the death of the late Sir Thomas Shard."

"You swear that?"

"I do."

"Prisoner at the bar, you have heard the evidence of the surgeon, and you can ask him any question you may please upon that evidence."

"I have nothing to ask."

"Do you admit the fact?"

"What fact?"

"That you murdered Sir Thomas Shard."

"No. Do you?"

"I?"

"Yes. Even you."

The magistrate shook his head.

"You may go down, sir," he said to the surgeon, and then he added, "she is, indeed, hardened in iniquity."

The bishop, in order completely to set the question at rest, as to whether the piece of lead produced by the surgeon was the identical one or not found in the corpse, volunteered his evidence.

He said—

"I saw the skull opened, and I saw that piece of lead taken from it."

Sir Ralph Shard then stepped forward, and was sworn. His evidence was just this—

"I saw the dead body from which that piece of lead was taken, and I swear that it was the dead body of my late nephew, Sir Thomas Shard, who was the husband, like a fool, as he was, of that bold, bad woman."

CHAPTER CIII.

THE CONDEMNATION OF THE LADY MARGARET.

HIS was quite conclusive.

A death-like stillness reigned in the court, and then, after a time, the justice spoke.

"Margaret Lassamour," he said. "Have you any hope?"

"Hope?"

"Ay. Hope of contending against such evidence as this?"

"What mean you?"

"I mean that you would do well to confess your great guilt, and call upon Heaven to extend its mercy to you."

"I am not in Heaven."

"Alas, no."

"Wherefore, then, should I call upon

Heaven to extend its mercy to me. It is man's mercy I require."

"We cannot show it."

"No. You call upon Heaven to do that which you shrink from yourselves."

"Will you plead guilty?"

"No."

"Then it is my duty to commit you to the common gaol, there to await your trial for murder, and which trial will take place with all convenient speed."

"Be it so."

"Have you no more to say?"

"What more can I have to say? I am one woman here among many men, who, it appears to me, have made up their minds to my death."

"No, no."

"Then I cry you mercy, sir, for it did, and it does appear to me to be so."

"It is not, indeed."

"What then?"

"There is no man here who has not made up his mind that you shall have full justice."

"Yes," cried Martin Lassamour, "and I will take care, Margaret, that you have such legal assistance as money can procure. You shall not be condemned, unheard, you may depend."

She turned a scornful glance upon him.

"Legal assistance? I need it not!"

"Refuse it not!"

"I do refuse it! Gaoler, lead on, I have no more to say here to these men who will take my life, or rather would if they could."

A very peculiar sort of smile crossed her face as she uttered these latter words.

"Stay — stay!" cried Martin Lassamour.

But she would not stay; she made an impatient gesture with her hand, and then was gone.

The certainty, now, of the guilt of the Lady Margaret led to the fact that her trial was rather hurried on; so, that on the fourth morning after this examination, and committal, she was again placed at the bar on the charge affecting her life.

The crowd on this more important occasion was so prodigious that a large force of military had to be called out to keep anything like order.

Those outside the court were so maddened at not being able to get in that they positively, at one time, stormed the building.

It was not until some cavalry had actually charged among them that they began to see the propriety of holding back, or rather, we may say, they began to see the danger of pressing on.

At rather a late hour, then, in consequence of the many disturbances, the trial commenced.

When the Lady Margaret was placed at the bar, no one would have imagined that she thought herself in any serious position.

Her face had a flush upon it that, if it was not the flush of exultation, looked very like it, indeed.

Before the commencement of the trial she addressed the judge, saying—

"My lord I have requested, in writing, that some books and some papers from my house at Pleasaunce should be brought to me, and I am told they are here.'

"They are here."

"Let me have them, then?"

"Will you say that they are necessary for your defence?"

"I will, and do."

"In that case, then, far be it from me to strain the law in any way so as to prohibit you from having them. In whose custody are these books and papers?"

"In mine, my lord," said the sheriff. "Since the prisoner so particularly asked for them, and particularised them, I went to the house and got them."

"You went yourself?"

"I did, my lord."

"And of what did they consist?"

"Some letters of the late husbands of the prisoner, my lord, and several books."

"Have you examined them?"

"Most carefully, my lord."

"And you can see no objection to the prisoner having them?"

"None."

"There are no concealed weapons?"

"None!"

"No poison?"

"None!"

"Then let her have them."

On the dock before the prisoner the books and the papers were now placed, and she took up one of the former and held it in her right hand with her fingers within it.

The trial now commenced.

It is not at all necessary that we should trouble the reader by a recapitulation of the evidence in this case.

The witnesses, with one exception, were the same that had been produced at the former examination, when she was fully committed.

That one exception, now, was Cyprian.

He, when called upon for his evidence, spoke as follows:—

"I saw more of this affair than many thought I did—that is to say of the late affair when Master Lassamour was in the state-chamber in a feigned sleep."

"What saw you?"

"All of it."

"How so?"

"I was, it is true, left in the corridor, but the fact is, I had lived so long at Pleasaunce House, that I knew some of its secrets."

"Go on."

"One of these consisted in the existence of a secret door from the Lady Margaret's bower-chamber to the picture-gallery, by which the latter could be reached without passing through the state bed-chamber."

"How long have you known of this door?"

"For a year."

"Proceed, then."

"When Master Lamont, then, and Lassamour went into the state bed-chamber, I said nothing to any one of my intention or my knowledge, but I ran round to the secret door."

"Alone?"

"Quite alone."

"Go on."

"I touched the spring of it, and it yielded at once, and I entered, softly, this private apartment of the Lady Margaret at the moment that she left it."

"You saw her, then?"

"I did."

"What had she with her?"

"A small ladle with molten lead in it."

"Did she speak?"

"She did."

"What said she?"

"She used these precise words—'This night renders me again a widow.'"

"Are you certain of the words?"

"As certain as that I live."

"Have you more to say?"

"No, that is all."

"Hold," said Lady Margaret, "Cyprian?"

He turned towards her.

"How long were you in my service?"

"Some eight years, madam."

"Was I kind to you, or harsh?"

"Kind, most kind."

"And thus you repay me?"

"Oh, madam, if the truth had had the effect of saving you, how much greater would have been my pleasure in uttering it; but I cannot help it. This is not a case or question of gratitude or not. It is one of crime or not."

"Go, I have no more to say to you."

Cyprian left the witness box.

This was the only fresh evidence, and in a few moments afterwards, as of course was to be fully and completely expected, the Lady Margaret was declared guilty of the wilful murder of Sir Thomas Shard, her own husband.

The penalty was death at the stake in those days.

CHAPTER CIV.

THE CONCLUSION.

DEATHLIKE stillness was in the court now, and the judge addressed the prisoner.

"Unhappy woman, have you aught to say why the dread sentence of the law should not be pronounced against you."

"I will say nothing, but one thing."

"What is that?"

"It is that I defy your sentence."

"Defy it?"

"Ay, I defy it, for I tell you now, my lord judge, and I tell all here, that you may sentence me to what you will, and yet I shall escape."

"Escape?"

"Yes, my lord, escape."

The judge shook his head.

"That hope is vain, let me tell you. Every sort of vigilance will be used to keep you safely, and so sure as that to-morrow's sun will rise, will you be led forth to death."

"No!"

"Unhappy woman, why will you persist in such a delusion? I will now pass the sentence of the law upon you."

She smiled.

"It is that you be taken, to-morrow morning, to the open area of Smithfield, and there tied to a stake and burnt to death!"

She smiled and bit the nails of her right hand, and then she smiled again.

"May the saints have mercy on your soul," added the judge.

"Amen," she said.

"Remove her."

"Hold! My lord, and you, Martin, and all here present, I have told you I should escape; I—I——"

She had to cling to the dock.

"I have escaped!"

She fell dead to the floor. A subtle poison had been concealed in the book she had asked for, and she had conveyed it to her mouth while the judge was passing sentence.

* * * * * *

Such, then, was the tragical end of the wife of seven husbands. She could perpetrate the dreadful crimes with the which she stood charged, but she had not the courage to suffer publicly for them.

It only now remains for us to possess the reader with what knowledge we ourselves possess of the different fates of our other characters.

Martin Lassamour, as regarded the large property that he came into possession of by the death of the Lady Margaret, was as good as his word. He made one clear half of it over to the church, so that a charitable institution should be founded with it.

The hospital at Blackfriars, which existed for many years, till what was called the Reformation, was wholly supported by that bequest.

The remainder he distributed with a liberal hand.

To Robert Lee he gave the acre of land, and the forty pounds a years he coveted, and Robert was happy as the husband of Amy Langdon.

Cyprian was wedded to his own gentle Patience, and likewise had a large share of the bounty of his former master, Martin Lassamour.

As for Martin Lassamour himself, he, for a time, appeared to be very unhappy, but at last a new hope appeared to spring up in his breast.

He and young Lamont were very busy.

It was soon found, then, that they were preparing for a long sea voyage; and, after a time, when Martin called upon old Sir Ralph Shard, he said to him—

"I have come to bid you good-bye."

"To bid me good bye—as how?"

"Why I am going from England for ever!"

"You don't mean it!"

"I do, indeed."

"Alone, too?"

"Oh no, Lamont goes with me."

"Good company, that; for, on my life, I do not know a more worthy and gallant youth! But whither go you, my good friend?"

"To the New World!"

"Humph!"

"Across the wide Atlantic. I will try and find a new home among those adventurers who are now hastening thither with such avidity. England is, after all that has happened, distasteful to me."

"Adzooks! if I were not so old——"

"What then?"

"I would go with you."

Martin Lassamour smiled, but he bade adieu to the worthy old knight, and in twenty-four hours more he and Lamont stepped on board their bark, and bade adieu to England for ever!

END.

PRINTED BY E. LLOYD, SALISBURY-SQUARE, FLEET-STREET, LONDON.